On Different Shores

Part One of

'For Their Country's Good'

By

Rebecca Bryn

This novel is inspired by the story of my great-great-great uncle, James Underwood, and his two cousins, Joseph Bedford and William Downing, of Yardley Hastings, Northampton, concerning John Dunkley, a gamekeeper in the employ of Admiral William Compton, 4th Marquis of Northampton.

Although I have used historical documentation to underpin the tale, and many of the locations exist, the names of the key players have been changed. The story surrounding the factual events of 6th October 1840 and the supporting characters portrayed within Yardley Hastings are fictitious, and any resemblance to people living or dead is unintended and entirely coincidental.

***

With youth comes knowledge: age brings the wisdom to use it.

***

For Elia, Becky, Molly, Riley, Charlotte, and Sophie Knight.

This fictional tale is based on your family history, and a lot of it did happen.

Editing by Kelly Hartigan (XterraWeb)

http://editing.xterraweb.com

Cover credits

Shutterstock 1153962727 standard licence 30.8.18 Signed model release on file with Shutterstock, Inc

Ship: Mr B's Photography on VisualHunt Creative commons attribution licence. Ship isolated from background.

Dreamstime royalty-free licence 15937999 bowie15/Dreamstime.com

Shutterstock 248334712 standard licence 2.5.16 Signed model release on file with Shutterstock, Inc

On Different Shores

You must travel where life takes you:
Bend, 'ere love breaks you
And tears the ties that bind you.
Though we dwell on different shores,
My heart's forever yours,
And one day, I shall find you.
~

Rebecca Bryn

Chapter One

August 1840, Northamptonshire, England:

One illicit kiss. Ella flicked back a wayward lock of auburn hair and glowered out of the coach window, her anger having barely abated during the hundred-and-twenty-mile journey. Ralph had told her she was beautiful, stolen one illicit kiss, and ruined her life.

The coach rumbled along a quiet, newly metalled road between broad verges. Hedges high with summer growth were festooned with blackberries and trailing wreaths of red bryony berries, reminding her of the picnics in the country she'd enjoyed as a child, when life had been simple, and she'd known her place in her small world.

The present reasserted itself. On her left, a grand gateway, flanked by gatehouses, opened onto a long avenue of trees that led to some unseen destination. To her right, the same avenue marched on across fields to distant woodland. Her mother had tried to mollify her anger at being sent away, exiled, with talk of the grand estate of the Marquis of Northampton. Her spirits rose a fraction. Was Castle Ashby to be her new home?

She took a deep calming breath as the coach rumbled on without pause, removing her from briefly imagined grandeur. Through gateways, she glimpsed men reaping with sickles. Children, released from school for harvest, bound the cut corn into sheaves and leant the bundles together in tall stooks. Farther on, gateways to her right showed green pastures in which cows grazed.

Houses came into view. Surely this wasn't her destination? She put a hand across her nose and mouth to ward off the less than savoury smell coming through the open window and stretched her neck to see what kind of place it was. Her heart sank; it looked like a bucolic backwater in the middle of nowhere, not the palatial estate of the Marquis of Northampton her mother had promised her, and nothing like the busy streets or grand façades of Bath where she'd grown up.

The coach turned onto a rougher surface. Wheels slowed, hooves danced, and harness jangled. The coach jerked to a halt, the springs protesting. Another turnpike? She stuck her head out of the window. 'Why are we stopping?'

A thump at the side of the coach was followed swiftly by another and answered her question. Her bags, second-hand and a parting gift from her mother's employer, lay where they'd landed on the grass at the side of the road. The coachman threw open the door. 'This is as far as you go, young lady.'

'But…'

'You'll have to walk from here.' The man pointed back to the white finger-post at the crossroads. 'Yardley Hastings. See?'

The lane into the village was striped with wheel ruts and muddy as if the stream alongside it had recently overflowed and the summer-baked earth had been unable to absorb it. She fumbled for her purse. 'I can pay you to drive me.'

'Much as I'd like to take your money, missy, these horses need a drink, as do I.' He nodded to the large stone and thatch building that stood a little way back from the lane. 'We're stopping for victuals at The Red Lion, and then I have a schedule to keep. Maybe, the people you're visiting will send a cart for you.'

She put her purse away, her cheeks warm with embarrassment at not having considered the four horses. They'd been trotting and cantering since five in the morning, when they'd left the coaching inn at Oxford. 'Of course. I'm sorry. It's not far.'

The coachman touched his cap and climbed back onto his seat. 'Get on, boys. Hi up.' The black, sweat-slicked geldings leaned into their collars, and the coach rumbled into the inn yard. It had disappeared before she looked around her. Cart? What had he meant by them sending a cart? Surely, Reverend Buchanan, who was to find her a position, would send a carriage.

The tower of the village church peeped shyly above trees weighed down with late-summer leaves, and a faint mist wisped from the rutted lane before her as the hot afternoon sun drove away the morning's rain. She picked up her bags, glad now that she'd travelled light, not wanting to bring reminders of her past with her. She'd determined to be philosophical, and make the best of her new situation, but she'd failed miserably; her spirits had lowered with every mile she'd travelled. She left the turnpike road behind and stamped north towards the centre of the village, past warm-stone, thick-thatched houses, her mood darkening further as she walked.

What right had they to send her away? She'd done nothing wrong, unless it was a sin to be born out of wedlock to a mother who'd refused to name the father. Mother had been lucky; women had been sent to the asylum or transported for that crime. She pursed set lips, her jaw clenched. All she wanted was to better herself, make a good marriage, avoid the life of drudgery her mother endured, and not die in the poorhouse like her grandmother. How was she supposed to do that now she'd been sent away from Bath and Mr Barton's social contacts?

A cart drawn by a chestnut horse splashed water from the ruts as it rounded the village green and rattled along the lane towards her. A young man with fair hair and ruddy cheeks sat atop the driver's seat. Had the reverend sent his man to fetch her? Better late than never, and a cart was better than walking. She stepped aside for the horse to pull the cart alongside her, and her foot slipped into a puddle. Wheels squelched past sending a sheet of water across her legs. 'Hey! Stop! I'm Ella Maundrell. Didn't Reverend Buchanan send you to fetch me?'

The man hauled on the reins, and the horse lumbered to a halt. 'Not me he didn't. No bugger sends me anywhere.'

Oh, besoms! She hid the expletive beneath her breath and brushed mud from her stockings with a white-gloved hand. 'You did that on purpose.'

He smirked down at her. 'Now, why would I do that? It rained. We get mud. Get used to it, and stay out of the bloody way of wagons, you daft mare.' He clicked his tongue and the horse trotted on.

She'd have to walk. 'You've got ideas above your station in life, young lady.' That was what her mother had told her, daily. She mimicked her mother's mocking voice again. 'Young lady.' That's what the coachman had called her, too.

Young lady: she clamped her jaw tighter. She was considered not good enough for the son of one, Josiah Barton, Esquire, solicitor of Bath: the man for whom her mother kept house. Was it her fault young Mr Ralph had fallen for a pretty girl beneath his station?

Enough men had told her she was pretty, winding their fingers in her long curls and gazing adoringly into her brown eyes, for her to believe it. Forewarned by her mother's romantic mistake, she hadn't fallen for their promises of marriage.

The master had seen to her education; she could read, write, and play the piano, and she knew how to keep house having helped her mother do the same for Mr Josiah Barton since she was tall enough to reach the sink on a low stool. She was a good catch: she had, with some considerable difficulty, kept herself for the marriage bed. Huh. Not a good enough catch, apparently. She had no land, no dowry, and no breeding.

She straightened her shoulders. No-one knew her here. She could be whoever she wanted to be. No, she wouldn't burden herself with a child out of wedlock and spend the rest of her life slaving for her keep, like her mother.

Another deep breath filled her lungs with cow muck and failed to calm her anger. It was she who'd had to leave her home. She stamped in another puddle, spraying mud across the cinder-strewn surface, and tried not to breathe the smell coming from the farmyard. Mr Josiah could have sent Ralph away to his London practice, if he'd wanted to keep them apart. For goodness' sake, Ralph was like a brother to her. She'd grown up playing hide and

8

seek with him, above and below stairs; she didn't want to marry him. Her heart quickened, her womanhood awakening despite herself: Ralph had stolen a kiss.

Pushing the feeling away, she glowered at the low thatched cottages. She'd been forced to leave her friends and the fringes of polite society, where she might have made a good match, to come to this filthy privy of a ... She tripped and fell headlong.

She removed her glove and wiped mud from her mouth with a wet hand. 'Oh besoms, besoms, besoms!' Her face hot with embarrassment, she got to her feet. Her coat was muddy and dripping. What would the reverend think? The letter in her pocket crinkled beneath her hand: hopefully, it would go some way to redress her appearance.

There was no sign of the rectory near the church. She accosted a young woman, who carried a child on her hip and looked at her with undisguised curiosity. The woman pointed the way to Rectory Lane, farther along the High Street.

At the gates of the rectory, her heart lifted somewhat. Set beyond a stone wall, the rectory was an imposing building of pleasing proportions with two above-ground storeys, an under-storey, and attic windows in the roof. Built of warm stone and mellow brick, and adorned with the dark green of clinging ivy, it was solid, warm, and homely but had style and grace. She pushed a lock of wet hair from her face and strode towards the house. The front door or the servant's entrance? She glanced down at her muddy boots: definitely not the front door.

The side entrance led to a cobbled courtyard with stables, coach house, and a small cottage built of the same warm stone. A horse whickered in the stables and was answered by another. The sound of singing, the smell of baking, and the noise of pots clattering invited her through an open door down some steps. She knocked tentatively, and the singing and clattering stopped.

'Lord luv us, what happened to you?' A short, dumpy woman with silver strands in brown hair tied back in a bun, and wearing a tight-bodiced, full-skirted grey dress, dried her hands on her

9

starched apron and looked her up and down. 'You fall in the brook?'

'I tripped in the road.'

'And you wearing no pattens –spoiled them fine boots.'

'I'm Ella Maundrell. I have a letter of introduction for Reverend Buchanan from Mr Josiah Barton of Bath.'

'Reverend Buchanan is expecting you.' The woman sniffed, but her face softened. 'You'd best come in, and I'll tell him you're here, Ella Maundrell, though what he'll think.'

The hallway, off which was a flight of narrow stairs, led to domestic offices.

The woman pointed to a high stool. 'Take off those boots, sit there, and don't you be touching anything.' She waddled away with a backwards glance, a swish of her skirts, and a discomforted sigh.

As Mrs Downs's footsteps receded along the passage, she looked around the kitchen; it was spacious, clean with the range newly blacked, and, with a tall window onto the courtyard above her, not as dark as the kitchen at Bath had been. A tray of small cakes tempted: she could smell cinnamon and ginger. Her stomach grumbled in anticipation.

Voices from beyond the kitchen door grew louder. She took the letter from her pocket and sat straighter. *You never get a second chance to make a first impression, young lady.* Right mess she'd made of that.

A tall man in his early fifties, with dark wavy hair and long sideburns, held out a manicured hand. She presented her letter. He smiled and took it, giving the wax seal a cursory glance, and she realised too late that he'd offered his hand in greeting. 'I'm...' Words stuck in her throat. 'Ella Maundrell.'

'Mrs Downs, bring a pot of tea and some of your wonderful cakes. And heat some water for Ella to wash her hands.' He looked at her coat. 'And put her coat by the range to dry. I'll be in the

10

study when she's cleaner.' He gave her a reassuring wink and left her to Mrs Downs's ministrations.

By the time she entered Reverend Buchanan's study, on the upper-ground floor, his easy smile had gone. He pointed her to a chair that sat across from his desk and faced a huge marble fireplace flanked by oak panelling and shelves of leather-bound books.

He stared at her over half-rimmed glasses. Evening sun slanted through the window and reflected in the metal rims. 'It seems you've been sent to me for religious instruction, to keep you on God's straight and narrow path for the sake of your immortal soul.' He reread the letter and looked up at her again. 'Well?'

'Yes, Reverend.' So much for being whoever she wanted to be.

'You have no explanation for your behaviour? You admit to being wanton?'

'Ralph kissed me, sir.'

'And you did nothing to encourage it, I suppose.' He laid the letter on the leather-inlaid desktop and sighed. 'Eve tempted Adam. Must I say more? Young men have their needs and are tempted by the flesh. You will learn how to behave like a respectable young woman. How old are you, Ella?'

Young men's needs were the fault of women? Did men really believe that? She unclenched her jaw. 'Are the immoral predations of men not the fault of those men, rather than the women on whom they prey?'

His expression darkened. 'Young women know nothing of such things. It is not seemly. They should be beyond reproach, for a reputation is easily ruined. I asked your age, Ella.'

She lowered her gaze. 'Seventeen, sir.'

'You are fortunate Mr Barton thought enough of you, for your mother's sake, to send you here for correction and not have you committed to an asylum for...' He paused and leaned across the desk towards her. 'I'm reading between the lines, here. Whoring is

11

not a word I use lightly but, from what Mr Barton intimates, this is not far from the truth. You have a chance to salvage your reputation here. To begin again with a clean slate.'

Whoring? What, in the name of all that was holy, had Mr Barton written? She bowed her head lower, it being prudent to hold her tongue. 'Yes, sir.'

'You will attend church on Sundays and come to me each evening for instruction. During the day, you will help Mrs Downs in the house. You will have Saturday afternoons free, but you will keep away from the young men of the village. They are not to be trusted with your virtue. I shall attempt to present you as a marriageable young woman and secure you a suitable husband, as Mr Barton requests, before you stray again. Is that clear?'

She looked up. 'A husband?'

'You are illegitimate, child. You have no breeding and no dowry to speak of. And don't think you would find a patron so accommodating as my good friend, Josiah Barton, should you find yourself in your mother's unhappy position. She's fortunate to have such a beneficent employer, one who is agreeable to keeping up her pretence of widowhood, as you are fortunate I am a man of God and have a charitable disposition. Josiah asks much of me.' He sighed and pushed the letter aside. 'I can't very well keep you locked up, so you must be married before your wicked lusts overcome you.'

She raised her head in defiance. 'I shall marry a man I love, and choose, or stay a spinster.'

He refolded the letter and returned it to its envelope. His face was granite, his voice implacable. 'You will do as you're told, Ella Maundrell.'

The rattle of china heralded tea and cakes; it might as well have been the rattle of chains. Mrs Downs set the tray on the desk and poured a cup. Reverend Buchanan pulled a pocket watch from his waistcoat. 'That's all, Ella. We'll begin your instruction at seven o'clock. In the meantime, Mrs Downs will find work for your idle hands before the devil does.'

Her stomach rumbled, too loud to be ignored. Mrs Downs pinched thin lips between a finger and thumb. 'I'll find her clean clothes and a bit to eat. Will that be all, Reverend?'

Her new employer waved the woman away. 'I'll ring if I need you, Mrs. Downs. Until seven, Ella.'

***

Harry Cartwright pushed his head into the soft flank of Bluebell, a Gloucester milk cow, and squeezed her teats rhythmically. She was a young cow, new to the milking herd, having given birth to her first calf in July, and wasn't producing a great yield yet. Glancing along the row of cows in the parlour filled him with pride. He and his father, John, had built the herd from nothing, and it was now one of the best herds in the county.

Bluebell lifted a leg, and he moved his hands away before her kick broke his arm. 'Keep still, fuck you.' A punch to her stomach would show her who was boss. She shuffled her hooves and settled again to lick at the remains of her cow-cake in the manger. 'Now, stand up, girl.' He warmed his hands under his armpits. Some young cows didn't like cold hands on their teats. He huffed a laugh. Some girls didn't like cold hands on their tits either. Not that they objected to the money he gave them to let him sow his wild oats. He resumed drawing down the milk, imagining he was fondling that stuck-up bitch who'd thought him a mere carter sent to fetch her at the reverend's whim.

He scowled. She wouldn't look twice at him, any more than any other woman would. His fingers traced the craters in his face; he didn't need a mirror to see the pockmarks left by smallpox, one of the illnesses that had damaged his boyhood. Was it any wonder no woman would accept his proposal of marriage and he had to resort to prostitutes for his pleasure?

His father had paid for his first prostitute when he was fifteen. He'd said she was reliable, and discreet, and would teach him all he needed to know. It was to be a secret between father, son, and the woman of the night and was to be kept from his mother. His manhood rose at the memory. Father knew every prostitute between Yardley and Northampton, and they'd visited most of them together.

At thirty, he should be married with an heir to take on the herd, as he'd take it on from his father one day. What was the point of building something if you had no-one to leave it to?

He'd thought young Cissy Walden might accept his advances. She might be a cart mare, compared to the reverend's auburn-haired up-herself blood filly, but he was sure she'd been about to say yes to a fumble that time behind the woodshed at the back of the Rose and Crown, if only the landlord hadn't interrupted them. Next thing he knew, Eric Meads was courting her, and they'd got married only last year. He'd lost his chance with Cissy, but maybe, one day, he'd find a woman to give him sons: one who might even come to love the man beneath the damaged skin.

He finished Bluebell off and moved to the next, Bluebell's mother, Damson. He threw her a scoop of cake, washed her udder and teats with near-scalding water, and settled on the stool. Damson had had a calf a year for the last nine years.

He ran his hands down her flank and along the prominent milk vein that tracked across her belly, and she turned liquid brown eyes to watch him. She was a good milker and a gentle cow. A warm, wet tongue curled around his hand: Damson didn't judge him by the pockmarks on his face. He'd always imagined his wife would be like Damson, like Cissy Walden was: someone who'd fit him like a comfortable glove. Gentle, kind, generous, hard-working, and dropping a calf a year: everything his mother wasn't. Was that why his father used prostitutes and he was an only child?

'Harry? You milking them cows or fucking them?'

'Nearly done, Father.'

'I'll open the gate to Top Field. They can graze that a bit tighter.'

'I'll bring them up in a bit. Ten minutes?'

14

'See you up there and get a move on. I've something to talk to you about. Something important. It'll make a man of you.'

His fingers clenched around Damson's teats. 'Make a man of me?' He glanced up to challenge his father's opinion of him, but he'd gone. Had he finally found a pretty young milkmaid to replace Mary, who'd made a sudden decision to go and stay with her aunt in Olney? His pulse quickened and his groin throbbed. He'd never had a virgin. Father usually broke in the maids; maybe, it was time he asserted his authority as heir to the Cartwright farm's tenancy and got in first. He'd show father he was as big a man as him, even if he didn't have a wife and sons. He loosened his breeches and pulled at his manhood until he moaned and ejaculated on the cobbled floor of the milking parlour.

***

Ella had an hour before her religious instruction with Reverend Buchanan. The silver polished, the copper buffed, and her expertise with a fulling iron and a smoothing iron demonstrated, Mrs Downs had relented and let her go out to stretch her legs.

'Stay away from them village boys. They mean no real harm, but some of them are a right handful and no better than they should be. A rough bunch, if I do say so myself as shouldn't.' Mrs Downs echoed her employer's warning. 'And be back before seven. Reverend Buchanan doesn't like to be kept waiting, and you're indebted to his charity, so don't think to abuse it.'

Mrs Downs thought she needed charity? She hadn't asked to be sent here, and she could work for a living. A horse whinnied from the stables, and another whickered in return: she crossed the yard to the stable block. Inside was dim and warm, redolent with fresh straw, warm dung, and urine. A tall black mare nickered to her in greeting, tossing her head against her pillar chains. She stroked the mare's nose and breathed in the warm smell of horse. 'I should have brought you a crust of bread or an apple, girl.'

'Her name's Ebony. She's the reverend's riding mare.'

The soft voice startled her. A lad of about her own age, or a

15

little older, smiled at her.

She smiled back. 'She's beautiful. Do you work here?'

'I'm James, James Weston. Everybody calls me Jem. I ain't seen you around here, before.'

'I'm Ella.'

'Just Ella?

'Ella Maundrell. I'm staying with Reverend Buchanan.'

James touched his cap and kicked at loose straw with a scuffed work boot. 'You his niece or something?'

She stared at her only pair of shoes, wishing she'd polished them. 'No. I'm not related to him. My mother...' She let the explanation hang. It was none of his business. 'I asked if you worked here, James.'

His smile faded. 'I'm doing repairs to the brickwork. Some of them are weathered and lost their face. Got about another week's work here, then I'm on the threshing unless I get work on the new house down the lane.' He ran a hand down the mare's flank. 'I like coming to see the horses.'

'They're lovely creatures.' It was a pity Jem was only a labourer. Muscles defined the outline of his thin shirt. His hazel eyes were soft and intelligent beneath black brows and a mass of black wavy hair and, despite a rather large nose and mouth, his smile had sat happily on his clean-shaven oval face.

She looked away, aware she was staring, as warmth flushed her cheeks.

Jem flexed a muscle, as if to impress, but she was saved from further embarrassment by Mrs Downs's chiding voice.

'Time you got yourself inside, Ella. And you get off home, young James. Your mother'll have your tea on, as well you know.'

Jem ducked his head. 'I'm going right off, Missus. Just got me tools to clean.' He risked another smile, his eyes crinkling with ill-

16

contained mischief. 'See you around, Ella.'

Her lips curved in a commiserating smile, but Mrs Downs took hold of her arm as if she were a naughty child. 'You're going to be a right handful, I can see.'

'I didn't know he was here. I came to see the horses.'

'Aye, likely story. I know why you were sent here, Ella. The reverend told me. If you want to make a good marriage, you must protect your reputation, not make eyes at the first youth who smiles at you. Lust is a sin, and Reverend Buchanan will beat it out of you, if he has to, to save you from the devil.'

'But…'

'You stay away from that James, my girl. Him and his cousins, Caleb and Nat, are trouble, a wild bunch, always egging one another on, and me Caleb's aunty, as shouldn't say so, and Nat a father now, as should know better.' Mrs Downs shook her head to drive home her point. 'No good'll come of 'em, you mark my words. No, you keep clear of young James Weston. Worry his poor mother into an early grave, he will, and her busy all the hours God gives making lace like our young queen had on her wedding dress, for all her ladyship's fine friends.' Mrs Downs paused for a hurried breath. 'Now go and brush your hair. You're here to be instructed. Start as you mean to go on, Ella. You've got looks and youth on your side. Take it from one as knows. Don't waste 'em.'

'Yes, Mrs Downs.' Her room was in the attic of a single-storey wing at the side of the main house and had a small, south-facing dormer window overlooking the front garden. Although she had to mind her head on the ceiling, it was a clean, comfortable room with a single bed, a clothes press, and a table in front of the window upon which stood a blue and white jug and basin. She washed quickly and brushed her hair, fastening her long curls back with clips and pins. Her mother had given her a small, silver-backed hand mirror as a parting gift. She prodded a wisp of hair and stared at her reflection as she ran a hand down the curve of her hip. Had Jem found her attractive?

17

She put the mirror down. Whatever the reverend and Mr Barton wanted, she wasn't looking for a husband. She'd come here to work, and anyway, a man like Jem wasn't what she needed. When she was ready to marry, she'd need a steady, upright man with prospects, if she wasn't going to be a drudge all her life with her looks ruined by bearing a child a year, not a grubby labourer with rough speech and rougher hands: one of a *wild bunch*. Something quickened low in her stomach. She took a deep breath and shook off the feeling. Reverend Buchanan awaited to rid her of sinful lust and improper thoughts.

Chapter Two

Harry sat opposite his father in front of the fire. He downed a mug of ale and waited for his father to speak, to find out what important matter it was that would '*make a man of him.*'

John Cartwright exchanged a glance with his wife. She got up from her chair and left the room, closing the door behind her and leaving him alone with his father. The older man cleared his throat. 'It's long past time you were married, Harry. You're thirty this year. You should have a son and heir by now. Hell, you should have half a dozen youngsters by now.'

'Fat chance of that.' He clattered the mug onto the hearth. 'What woman will look at me?'

'A woman who wants security and a comfortable life in a prominent family. A woman like the pretty little thing the rector has staying with him.'

He laughed. 'I saw her when she arrived, all dressed up and stuck up. She's only a child.'

'She's seventeen, which is quite old enough for your purpose. Think of that young, firm, virgin flesh, Harry. And she'll still be young enough to look after you when you're an old man.'

'I suppose. How do you know about her?'

'Reverend Buchanan is to find a husband for her. Seems she's a spirited girl and not averse to the male sex.'

'You mean she's a whore. I thought you said virgin flesh.'

'No, not a whore. The reverend swears she's a virgin. She got a bit too friendly with the son of her mother's employer, that's all, and was sent here out of harm's way. She's young, strong, and easy on the eye. She'll bear you strong sons.'

'What if I don't like her?'

His father let out a deep breath. 'It's best you don't fall in love with the woman who'll bear your children. I made that mistake. Having you nearly killed your mother. Why do you think you're an only child? Why do you think I use whores? Do you know how many women die in childbirth? No, take my word for it – it's best you find a woman you can fuck and not grieve over. And, like I said, this one's a virgin, and *you* get to take her virginity.'

'A virgin.' The bulge in his breeches hardened. 'She is pretty, but she may not agree to marriage.'

'I doubt the rector will give her a choice from what he told me. She's to be married, whether she wants it or not, and Reverend Buchanan thinks you'll be a suitable match.' His father frowned. 'Let's face it, Harry. You said it yourself. What woman would look twice at you of her own accord.'

It was true. 'My own personal whore, and I won't have to pay her.' He smiled a slow smile. 'And a virgin to break.'

***

The inside of The Red Lion was thick with wreathing smoke and the smell of pipe tobacco. Jem drew a long draught of beer from his pint tankard and slapped the vessel onto the table. 'By the Lord, I needed that.'

Caleb Brafield, nearly a year younger than him, having only just had his twentieth birthday, nodded at the barkeep's daughter. 'I wouldn't mind a tumble in the hay with that one.'

He frowned. 'Mind your mouth, Cal. Her old man's right protective of her. If he hears that sort of talk…'

Nathan Denton, ten years his elder and married a twelvemonth with a young baby, wiped foam from his lips and laughed. 'She's a hot 'un, all right, but you wouldn't stand a chance with her, Cal. Old man or no old man.'

Caleb pouted. 'And you would, of course?'

Nat began to stand up. 'Absolutely. Watch.'

'Don't encourage him, Cal.' He put a hand on Nat's broad shoulder and pushed him back in his chair. 'She ain't worth getting beat up over, cousin. Your Sarah'll take a copper stick to you if she hears you're messing about.'

Nat raised an eyebrow. 'And you'd know this, how?'

He feigned innocence. 'About your Sarah?'

'No, pillock. About her over there not being worth it.'

He buried his admission of guilt in another swallow of beer, but his cousins didn't miss the evasion. Cal and Nat's lips moved in time. 'You haven't, Jem?'

He nodded, studying beer stains on the oak table top. 'As much fun as a barrel of salted trout.'

Nat thumbed tobacco in the tiny bowl of a clay pipe. 'I heard Joe Upton had a fling with her.

He frowned. 'That's just gossip. Anyway, Joe's married.'

Cal laughed. 'When did that ever stop a man?' His cousin's laughter died. 'You don't want to get the wrong side of Upton, Nat, spreading stories as ain't true. You neither, Jem.'

'Me and Nat are already on the wrong side of that one, Cal.' He grunted mirthlessly. Upton was one of his lordship's gamekeepers and had got him a huge fine, two years back, for poaching. He was still paying the bugger off. 'All we want to do is put food on the table. Why should that be a crime?'

'Don't start, Jem. You know damn well why. The game belongs to the estate, as do we all. You'd walk half a day to get clear of His Lordship's land and His Lordship's gamekeepers.' Cal lowered his voice. 'You think I'd poach if our little 'uns weren't hungry?'

Cal was right: the marquis had so much, and the villagers had so little. 'That's true enough, and it won't stop a keeper peppering your arse with his twelve bore if he catches you, Nathan.'

21

Nat blushed scarlet, but his knuckles around the pipe stem bled white. 'I still owe Upton for nearly getting me a month in jail. Bastard said he saw me carrying a gun.'

'Pipe down, Nat.' He pushed his mug towards Nat. 'And keep quiet about me and her, right? Upton and her dad are mates. Upton could fit me up, like he tried to do to you.' He pushed the tankard closer. 'It's your round, Nat.'

Nat cursed and waved the pipe aimlessly. 'False evidence.'

'Yes, you've said as much a hundred times.'

Nat wasn't to be deflected. 'Previous good character, that's what the judge said when he let me off.' He got to his feet unsteadily. 'Last I'm buying tonight, Jem. Quarter's rent's due come Michaelmas, and Sarah'll have me guts for garters if I don't raise it. Good character, see. I'm a reformed man.'

'Yeah, till you get caught.' His thoughts returned to the girl with auburn hair and sparkling eyes. Ella wouldn't be like a barrel of salted anything. She had an unattainability that challenged his need for a sexual conquest, but she touched him on a deeper level, too. If she wasn't related to Reverend Buchanan, who was she? 'Cal, your aunty works for the rector.' Nat slid a tankard across the table towards him, and he nodded his thanks. 'You know who the new girl is at the rectory?'

Caleb leaned closer. 'I heard Aunty Ev talking to Ma afore I came out. You mustn't say nothing though. She's been sent here. Got into a spot of bother with her employer's son, by all accounts. The rector's to find her a husband.'

'A husband?' The thought of her married off, beyond his reach, to some stuffed shirt made him feel sick. But she might not be so unattainable, after all, if she were soiled goods and Reverend Buchanan was looking for a husband for her. And her smile had meant something. She liked him. Surely, a come-on? 'She with child do you think? They trying to palm her off on some poor, unsuspecting fool?'

'Aunty Ev didn't think so.'

22

He let out a held breath between his teeth. He didn't particularly want another man's child to bring up, but that would make it more difficult to find a willing husband for her, which would surely give him more of a look in. He creased his brow. A husband? Marriage? When had he started thinking like that?

He was twenty and single, he had plenty of time to settle down, but there was something about Ella Maundrell. He didn't want a quick romp in the hay with this girl: he wanted all of her. His heart thudded. He looked from Caleb to Nathan. 'I'll wager you both a week's wages I'll have her afore Michaelmas.' And, if she was as willing as he suspected, she'd be happy to lie with him, wouldn't she?

He downed his third pint and fetched another round. Cal was swaying like a pig drunk on fermenting cider apples. His cousin's reedy voice broke out into a taunting song. 'On yonder hill there stands a creature, who she is I do not know, Jem will court her for her beauty, she must answer yes or no.'

Nat joined in the chorus, laughing. 'Oh, no, Jem. No, Jem. No, Jem. No!'

The two of them dissolved into laughter.

'I'll show you, see if I don't.' But their laughter was infectious, and he joined in yelling Cal or Nat, where they yelled Jem.

'Put a lid on it, boys. We can't hear ourselves fart, over here.' Joe Upton's moustached face wore a patronising smile.

'You can sure smell 'em, though.'

Joe shook his head. 'Less o' your cheek, young Weston.'

Ernest Barritt, his lordship's head gamekeeper, put down his pint. 'You boys had better get off home before ale-talk gets you into trouble.'

The innkeeper looked up from serving his customer. 'You've had enough, Jem. All three of you have. Go home, peaceably, before I have to throw you out.'

23

'Come on, Jem. Ain't staying where I'm not wanted. Come on, Cal.' Nat emptied his tankard in one gulp and slammed it on the table. 'We'll go serenade the village or nip in the Rose and Crown.'

Arm in arm, they sauntered through the village, singing tunelessly.

'Oh, madam, in your face is beauty.

'On your lips red roses grow.

'Will you take me for your lover?

'Madam answer yes or no.

'Oh no, Nat. No, Cal. N*o, Jem. No!*'

He woke with a sore head, sprawled across his bed, and still fully dressed. He hadn't even taken his boots off. Four small squares of bright light made his eyes smart. It must be time he was up. 'Oh no, Jem. No, Jem…' The words battered his brain like a threshing machine. Every noise he made was like the blast of a shotgun.

He rubbed his neck and squinted at the sunlight slanting through his window. 'I ain't never getting drunk again. Never.' How many times had he said that? He removed his beer-soaked jacket and trousers and splashed water from a jug across his face and neck. He drank enough, straight from the jug, to wet his throat and then dressed in his work clothes and thudded down the oak plank stairs to the kitchen more quietly than usual.

His mother held a crusty loaf to her full bosom and ravaged it with quick, stabbing movements of a long bone-handled knife, the blade sharpened over the years to a scimitar shape. One of these days, she'd cut her throat with it. She glared at him. 'You made enough noise to wake the whole graveyard, coming in drunk. And I saw Joe Upton's mother, first thing. She tells me you got thrown out of the Red Lion for unruly behaviour. You boys'll be the death of me.'

'Sorry, Ma.' He filched a doorstep from beneath her angry

blade and slapped a wedge of butter on it.

'There's cheese on the slab.'

He took his knife to the pantry, lifted the muslin covering, and cut a thick slice. 'I'll eat it on the run. Don't wanna be late for the reverend.'

'Dear Lord in his mercy...'

The rest of his mother's plea to her redeemer went unheard as he tore at a chunk of his breakfast and slammed the door behind him. He cringed as the noise crashed into his head. 'Jesus Christ.' His voice was a pained whisper. 'Definitely going on the bloody wagon.'

***

Mrs Downs had sent Ella along the lane to the bake-house. She was on her way back through the stable yard with two warm, crusty loaves when a familiar voice stopped her.

'Nothing like the smell of a loaf straight from the bake-house, Ella.' Jem straightened, a brick in one hand and a trowel in the other.

Why did her cheeks go hot and her stomach clench at the sound of his voice? She took a deep breath: he was only here for a few more days. 'Mrs Downs is waiting for me.' She took a step towards the kitchen door.

'Unless it's the smell of bluebells in spring, or fresh earth and autumn leaves in the Chase.'

She turned despite herself. 'Anything's better than the smell of manure.'

Jem grinned. 'True enough.' He buttered a brick with mortar and tapped it into place with the handle of his trowel before scraping away the excess and flicking it back onto his spot. 'I could show you the Chase, if you like. It's beautiful this time of year. The autumn colours are starting in already. There's fox earths and badger setts all over the Chase. Squirrels, too, and jays. We could find blue jay feathers for your Sunday hat. Collect chestnuts?'

Maybe, he was more than a labourer. He had an appreciation of nature. The corners of her mouth turned down. 'I'm not allowed.'

He raised a black eyebrow and winked. 'Don't ask, then. You gets some time off, don't you?'

'Saturday afternoon, but…'

Jem finished pointing the joints around the brick and stood back to check his work. 'But nothin'. Your life is yours to live, Ella Maundrell. It ain't no-one else's.'

The blinkered truth of this simple statement shocked her. 'It might be so for you, Jem Weston. You ain't – you're not a woman. A young woman.'

Jem patted up and down his chest with his hands and looked at her with mock surprise. 'So I ain't.'

She laughed, and the devil slipped past her guard. Where was the harm in exploring the countryside? She lived here after all, she needed to get to know her surroundings, and Jem obviously knew the Chase well. Even Mrs Downs said Jem meant no harm, was just a bit wild. She longed for an hour or two of wild freedom away from the confines of the rectory and Reverend Buchanan's moral sermons. 'Saturday, after lunch.'

'I'll meet you up The Greenyard. No, thinking about it, that's too close to the rectory. Meet me at the far end of Church Lane. We'll go to Cold Oak Copse. It ain't but half a mile, and the track's good, us not having had much rain over the summer, though we'll have to cut across a bit of pasture if we go that way. Two of the clock?'

She mentally bit her lower lip in silent apprehension. 'Two o'clock, then, at the end of Church Lane.'

***

Ella fastened her coat and slipped on her newly polished boots. Her new mistress had kept her hands busy from dawn to dusk, and even then, her rest time after her nightly instruction was occupied with mending and sewing. Saturday afternoon hadn't come a moment too soon. Would Jem be waiting?

Mrs Downs looked her up and down. 'Where are you going, Ella?'

'I thought I'd get to know the village, Mrs Downs. I haven't seen much of it since I got here. Only the bake-house and the High Street. And I'd like to spend some time in the church, thinking.'

The housekeeper nodded her approval. 'Reflecting on Reverend Buchanan's words will do you no harm. No harm at all. Be back in time to help me get supper.'

'I will, I promise.'

'Good girl. And don't get them boots and coat all dirty again.' Mrs Downs smiled. 'You was a sight when you got here, and no mistake.'

'I'll try to stay out of the mud.' She smiled back, guilty at the deception; Mrs Downs had a soft side and only wanted what was best for her. A pity they didn't agree on what best was. She walked across the stable yard and onto the lane. Heavy horses crossed the High Street ahead of her pulling a huge cart piled high with long-shafted wheat: harvest was in full swing, and every available man, child, and horse was bringing it in.

Jem lounged against a gate at the end of Church Lane, a straw between his lips. He turned when he heard her coming and spat it out.

She looked where he'd been looking, to rows of men scything in unison. Swaths of pale gold fell hypnotically beneath their blades. 'Shouldn't you be in the fields helping?'

'I wangled an hour off.' He grinned. 'Bellyache… Don't worry. I shall be busy all hours when they start threshing.'

'Why do I feel you're a bad influence, Jem Weston?'

27

'You're a free spirit, Ella. You want to live life or regret not living it? It's up to you.'

The woods tempted. She had a lifetime in which to wash clothes and scrub floors. 'I want a blue jay feather for my Sunday hat, remember?'

'We'd best shake a leg, then.'

Cold Oak Copse shimmered with the greens and golds of oak and beech leaves, the ground already scattered with the leaves of sycamores and ash, not unusual after a hot and mostly dry summer. Pale trunks of white birch and smooth silver-grey beech gleamed in the sun, and she breathed deeply of the scent of leaf mould. A squirrel stood on its hind legs on the riding before her and then bounded across the ground and up an oak to disappear among more stubborn leaves.

'Hush.' Jem stilled and put a finger to his lips, pointing carefully. A deer blended with its background, barely visible in the dappled light. It moved silently away, and Jem's stance relaxed. 'Come on.'

She followed him farther into the copse, enchanted by the silent wilderness and careless that she was alone with him. A flash of white winged away through the trees.

'Jay.' He searched the ground in front of him. 'No feathers, sorry. That's a badger sett.' He indicated a wide hole in an excavated bank, the mouth to it worn smooth. 'Tracks.' He pointed to a narrow path between brambles. 'The Chase is criss-crossed with fox and badger runs.'

A loud squawk and a flurry of movement startled her. A large bird rose clumsily into the air and whirred away, followed by two more.

'His lordship's pheasants.' He winked at her. 'Right tasty they are too.'

'Reverend Buchanan enjoys pheasant, too, courtesy of the marquis.'

'Aye. Difference is I'd likely get hung now if I got caught poaching one.'

'Hung for taking a wild bird?'

'His lordship's bird. They're bred, not wild. He has eighty keepers watching the Chase and raising pheasant for his sport. We take one bird to help feed our hungry families...' He shrugged. 'We try to make sure as we don't get caught, that's all.'

'That doesn't seem fair, if he has so many.'

'Nowt's fair in this life, Ella. Nowt's fair at all.' He looked up through a gap in the canopy. 'Best be getting back, or I'll be missed, and there'll be hell to pay. He'll have me guts for garters.'

'I still haven't found my feather.'

He turned to face her. 'Maybe next time. Will there be a next time, Ella?'

She studied her boots. 'I shouldn't. The reverend wouldn't approve, but thank you for showing me the copse.'

'I don't want to get you into trouble, Ella.' Jem turned towards the village. 'If you change your mind – well, I'll be around. Sure to bump into each other.' They walked back across the pasture to the end of Church Lane. He stopped by the gate. 'You walk on. It's maybe best you're not seen with me.'

'Yes, maybe.' She paused, not sure if she should offer her hand. 'Thank you, again.' She walked on and didn't look back.

***

Jem watched Ella's swaying hips as she walked along Church Lane and then followed her at a discreet distance. He strolled back to the field where he should have been working, stubble scrunching beneath his feet. His scythe was where he'd left it, and he joined the row of reapers who swung their way across the cornfield cutting a swath in the swaying corn. The slow, simple rhythm soothed him, his muscles flexing and relaxing, step, swing, and back, step, swing, and back. Would he see Ella again? Would he

29

win his bet? She was a pretty girl: a cut above the local maids. Too good for the likes of him, that was for sure.

He was chasing hares in the moonlight with a three-legged dog. Ella had an independent spirit that wouldn't settle for the boredom of village life. The corn fell before him, as he kept pace with Old George on one side and Herbie Longfellow on the other and tried to copy their smooth, deliberate action. Did they find village life boring? A bit of poaching up the Chase was as much excitement as most of the lads of Yardley ever got – that and taking a willing girl behind the Rose and Crown privy for a kiss.

Ella Maundrell wouldn't be the sort of girl to give him a kiss behind any privy or help Ma with scrubbing floors and the weekly wash. No, Ella wasn't the right sort of girl for the likes of him. Forget Ella. Forget the bet. Louisa, the Cartwright's scullery maid, was pretty and not promised to no-one, as far as he knew.

***

Ella was on an errand for the reverend, taking a basket of vegetables from the rectory garden to an old lady in one of the cottages in the High Street. She stepped aside at the sound of voices and the rumble of wheels. Three youths sat atop a loaded hay cart pulled by a roan mare.

One of the lads whistled. 'Fancy a roll in the hay, sweetheart?'

Her cheeks heated with embarrassment, but before she could think of a scathing reply, one of the lads jumped down. It was Jem.

His shirt sleeves were rolled up, and his collar was undone, showing tanned skin. 'Take no notice of my idiot of a cousin, Ella.'

'I didn't intend to.'

Jem continued, unabashed. 'He's Cal, and the other one is Nat. He's my cousin, too.'

She clutched the basket tighter. 'Mrs Downs is Cal's aunt, I think.'

30

Cal and Nat jumped down. Nat smiled broadly. 'So this is the lovely Ella?'

Jem's brown face reddened. 'Ella Maundrell, meet the village idiots. Caleb Brafield and Nathan Denton.

She held out a clean hand in greeting and was rewarded with two grubby ones in return. 'Nice to meet you both.' She refrained from wiping her hand on her dress. 'I'm off to visit Eliza Payne. I must be going. The reverend is expecting me back.'

'See you around, Ella.' Jem paused as if making a decision. 'Fancy going to the copse again, find that jay feather? This evening?'

She shouldn't, but something inside her, body or heart, made her nod. The reverend would want her in his study around seven. She'd need a bit of fresh air after that. 'I can get out about eight o'clock?'

'I can make that. Same place?'

What on earth was she doing? 'Church Lane, eight o'clock, then.'

Jem clapped Cal on the shoulder, and the three lads ran after the hay cart. He turned and waved, blew her a kiss, and then ran after Cal and Nat.

The feeling that the memory of Ralph's kiss had stirred trembled through her. This was wrong and, yet, why should she deny her womanhood?

She found it hard to concentrate on the reverend's sermon that evening. It was something about duty and diligence and trusting in her saviour, and she promised to read and inwardly digest the texts he'd bookmarked for her in her Bible. At last, he let her go, and she ran out through the kitchen door before Mrs Downs found work for idle hands.

Jem was waiting for her. 'I thought we'd go and see if there are newts in the pond.' He led the way across two fields. In the middle of the second was a small group of trees. Beneath their shade, the water was dark. A duck took to the water, followed by half-grown ducklings, and a croaking noise suggested frogs. Jem bent down at the water's edge and beckoned her. 'You sometimes see newts here, if you keep very still.'

She sat beside him and stared into the water. His closeness made her uncomfortable, but it seemed rude and standoffish not to sit where he'd suggested, and, anyway, she wouldn't see newts unless he pointed them out.

He was silent for a long moment. 'There look.'

'I see it.' She smiled. 'I've never seen one before.'

'I can show you all the wild places, Ella. There's badger cubs the far side of the copse.'

'I should get back. Mrs Downs will be looking for me.'

He got to his feet and held out a hand to help her up. His hand was strong and sure. She smoothed her skirts and followed him through the trees and back into the field.

'I really like you, Ella.'

His finger caressed her chin and lifted her face towards him. He wasn't much taller than she was. He cupped her cheeks in broad hands, and his lips brushed hers, sending shivers through her body. He withdrew, his eyes teasing, an eyebrow raised in question.

She lowered her eyelashes, sure she was blushing. 'Next time, I want a blue jay feather.'

He pulled her close and rested his chin on top of her head. 'I shall make sure you have one, Ella. I shall make sure you have everything you ever need.'

Her knees trembled as her lips sought his, hers tentative, gentle, and his firm and demanding. She surrendered herself, body and soul. He let her go at last, leaving her breathless and shaking, and pressed his lips to her hand.

If this was sin, she would gladly burn in hell for all eternity.

32

Chapter Three

Stained glass in the west window painted the sunlight red, yellow, and green across Ella's hands, clasped in prayer and still burning from the brush of Jem's soft lips. St Andrews was silent, its oak pews empty but for her and her churning thoughts. Below the altar, someone had left wheat and barley sheaves, anticipating September's harvest service. Mrs Downs would soon begin baking for harvest supper, and the next full moon would be a harvest moon.

She'd left Jem at the gate, as before, so they wouldn't be seen walking through the village together. Her stomach clenched, heart thudding, at the memory of his parting kiss: the stone walls of the church swam in and out of her vision. Was this love or lust she felt for Jem, and if it wasn't her body betraying her with lust, surely love could never be wrong? It felt so right. Jem felt so right.

Unless his intentions weren't honourable. Her mother had warned her often enough of men who promised the world to get what they wanted and gave nothing in return. Many a young woman had lost her virginity to a lustful man and lived to regret it.

She ran her hands across her flat stomach, imagining it swelling with Jem's child. It was obvious he had feelings for her, wasn't it? Would he offer marriage? If she gave him her body, would she be left holding the baby like her mother? She didn't believe Jem would shirk his responsibility despite Ev Downs's poor opinion of him.

If he proved himself worthy, would Reverend Buchanan agree to a union between them? She would fish, discreetly, into her mentor's intentions for her. It would be wrong to encourage Jem further if there were no hope for them. The thought made bile rise in her throat. Who was the reverend, or her mother, or Mr Josiah, to control her life so? Jem had a wage, he worked, but could he support a family?

The coloured pattern of the stained glass had moved from her hands to the column at the side of her. She let out a long slow breath, shocked by her own thoughts. Was she seriously contemplating the very thing she'd determined not to do? She wanted to better herself, make a good match. Love didn't feed a baby or clothe it. Love wouldn't put a roof over her head. Love wouldn't stop her working her fingers to the bone or dying in the poorhouse.

She got to her feet, kicking aside a kneeler. She'd told the reverend she'd marry for love, but he was right to deny her wish. She was a silly, childish girl. What had love got to do with the harsh realities of life? Her iron-shod boots clattered across the tiled floor. Mrs Downs would be wondering where she was.

***

Seven o'clock the next evening, Reverend Buchanan was waiting for Ella in his study. He motioned her to her chair and studied her over his spectacles. 'So, Ella, what have you learned since we last spoke?'

She considered the question for a long moment. 'That I'm not sure I know the difference between love and lust.'

He raised an eyebrow. 'An insightful statement from one so young. What prompts it?'

A rough fingernail absorbed her attention.

'Well? Speak up, Ella.'

'I was thinking of Ralph. I love him as I'd love a brother, not how I feel I would love a husband.'

'Brotherly love is to be commended, but the love of a woman for her husband should be a pure and unconditional gift kept only for him.' He gazed at his Bible as if able to see through the leather binding. 'Hebrews thirteen, verse four. "*Let marriage be held in honour among all, and let the marriage bed be undefiled, for God will judge the sexually immoral and adulterous.*'" He patted the good book. 'Marriage is a life-long commitment, Ella. Lust should not be a basis for it. Many a happy marriage has been arranged where the parties have grown to love one another. Many a marriage based in lust has been a path to adultery, immorality, and disaster.'

'How can I know if a man looks at me with love not lust?'

Reverend Buchanan contemplated her, his head on one side like a curious robin. He straightened. 'Matthew five, verse twenty-eight. "*But I say to you that everyone who looks at a woman with lustful intent has already committed adultery with her in his heart.*"' He lowered his eyes, appearing to compose himself before moving to the window that looked out across the lawn. 'A man who will wait until the marriage bed is one who loves you, not the man who asks you for favours you shouldn't give. Keep yourself pure, Ella, and love will come. Psalms 119, I think. "*How can a young man keep his way pure? By guarding it according to your word. With my whole heart I seek you; let me not wander from your commandments.*" Seek God, Ella, and he will guide you.'

'I shall try, Reverend.'

He nodded and turned back to her, smiling. 'I'll see you in church tomorrow. I have someone I want you to meet. His name is Harry, and his family are tenant farmers over at Newhay. They're a good family but not too far above your station. He's a little older than you, a steady lad, and he'd be a good match. Make sure you look your best. Don't let me down, now.'

Her heart missed a beat. She schooled her features carefully. 'No, Reverend.'

'And remember Galatians five, verse sixteen. "*But I say, walk by the spirit and you will not gratify the desires of the flesh.*"' Reverend Buchanan sighed. 'It's not always easy, Ella, I'm a man like any other, but we must all strive to obey Our Lord.'

Sunday arrived with a shower. Talk was of the harvest, corn-ricks, the weather, and preparations for the next month's harvest

35

supper. It seemed all the village women were baking or preserving: salting, pickling, smoking, hanging, or curing, while their menfolk were reaping, stooking, and loading sheaves ready for threshing.

Reverend Buchanan met her by the church's south porch. He reached out and pressed one of her hands between both of his. 'You look lovely, Ella. Any man would be proud to have you on his arm.'

She forced a smile. She didn't want to be an ornament to any man's vanity.

'Ah, here's Harry now. Give him a chance and don't judge him by his looks. They've scarred more than his face.'

The young man walking towards her looked about thirty, thick-set with fair hair and pale blue eyes. His face bore the marks of smallpox: probably, she thought with some compassion, why he was still single.

Reverend Buchanan greeted him warmly. 'Harry, I'd like you meet my protégé, Miss Ella Maundrell. Ella, this is Harry Cartwright.'

Harry held out a hand and smiled. 'Pleased to meet you, Miss Ella. I see you managed to get dry.'

'Dry?' Her throat was as parched as the word she croaked.

'I met you the day you arrived off the coach. I'm afraid I splashed you with the cartwheels.' His hand was warm, broad, and callused. He released her fingers and turned to the couple beside him. 'My mother and father.'

He'd called her a daft mare. She swallowed. 'Pleased to meet you.'

'Ella.' Harry's mother looked her up and down with taut lips, as if she were a prize heifer or a brood mare.

His father's eyes twinkled. 'Honoured to make your acquaintance, Miss Maundrell.'

She repressed an urge to curtsey. 'Mrs Cartwright... Mr

36

Cartwright…'

Organ music flowed unharmoniously from the church door. Reverend Buchanan raised his eyes to heaven and held out an encompassing arm. 'We should go in.'

The church was almost full. Jem sat in his Sunday best at the rear of the church with young men she assumed were relations. She met his eyes, struggling to keep her expression neutral and the thumping of her heart steady. Mrs Downs, sitting with several women who looked like sisters, nodded to her encouragingly. Something deep inside screamed at being herded to a future over which she had no control. She found herself on the third row of pews, two rows behind the fourth Marquis of Northampton and his family, and next to Harry's mother.

The reverend's voice droned on, and her attention wandered. Strange gargoyles grinned down at her, taunting and warning her. She imagined walking down this aisle in her wedding dress with Harry waiting at the altar and having Harry's children baptised in the ancient font. Her life stretched in an endless dark tunnel of duty and regret for what might have been. Could she grow to love this man she didn't know? After one blissful kiss with Jem that had tingled through every fibre of her body, should she even try? The walls of the church closed around her, blotting out the wild, woodland canopy and the earthy smells of the Chase with cold stone and the mustiness of a living grave. Voices rang in her ears, loud in prayer: her funeral dirge, her life over before she'd even lived it. She swayed on her feet and clutched the back of the pew in front of her. She had to get out into the fresh air.

'Are you unwell?' Harry's quiet voice offered her a way of escape.

'I feel faint… I need air. I'm sorry.' He rose to accompany her, but she shook her head and kept her voice to a whisper. 'Stay here. I'll be fine.' She pushed past him to the side aisle and left the church by the south door. Leaning against the church wall, she took several deep breaths. 'Besoms, besoms, *besoms*…'

'Not very ladylike language, Ella?'

Jem's amused tone made her fingers curl. 'This isn't funny, Jem. They want me to marry that man.'

'Harry Cartwright?' Jem's face reordered itself. 'They can't force you against your will.'

She earned nothing from her work for Reverend Buchanan. Her only means of support was an allowance from her mother's employer: a small amount but a generous gesture considering he was probably also recompensing the rector for his expenses in keeping her. 'They can cut off my allowance, refuse me permission to marry anyone else – I'm underage, Jem. I'd be destitute. You don't know what it's like being dependent, a mere girl to be married off.'

'You can work, can't you? Or don't women work where you come from? Ma could teach you lacemaking. Most of the village women do it to make a little extra money.'

Jem's gibe cut deep. *Ideas above your station in life, young lady.* She wouldn't be mocked. 'I wanted...'

'You wanted a rich husband?'

'Is it wrong to want my children to have a decent home, enough food, and a good father?'

Jem fiddled with a shirt button. 'Harry's not a bad chap. His dad's a bit of a ladies' man, by all accounts, but you could do worse. It's a lot of work being a farmer's wife, but they have help in the house at Newhay, as well as on the land. They're respected round here. A good family. Harry has prospects. You wouldn't go hungry. Yes, you could do a lot worse.'

'I don't love him. Jem...'

Jem's face softened: he put a finger to her lips, as if hearing what she would say would cast their futures in stone. 'I know what I promised, but I lied. I ain't got two ha'pennies to rub together. Never will have. Hell, I owe the court nearly half a year's wages. I can't give you what you want, what you deserve, Ella. Only a life of hardship and never knowing where the next meal or the next quarter's rent is coming from.'

She brushed his finger aside. 'But we kissed. Jem, I...'

'No. Don't say it.' He looked past her, over her shoulder. 'It was just a kiss. It meant nothing.'

'I don't believe you.'

'It's true. If I married every girl I kissed or rolled in the hay with...' He shrugged. 'I'm not the marrying kind, Ella. Give Harry a chance. Get to know him.'

'But...'

'I like you, Ella, but that's all.' His voice was cold, his face expressionless. 'I can't marry you. I don't want to marry you.'

She backed away from him, her heart lurching from despair to anger. She'd almost made the mistake of her life in trusting a man she'd only just met. Worse, she'd let herself fall in love. She turned and ran back to the rectory, not stopping until she was in her attic room. She flung herself onto her bed and sobbed until her throat was sore and her chest ached.

***

Jem slumped at the foot of a gravestone, holding his head in his hands. He'd done the right thing, so why did he feel so empty, so angry, and like a complete bastard? Ev Downs had been right when she'd called on Ma and Dad, and talk had turned to Ella. The reverend had told Ev he was duty-bound to find the girl a good husband and fulfil the obligation Ella's benefactor had placed upon him. Ev Downs had made it quite clear that the likes of Jem Weston wouldn't be acceptable and had promised the reverend's anger if he interfered with Ella's future in any way; Jem Weston wouldn't, Ev had assured him, be doing Ella any favours.

He'd given Ella a life. She was educated and refined: he couldn't see her with her hands raw from handling cotton threads and bobbins all the hours God gave, like his mother's, or red from having them in hot wash water all day, her fingers and knuckles swollen with arthritis and rheumatism. Harry would treat her fairly.

39

Jane Cartwright, Harry's mother, had a hard exterior, but she wasn't a bad person: she had a dairymaid, scullery maid, and housemaid to keep in order. Ella would learn to run her own household at Jane's apron strings.

Harry's father, John, was forward thinking, like the marquis, and keen to buy one of those new-fangled horse-drawn reapers. He'd already purchased a fine Percheron mare from the Northampton horse fair to pull it. Harry was a good stockman in his own right, having built a herd of beef and dairy Gloucesters from next to nothing. Newhay was well-set and offered Ella a decent life and a secure future. It was the likes of him, Jem Weston, as would never amount to nothing more than a labourer, a hired hand, for the likes of Harry Cartwright. Cal's Aunty Ev was right: Jem Weston had done Ella Maundrell a favour.

He brushed dampness from his face with a rough hand. What was done was done: it was for the best. Ella was young, she'd get over him in next to no time, and she'd have babes soon enough to keep her busy. He picked up a stone and hurled it at a leaning gravestone, the resting place of Harry's grandfather.

Why did Ella have to come into his life? Her soft lips and smooth skin, the smell of her hair, her gentle innocent smile: the taste of her. And Harry and Ella making love, love that was rightly his, made him sick to his stomach. The tenor bell chimed the hour. The service would be over, and worshippers would be coming out. He didn't want to see Harry Cartwright in his fine Sunday coat and breeches. He shambled from the churchyard with the steps of an old and broken man, stumbling towards the solitude of Cold Oak Copse and his memories of that last, long, sweet kiss. He rubbed away another tear. If he couldn't love Ella, he'd love no-one.

Chapter Four

Harry left the church at the end of the service, but Ella was nowhere to be seen. He shrugged. The girl was pretty, and as his father had said, she looked strong enough to bear children. Her hips weren't narrow, like some girls he'd had, and her breasts were full, her skin smooth. Yes, she was ripe for taking. He whistled as he helped his mother onto the pony trap.

His father spoke first. 'What do you think about young Ella, Harry? Pretty little thing, isn't she?'

His mother didn't give him a chance to answer. She glared at his father. 'Do you think she can work? Or does she think herself too genteel for that? I need help in the house, so I can let Louisa go, not someone who expects to be waited on.'

His father laughed. 'Her mother's a housekeeper, Jane. A widow, I believe, not the wife of the rector's acquaintance. She keeps house for a widower, a solicitor in Bath, who is a good friend of Reverend Buchanan. Ella's used to work. She also knows how to conduct herself in polite society. She'll be an asset to this family. I think the boy should wed her and be quick about it.'

'Do I get a say in this, Father?' He tickled the pony's rump with the whip, and it set off at a smart trot. 'I'm not a child to be told who to marry.'

His mother huffed her disapproval. 'Until you can produce a son and heir, you have no say in what goes on in this family.'

He clamped his lips. He'd had a handful of the less pretty village girls behind the privy of the Rose and Crown, and none of them had come running to him claiming pregnancy. As far as he knew, none of the whores he'd fucked had borne him children, whereas his father had bragged to him about having bastards all over the county. Bastards his mother knew nothing about.

He pushed away the niggling thought that his childhood illness had left him infertile. The village girls had been young, maybe too young for childbearing, and maybe whores went to the woman in Denton and got rid, afraid his pockmarks would disfigure their children, or so they could keep working.

He'd show the women who'd turned him down, and the whores who'd showed him pity, he could snare a beautiful woman. He needed a strong son to show his parents he was the son and heir they'd hoped for: the man his father refused to see. 'I shall marry this Ella, and I shall get her with child within the month. See if I don't.'

His father smiled. 'Then I shall inform the reverend we'll have the girl. Turn us around. The sooner the reverend knows, the better, before someone else snaps her up.'

***

Ella held up the dress that had arrived by carrier from Bedford. Cream, with tiny green leaves and pink flowers embroidered all over, it was of a quality she'd never expected to wear. It was a gift from her mother, but her excitement at wearing it to afternoon tea was tempered by the fact that Reverend Buchanan had invited the Cartwrights.

She held the dress against her and swirled the full skirt around before slipping the garment over her head. The bodice looked rather daring, the neckline revealing. She raised her chin, her fingers clenching the finely woven fabric. Jem had made his feelings clear enough; she'd show him how little she cared.

Opening the door to the drawing room, she paused, smoothed her dress, and adjusted her bodice. She pushed the door wider and smiled.

'Ella, my dear.' Reverend Buchanan beckoned her. 'Come and sit by Harry.' Harry hastily pulled out a chair for her. The reverend nodded and rubbed his hands together as if cold. 'Mrs Downs will bring tea shortly. Now, Mrs Cartwright. How are preparations for

42

harvest supper coming along? Mrs Downs tells me Ella here is quite accomplished in the kitchen.'

Mrs Cartwright adjusted the high neck of her dark gown and looked down her aquiline nose. 'Running a household is more than being a good cook.'

Harry smiled at her with an expression of commiseration. 'Being a good cook is a very good start, wouldn't you say, Ella?'

She smiled back, gratefully. 'I'm sure I have a lot to learn.'

Harry's mother nodded. Agreement or a slight softening of her superior attitude? 'You're very young, Ella. It takes years to acquire the skills needed to run a household like mine.' She emphasised the word mine as if to establish her position as head of the household and put her firmly into her place.

'You look very beautiful, Ella.' Mr Cartwright's attempt to ameliorate his wife's words was met with a glare, but he ignored it. 'Wouldn't you agree, Harry?'

Harry glanced at his father and nodded, apparently lost for words and looking slightly uncomfortable.

Mrs Cartwright had no such problem. 'Reverend Buchanan tells us you're from Bath. I dare say you find our fashions rather dull, Ella. Thrift, diligence, modesty, and sobriety are my bywords. Plain food, hard work, plain dress, and abstinence.'

She glanced down at the bare flesh above her neckline, flushing. 'The dress was a gift from my mother. It's the latest fashion in *polite* society.'

Mrs Cartwright bridled at the intended slight, but Mr Cartwright forestalled his wife's next comment and leant across Harry. 'We're too stuck in our ways, Ella. Still in the eighteenth century. You're a breath of fresh air, fresh young blood like our new breeding stock. Just what Yardley and the Cartwright family needs. Isn't that right, Harry?'

Harry's cheeks reddened, and he stiffened in his seat. 'Yes, Father.'

She forced a polite smile, and conversation turned to the new McCormick reaper being developed in America that Mr Cartwright had seen spoken of in *The Mercury*. She let her thoughts wander back to Cold Oak Copse and her first and last real kiss.

'Ella?'

'Pardon?'

'You've hardly eaten anything. Mrs Cartwright was asking if you'd like to take tea with them tomorrow.'

'I'm sorry. Yes, that would be delightful.'

Mrs Cartwright smiled with as much warmth as a slab of marble. 'Harry can show you the farm and the copse.' The marble warmed slightly. 'Shall we say four o'clock? I'm sure Mr Cartwright can spare our son for an hour.'

***

Jem straightened from mixing lime mortar for the wall he was repairing in the lane. The reverend's pony trap was leaving the rectory with Ella and Reverend Buchanan sitting side by side. Ella should be helping Mrs Downs get the reverend's afternoon tea at this time of day, so where were they going all dressed up? Newhay? He cleaned his trowel and shovel in a bucket of water and leaned the shovel against the wall. If anyone asked, he could say he was fetching more lime or bricks.

At the turnpike road, he crossed and took a path across the fields, following the brook towards Newhay. He stopped and looked back at the village: he should let Ella get on with her life. The chimneys of Newhay stood pale against the backdrop of the Chase. He couldn't bear to think of her with another man.

He paused for breath by the side of the track that led to the farm buildings. Jesus Christ, what did he think he was going to do? Drag Ella home? She was free to make her own decisions. That didn't mean he couldn't watch over her and be there if she needed him. He slipped behind a length of unlaid hedge. Harry Cartwright had better be treating her right, or he'd answer to Jem Weston.

Brambles tore at his jacket, fallen crab apples crunched underfoot, and branches snagged at his hair. He melted into the undergrowth and waited.

The farmhouse door opened. Ella came out followed closely by Harry. Ella was smiling. His heart constricted. Harry put a hand on her arm and pointed to a long stone barn. They walked towards it. Not altogether trusting what Harry had in mind, he moved position for a better view.

Creeping closer, along the hedge line, he tried to put Ella's soft skin from his mind. The barn door opened inwards, and little light fell into the interior through the long, narrow slits in the stone that let in fresh air. All he could see was Ella's pale dress against an oblong of black. He crept closer still. Voices, laughing.

'She was born in July.' Harry's voice. 'She'll join the milking herd when she's old enough to calve.'

He let out a held breath: not a hay barn and wicked seduction. Harry was showing her the calves.

'She's beautiful. Has she got a name?'

'You're beautiful, too, Ella. I think I'll call her Ella, after you. Or you can name her if you like.'

Ella laughed again. 'I've never had a cow named after me.'

He ducked back to cover when figures moved in the doorway. Harry was close to Ella. She didn't respond when Harry kissed her cheek, but she didn't pull away either. Apparently encouraged, Harry pulled her closer and kissed her lips. It seemed Ella had made her choice.

***

Ella stared out of her window, biting her top lip. She'd made her decision, not that she'd been given much choice, and now she must stand by it. The betrothal was to be announced in church tomorrow and the marriage banns read. Letters had been dispatched, post-haste, to obtain her mother's permission. Neither she nor the rector doubted it would be swiftly forthcoming, a fact that had put a smile on the reverend's face and a bustle into the steps of Mrs Downs who had a wedding feast to plan.

Harry had been kind to her, and she hadn't lied to him about her feelings for him. Love, he assured her, would follow when they knew one another better. She wondered, briefly, about the need for haste but put it down to Harry's urgent desire to bed her and the rector's eagerness to have someone else responsible for her 'wanton lusts'.

She turned back to her room, only now realising that she would soon have to leave what had become her sanctuary, her own safe, private place, to share her life with people she'd only just met. Her heart thudded beneath her ribs. She had to give her maidenhood to a virtual stranger. He was thirteen years her senior. Would he be a patient lover? A year from now she could be a mother. Seventeen years old, and her life was mapped out: the farm, Harry, and a brood of children, for Harry would need sons. She shrugged off a feeling of entrapment, instead counting blessings. Life could hold worse: a lot of women would be thankful to have such a secure, settled future, a husband who wanted her, and the chance of children to love and to keep her in her old age.

She raised her chin in defiance. Jem wasn't hers and never would be. She must make the best of it or wallow in self-pity, and self-pity wasn't her way. Tomorrow, in church, Jem would learn of her betrothal. Maybe he'd regret letting someone else have her. If he did, it would serve him right.

The light was failing: she'd take a brisk walk, before it got too dark, and clear her mind of both Harry and Jem. The fresh air would do her good. Her steps took her along Church Lane, past stone cottages, towards the gate that led to Cold Oak Copse. The smell of cooking wafted from an open window and reminded her Mrs Downs would soon need her help. She strode on, a breeze on her cheek, breathing in the scents of freedom it carried. Birds, silhouettes in black, flocked towards the copse looking for an evening roost: tiny specks in the sky, they rose and fell, turning as one like a shoal of fish in water and rippling like water around

46

stones. The sight transfixed her.

'Starlings.' A breath at her side made her heart lurch. Jem's face held an expression she couldn't read.

She pushed down a desire to fold herself into his arms. 'How do they move together like that?'

He shrugged. 'God's truth? I've no idea.'

She smiled and leaned on the gate. If anyone saw her here, alone with Jem, her honour would be in question. Did she care? He'd hurt her, but she reached for him with her heart. 'You promised me a blue jay feather.'

He shrugged again and let his hand fall to his side. 'Ain't found one yet. Anyways...'

'Harry and I...'

'I'm happy for you.' His smile didn't reach his eyes.

'But?'

'But nothing. You'll be mistress of your own household. I'm happy for you, truly.'

He'd thrown her lifeline back to her, ungrasped. She turned from him. 'You'll be in church, tomorrow?'

'Of course.'

She looked away, fingers clenched. 'I pray God will grant you a happy life, James Weston.' She threw the comment over her shoulder and strode back along the lane, letting silent tears fall.

***

Jem fidgeted on the hard pew, twirling the blue jay feather between fingers and thumb. He could have given it to Ella yesterday in the lane: maybe, he should have. He would, at least, have kept one of his promises to her. He tucked the feather out of sight inside his inner breast pocket: now wasn't the right time. He'd wait for her outside after the service and slip it into her hand. The church was filling with folk. The Cartwrights were towards the front of the

47

church, as usual. Ella, and Mrs Downs, who was doubtless acting as her chaperone, sat with them. He glowered at Harry, who leaned back in the pew, his arm stretched across the low back behind Ella in a gesture of possessiveness.

Cal dug him in the ribs with his elbow and nodded towards Ella. 'Looks like you're going to owe us a week's wages, Jem.'

Nat followed where they looked. 'You gonna win that bet or what? That Harry'll have her if you don't. I heard…'

Reverend Buchanan turned from the altar to face them. Nat fell silent and they stood and bowed their heads.

'Please be seated.' The reverend surveyed his flock, waiting for the shuffle of feet to quiet. 'Today's sermon has a special theme. Thanksgiving for getting in the hay, and a prayer and thanks for a good harvest. Not just the harvesting of crops planted and tended with love, but the planting, tending, and harvesting of love itself.'

Ella had planted a seed of love. Could he make something of himself and be a worthy husband for her? He would give her the jay feather.

Reverend Buchanan smiled and looked towards the Cartwrights. 'Today I'm happy to announce the betrothal of Harry Cartwright, of Newhay, and Ella Maundrell, who has been staying with me at the rectory. Today we pray for the growth of the seed of love for Harry and Ella as they enter into God's holy estate of marriage. I shall read the banns at the end of the service, and the wedding will take place in three weeks' time.'

So soon? He bowed his head to hide his grief. He'd thought he'd have time to win Ella back. His fingers smoothed the filaments of the jay feather; it was too late. There would never now be a right time to give it to her.

Chapter Five

My dearest Ella. I am so happy to hear of your betrothal to Harry Cartwright. Reverend Buchanan assures me he is eminently acceptable, a young man of good family with prospects. You have my blessing and the approval of Mr Josiah, who has kindly agreed to do you the honour of giving you away, and we hope to travel by coach the day before your marriage to be with you. Perhaps, the reverend would be kind enough to send a carriage to meet the Oxford coach at Northampton and arrange lodging for us in Yardley Hastings.

Her mother's letter in her hand, Ella fidgeted on the hard chair in the housekeeper's small sitting room as Mrs Downs attempted to cajole wayward wisps of her hair into a neat spiral. The letter of permission had arrived only that morning, and there was scant time to send a reply before her mother left Bath. She couldn't help feeling Mr Barton was coming merely to ensure she was safely married and away from Ralph.

Her wedding was still some days away, but her stomach churned with apprehension. This evening's harvest supper and dance, to be held in a huge barn on the Castle Ashby estate, was to be her first public appearance with Harry, as a couple. Butterflies danced in her stomach. 'Ouch.'

'Keep still, girl, then it won't pull.' Mrs Downs passed her a hand mirror and looked over her shoulder into it as she held it in front of her face. 'There now, Ella. Don't you look a picture?'

She had to admit the woman had a way with hair and clothes. She looked quite presentable. 'Am I doing the right thing, Mrs Downs?'

Mrs Downs laid a hand on her shoulder and squeezed reassuringly. 'You're bound to feel nervous, Ella. It's only natural seeing as your mother ain't here.'

'She writes that she'll be here for the wedding.'

'We'll give the spare room a good bottoming, come Monday, ready for her. It'll keep your mind off the wedding. Mrs Cartwright can be a bit of a harridan, but young Harry's not a bad lad, you know, and a hard worker. Better than some I could mention.'

Mrs Downs was alluding to Jem. She tried to keep her face neutral. Nothing could keep her mind from the wedding or, to be more truthful, the wedding night. 'I wish Mother were here now. Mrs Downs...' How could she ask Mrs Downs what it would be like?

The housekeeper seemed to read her mind. 'A girl needs her mother at such a time and at birthing. The first time he lays with you – well, it may hurt a bit. After that...' She patted her shoulder. 'It'll be fine. You do your duty, as and when required, and bear what you can't enjoy with fortitude.'

'Enjoy?'

Mrs Downs fiddled with a curl; her face in the mirror was red. 'A body given in love – well, that's whole different thing, Ella.'

Would she ever experience that? Her stomach spasmed at the memory of Jem's one kiss and her cheeks heated. 'I don't love Harry. I told him as much.'

Her face must have betrayed her, because Mrs Downs frowned. 'Marriage can be based on mutual respect. Love can follow on its heels. But that isn't what you meant, is it?'

'Not really.' She fingered the cameo at her throat, a gift from Harry: his grandmother's. 'It's not important.'

'If you're mooning over young James – well, all I can say is the sooner you're married to Harry, the better.'

'He doesn't love me.'

'James or Harry?'

The truth struck her like a shower of hail. 'Neither of them.'

Mrs Downs gave her a brief hug. 'There, there, Ella. Don't fret over it. Even queens and duchesses don't get to marry for love. They marry for duty. Why should you fret over marrying young Harry? Just because his face is like it is.'

His pockmarks didn't bother her. It was the lack of spark between the two of them. 'Our queen married for love, they say.'

'Then she's a lucky woman, and long may she be happy, God bless her.' Mrs Downs glanced at the grandfather clock in the corner. 'Now, I must get on, Ella. It's eleven o'clock and not a poe emptied.'

Would God bless Harry and Ella Cartwright?

***

The trestle tables had been cleared away and the benches arranged around the walls of the barn. The roof timbers were hung with lanterns and decorated with corn dollies. A trio of fiddlers was setting up in one corner. Jem glared across the room at Harry, who had an arm around Ella and was talking across her to Joe and Elizabeth Upton. She glanced around and caught his eye but looked away. He had a sudden urge to hold her in his arms one last time. Maybe he'd ask her to dance *Strip the Willow* or the *Gay Gordons*.

The fiddlers struck up a tune. He looked around for a suitable partner as Harry led Ella onto the dance floor. Louisa, the Cartwrights' scullery maid, didn't have a partner. Guilt at using her was overridden by the need to be close to Ella. He whirled Louisa round, picking out Ella among the couples. Their eyes locked over Harry's shoulder and his guts constricted.

The reel ended and he thanked his partner for the dance, bowing to her as he'd seen Harry do to Ella. He glanced across at Harry, who was downing a tankard of beer. Ella looked lost. This was his chance; he crossed the room towards her, and as the fiddlers began the next reel, he held out his hand to her. She glanced over her shoulder, uncertainly, but Harry was laughing with Joe. She took his outstretched hand, and he led her onto the floor.

The music soared in his head, urging him on. Her hand was warm and soft in his, her waist supple and slim beneath his arm, and her breath on his neck too close for comfort. He looked into her eyes, deep, fathomless pools of desire. A rough hand on his shoulder broke their gaze.

'Hands off, Weston. This girl's mine.' Harry grasped Ella by the arm and dragged her away, swinging her around in time to the music.

He stared after Ella, barely aware of Harry's scowl, until laughing made him realise he stood partnerless in the centre of a swirl of beer-fumed, sweating bodies. He dodged the whirling couples and made for the bar, a series of trestles with barrels and rows of tankards set on top of them. Beer was free tonight, courtesy of the marquis. He downed three pints in quick succession; he needed to get seriously drunk.

'Steady up, Weston. You'd think the beer was running low the way you're going at it.' Joe Upton knocked a tap into a new barrel with a mallet. 'I see Harry got his girl back. I reckon that one's got wandering eyes, Jem.'

'Don't talk about Ella like that.'

Joe smiled a slow, teasing smile. 'What, you sweet on Ella? That's it, ain't it? You're sweet on Harry's girl.'

'No, I ain't.' He tore his eyes from Ella and drowned his desire in his beer. 'But she's a nice girl. She needs treating right.'

Joe smirked. 'Oh, Harry'll treat her right. You ask the girls…' Joe turned away.

He grabbed Joe's arm. 'What girls? Harry's getting married on Saturday, for God's sake. What girls?'

Joe snatched his arm free. 'Grow up, Weston. What sort of girls do you think a man with a pocked face finds? Girls who'll take his money, like she will. Whores.' He pointed to Ella. 'He'll make sure she stays home at nights, but he won't give up his whores for

52

any woman.'

'Damn Harry Cartwright.' Bile rose in his throat. He had to talk to Ella. Warn her. The music stopped, and Harry steered Ella away from him towards the bench where the Cartwrights sat with the Newcombes from Roundhay. Louisa caught his eye and smiled; maybe she knew what went on behind closed doors at Newhay.

***

Ella watched Jem, who was deep in conversation with a dark-haired girl. Jem and the girl had been dancing together earlier, and as the music struck up again, he led her back onto the dance floor. Was she one of the girls Jem had rolled in the hay with? She bit her lip. What would it be like with Jem?

'Ella?' Harry's voice shocked her back to the present. 'I asked you if you wanted something to drink.'

'No, thank you. I think I've had enough.'

Harry frowned. 'Is that your way of saying you think I've had enough?'

'That's for you to decide.'

Harry looked across the room. 'I see our scullery maid has found her level. If James Weston asks you to dance again, you refuse. Do you understand? It's not becoming of a future bride to put herself about like that.'

Put herself about? 'Yes, Harry.' She lowered her gaze, glancing sideways as Jem twirled Louisa closer. He smiled at her and glided away.

'If he comes near you again, I'll smash his teeth down his throat.'

Harry was plainly drunk and full of bravado. This wasn't the place or time to disagree with him. 'I'll make sure I stay close to you, Harry.'

Jem made several attempts to catch her eye, but she ignored him. She didn't want him having to defend himself against Harry, who was taller and broader. This was her fault for dancing with Jem earlier, and it wasn't fair on either of them. Jem and the dark-haired girl left the barn, and a pang of regret spasmed through her. She'd have given her whole future with Harry for one roll in the hay with Jem. The rector's words rang in her head. "But I say to you that everyone who looks at a woman with lustful intent has already committed adultery with her in his heart." It wasn't just men who had lustful intent. She would grow to love Harry, as she must, but she'd just committed adultery in her heart.

Chapter Six

'Ready for your big night, son?' John Cartwright adjusted his son's cravat.

Harry brushed his father's hand away. 'I'm quite capable of tying it myself. I don't need your help, Father.'

His father dropped his hand to his side and smirked. 'You need my help bedding young Ella?'

'No. This one's mine, Father. Her virginity is mine to take, not yours.'

His father hadn't finished with his taunts. 'You have any trouble, boy, I'll be glad to finish a man's job for you.' John patted his shoulder. 'I'll be listening to make sure you do it right, son.'

'Oh, I'll do it right. Your whores taught me how to pleasure them.'

'And a man with my experience could teach the girl how to pleasure you.'

He clenched a fist. 'Leave it, Father, or so help me...'

John Cartwright laughed. 'You haven't got the guts, boy.' He shrugged. 'Remember, if you can't manage to get her pregnant, I'll be happy to oblige. If Jem Weston doesn't get there first.'

'I said leave it. Ella's mine, not yours or Jem Weston's, and I'll get a whole litter of children on her, not just one disappointment of a son.'

'I'll be proud of you when you can show me you're a man, Harry, and not until.'

He pushed past his father and out into the yard, where the pony and trap stood ready to bring his bride home. Bride! His virgin bride. He wished he'd had a virgin before, so he knew how she'd react. Would she be afraid? She was young, innocent. He hardened in anticipation. He'd make her beg him for more and make sure his father heard and knew he was doing her right. Doing a man's job. And he'd make sure Jem Weston heard what a good fuck she was.

***

Ella arranged mauve Michaelmas daisies into a small bouquet to match the ones Mrs Downs had kindly woven into her auburn hair. Lace, purchased from lace makers in the village and sewn with tiny stitches by Mrs Downs and herself, had turned her best dress into something special for her wedding. She took a deep calming breath. In a little less than an hour, she'd be Mrs Harry Cartwright.

A knock at her door startled her. 'Ella?' Her mother's voice.

'Come in.'

Her mother held out a small purse of cream silk on a long silver chain. 'You might like to have a handkerchief or some smelling salts. I thought this would go with your dress.'

She took the purse and gave her mother a long hug. 'I am doing the right thing?'

Her mother arranged her full skirt and sat carefully on the chair in the corner. 'Ella, Harry is a better match than I could have hoped for you. He's a decent man, according to the rector. A farmer's wife is a step up from a housekeeper, and he'll provide for you and be a good father to your children.'

'I want my children to have a father.' She didn't even know who her father was. 'Is that all that's important in a marriage?'

'No, but it's a good foundation to build on. You're so lucky to have Reverend Buchanan to marry you and Mr Josiah to give you away. No broomstick marriage for my daughter.'

'Why didn't you marry my father?' The words were out before she could stop them. 'I know Mr Josiah calls you Mrs Maundrell, but that's just convention because you're his housekeeper. You weren't married when you had me.'

56

Her mother picked fluff from her sleeve. 'I would have married your father if it had been proper to do so. The circumstances...' Her mother sighed. 'We loved each other, but he was above me socially. It would have ruined his reputation. His career.'

'Did he know about me?'

'Yes, Ella, of course, he knows about you.'

She swivelled on her heel. 'He knows? So who is he? Why isn't he here?'

'I can't tell you, Ella. It's like I said. His career would be ruined if it were known he had an illegitimate child.'

'And you've kept quiet all these years to protect him?'

'It's what you do when you love someone, Ella. Protect them.'

'And what about me? What about protecting me?'

'The less you know, the better. It's why I wanted you away from Bath, away from vicious tongues. Harry will protect you as I can't.'

What was so dangerous about Bath? It didn't make sense.

Another knock interrupted her thoughts, and Mrs Downs's head appeared round the door. 'Oh, my Lord, you look beautiful, Ella Maundrell.' The housekeeper fussed at the lace adorning the wedding dress's long sleeves and stood back, looking her over critically. 'Perfect. Are you ready for your big day? The reverend has the pony trap at the front door, and Mr Barton is waiting.'

'Please tell Reverend Buchanan I'm ready.' She straightened and smoothed the lace on her bodice. This was it. This was the first day of the rest of her life. *Till death us do part...*

***

It was September twelfth, seventeen days before Michaelmas, and tonight would be a harvest moon: a good night to set some snares and get a rabbit or, if there were no keepers about, maybe a hare or even a pheasant. It was also the day Ella married Harry Cartwright

57

and put herself forever beyond Jem's reach.

Jem rotated the blue jay feather in his fingers, its bands of iridescent blue sparkling in the morning sun. He'd tried to call on Ella at the rectory, after he'd spoken to Louisa, but had been turned away by Cal's Aunty Ev.

What Louisa had told him weighed heavy on his heart. She knew nothing of Harry's indiscretions and had thought Joe was making it up to taunt him, which calmed his heart a bit, but she'd let slip that Mr Cartwright wasn't to be trusted around the maids, and that Mrs Cartwright had let her go as she wouldn't be needed once Ella was in the house. She'd said Mrs Cartwright had been quite blatant about Ella being young, strong, free labour in the scullery and would be firmly under her command. Free labour. Was that all the Cartwrights wanted? Free labour and a breeding bitch for Harry's whelps.

He'd thought he was doing right by Ella, not giving her the feather he'd promised her, but now he wasn't so sure. He'd found it for her and had made a special trip to look for it. If he'd given it to her weeks ago, before she'd met Harry, things might be different now.

The church door stood open. Inside had been decorated with Michaelmas daisies and had flowers, sheaves of wheat, oats, and barley, and stacks of vegetables ready for the harvest service. He walked down the aisle and stood before the altar. It should be him standing here waiting for Ella, not Harry. The arrangements were all made; the banns had been read three times. There was nothing he could do to stop this.

Ella had made her decision: if he made a public approach to her before the wedding, it would only embarrass her or, worse, harm her reputation and make him look a desperate fool. He had nothing to offer her but love; he must let her go. He smoothed the jay feather between his fingers. Jays were beautiful birds, but they were corvids, like jackdaws, crows, and rooks, and robbed eggs and chicks from the nests of songbirds. He let the blue feather float to the floor and strode from the church.

***

Ella walked down the aisle of the church with Mr Josiah Barton at her side. She wished it had been her father giving her away. Why hadn't he come? Harry stood facing the altar, his broad back to her. His shoulders looked tense and stiff. Was he as nervous as she was? The church was full. The entire village seemed to have turned out; they hardly knew her so they must have come for Harry.

She searched the faces that turned to watch her progress. Was one these men her father, come here incognito? There was no sign of Jem. She wasn't sure she'd be able to go through with it if he were there. Was she glad or disappointed he hadn't come?

Mrs Downs smiled at her as the distance closed between herself and the groom. Her heart thumped in her ears as if she'd run all the way from the rectory. *Thump, thump, thump.* She stopped at Harry's side.

She was to be Harry's property, with no rights or possessions of her own, no right to refuse him sexual advances, and no right to object to him punishing her physically if he so chose.

Thump, thump.

Harry turned to look at her and smiled.

Thump.

Reverend Buchanan clasped his hands. 'Dearly beloved, we are gathered here today, in the sight of God…'

She bowed her head. *Thump, thump.*

'And in the face of this congregation…'

Thud, thump, thump.

'…carnal lusts and appetites. Like brute beasts…'

Thud, thud, thump.

'Into which holy estate these two persons come now to be joined. Therefore, if any man can shew any just cause why they may not lawfully be joined together, let him now speak or else, hereafter, forever hold his peace.'

Thud. Her heart was deafening in the silence. Was she hoping Jem would stand up and cry out? Would he come?

'I require and charge you both, as ye will answer at the dreadful day of judgement, when the secrets of all hearts shall be disclosed, that if either of you know any impediment why ye may not be lawfully joined together in matrimony, ye do now confess it.'

Was them not loving each other an impediment? She glanced at Harry, but his face was rigid.

'Harold Henry Cartwright, wilt thou have this woman to thy wedded wife, to live together after God's ordinance in the holy estate of matrimony? Wilt thou love her, comfort her, honour, and keep her, in sickness and in health; and, forsaking all other, keep thee only unto her so long as ye both shall live?'

There was something on the floor in front of her.

Harry cleared his throat. 'I will.'

He'd vowed to honour her. Could she do less?

'Ella Maud Maundrell, wilt thou have this man to thy wedded husband, to live together after God's ordinance in the holy estate of matrimony? Wilt thou obey him, and serve him, love, honour, and keep him, in sickness and in health; and, forsaking all other, keep thee only unto him so long as ye both shall live?'

The thing on the floor was blue.

Reverend Buchanan coughed quietly. 'Ella?'

She looked up. Everyone was waiting. 'I will.' Something nagged at her mind. The words of the service faded. Her attention was drawn back to the blue thing on the floor.

'Who giveth this woman to be married to this man?

'I do.' Mr Josiah took her hand and placed it in the reverend's. Their hands were soft and warm, not work-hardened like Jem's and Harry's.

Harry's voice was quiet and distant.

Reverend Buchanan put Harry's hand in hers. 'Repeat after me, Ella.'

Something borrowed, something blue. Words stumbled from her mouth. A cold band of gold slipped over her finger. The blue thing at her feet floated briefly as the reverend turned slightly and his robe swept past it.

Harry's voice, stronger now. 'With this ring, I thee wed, with my body, I thee worship, and with all my worldly goods, I thee endow. In the name of the Father, and of the Son, and of the Holy Ghost. Amen.'

The reverend indicated that they kneel. She could see the *something blue* more clearly now.

'Let us pray.' The reverend's voice droned on.

It was a feather.

'Those whom God hath joined together let no man put asunder...'

Understanding came in a sudden flash of heartbreak. It was a blue jay feather. She grasped it and everything it stood for.

'I pronounce that they be man and wife together, in the name of the Father, and of the Son, and of the Holy Ghost. Amen.'

No, no... Oh, Jem. The church dimmed and swayed. 'No.' Hands caught her as she fell.

***

The bedroom Ella was to share with Harry was small compared to the large bedchambers she'd helped clean at the rectory. A bed, crisp with fresh linen and covered with a grey woollen counterpane, dominated both the room and her fears. She looked away, her hand going to her breast where the blue jay feather nestled against her heart. As her mother would have said, she'd made her bed and now she must lie in it: this was her home.

Newhay Farm was situated down a long track off Howcut Lane, which led off Chase Park Road, south from the turnpike road that led from Bedford to Northampton. Fields and copses surrounded it, and the roofs of another farm could be seen above distant hedgerows. Her window looked towards Newhay Copse to the south and would catch the sun from midmorning.

Morning, and her first night with Harry would be over. Morning, and the list of jobs her mother-in-law had compiled would need starting. The list looked endless, the rules longer, and it didn't look as if she'd have much time to herself or the freedom to explore the woods.

The door opened, and Harry strode in; it clicked shut behind him. He smiled, removed his jacket, and motioned for her to unbutton his shirt. She forced a smile in return. She'd promised to obey.

She scattered meaningless words into the awkward silence as her fingers fumbled. 'It's a nice room. I put my clothes in the press. You must tell me if I should move them.'

'They're fine where they are.' He slid his hands up her arms and held her fast. His lips pressed hard against hers, making her take a step backwards.

He released her at last, leaving her breathless. He smelt of beer. 'Harry…'

He placed a finger on her lips. 'It's all right. I'll be gentle with you.'

He shrugged off his shirt and pointed to the buttons on his trousers: her hands shook as she unbuttoned them. His fingers worked at the laces of her bodice, revealing a shoulder. Soft lips explored her neck, moist across the bare flesh. Something inside her shuddered. He cupped her breast and eased her backwards onto the edge of the bed. A callused hand snagged on her stockings as he pushed her wedding dress up around her hips. She held out a hand to stop him: the dress would crease, and she could get onto the bed properly. 'Please, Harry.'

62

'Your right to refuse me ended when we married, Ella. I want you, and I want you now.' He stood over her and pulled down his long pants, releasing his manhood.

She'd never seen such a thing before. Her heart thudded and her stomach clenched.

'I expect you to cry out with pleasure, Ella. Loudly, so the old man can hear. I want him telling Joe Upton and that pig's breath, Jem Weston, how he heard me take your maidenhood.'

Her reticence had made him angry. 'Please, Harry.'

'I saw how he looked at you, Ella.'

'He?'

'Jem Weston. And how you looked at him. You won't want another man after I've broken you in.'

'I'm...

'Scared? Don't be, Ella.' He leant forward and kissed her gently. 'Don't worry. I know what I'm doing. You're not my first, and I dare say you won't be my last. I, however, will be your first and your last.'

She closed her eyes. This was her duty. She must bear it till death.

'Look at me, Ella.'

Her eyes jerked open: fear clenched her guts. 'I'm sorry... I...'

'Shush.' Harry's free hand pushed her torn undergarment aside as he lowered himself between her thighs. He pushed against her with his manhood. She bit her lip, determined not to give him the satisfaction of her crying out as he pierced her maidenhood. A muffled cry escaped despite her resolve. He thrust at her, one hand beneath her hips, lifting her to him. 'Relax, Ella. Move your hips... Move with me. You're like a pail of pig swill.'

She moved, gradually matching his rhythm, his thrusting deeper and deeper, and more and more urgent. She hadn't thought it would hurt like this.

He gripped her knees, holding them up and pushing them farther apart, to thrust ever deeper. 'Cry out, Ella.' He dug his fingers into her legs. 'I want Father to hear you begging for it.'

'No. Please, Harry... Please stop.'

'Louder. I want him to hear.'

'*Harry, please.*'

He tensed, shuddered and moaned, and then collapsed on top of her, crushing the breath from her body.

It was over. She couldn't breathe; she no longer cared if she ever breathed again. Used, trapped and helpless, wetness trickled down her thighs as tears trickled down her face. A text the reverend had quoted came unbidden, bringing with it guilt and shame. '*But each person is tempted when he is lured and enticed by his own desire. Then desire when it has conceived gives birth to sin, and sin when it is fully grown brings forth death.*' This was her own doing: she'd tempted Harry with her low-cut neckline and false smiles, when she didn't love him. Her selfish, snobbish desire for a suitable match had brought her everything she deserved.

Chapter Seven

Ella woke stiff and sore. It was barely light, but the bed beside her was empty. Memories of the night before crushed her. Beneath her pillow, the blue feather was but a painful reminder of what could have been. Sounds from the other side of her bedroom door suggested Harry wasn't the only one up and about.

'Let her sleep. She had a hard night.' Harry's laugh sent a chill through her.

'The lazy mare has to learn what hard work means.' Harry's mother didn't sound in a good mood. 'Spare the rod and spoil the child.'

'She's not a child, Mother. Give her a chance. If anyone's going to beat her, it'll be me. She's going to give me sons and daughters to work the farm, after all. After last night, she's probably with child already.'

His mother laughed bitterly. 'Sometimes bearing children isn't that easy, or you'd have brothers and sisters.'

'She's not you, Mother.' Harry's tone was provocative, disparaging. 'No reason why she can't have more than one.'

'Having you all but killed me, Harry.'

The silence suggested this didn't concern Harry overmuch. 'I'll get her up.' He laughed again, and the doorknob rattled. 'After I've got up her.' The words fell into a taut silence. The bedroom door opened and Harry came into the room. He removed his breeches; he didn't speak but threw back the covers and stared at her body. She moved her hands to cover her nakedness. He was erect and ready.

He pushed aside her hands and ran his fingers over her breasts and hard nipples and then knelt between her legs, lifting them as he had the night before. She braced herself for his thrusts as he went deep inside her, making her cry out again. When he was done, he rolled off her and threw her some clothes. 'I've milking to do. Mother needs you in the kitchen.' He pulled on his breeches, strode from the room, and closed the door behind him. He hadn't looked her in the eye or asked how she'd slept. It was as if she'd stopped being a person and had become breasts, belly, and open thighs: somewhere merely to plant his seed and satisfy his carnal lust.

She washed herself, scrubbed the blood from her thighs, and dressed in the work clothes Harry had left for her. Her insides hurt, and her back and legs were stiff and bruised. *A hard day's work will make you forget your troubles.* Another of her mother's sayings.

'Lazy mare.' She drew herself up, flexing sore muscles. She'd show Mrs Cartwright, senior, she wasn't afraid of hard work.

***

Jem lifted the leather-jointed flail above his head and brought it down with all his strength on the loosened sheaf on the threshing floor. Grains of wheat leapt into the air and fell again among rising dust. *Harry bloody Cartwright.* He lifted it again, letting the head-stock fold back against the hand-stock before propelling it forwards again. It met the floor with a crack, and more grain loosened from the husks. *Joe fucking Upton.* He swung it again with scarcely less venom. *Reverend unholy Buchanan.*

'What in the name of all the saints are you doing, Jem?' Cal stood in the wide doorway of the threshing barn. 'The threshing machine's coming next week. Ain't like you to be doing it by hand, as ain't needed no more, and, the amount you put away last night, I'm surprised you're even standing.'

'Get lost, Cal.' He straightened, chest heaving with exertion, his head pounding. Cal was right. He'd drunk himself into oblivion. Oblivion being the only place where Harry wasn't fucking Ella, and Harry and Joe weren't laughing and bragging about it in the pub. They'd guessed how he felt about her and knew exactly how to wind him up.

Why had he let her think he didn't care? He raised the flail again, a scream welling in his throat. Crack.

Cal put a hand on his arm. 'This is about that girl, ain't it? The one as married Harry.'

'If he hurts her, by God, I'll kill him.'

'Why would he hurt her?'

'Me and her... I kissed her... before her and Harry.' Ella had locked eyes with him. She loved him and he'd hurt her, like Harry would if he discovered the truth about her feelings for one Jem Weston. 'He's the jealous sort, and that Joe Upton loves stirring things.'

'Then if you've got feelings for her, you'd best stay out of her way and theirs, Jem.'

'I'll find a way to make them suffer, if they don't treat Ella with respect.'

***

Harry whistled as he threw buckets of water across the cobbled floor of the milking parlour. He picked up the stiff-bristled yard brush and swept the floor clean of cow shit.

'You sound happy this morning. The girl performed well?' His father smirked. 'Was she a virgin?'

'She was, but she isn't now.' He smiled, reliving the feel of her young, smooth breasts and thighs, not sagging, fat, and sweaty like the whores he was used to. 'Screamed like a rabbit caught by a stoat. She's green but she'll learn.'

'Cowslip and Kingcup are bulling. I'll bring Marquis in, ready.'

'I'll be with you in a minute, Father.' He grinned. What Lord Northampton would think if he knew they'd named their best bull after him, he dreaded to think. He shovelled the last of the shit into a barrow, wheeled it to the muck heap, and then washed his hands at the dairy pump.

His mother was pouring milk through the cooler. 'Lucy Chambers might be starting as dairymaid tomorrow. She'll be here at five for a trial. It's a good job I have Ella in the house today, or I'd be run off my feet. I'll check on her when I've finished here, make sure she's doing a thorough job.'

'I'm sure Ella will be just fine, Mother. You've got your hands full here for a couple more hours. Leave her be.' He dried his hands on a roller-towel on the back of the dairy door. 'Got to give father a hand with the bull.'

Marquis stood impatiently in his pen, tasting the air and bellowing. A hooked pole through the ring in the bull's nose would control him. Cowslip was tethered in the yard, calling for her mate.

'Open the gate, Father.' The bull surged forward, but he held hard to the pole, swinging the animal round by his nose.

'Hold him while I clean him off, Harry.' His father washed the bull's erection, dodging pawing hooves and flailing horns. 'All done.'

'Stand clear, Father.' He walked the bull forward. The beast's eyes showed their whites, drool hung from his mouth, and his thick neck strained.

His father dropped the heavy wooden bar across the cow's hocks, to stop her kicking and injuring the bull, and then stood in front of the cow, holding her halter to keep her from pulling away. 'Ready. Let him come.'

Cowslip reminded him of Ella, helpless in the face of male domination. A useful cow to be mated. Marquis was erect and huge. He stood aside as the bull mounted the cow. He guided Marquis's organ into Cowslip, so as not to damage the prize bull's equipment. His own organ responded as the cow braced herself. He didn't need his father to find him a whore now. He had his own Cowslip to mount when he pleased. Hooves clattered to the cobbles as Marquis withdrew.

Father patted the bull's neck. 'We'll give him half an hour and then see if he'll do Kingcup. I'm going to check on the new calf. Turn Cowslip out and get Kingcup ready and then stay with Marquis. Keep him calm or he'll be injuring himself.'

One of these days it wouldn't be Father giving the orders; it would be him. Ella would be pregnant soon, and then his father would see him for the man he was.

***

Harry and John had been out since first light. Mrs Cartwright was busy in the dairy and had demanded the tasks she'd set be finished when she returned: Ella was not about to give her mother-in-law cause for complaint. She wiped sweat from her brow and straightened as a shadow darkened the scullery doorway.

'You settling in all right, Ella?' Harry's father's voice was soft, kind.

She smiled. 'I'm finding my way about, John. Thank you.'

'Jane not working you too hard, I hope?' He came closer and looked at her face. 'You've been crying?'

'I don't mind hard work. I'm a bit homesick for Bath, that's all.' It was a plausible lie.

He put a hand on her shoulder. 'I reckon our Harry's found us a good 'un this time.'

'This time?'

He squeezed her shoulder. 'His women – well, his face puts them off. That and...'

She frowned. 'And?'

'Me and Harry have the same taste in women. I usually break them in for him. The missus – she knows her place, like I'm sure you do.'

'What do you mean?'

One finger trailed down her arm. 'He had you first. Only right

69

he took your maidenhood, you being his wife, but now I reckon it's my turn. Show you what it's like to have a real man.'

Surely, she'd misunderstood him. 'I have to tend the range. It's time to start breakfast. Harry will be hungry.'

He put a hand across the doorway. 'You promised to obey. You're going nowhere.' He pushed her back against the wall of the scullery.

'I promised to obey Harry.' Stones dug into her spine. 'Please, let me go. Mrs Cartwright won't be pleased if I'm behind with things.'

He breathed pickled onions and cheese into her face. His weight pinned her. He pushed up her skirt and jammed his knee between her legs. 'Made me hard as his lordship's rutting stags hearing you two at it last night. Been thinking about it all morning. Seeing the bull serving one of the cows just now only made me harder.'

She pounded at his back with her fists. 'Stop it. Please stop.'

John yanked down her undergarment and grasped her buttocks, lifting her onto him. His manhood pushed against her. She struggled and kicked but it only served to excite him more. Please, let Harry come home early. John pushed inside her and thrust, grunting like the pig he was. A metal colander hung on a hook on the wall. She reached for it with outstretched fingers, unhooked it, and crashed it hard into the side of Mr Cartwright's head. He looked at her with a moment's surprise and then slumped to the floor.

She retched into the scullery sink, then adjusted her clothing, and ran up the stairs to her room. She tugged her bags from under the bed and threw in her clothes; she wasn't staying here a moment longer. At the door, she paused to look around the room. There was nothing she wanted to take with her, except the blue jay feather that lay beneath her pillow. Jem had felt something for her, hadn't he? Why else had he left her the feather? She threw aside the pillow, grabbed the feather, and crept down the stairs. The house was deathly silent. Suppose she'd killed John?

She let herself out of the front door and ran along the lane. She didn't stop running until she collapsed, breathless, on Jem's mother's doorstep.

***

Mrs Weston, Jem's mother, answered the door to Ella's knock. 'Well, I'll go to the foot of our stairs. If ain't the reverend's young girl. You look done in. Whatever's the matter?'

'Is Jem here?'

'No.' She frowned. 'What would you be wanting with our James?'

'I…' Why had she come here? What did she expect Jem to do? She was a married woman now. Involving Jem in her problems would only make trouble for him. Harry was a jealous man: he might kill Jem. 'It doesn't matter. It's not important.'

'I'll tell him you called. It's Ella, ain't it?'

'Yes.'

'Are you sure nothing's wrong?'

'Quite sure, thank you.' She didn't know where to go, what to do. The only other person who cared for her was Mrs Downs. She ran along the lane and into the rectory yard. She threw open the kitchen door.

Mrs Downs looked up. Her eyes opened wide in shock. 'Lord, luv us, Ella, what's happened? Has Mrs Cartwright sent you? Has there been an accident?'

'I've run away.' She leant back against the kitchen door, her breathing ragged, her bags clutched in her hands. 'I can't stay in that house, Mrs Downs. I just can't.'

'Oh, you poor lamb. Come here.' Mrs Downs gave her a hug, her ample form soft and comforting. 'Sit yourself down, Ella. I'll make us a cuppa with some of the reverend's best tea. He won't know as how as we've had it, as shouldn't, it being his favourite and costing so much. When you've caught your breath, you can

71

tell me all about it.'

'I can't.'

'My lips is sealed, Ella. I ain't no gossip.'

'I...' She forced a smile. 'You're so kind. It's just... It's too awful.'

Mrs Downs set a cup on the table in front of her and pursed her lips as if wondering how to broach a delicate subject. 'It's been one night, Ella. Your wedding night? I know as you didn't know what to expect. I did say it might hurt, the first time. Did Harry hurt you? Is that why you've come home?'

'Home? But this isn't my home, is it? Maybe that's what I should do. Go home to Bath.'

'Ella, you belong to Harry now. Newhay is your home. You must go back afore you're missed.'

'I'm not going back to be...treated like that. I won't be any man's property.'

'But you are, Ella. It's his right and your duty, whether he hurt you or not.'

She covered her face with her hands. 'He forced me.'

Mrs Downs sighed. 'Not all marriages are beds of roses. Next time won't be so bad, believe me.'

'It was as bad. It was worse. Harry treated me like a breeding sow and his father... Oh, dear God. How could he do that to me?' Tears streamed down her cheeks. 'I won't go back. John's a lecher.'

'Old Mr Cartwright's a bit of a lady's man. Everybody knows that. He don't mean no harm by it.'

'No harm?' His hands had been rough, like Harry's. His breath had made her want to vomit. Her stomach revolted and she swallowed bile. 'He waited till I was alone in the house, then he pinned me against the scullery wall, and... He had his way with me.'

'Ella Maundrell – I mean Cartwright – wash out your mouth with soap and water.'

'It's true. I tried to fight him off.' The memory froze her. 'I hit him hard over the head with the colander. Suppose I've killed him?'

Mrs Downs covered her mouth with her hand, her eyes wide. Her maternal bosom heaved. 'Oh, Lord love us. Ella, what have you done?'

***

'Harry! Harry, where are you?'

Harry had never heard his mother sound so panicked. He put Marquis back in his pen and crossed the yard at a run. 'What's up, Mother?'

'Come quick. It's your father. I think he's dead.'

'Where?'

'He's in the scullery. Quickly.'

He took his mother by the elbow and hurried her homewards. 'He said he was going to check on the new calf. What was he doing in the scullery? What happened?'

His mother was silent for a moment too long.

Louisa had been scullery maid before Ella. He'd heard his father fucking the girl in there when his mother was out. 'What *was* he doing in the scullery?'

'You'd better see for yourself.'

His heart sank. 'Where's Ella?'

'She's not in the house. I think she's gone.'

'He wouldn't, would he?' His fingers gripped his mother's elbow harder. 'Ella's mine. If he's touched her... If he's not dead, I'll kill him myself.'

The back door to the farmhouse stood open. He pushed his mother aside and ran into the scullery. His father lay on the stone flags, blood covering his head and face. A bloodied colander lay at his side, but that wasn't what riveted his attention. His father's breeches and pants were round his ankles.

'Is he dead?'

He felt for a pulse. It was weak and fluttering. 'No, but he's going to wish he was.' He fetched an enamel jug from a hook on the wall, pumped up a jug full of water, and threw the contents over his father's face and limp privates. John Cartwright twitched and spluttered. Grabbing his father by his jacket sleeves, he hauled him upright. 'Wake up, you bastard.'

His father opened his eyes and stared around vacantly. 'What happened?'

His mother glowered down at her husband. 'Did you try to have your way with Ella?'

John Cartwright put a hand gingerly to his head and winced. 'The bitch hit me.'

He gripped his father's shirt front and dragged him to his feet, towering over him. The man was smaller than he'd realised. 'Did you fuck my wife?'

'I let you have her first. You took her virginity. What's the problem?'

'She was mine!' His fingers tightened, twisting the fabric against his father's throat, making him choke. 'I'll kill you. I'll fucking kill you.'

His father waved a hand wordlessly.

'Harry, no.' His mother tugged at his fingers, trying to unclench them. 'Harry. This isn't his fault.'

He turned on her. 'Are you telling me Ella was a willing party?'

'No… Harry, your father has his needs. If it hadn't been for you, this wouldn't have happened.'

74

'Me? What have I done?'

'You almost killed me, Harry. That's what you did. I almost died. John won't risk my life again. That's why he uses whores and the maids. That's why he took Ella.'

'You mean you know about his whoring?'

'Of course, I do. He thinks I don't but...'

John Cartwright waved his arms desperately.

'Harry, you're choking him.'

He released his grip slightly. 'You're as bad as each other.' He shook his head, tears blurring his vision. 'Ella is my wife. Mine. You had no right.'

His father gasped a deep rasping breath. 'But you don't love her. I didn't think you'd mind. It's not as if we haven't shared plenty of women in the past.'

'You don't get it, do you? Ella was pure, my first virgin. She was meant only for me, no-one else. She belongs to *me*.'

'I'm sorry, son. I didn't realise you'd fallen for the girl.'

He hadn't, but she was his property. He drew back his arm, clenched his fist, and slammed it into his father's face. 'You will never touch what's mine again, ever.' He let his father fall limply to the floor and stormed out. Ella had gone, and he wanted her back, despoiled though she was. She was the only thing he had that truly belonged to him.

***

There was blood in the chamber pot. Ella covered the pot with a cloth and took it downstairs to empty. Relief at not carrying Harry or John Cartwright's child fought with the fear of retribution. Morning had brought her no closer to a solution.

She drew water from the pump and set a kettle on the hob to boil. 'Mrs Downs, what am I going to do?'

Mrs Downs tended the range. 'You can't go back to Newhay, or

75

not alone. And you can't stay here, if...'

The woman's words hung unspoken: if she'd killed John Cartwright. And if she had, they'd find him with his breeches down round his ankles.

'Maybe, you should get the coach back to Bath. Yes, that's what you must do. Get away from here.' The decision made, Mrs Downs took charge. 'You can stay here, till then, up in the attic. The reverend won't deny you a roof over your head. We can't keep this from him, Ella. You have to tell him. I'm sure he'll give you the fare. You can repay him when you're able.'

A knock came at the door. Mrs Downs put a finger to her lips and then motioned her away before opening it. She backed out of the kitchen, trying to think of somewhere to hide in case it was the sergeant come to arrest her. The voice at the door was familiar. Jane Cartwright? She squeezed behind a cupboard door and listened.

'Is Ella here?' The woman sounded anxious.

'I ain't seen her, dear. Not since the wedding.'

'Where else would she go but here? I'm not here to cause trouble. I know what happened. I really need to talk to her.'

'What happened?' Mrs Downs's voice was all innocence.

'She gave my husband a crack on the head.'

'Is he all right?'

'Got a right headache. I know Ella's here. Like I said, I'm not here to cause trouble. I want to hear her side of the story.'

A door closed. 'Ella, you'd best come in here.'

She took a deep breath and went back into the kitchen. Mrs Cartwright looked pale and drawn. She almost felt sorry for the woman. 'I'm not coming back. You can tell Harry that.'

Mrs Cartwright dry-washed her hands. 'I'll speak to Ella alone. Ella?'

76

'No.' She shook her head. 'Mrs Downs knows. I told her.'

Mrs Cartwright pursed her lips. 'I hope we can count on your discretion, Mrs Downs. I found John senseless, in the scullery. I need to know exactly what happened, Ella.'

'You were in the dairy. Harry was out with the cows. I was in the scullery when John came in. He said he and Harry had the same taste in women. He said lewd things. He... I tried to fight him off. He wouldn't stop, so I hit him.'

'But you did stop him?'

She looked up at Harry's mother, seeing her pain and something else. Guilt? 'He had his way before I managed to hit him.'

Tears shone on her mother-in-law's cheeks. 'I'm so sorry, Ella. I'm so very sorry. I thought, you being Harry's wife, you'd be safe. You're not the first.'

'You know he does this and you've said nothing?'

'I almost died having Harry. John vowed not to put me in danger ever again. We don't... We haven't for more than thirty years. I've turned a blind eye to his whoring though it makes me sick to my stomach, even if the girls are willing. He's gone too far this time. Harry found out what he'd done. He's given John a black eye.'

'I'm still not coming back. I might as well be a breeding sow for all the care Harry shows me. I have feelings... I won't be used.'

'You're still Harry's wife. You promised to obey him. Give him another chance, Ella.'

She took the ring from her finger and threw it at Mrs Cartwright's feet. 'I want nothing from him except my freedom.'

Mrs Cartwright shook her head and bent to pick up the ring. 'I'll tell him. I shan't say anything to anyone about you hitting John, and I'm sure he and Harry won't either. What you say about him is up to you. If there's a child...'

'There's no child.'

The woman sighed. 'It's for the best. There are enough of John's bastards, as it is. Goodbye, Ella. I can't tell you how sorry I am.'

She sank onto a chair by the table and let her tears fall. Mrs Downs put an arm around her and held her against her bosom while she sobbed.

Chapter Eight

Reverend Buchanan sat at his desk, his hands steepled, fingers entwined, as if in prayer. He looked at Ella over his spectacles. 'I'm at a loss to know what to do with you, Ella.'

'You can't make me go back to Newhay.'

He shuffled uncomfortably in his chair and looked down to his closed Bible. 'You have a way of inflaming men's passions, Ella. Your immodesty does you no credit. No credit at all.'

She leant towards him, palms flat on the desk, her chest heaving with barely contained rage. 'In what way am I immodest?'

His eyes fixed on her low-cut bodice, chosen because the day was warm and the range made the rectory kitchen uncomfortably hot. 'You dress provocatively. You are showing far too much flesh for any man to bear.'

She looked down at her dress to the swell of her breasts and straightened, flushing. 'Am I to die of overheating because men can't control their animal passions?'

'Silence, girl. You know nothing of what you speak.'

'Oh, I know about men's lusts. I know how they use innocent girls for their own pleasure and be damned. I've heard the excuses they make to justify rape.'

'Ella!' Reverend Buchanan rose to his feet and towered over her. She flinched; for a moment, she'd thought he was going to strike her. He sat down again but not before she'd noticed a bulge in his breeches. 'You're Harry's wife. You can't stay here, and you can't go back to Bath.'

It was obvious why she couldn't stay at the rectory, but Bath was her birthplace. 'Why not? My mother and Mr Josiah wouldn't deny me a home.'

The reverend looked at her pityingly. 'There's no place for you there. Josiah Barton made that quite clear to me in his letter. I shall write to him and acquaint him of the circumstances, of course, but don't expect an invitation from him or your mother.'

She slumped into the chair by the desk. Where was she to go? She was thankful she wasn't carrying a child, and she realised now how fortunate her mother was to have found Mr Barton to take her in as housekeeper. She still didn't understand why she'd had to leave. Ralph would have taken no for an answer, even if she did 'inflame men's passions'. Was it Mr Barton's passions she'd inflamed?

'Was it my fault Mr Barton sent me away? What did I do wrong?' Her voice was flat with defeat. Her life had fallen apart, and she needed to make sense of it.

'Colossians three, verse five.' The words were muttered like a mantra.

Was that something she was meant to hear? 'I beg your pardon.'

'"Put to death therefore what is earthly in you: sexual immorality, impurity, passion, evil desire, and covetousness, which is idolatry."' Reverend Buchanan smiled, a small sad smile. 'You're an innocent, Ella. Truly you are. A beautiful innocent. You don't know your power to make men feel desire. The world is full of men who'll take advantage of your youth and naivety to satisfy their evil lusts. The devil is your eyes, Ella Cartwright. It's he who tempts men to leave God's holy path. You must learn more modesty and hide your beauty from all but your husband, or things will not go well with you. You need a man's protection. A husband's protection.'

'I won't go back to Harry.'

'No. I can see you're adamant, and perhaps, in the circumstances... I'll see if I can find you lodgings in Brafield or Olney. Someone may need a servant, and it'll be far enough away from the Cartwrights. I'll speak to Harry, but you know there's no chance of a divorce for someone of your station. Even if you were gentry, and your husband beat you daily, the church frowns on divorce, and the cost would be prohibitive.' He sighed. 'I'd hoped for better for you than this, Ella.'

***

Jem checked his traps and snares and moved on silently through the undergrowth. He loved these quiet moonlit nights in the Chase, with the stars sparkling in a midnight sky. It was an in-between time, a time of freedom. An owl *Ku-wikked*, the call rising at the end as if in question, and its mate answered with a long affirming *hoowooo*. A nightjar called from somewhere deep in the copse. He smiled; the noise always made him think of Cal farting after too many beers in the Rose and Crown. Moonlight shone briefly from a pair of pale eyes, blinking out as quickly as they'd appeared. A fox, probably, after his lordship's pheasants. As was he: the deep pockets of his poaching jacket held a hare and two young cock birds.

A crack of a twig froze his steps. He listened, breath held. Another crack, closer, and the quiet exhale of a breath. Another poacher or one of his lordship's keepers? The sounds of stealthy feet moved away, and he let out a slow breath. Time he made himself scarce. Patterns of moonlight showed him the way back to the edge of the wood. He pushed through a gap in the hedge and out onto the track.

'Hey!' The shout behind him propelled him into a run. A shotgun blasted over his head. 'I'll get you, you young bugger!'

'Not if I can help it.' The words were muttered, too quiet for the man to hear; he was faster on his toes than Joe Upton. The keeper had put on a couple of stones since Elizabeth had been cooking for him; marriage to a good woman had made him far too comfortable. He grinned; Joe wouldn't know for certain who the poacher was in the dark, and it would be the keeper's word against his. He muttered beneath his breath as he pounded down the track to the village. 'You gotta catch me first, Joe Upton. You're...' *Puff.* 'A-getting slow, old man.'

***

Ella bowed her head as she walked to the bake-house to fetch the loaves for the rectory. A shawl, borrowed from Mrs Downs, covered her shoulders and arms despite the warmth of the day. It being early, not many folk were about. Those that were didn't speak to her, and she didn't raise her head to catch their eyes, but she was sure they whispered together as she passed. It didn't matter what she thought of men's wanton lack of control: she had to be seen to be protecting her modesty, however much the necessity irked her.

'Ella?'

Her heart faltered and thudded, but she kept on walking, head down, pulling her shawl tighter.

'Ella!'

'You shouldn't be talking to me.'

Jem caught her elbow and turned her to him. 'No bugger tells me who I can talk to. I heard you came looking for me.'

'I shouldn't have. I'm sorry.'

'Come on, Ella. If I heard right, you've left Harry Cartwright.' He put a finger beneath her chin and made her look at him. 'What happened, Ella?'

'Let me go.'

'Not till you tell me. If Harry didn't treat you right, I'll kill him.'

'Harry…' There was no point in making Jem angry with Harry or John. That way lay trouble she didn't want to be responsible for. 'We didn't get on, that's all. It isn't Harry's fault I don't love him.'

Jem's eyes held hers. 'I should never have let you go. I thought I could but you and Harry… I ain't slept since, thinking of you and him together.'

He did care? 'The blue jay feather…'

82

'You found it?'

'It was too late. I'd said my vows.' Her sigh was heartfelt. 'Jem, why did you have to leave it? How could I live with Harry thinking there was still a chance you might love me? Wishing...'

'I'm sorry. I thought I was doing the right thing, letting you have a better life. I couldn't stay to see you wed Harry. I dropped the feather and went and hid in Cold Oak. Sat beneath an old oak and wept like a baby. I've been a fool, Ella. A stupid, pig-ignorant, bloody fool.'

Her fingernails dug into her palms. 'If you'd only told me how you felt, Jem, none of this would have happened.'

'Forgive me?'

She smiled. He'd sacrificed his own feelings for what he'd perceived to be a better future for her. That had to the greatest love a man could give. It wasn't his fault Harry and John weren't fit to be around a woman. And she couldn't fault Jem for weakening at the end, when she'd have done the same had she seen the feather sooner. With Jem's love, anything was possible. 'I love you, James Weston.'

He took her in his arms. His lips covered hers, and the shawl fell to the ground as she lifted her arms around his neck. He smelt of wood smoke and brick dust and something animal.

He released her at last. 'I ain't got much to offer you, Ella. Hard work, a tiny room in a cottage I share with Ma and Dad, and my love every day for the rest of my life. I want to marry you.' He laughed suddenly. 'I reckon I might have a bit of extra cash coming my way. Cal and Nat are going to owe me a tidy sum.'

'How's that?'

He grinned and tapped a forefinger on the side of his nose. 'I'll tell you after Michaelmas.'

Her smile fled. 'I'm already married, Jem.'

'We'll live over the brush. I don't care. I want to be with you.

83

I'll never love anyone else.'

'Harry hates you already. He won't let me go. Reverend Buchanan will be furious. It'll only cause trouble.'

'The buggers can lump it, then. It's your life and your decision, but I mean what I say. I love you, Ella. I think I've loved you since I first saw you in the reverend's stable.'

Her heart thumped erratically: this was a life-defining moment, a dangerous decision she shouldn't even be considering. Jem kissed her again, and her resolve melted, her caution swept away on a storm of desire. 'And I you.'

His lips brushed her cheek. 'Where's your stuff?'

'At the rectory.'

'Go and get it. I'll wait for you. You're coming home with me.'

***

Ella followed Jem through the front door of the Westons' home. It was in a row of thatched cottages, small-windowed and low-ceilinged, with attic bedrooms. The rooms were cramped and dark, the hearth smoky with a tiny range upon which all the cooking was done. Jem had told her one outside privy, with two holes in a plank seat and buckets beneath, served the whole row.

The living room was also Charlotte's workroom. Upon plump pillows were spread finely wrought pieces of lacework in varying stages of completion; pins and intricately carved bobbins of wood and bone kept the work in shape and the threads in order.

'Ma must be out. Go on up the stairs. I'll bring your stuff.' Jem followed behind her up stairs steeper and narrower than the back stairs of the rectory.

'Will they mind me being here? I mean, there's not much room.'

Jem frowned. 'Course not. Ma brought up six of us here. There's only her and Dad and us two now.'

84

'You have brothers and sisters?' She'd been an only child and couldn't imagine a houseful of siblings.

'Two brothers and three sisters. Jane, she's eight years older than me, lives in Denton.'

Denton was a village the far side of the grand avenue that swept down to the front of Castle Ashby, the seat of the fourth marquis. She couldn't help compare the fine house to the cottages rented to his lordship's tenants. 'How did you get eight of you in here?'

'Us kids were chucked out first thing, all weathers, to play out in the lane or up the woods. Or else, we were head to toe in our beds.' He glanced around the room she was to share with him. 'We had four beds crammed in here, two to a bed for the four younger ones. Jane, and Tom, my oldest brother, had a bed each.'

'There's only the two bedrooms?'

Jem laughed at her surprise. 'It's all we ever needed. It were cosy.'

A noise downstairs made her start.

'That'll be Ma now.' He cleared a space in a chest. 'Shove your things in there, Ella. I'll tell her I've found me a wife.'

'A wife?'

'Over the brush, remember.' He fetched a broom from the landing and laid it on the wooden boards. 'Ready?'

She bit her top lip. This was as important a commitment as saying her vows before God, and she'd already broken those. God would surely judge her. 'Ready.'

'Sure?'

She nodded. 'We should say something.'

He grasped her hand. 'I will love and protect you till the day I die.'

His hand was warm and strong around hers. 'Whatever life holds, wherever it takes us, I'll always love you.' She squeezed his

85

hand and together they stepped over the broom.

He kissed her gently. 'You're Ella Weston, now.'

She put away her clothes for the third time in as many days: the drawers smelt of camphor and lavender. She gave Jem five minutes to talk to his mother and then padded down the bare wooden stairs.

Charlotte Weston, Jem's mother, stood in the middle of her living room with her hands on her hips. She shook her head. 'This is a fine to do, I'm sure. What the reverend would make of me taking you in, I don't know. I have to live here, Ella Cartwright, and God will judge me, as will the good folk of this village.'

Tears welled in her eyes. 'I'm sorry, Mrs Weston. I should go. I didn't think how having me here would affect you.'

'There's talk enough, already. I don't want no trouble and what Jem's father would reckon, I can't say.'

'I'll get my things. The reverend will find me a place. It isn't right me staying here.'

'You'll do no such thing.' Jem barred her way. 'She's Ella Weston now, Ma. My common-law wife. She didn't leave Harry without a damn good reason.'

A reason she didn't want Jem to know for fear of what he'd do. 'No, Jem. This isn't fair. I can't put you and your parents in the wrong like this. I'll go and stay with my mother.'

'But, Ella. Over the brush, remember. You promised.'

She shook her head. 'I know what I said. "Whatever life holds, wherever it takes us, I'll always love you." But I can't stay, Jem. We can't be together. I see that now. It would cause too much trouble for your family.'

Charlotte Weston nodded. 'I'm sorry, child, but you have the truth of it. It's best you go back to your mother, and I'd do it before Harry comes looking for you.'

***

86

Harry finished the afternoon milking and opened the gate to the yard to let the cows out onto the lane. Father had already gone to open Top Field gate for them, and the herd knew its own way well enough. He set to scraping and swilling the parlour, a twice-daily chore he did without complaint. Ella would be home by now or would be once she'd got over her fright. She was his wife, after all, and where else would she go?

He'd pushed his father's explanations and apologies aside, refusing to speak to him for fear he'd hit the old man again. How was he to prove himself a man if he didn't even know if his own wife bore his child or his father's? He'd seen his father as he really was for the first time: a selfish, greedy, dirty, old man. The knowledge gave him power. He was the better man, and it was time to take his proper place in the running of the farm and make his father do his bidding. Ella had given him this power, though not in the way she might have chosen.

No matter. The girl would get over it and might even turn to him for protection, as was his duty as a husband. She would grow to love him if she saw how he hated his father for what he'd done. He stood taller. His fingers clenched the shovel handle, and the blade edge dug into the hard-packed dirt between the cobbles. He'd failed her as much as his parents had failed him.

He stood up the shovel and headed for home, not bothering to wait for his father's say so as he usually did. He wanted to make sure Ella was where she should be. He pushed open the door. 'Ella? Mother?'

His mother hurried from the kitchen. 'She's at the rectory, Harry. I spoke to her. She was very upset.'

He frowned. 'I'd better hitch up the pony and fetch her home.'

'Your father'll apologise to her when he comes in. It's the least he can do.'

'Apologise? Tell him to stay away from her and me.' He turned and slammed the door back on its hinges.

He filled a shallow pan with horse nuts and grabbed a halter from the tack room. 'Dolly!' He pushed open the paddock gate and rattled the nuts in the pan. The old grey pony nickered and trotted towards him. He slipped the halter rope round her neck while she ate the nuts and then pushed the halter up over her nose and eased her ears through the headpiece. 'Come on, old girl. Let's go and fetch the mistress home.' The mistress. He liked the sound of that. Master and mistress of their own domain.

Dolly stood patiently while he harnessed her to the pony trap. 'Get up, girl. Get up.' He tapped her rump with a flick of the whip, and she broke into a lazy, Sunday trot. He flicked her again. 'Get up there.' Her ears flicked back, and she smartened her pace. He crossed the turnpike road into the village and pulled her to a halt outside the rectory gates. 'Wait there. Stand.'

He left Dolly grazing the verge outside the rectory's garden wall and marched up the path to the front door. It opened to his knock. 'Mrs Downs, I've brought the trap for Ella.'

The woman frowned. 'She's not here, Mr Harry. She took her things and left, must be three hours since.' Mrs Downs looked at him knowingly. 'There's been a bit of a to-do by all accounts.'

'It's none of your business. Did she say where she was going?'

'Not a word, Mr Harry. But she were right upset.'

'Where do you think she's gone?'

'She went out for a walk to clear her head. I couldn't say where she went after that.'

'You're lying.' He stepped closer and bent to breathe in the woman's face. 'You know very well where she is. Has she gone back to Bath? Or do you want me to rip the rectory apart looking for her?' He pushed past her into the hallway.

'She ain't here, sir. She's...'

'Yes?'

The housekeeper put her hands on her hips. 'I think she's gone to the Weston's.'

'Jem Weston's?'

'She took a liking to the lad.'

And he to her. He'd kill him. 'Not a word about this to anyone. She's my wife and she belongs with me. I don't need gossip. Do you understand?'

'Yes, Mr Harry, sir. If the village hears about her leaving you after one night, for a labourer like Jem Weston, it won't be from me.' There was a subtle satisfaction in the woman's voice that irked him.

He drew his eyebrows down over his eyes. 'I'll know who to blame if this gets out, Ev Downs, and you'll live to regret it.'

Mrs Downs bristled. 'You don't frighten me, young Harry Cartwright. I knew you when you were in napkins. You treat that poor girl right and keep your father's hands off her, and I won't say a thing. You hurt her one more time, and the whole county will know it.'

He swivelled on one heel and strode from the rectory. Lashing Dolly across the back, he cantered her to the Weston's door and hammered on it. It opened, and Charlotte Weston looked up at him expectantly. He didn't want to air his grievance in the street. 'Can I come in?'

She opened the door wider and stood back. He pushed past and looked around. 'Where's Ella?'

'Ella?'

'My wife, Ella Cartwright. Mrs Downs said she was here.'

'She was, for a short while, but we only have two rooms upstairs. We don't have room for no guest.'

There was a door at the side of the hearth. 'What's in there?'

'It's the pantry. You can look if you like.'

There was no sign Ella had been here. There was a thump from upstairs, and he raised his eyes to the low ceiling. 'Is she up there with him?'

'With him?' Charlotte Weston's tone was altogether too innocent.

'With Jem.'

'I told you. Mrs Cartwright ain't here.'

'So where is she?'

'I don't know where your wife may be. Perhaps, you should'a took better care of her.'

He raised a hand but let it fall impotently. He wasn't a man to strike a woman unless she was his to discipline. 'Tell her I want her home. Tell her I forgive her.'

Charlotte Weston's eyebrows rose, but she said nothing.

'Tell her my father forgives her, too.'

'Should I see Mrs Cartwright, I'll pass on your message. Now, I'll bid you good evening, Mr Cartwright.'

He made towards the stairs, but Mr Weston's bulk filled the narrow staircase. 'You want to search my home, Mr Cartwright, you'll need his lordship's say so afore you get past me. Now please do as my wife asks and leave us be. Ella Cartwright ain't here.'

'So you say, Mr Weston.' He backed away, unwilling to take on a man with Bill Weston's reputation of bare-knuckle fighting. 'Don't think you'll get away with hiding her. If she doesn't come home with me, now, I'll ruin your family. No-one here gets to live in peace until she's back where she belongs. Tell her I give her until dark, or you'll all regret it.' He strode towards Joe Upton's cottage close to the woodland's edge. Upton had no love for Jem Weston, poacher and probable adulterer.

Chapter Nine

Ella had a few pounds left from the allowance Mr Josiah had given her, kept safe in the blue purse Jane Cartwright had pushed into her hand for her *something blue*. She paid the carter for her journey to Bedford and used a little money for a room at the coaching inn. She didn't believe her mother would turn her away, and she'd decided that her first, ill-fated brush with the male sex would be her last. She would stay in Bath and live as a widow: without a child to encumber her, she'd find work as a housekeeper or maid and put Harry and Jem behind her. It wasn't the life she'd hoped for, but it was better than being abused at Newhay or causing trouble for the Westons.

She caught the mail coach at daybreak, and the journey, accompanied by guards sounding warning blasts on the post horn, was non-stop apart from changes of horses every few miles. It was a rough and uncomfortable way to travel, but she was in Bath by nightfall.

Gas lamps lit her way to the house where she'd grown up: home. The word failed to fill the empty void in her heart. It wasn't her home anymore, and she wasn't sure of her welcome. She pulled the bell pull and listened to its distant jangle. The door opened.

'Can I help you?' A young girl in a grey dress and white apron waited for her answer.

'I'm Ella Weston, Mrs Maundrell's daughter. Is she in? Is Mr Josiah here?'

'Oh, you're Ella. Mrs Maundrell talks about you all the while. Come in. I'm Annie, Mr Barton's housemaid.'

'I'm pleased to meet you, Annie.' She held out her hand and

forced a smile. It wasn't unreasonable for Mr Barton to have replaced her with Annie.

'You're not expected, I'm sure, or I'd have a bed made up for you, ready.'

'A letter would have taken as long to get here as I did. Please, don't go to any trouble. I can make my own bed.'

'Your mother's in her parlour. She'll be over the moon to see you.'

'Thank you.' She doubted her mother would be pleased. She walked into the parlour. 'Mother?'

'Ella? What on earth are you doing here?' Her mother hugged her.

'I've come home. I can't live with Harry, and I can't stay in Yardley Hastings.'

'Why ever not, Ella? What's happened?'

'I've fallen in love, Mother, but not with Harry. With Jem Weston. He's a labourer, but I've caused so much trouble. I had to leave.'

Her mother sighed. 'I'll fetch Josiah.'

'Do you have to tell him?'

'I can hardly hide you away. He has to know. He took a great deal of trouble to arrange this marriage. I think you owe him an explanation, young lady.' Her mother clacked along the passageway, voices rose in argument, and footsteps clacked back. 'Josiah will speak to you in his office, Ella. He's not happy.'

'I don't suppose he is.' She took a deep breath. Ralph had played hide and seek with her along this passageway. There was nothing to fear. She knocked and entered. 'You wanted to see me, Mr Josiah?'

Mr Barton pushed aside a pile of papers. 'Sit. Explain yourself, Ella.'

'I can't.'

'Can't? You've deserted you husband. Do you think this is the action of a dutiful wife?'

'No, sir.'

Mr Barton undid a couple of coat buttons and did them up again. 'You expect to come here and live on my charity and goodwill?'

'No, Mr Josiah. I can work.'

He took out his pocket watch and laid it on his desk. 'I have a housemaid. I don't need another. Your place is with your husband.'

'I won't go back to Harry, sir.'

'Why not?'

'He… His…' She couldn't bring herself to unburden herself to this man who'd been the nearest thing to a father she'd ever had. 'I can't say.'

Mr Barton looked up from his pocket watch and frowned. 'If you can give me no reason, you leave me no alternative. You must return to your husband.'

'Please, Mr Josiah.'

'I'm sorry, Ella.' His tone softened. 'I have no choice in the matter and neither have you. You belong to Harry. It's my legal responsibility and my Christian duty to return you to him.'

'Your Christian duty? You're sending me back to be…' Her voice faltered.

'To be a dutiful wife. You made vows before God. You cannot break them on a whim. This story of you falling in love…' He waved a dismissive hand. 'It's a passing fancy. You're too young to know what love is, never mind ruin your life over a man of low station whom you can barely know.' He sighed and put the watch back in his breast pocket. 'It's an offence before God, child, to

93

break your marriage vows. Your immortal soul is in peril. I'm not sending you back. I shall take you back, first thing in the morning, and I shall take you back because I love you like a daughter. It's for your own good, Ella. You don't know your own mind.'

She ran from the room and pounded up the stairs to her old room. It was as she'd left it, except it felt empty and strange. She sat on her bed and wept like a child. She had nothing and nowhere to go. There was to be no escape from her doom.

**

The coach to Oxford had left at first light after a night when Ella had had no sleep. She'd tossed and turned while the moon tracked a path across the night sky beyond her window. Josiah Barton sat stiff-backed at her side on the thinly upholstered seats of the stagecoach, their conversation having long since lapsed into an uneasy silence.

Fields and hedgerows swept past at the pace of cantering horses. Last time she'd made this journey, she'd been angry at being sent away but hopeful of a future: now she was just plain angry.

The grand gates of Castle Ashby once again came into sight, and her heartbeat quickened. Harry would be furious.

'Do you think he'll beat me, Mr Josiah?'

'Harry?' Mr Barton continued to stare out of the window. 'He'd be within his rights, Ella. You have offended his person and God. You must bear whatever punishment he sees fit.'

'Even if...'

'I'm sure he'll be glad to see you home safe, Ella. His anger will be short-lived.'

They left the coach at the crossroads, where Mr Josiah paid the coachman for the last stage and tipped the guards. He turned to her, an overnight bag in his hand. 'Now, where is the Cartwright's farm?'

She pointed down Chase Park Road. 'It's a fair walk.'

94

'The walk will do us good. Stretch our legs after being cooped up like chickens for two days. Come along, Ella.'

A sigh escaped her lips. Whatever Mr Josiah thought, Harry would want his pound of flesh, and he'd make sure he got it.

The farmhouse loomed large in front of her. John and Harry were in the yard working on a piece of machinery. The chestnut cart mare and the Percheron were tethered nearby. She swallowed and hesitated.

Josiah took hold of her elbow and propelled her forward. 'You have to face him, Ella. You may as well get it over with.'

Her heart pounded like horses' hooves galloping on a hard-packed dirt track.

Harry walked towards her. 'Ella.'

Josiah Barton smiled. 'I think Ella got a little homesick, Harry. Understandable in one so young, on her first time away from her mother, wouldn't you say?'

Harry's face juggled a variety of emotions. 'Quite understandable. It's good to have you home, Ella.'

She bowed her head. 'I'm sorry, Harry. I was scared.'

Harry laughed. 'Scared? Of what? Me? My dear girl, you have nothing to fear at Newhay.' He put a finger beneath her chin and lifted her face to look at him.

What could she read in his eyes? Not love. Not hate. Nothing? Nothing was somehow more terrifying than anger. 'I've been stupid, Harry. Please forgive me.'

Mr Josiah exhaled loudly. 'There, you see, Ella? I told you Harry would be pleased to see you.'

Her head swam. 'Yes, Mr Josiah. I'm sorry to have caused you trouble.'

'Pay it no heed, Ella. I shall enjoy a short visit with Charles Buchanan while I'm here. Now, I'll bid you farewell. Be a good

95

wife, Ella, and Harry will be a good husband. Mark my words.'

'I'll try, sir.'

Her last link with Bath turned away and marched back towards Yardley. Harry gripped her arm. 'Get upstairs.'

'Yes, Harry.'

John Cartwright had been silent up to now. 'Ella can wait, Harry. We need to get this job finished.'

'I'll be back in a minute, Father.' Harry marched her across the yard and in through the front door of the house. 'Get up those stairs.' She resigned herself to her fate and trudged up the stairs. Harry opened the bedroom door and thrust her through it. 'I'll deal with you later.' The door slammed behind her, and the key clicked in the lock.

He'd locked her in? She pulled at the door handle, turning it both ways. 'Harry, let me out.'

Her answer was hobnailed boots crashing down the stairs. The window offered a small square of hope. Throwing it open, she peered out. How far was it to the ground? Ten feet? She knelt on the wide windowsill, threw her bag to the ground, and gripped the frame. She could do this. She turned and backed out through the small gap, lowering herself down until she was clinging to the frame by her fingertips. She looked down, swallowed hard, and let go. The ground hit her back like a carpet beater on a dusty rug and knocked the breath from her body. She gasped, unable to breathe, and took another desperate gulp of painful air.

There was no-one in sight. She grabbed her bag, bent double, taking ragged breaths, and ran through an open gate into the field beyond the house. Following the hedge lines and climbing over fences and through hedges that tore at her clothes and snagged in her hair, she made her way to the turnpike road.

Now what? She collapsed onto the grass verge. The only person who would help her now was Jem.

***

96

'You again.' Charlotte Weston's brow furrowed as she looked Ella up and down. 'I thought you were staying with your mother?'

Ella shook her head. 'Mr Barton, my mother's employer, brought me back to Harry. He locked me in the bedroom.'

'Mr Barton did?'

'No, Harry did. I climbed out of the window and ran across the fields.'

'You look like you've been dragged through a hedge backwards.' Mrs Weston shook her head. 'Oh, Ella. Does Harry treat you so badly?'

'It isn't just Harry. It's John. And, anyway, I love Jem. I'm sorry, I shouldn't have come, but I didn't know where else to turn, Mrs Weston. If Harry finds me…'

A shadow darkened the room. 'Harry will have to get through me first.' Jem's determined smile lit her soul.

'Jem.' She ran into his arms. 'Please, I can't go back to Newhay.'

'What the hell happened to you, Ella?' Jem turned to his mother. 'We can't turn her away, Ma, not in this state.'

'I didn't say she had to go, Jem.' The furrows on Mrs Weston's brow deepened. 'John Cartwright's no better than he should be when it comes to young girls. It's said he has four bastards between here and Olney. Is that what happened, Ella, the first time you ran away? Did he try to force his attentions?'

She nodded, but she wouldn't admit to the whole truth: John's lecherous intent would surely be enough reason for her flight. 'I can't go back there.'

Mrs Weston gave her a shrewd look. Had she guessed the truth? 'And Harry?'

She nodded again, tears streaming down her cheeks. 'He was…' Her words came out in a whisper.

97

Mrs Weston's arms came around her. 'Enough said, child. No woman should have to endure such treatment. Get that kettle from the range, Jem. Can't you see the poor girl needs a cuppa?' Mrs Weston steered her to a chair by the hearth and then fetched a small box from a shelf, took out a small gold ring, and gave it to Jem. 'You said you and Ella had married over the brush, son. This was my mam's. She'd have loved to have met you, Ella.'

'Ella?' Jem knelt at her feet and slipped the ring onto her finger. 'There, no bugger can say we ain't wed now.'

'It's beautiful. Thank you, Mrs Weston.'

Jem's mother smiled. 'Call me Charlotte, Ella Weston. Whatever trouble's coming our way, we'll face it together.'

A loud hammering crashed on the front door. 'Quick, Ella. Hide in the privy and lock the door.' Jem threw open the back door and pushed her outside, throwing her bag after her.

She ran down the garden path and sat on one of the two holes, trembling. Muffled shouting came from the cottage. Harry had come to claim his bride.

***

The last oil lamp was put out, and Ella climbed the stairs, Jem holding a chamber stick above his head to light her way. She'd viewed Jem's father, William, a brickmaker, with some suspicion, but the man, though coarse of speech, had been welcoming and quietly courteous towards her, and he and his wife had vowed to protect her from Harry and John.

She felt guilty about making them lie for her, but Jem's parents had insisted they hadn't lied when they'd convinced Harry they hadn't seen Ella Cartwright. Ella Cartwright didn't exist anymore, they assured her; she was Ella Weston now. William had laughed and shown her his fists. He told her he was bare-knuckle champion, as Harry well knew, and Harry had backed down fast enough when faced with rolled-up sleeves and brawny arms.

She'd asked Charlotte to teach her the rudiments of lacemaking, in order to help earn a little extra money for the family, but she'd been happy to do what chores she could that evening to let Charlotte's nimble fingers work at her lace while there was daylight enough by which to see.

Charlotte and William had retired early, giving her and Jem precious time to themselves, but now it was time to face her demons. Jem undressed down to his pantaloons and threw back the sheet on his bed. 'I'd have got clean linen if I'd known as how as you were going to be sharing my bed. You rather be this side or to the window?'

'The window?' Her voice had a barely controlled tremor.

'It'll be all right, Ella. Things'll settle. You'll see.'

She pulled her dress over her head and stood in her shift. Jem didn't move towards her but climbed into bed.

'You got enough room?'

The mattress was made of straw, not feathers, and the linen was coarse, but she lay down next to Jem, stiff with mixed dread and longing. 'It's fine.'

Jem rolled on his side to face her. The candlelight flickered across his features, sending his eyes into deep shadow and highlighting the curve of a smile. He put one arm across her waist and the other cradled her head so that her face was nestled against his shoulder. She laid a hand upon his chest, feeling the gentle rise and fall of his ribs.

His lips brushed the top of her head. 'I can wait until you're ready, Ella. We have the rest of our lives for making love.'

***

Ella's first night with Jem had been a haven of peace. He'd held her in his arms and let her sleep: safe, demanding nothing and giving only his love. He didn't touch her intimately, apart from kissing her lips and tangling his fingers in her hair, respecting that her mind needed time to heal. She loved him all the more for his kindness, patience, and compassion.

Sunday arrived unbidden and, with it, the necessity of braving the village. All faces turned towards the Westons as they slipped into their pew at the back of the church. The reverend's sermon was about marriage, obedience to God's holy ordinance, lusts of the flesh, and the descent of the adulterous into hell.

The reverend cleared his throat and looked directly at her. 'Let the social evil that is prostitution be a punishable offence by law, which adultery is already forbidden by God's Holy Commandments, as much as murder, theft, or any other offence.' He made it quite clear he'd washed his hands of Ella Cartwright who was damned to suffer the wages of sin and eternal torment.

She sat, head bowed, at the rear of the church as far from the centre aisle as possible, next to Jem and his parents, and let the words wash over her. She knew the truth, and God would judge her and the Cartwrights.

The sermon over, they sat quietly waiting for the villagers to file out. Word had obviously got around. Some smiled sympathetically and others glowered: divided loyalties, a village split. Harry slowed and stared at her and then shrugged his shoulders as if he didn't care. He'd cared enough to try to find her. Well, he knew where she was living now if he dared to face Jem and the Westons. The man with him, Joe Upton, made as if to spit at her. 'Whore.'

Jem leapt to his feet, but she put a hand on his arm. 'Leave it, Jem.'

'What's it got to do with Joe Upton?'

'He's a friend of Harry's. He'll have heard Harry's side of the story.'

'Which is?'

'Probably not the same as mine.'

'Which is?'

'It's in the past, Jem. I don't want to think about it. Let it lie.'

100

'No-one calls you a whore and gets away with it. I'll teach that bastard some manners.'

'Please, Jem. Leave it be. Joe doesn't know what went on in that house. And I've no wish to relive it.'

Jem put a hand beneath her arm and helped her up. 'Come on. I ain't hiding in here as if we've something to be ashamed of.'

She raised her chin. Jem was right. She'd done nothing wrong. People were bound to gossip and speculate. If Harry or John spread scurrilous rumours about her, she'd spread some stories of her own: true ones.

***

Harry waited outside the churchyard. 'Just because I didn't make a scene in church doesn't mean I'm leaving without my wife.'

Joe Upton flexed his muscles and turned to his wife. 'Go on home, Elizabeth. This isn't woman's work. I've been waiting for a reason to punch Jem Weston since he was old enough to lay a snare. You ready, Harry?'

'I'm ready, Joe.' He removed his Sunday jacket and hung it over a leaning gravestone. 'I'm more than ready.' There was going to be a fight: him and Joe against Jem Weston. People gathered in small groups, exchanging gossip. He went hot under the collar; the gossip would be about him, Harry Cartwright, and Ella. Damn her for walking out on him. The groups split and drifted away. Ella appeared in the church doorway, Jem at her side.

'We don't want no trouble, Harry.' Jem Weston drew himself up to his full height, still a mere five feet four inches.

Weston was no match for him and Joe. 'Get up on the trap, Ella, and there'll be no trouble. We'll call it even.'

Jem moved to stand in front of Ella. 'She makes her own choices, Harry. I won't have you forcing her hand.'

'She's my wife. She promised to obey me, and obey me she will.'

101

'I don't think so. I don't believe she's safe under John Cartwright's roof, Harry.'

'She's safe under *my* roof.' He gritted his teeth. While his father lived, his shadow would always cut the light from his life. It was a pity Ella hadn't killed the bastard with that colander. 'Ella, get on the trap.'

'No.' Ella moved to stand beside Jem, who grasped her hand. 'I won't. Jem and I married over the broom yesterday. I'm Ella Weston now.'

His head thumped as if it would explode. 'I'm your legal husband. You're mine. Now stand aside while I beat the shit out of this apology for a man.'

Ella stood in front of Jem. Anger overcame propriety. 'You'll have to beat the shit out of me, first.'

Jem pushed her aside and unbuttoned his coat. He tossed it on the grass and rolled up his sleeves. 'Come on, then, Cartwright. You, too, Upton.'

'Jem, no. Please, Harry.'

He liked to hear her beg. He smirked. 'That's what she said on her our wedding night, Jem. Begging for it, she was. "Please, Harry."'

Jem's fist connected with his nose, sending him reeling. He staggered upright, but not before Joe waded into Jem, fists flying. Jem ducked and danced. Weston had obviously picked up some tricks from his father, Bill, bare-knuckle champion of the county.

Jem stood with his fists raised, deflecting Upton's blows. 'Getting Upton to do your dirty work, Harry. Come on, then, coward. You want her or not?'

'Stand aside, Joe. No bugger calls me a coward. Ella's mine. I'll show her who the master is here.' Blood oozed from his nose; he wiped it away with the back of his hand and raised his own fists, mimicking Jem's stance, and they circled one another, jabbing and ducking aside.

Ella was crying. 'Stop it, both of you. Jem… Harry…'

He ignored her but Jem, distracted, glanced towards her. Taking advantage of Jem's lapse, he moved in fast and got in a heavy blow to Jem's gut and another to his temple. Jem folded and almost fell but regained his footing and jabbed back at his face, trying to further damage his nose. He deflected Jem's punch and slammed in a right hook. Ella collapsed at his feet.

Jem fell to his knees beside her. 'You bloody idiot, Harry.'

'It wasn't my fault I hit her. She got in the way. Daft mare.'

Jem bent close to listen for a breath. 'Get the doctor.'

'She's my wife. I'm staying with her. You run and fetch the doctor if you want one.'

'For fuck's sake, Harry.'

'I'll go.' Joe Upton broke into a run and disappeared towards the doctor's house.

'Harry.' Jem stared at him coldly. 'This isn't Ella's fault, as well you know. I let her go because I thought you could give her what I couldn't. A good life. I entrusted her future to you. What happened to make her leave you?'

'It's none of your business.' The Cartwrights didn't need any more gossip of the kind his father engendered. He smirked. 'She was probably frightened by the size of my todger. She'll be fine now I've broken her in. Sooner I get her home, the better.'

'You're taking her nowhere. She loves me, Harry, and I love her. You don't care a toss about her. All you want is a skivvy and a milk cow.'

Ella moaned and brought an end to the argument. 'What happened?'

'Harry hit you.'

'You got in the way, you daft mare. I was aiming at Jem.'

'Let me go, Harry. Please, before anyone else gets hurt.'

103

'Come home, and no-one else will get hurt.'

She sat up as Doc Hayes hurried through the gates to the churchyard. The doctor bent over her. 'That's quite a bruise, young lady. Did you fall?'

She looked from her legal husband to Jem and back again. 'I tripped.'

'Were you unconscious?'

'I don't think so. Just feel faint.'

The doctor examined her head and felt her neck. 'I don't think there's serious damage. You'd better get your wife home, and see she gets some rest.'

'I need to sit down for a bit, Harry.'

He hauled her to her feet. 'You're coming home with me.'

Doc Hayes frowned. 'What she needs is a cup of sweet tea and a cold compress on that bruise. The road is very bumpy between here and Newhay, Harry. Maybe, she should rest up for a while first.'

'She ain't going with Harry. She wants to be with me.' Jem staked his claim by laying a hand on Ella's arm. 'I'm taking her home.'

The doctor attempted to calm the situation. 'I'm sure Charlotte Weston will make you a cup of tea, Ella. You'll feel fine in no time, and Harry can take you home when you feel ready.'

Ella nodded and allowed herself to be escorted to the Weston's cottage.

'Wait, Harry.' Doc Hayes put a restraining hand on his arm. He tried to shake it off and push inside the cottage after Ella and Jem. Doc Hayes held his arm tighter. 'Give her some space, Harry. I heard Ella left you for James Weston. If you did this to her, be warned. I'm watching you. I don't agree with hitting women, even if it is your wife. Now, go home. If Ella wants to come back to you, she will. Personally, from the gossip I've heard flying around

104

the village, I wouldn't blame her if she didn't.' The doctor gripped the handle of his bag more firmly. 'I suggest we go to my surgery, and I'll take a look at that nose. You've been fighting James? I think he's broken it for you.' He sighed. 'Two young lads and one pretty girl. Bound to cause trouble.'

'I'm not leaving without Ella.'

Joe touched his shoulder. 'Leave it, Harry, and go with the doc. There's more than one way to skin this rabbit. Jem Weston will put a foot wrong soon enough.'

He smiled and nodded. Jem was a poacher. Joe had a shotgun and the game laws gave him legal cause to use it.

Chapter Ten

The candle on the table at the side of the bed guttered. Dancing shadows flickered across the walls and ceiling, ephemeral and fleeting like life. Ella gazed at Jem. She'd given him her heart, and now... She let her fingers travel down his chest until he caught them with his own and kissed them. She drew his hand across her and laid it on her naked breast. He caressed it gently and leaned over to kiss her.

She moved her body closer, and his hardness against her was obvious. 'Jem...'

'Only if you're sure.' His whispered breath set her heart racing.

'I want you.'

Her skin tingled, every nerve alive, as his lips explored her body. His muscles were firm and strong: the arch of his back and the swell of his buttocks under her hands excited her.

'I love you, Ella.' He took her gently, slowly, murmuring to her, caressing her, and building a slow fire of need.

She moved with him, pressing him closer, her movements ever more urgent as she matched his. He responded to her passion with his own, taking her to a place she'd never imagined possible. Desire exploded, leaving her breathless and spent, and Jem sagged against her, exhausted. Tears ran unheeded down her cheeks. To think she might never have known love like this.

Jem thumbed away her tears. 'I hurt you.'

She smiled. 'No, you healed me. You've shown me what love is. Whatever trials our being together brings, I'll never regret one night of our love nor trade one moment with you for all the riches in the world.'

Jem left the cottage at first light with the tools of his trade in a bag and a whistle on his lips. He'd left Ella lighting a fire under the boiler in the outside washhouse, ready to tackle the weekly wash. She'd only been in the cottage for three weeks, and he couldn't imagine life without her; already his mother relied on Ella to do much of the work, freeing her hands for lacemaking. Three weeks of looking over his shoulder for Harry Cartwright were nothing compared to three weeks of loving Ella. Maybe, Harry had accepted he'd lost Ella and moved on. Or, maybe, he was biding his time.

It was another Monday morning, and months of hard labour lay ahead. He had bricks to cart from the brickworks for the new house he was helping build west of the brook. It was several months of guaranteed work, if the weather let them get on with the groundwork, and wages he and Ella desperately needed if they were to afford rent on a home of their own. He walked with a jaunty step, whistling louder. Ella loved him, she'd lit a fire under his boiler nothing would put out, and all was right with his world. Anything was possible.

He arrived at the building site to find the foreman already there. He approached the man. 'Do you want me to fetch the horses for the cart, right off?'

The foreman shook his head. 'I'm going to have to let you go, James.'

'Let me go where? What do you mean?'

'There ain't any work for you here.'

'But, I'm a good worker. The new house…'

'I'm sorry, lad. It ain't my choice. You and young Harry's wife ain't none of my business, but I got a big job coming up at Newhay. Some barns as need repairing and reroofing. John Cartwright's threatened to tell his lordship's estate manager to give the job to Furnell's, over Brafield way, if I employ you.'

'He can't do that.'

'Seems he can and he has. He says you got to go. I can't put the other men's livelihoods in danger. Old man Upton's cancelled a job as well.'

He spat at the ground. 'John Cartwright ain't got no cause to do this. It's him and his Harry as upset my Ella. And it's none of Upton's bloody business.'

'Look, lad. There's plenty of work at the threshing, I hear, and Isaac Ruddle's paying two shillings and eleven pence a day, which is more than I can pay you. Why don't you go down and ask? Them cousins of yours, Caleb and Nathan, have got work there. You can tell Ruddle I'll put in a good word for you, if he asks.'

'Thanks.' He couldn't ask the man to jeopardise his workers. The last few stooks of corn needed bringing in from the rick-yards to be stacked ready for threshing. Then there were the teams of horses to handle on the sweep that powered the machine or pitchfork work throwing up sheaves to the top of the thresher, grain skips to be emptied into sacks, and waste straw to be forked away and restacked or loaded onto carts. Yes, a lot of strong arms would be needed, and harvest rates were the best pay he'd get all year. Maybe Isaac Ruddle wasn't in the Cartwrights' pocket. Harry and John could do their worst. Nothing would make him give up Ella.

Ruddle greeted him with a grunt. 'I'll put you on pitching-up with Caleb. That's a job for young arms.' He paused and looked at him quizzically. 'I hear as how as you've gone over the brush with the rector's young girl. It ain't none of my business, but it doesn't surprise me she didn't stay at Newhay. Harry Cartwright's used to getting what he wants and never mind who gets hurt.'

'What do you mean?'

'Him having had the pox as a young un? He usually has to pay for it, I heard. That must be hard for a man, and that family like their money's worth. You ask Louisa as worked for them. And as for John…' Isaac lowered his voice. 'It's common knowledge he can't keep his hands to himself where young girls are concerned. None of them are kept on long enough to show they're pregnant. Has more bastards than he has horses, I heard.'

'I heard that, too.' He frowned. 'You think John might have interfered with Ella? You think he'd touch his son's wife?' Louisa had said John wasn't to be trusted.

Isaac shrugged. 'She left after one night, didn't she? Something must have happened.' Isaac coughed and spat. 'Damn dust... I get this cough every harvest. Time we got started. Help Seth harness the horses, James, and haul the sweep out. Tell him I need four pairs. Put the grey and the roan together. The roan's young and the grey's steady. The two Suffolks work best as a pair, and keep the black Shire geldings apart or the buggers'll fight.'

'Right, Mr Ruddle.' He hurried away to fetch harnesses for the heavy horses. He'd kill John Cartwright and Harry, if what Isaac suggested was true. And Joe Upton had better watch his back as well.

*****

Ella wiped sweat from her brow with the back of a reddened washday hand and pounded and twisted the scrubbed whites in the dolly tub with a work-bleached dolly-stick. The smell of soap suds and boiling linen took her back to Mr Barton's residence and her ritual Monday washdays with her mother, though the linen she washed now was heavier, greyer, and coarser and she only had one pair of hands.

She didn't care. She'd sleep on a hessian sack on the floor with Jem, rather than on smooth linen and a feather mattress with Harry. Her mouth twitched into a smile. These last weeks with Jem had shown her what true happiness was: how stupid she'd been to agree to marry a man she didn't know, let alone love. Her smile faded. Harry had made little attempt to get her back after Jem had broken his nose. She touched the faded bruise on her forehead. Would Harry stay quiet about her hitting John when he'd raped her, or would he cause trouble for them out of spite, to save face?

109

She'd known Jem such a short time, and yet he felt right. He was a good man who loved her: passionate and thoughtful. Her cheeks flushed warm at the thought, and her stomach muscles tightened; it would be fun getting to know him better. She stifled a guilty laugh; she could imagine the reverend's sermon on the subject of wantonness, lust, and adultery. Had Reverend Buchanan ever known true love? He'd been eager enough to marry her off to Harry, but did he have any idea of what he preached?

She lifted a steaming sheet from the tub and dragged it to a cast-iron mangle that stood close by. Feeding a bulky corner between the wooden rollers, she turned the handle, letting the squeezed and flattened linen fall into folds into a long stone sink on the other side as the soapy water flowed down a wooden board and back into the boiler.

She drew buckets of cold water from the pump and emptied them into the sink. The bending, as she swished the sheet around, pummelling, squeezing, and wringing it with her hands to force out the suds, made her back ache.

Her arms and wrists burnt by the time the last pair of breeches was rinsed to her satisfaction and had been wound back through the wringer twice. She dropped the breeches into a two-handled wicker basket and carried her load out to the backyard. A bacon pig grunted in greeting from the sty at the end of the yard, standing up on its hind legs to see out, its snout snuffling. Birds sang from trees beyond the sty, and the sound of babies crying and children shouting drowned out the flapping of sheets.

A glance down the row of backyards showed other wives already had their washing blowing in the midmorning sun. She pegged sheets, shirts, and underwear onto a rope line tied between two trees and compared her efforts to that of her neighbours. Next week, she would rise earlier and expend greater effort at the washboard. She'd do her bit for her new family and make Jem proud of her. She'd make sure they never regretted taking her in, if she had to work all the hours God gave.

***

Jem woke at cock crow. He opened one eye and turned towards the pale square of daylight that filtered through the curtains. Ella lay on her back, sleeping. Her face was silhouetted against the window, and her breasts rose and fell beneath her thin nightdress, her nipples making tiny points in the fabric. The swell of her belly was hidden beneath the blankets. He ran a gentle hand down her hip and across her stomach, letting it rest on the small mound above the juncture of her thighs.

Ella made a low sound and turned towards him. He traced the shape of her thigh until he reached the hem of her nightdress and let his hand wander upwards beneath it.

She opened her eyes and smiled. 'It's almost light.'

'We have time, don't we?'

She shook her head playfully. 'I have the starching and ironing…'

His hand found the moist place between her legs. 'I don't need nothing ironed nor starched…'

'I won't have folk saying I don't know how to look after my man. And you have another hard day's work.'

His fingers delved gently. 'And I'll do it all the better after making love to my beautiful wife.'

She let out a small moan and arched her back. 'You're a bad influence, Jem Weston.'

He kissed her neck. 'Ain't I just? And you're a wicked temptress, Ella.'

She ran a hand down his stomach and giggled. 'Ain't I just?'

He covered her with his body and she accepted him, moving with him, her muscles driving him onwards, hard and urgent inside her. He spent his seed and lay against her, heart thumping and chest heaving.

He withdrew, and she rolled against him and rested her head on his chest, her long auburn curls spread across his shoulder. He stroked her hair. 'I love you, Ella Weston. I love you so much.'

The sound of footsteps on the stairs reminded him he had work to do. He kissed her slowly and then reached for his shirt. 'I'm threshing all day again at Ruddle's. Tonight, I'm thinking of going up the Chase. Bring us home a couple of rabbits, or maybe a pheasant.

Ella shrugged her shift over her head and reached for her hairbrush. 'Jem, be careful.'

'Rabbits ain't game. Any road, it'll take a better man than Joe Upton to catch me, don't you worry. I'll see you later.' He kissed her again and paused. She'd be mad if she heard this from Cal or Nat. 'About Michaelmas…'

'We paid our share of the rent, didn't we?' She arched an eyebrow. 'Is this about that money you said you had coming?'

He nodded and arranged his features in an expression he hoped was shamefaced. 'I had a bet with Cal and Nat, and…'

'And?'

'You should hear this from me.'

She paused in the act of brushing out tangles. 'Now you're worrying me, Jem. Don't tell me you've lost your wages.'

'I bet them a week's money I'd… We'd make love afore Michaelmas.' He stared at his boots.' I won the bet, didn't I?'

Ella flung the hairbrush across the room towards him. 'Jem! How could you?'

He ducked. 'That isn't why I…'

She stood with her hands on her hips, failing to look cross. 'You are in so much trouble, Jem Weston.'

'I know.' He couldn't help grinning. 'You can punish me, tonight.' He thudded down the stairs with a smile on his face.

Old man Ruddle was in the yard when he arrived with Cal and Nat. He touched his cap. 'You want us to drag out the sweep, Mr

112

Ruddle?'

Ruddle looked at the sky and grunted. 'Reckon it'll be fine all day. Let's get started. Get them teams hitched.'

'The Suffolks together, the grey with the roan, and keep the black Shires apart.'

'Good lad.' Ruddle tugged at a belt on the thresher and cleared straw from the chute. 'Nat, give us a hand connecting the drive shafts.'

He left Nat and Ruddle to it and harnessed the Suffolk Punches, a pair of compact, well-muscled chestnut mares, and backed them up to the sweep, one either side of the centre pole. 'Steady, my girls. Whoa there.' The mares stood quietly while he hitched them to the machine. He patted a shining neck. 'Walk on.' The horses leaned into their collars and the sweep rumbled out into the yard. Careful manoeuvring brought the drive gears in line with the shaft that connected the sweep to the threshing machine.

Cal beckoned with a raised hand. 'Back a bit. Stop! That's it.' Cal straightened and then lowered the arms of the sweep, ready for him to hitch the teams of horses.

It was a clever contraption, even if its introduction had caused riots only a few years earlier. Four or five teams of horses or mules, hitched to long arms, walked in a large circle to rotate a cog that turned a drive shaft that ran along the ground to another set of cogs that, in turn, drove the thresher. It had been feared it would put thousands of labourers out of work, but men were still needed, and the work was less back-breaking than with a flail.

Ruddle had put him and Cal on pitching-up again, one of the most tiring jobs. Nat was on top of the thresher filling the grain tubs and replacing them with empty ones. The horses moved forwards, led round by some of the older workers. A low rumble of shafts turning and cogs whirring grew into a whine. Belts, and moving parts on the thresher, flapped and clattered making talking impossible and filling the air with the smell of hot grease. Nat signalled that he was ready so he tossed up a sheaf of corn. Dust

113

billowed down.

Midmorning, and the thresher ground to a screeching halt. Ruddle scratched his head and re-positioned his cap. 'Reckon something's jammed. Unhitch the teams, Jem, and let them rest. Feed and water them, and then you'd better all have an early bite while I see what's up with this infernal thing.'

'Right away, Mr Ruddle, sir.' He leaned his pitchfork against the thresher and hurried to see to the teams. He led them to the trough in turn and then scooped corn from the bin into mangers in their stalls. He patted the big black, checked the half-hitch on the rope was secure, and went outside to fetch his lunch tin. Bread, cheese, and an apple straight off the tree in the backyard, and Ella had put up a flagon of beer.

Threshing was hot, dusty, thirsty work, and they were all parched. He downed his second pint, refilled his tankard from the flagon, and glanced around. 'I'm going up the Chase tonight, see if I can bag me a rabbit. He lowered his voice. 'Or, maybe, a hare. You wanna come?'

Cal nodded and took a bite of the bread and cheese his mother had brought him. 'I'll bring a gun along.'

Nat leaned forwards. 'I'll bring the one your dad lent me, Cal.'

Cal nodded. 'How about you, Jem?'

'I'll see if I can borrow one. It'll be surer than snares.'

Nat belched loudly. 'We'd better see what's happening. Old man Ruddle'll be as hopping as a bucket of frogs if we set here all day.'

Ruddle grunted. 'The man as made the thresher has come and taken the bugger to bits. We've gotta haul it to the blacksmiths for him to make a new part. Fetch the Suffolks out, Jem.'

'Right away, Mr Ruddle.' He led out the chestnuts and helped Cal and Nat hitch them to the heavy machine and lead them across the village to the blacksmith's shop.

The blacksmith pointed, and Ruddle squatted to look at the broken part. Ruddle grunted again. 'Take the horses back and then get yourselves off. There'll be no threshing done this afternoon, lads.'

***

Two thirty, and in the Rose and Crown the afternoon was still young. Jem ordered another round of beers, and the barmaid brought a fresh flagon. He filled his tankard and placed a domino on the table. 'Cal, you sure you can't find another gun?'

Cal wiped froth from his top lip, checked his pieces, and knocked to show he couldn't go. 'Quite sure.'

Nat laid his domino and lifted his pint. 'Ask old Herby.'

He nodded to Herby Longfellow, who was also having a long lunch. 'Herby, you got a gun I can borrow? I wanna bag me some rabbits.'

'No, boy, I ain't.'

'Well, have you got one I can buy then?'

'No, boy.'

'Come on, Herby. I need one. We're going on a bit of a spree tonight. Just rabbits, honest. Rabbits ain't game.'

'Answer's still no, young Jem.'

The clock above the bar said it was half past five by the time they'd spent the morning's wages and finished the last game. Jem wiped beer from his lips. 'I reckon that's settled the dust in our throats. You two coming? I fancy rabbit stew for supper.'

***

Jem breathed in cool air. It had an October bite and was clean and fresh after the smoke-wreathed room in the Rose and Crown. He'd gone with Cal to fetch a gun and have a bite of food while Nat had gone home for his tea. He and Cal walked along the turnpike road together to meet up with their cousin.

115

Cal pointed. 'Ain't that Nat up ahead?'

They quickened their pace to catch up with the stouter figure. Nat patted his pockets; the barrel of a gun stuck from the top of one and the stock from the other. 'You bring your snares, Jem?'

'Yeah.' He wished he had a gun. Next time he'd make sure he brought one. He had his snares, because he'd promised Ella he'd bring something home, but it meant having to snare all the escape routes as the guns would scatter any hares and rabbits in the stubble like chaff in the wind. Rabbits weren't illegal to take, but hare tasted better. 'I reckon as we should make for Newhay Copse. I've seen hares a plenty in the stubble down that way.'

They took the Olney Road to come at the copse from along the edge of the woods, and they got to Letts Close before they saw a soul, and then it was only old George Whitehouse, a labourer at the brickworks.

George hailed Cal. 'If you're going across there, you'd better take care. Keepers have gone that way.'

Cal spat on the grass. 'Damn their eyes. They'd better take care of themselves.' Cal turned back to him and Nat, obviously annoyed. 'Why the hell don't you two come on? We shan't get the taters dug for Sunday dinner at this rate.'

'We're coming, Cal. What's the hurry?' He quickened his stride, but Nat stopped by the gate and took the stock and barrel from his pockets. 'I'll catch you up, Jem.'

He left Nat assembling and loading his gun and walked along the rows of spiky wheat stubble, scrunching them beneath his boots. Cal was working the grass between the stripe of plough and the edge of the wood, so he crossed to the wood's edge and set a couple of snares in likely looking runs through the hedge.

A hare stood on its hind legs among the stubble, ears twitching to catch every sound. He raised an arm slowly and pointed before realising any keeper in Newhay Copse would hear the shot and know they were close by. Cal nodded and aimed before he could stop him. A shot rang out, and the hare leapt into the air before

116

bounding into the wood. Damn, it had missed the run he'd snared.

'You hit it, Cal. It won't get far.' He turned to follow it. 'Come on, quick afore the keepers spot us.'

Nat puffed up to them, waving. 'Keeper! Get over the hedge. Hide!'

'Shit!' He pushed Cal forward and scrambled over the hedge and into the wood after Nat.

Cal climbed onto a bank. 'It's Upton!'

He pulled at Cal's jacket. 'Get down, you bloody fool. He'll see you.'

Cal jumped down. 'I ain't afeared of Joe Upton.'

Neither was he, but there was no point looking for trouble. 'We'd better split up. Make ourselves scarce.' Cal ran down a riding, but he turned deeper into the copse, the sound of Nat's boots thudding behind him. Two gunshots blasted through the trees, fired in quick succession, followed by loud swearing. He skidded to a halt. 'What the hell?'

'Upton?' Nat's face was pale. 'If he'd been firing a warning shot…'

'Cal!'

They ran towards the riding where the shots had sounded. Cal staggered to his feet holding his arm. His jacket was bloodied and peppered with holes.

'Christ, Cal, has he shot you?'

Cal held one arm. 'I think he's broke me shoulder all to morsels.'

Nat's finger tightened on his trigger. 'The bastard won't get away with this.' Nat ran up the riding looking for Upton.

'Nat, come back.' He'd heard two shots. 'Where's Upton? Cal, did you shoot him?'

'I missed. The bastard just swore at me and left me here to

bleed to death.'

Blood oozed from tiny holes in Cal's jacket. Peppered but not life-threatening. Though it'd take Doc Hayes a while to pick out all the lead shot. 'Shit, we'd better go after Nat. If he catches up with Upton…' He pounded after Nat, Cal breathing heavily at his back.

Ahead of them, the keeper jumped a ditch onto the riding and stood in front of them, his shotgun in his hands.

Nat strode on, regardless, and grabbed hold of Upton by the collar. Upton shook Nat off and raised his gun. If Upton had his other barrel loaded, he could kill someone.

'Joe, Nat… No.' He dashed forward and took hold of the gamekeeper's jacket.

Undeterred, Upton shoved him aside, levelled his gun at Nat, and glowered down the barrel, his finger on the trigger. 'You mean to stand this, do you, Nathan?'

Cal grabbed the muzzle of Upton's gun with his good hand and thrust it aside, knocking the keeper off-balance: at the same instant Nat stepped backwards and fired. At almost point-blank range, Nat couldn't miss.

Blood sprayed. For a brief moment, Cal and Nat seemed to freeze. The taste of blood, burnt flesh, and powder made him gag.

Cal's fingers still gripped Upton's shotgun by its barrel, and, knuckles clenched, he swung it at Joe's head with his good hand and then smashed it against the ground, shattering the stock with the force. Cal threw the gun down, breathing heavily, his face sweat-beaded with exertion and drawn with pain.

The bugger had shot Cal and would have shot Nat. Blood thundered through Jem's head: everything seemed to slow. Upton lay at his feet. He kicked out with his foot, catching Upton hard. The man had gone too far: tangled with him once too often. Upton struggled, as if trying to get to his feet. The bastard had called Ella a whore, spat at her, helped lose him his job, had taken Harry's side against Ella, attacked him, accused, and taunted him. He took

118

a deep breath. This time the bugger would stay down. His fingers closed around the gun barrel: he brought it down on the prone man's skull with a dull crack, and Joe Upton lay still.

For a long moment, no-one moved: no-one spoke. Then Nat got hold of Upton's legs. 'Give us a hand, Jem.'

'What...' Bile rose in his throat. He grabbed one of the man's limp hands, recoiling from the touch: together he and Nat dragged him out of sight of the riding. Joe's head was bloodied, his hair matted with gore, and a dark stain spread across his neck and shoulder. Had they killed him? What if Upton lived to tell the tale? A shiver ran through his body, cold and violent, and his hands began shaking. 'Jesus Christ, what have we done?'

Nat just stood there, staring, but Cal snatched Nat's gun from the ground and walked away. He and Nat followed in stunned silence.

They didn't stop walking until they were almost at Olney. Cal tucked the gun into the hedge at the side of the road. Nat had got rid of the other one somewhere along the way. Cal pulled his coat collar round his ears and glanced over his shoulder. 'I need a bloody drink.'

They sat in an ill-lit corner of the pub bar, keeping themselves to themselves and their voices low. Cal and Nat looked as pale as he felt. He downed a pint in one gulp despite shaking like a poplar leaf in a breeze. Jesus, what had he done? He glanced around the room furtively and voiced his fear. 'What if we've killed him? We could all hang for this.'

Nat blanched. 'It were Upton's fault. It were him as shot Cal. We wouldn't have had a go at him, otherwise.'

Cal nursed his shoulder. He moved his arm and winced. 'There ain't nothing to connect us to it if I keep quiet about this lead in my shoulder. Ma'll pick it out for me when I get home.'

There were spatters of blood on Cal's coat, where Joe had peppered him with shot, and dark stains on Nat's: Joe's blood.

119

Cal winced again. 'But no bugger saw what happened. We're far enough from the Cartwrights' house not to have been seen. And I don't reckon Joe's in a state to be saying nothing to no-one.'

'Old George saw us going that way, Cal.'

Nat swigged at his beer and wiped his mouth with his hand. 'We just gotta keep our heads down, Jem.'

His heart thumped erratically. Hot and cold sweats shivered through his body, and his mouth tasted bitter. Life had turned on a sixpence; in a moment of madness, he'd killed a man. How, in God's name, would he face Ella with that on his conscience?

Chapter Eleven

Ella turned over and stretched, opening her eyes slowly and reaching for Jem. His side of the bed was cold, empty. He'd come in very late and gone straight to bed. He'd seemed preoccupied and, when asked, had said he'd had a hard day and needed to be up early to go to Ruddle's. Was he tired of his new wife already?

She was being unreasonable: Jem worked hard from dawn to dusk and had spent half the night trying to catch much-needed food for the table. The fact that he'd failed wouldn't have improved his mood. She washed and dressed. She'd be early at the bake-house and go to Ruddle's before eight to take Jem his breakfast, lunch, and a bottle of cold tea.

Charlotte was already at her lace, her nimble fingers flying across the threads, over and under, back and forth, moving the bobbins and pins as she worked. She didn't look up. 'Jem was out early, Ella?'

'He looks pale, worn out, Charlotte.' She knelt to clean out the fire, ready for relighting. He's up early, comes home late. He hardly had the strength to talk to me last night. And I don't think he slept that well, either. Nor stopped for breakfast by the look of it.'

Charlotte straightened her back for a moment before resuming her work. 'Harvest's a difficult time. Relentless. It can break the strongest man, even a young 'un. I'm lucky my William's a brick maker. It's hard work but steady.'

'I'm going to take him some food over when I've been to the bake-house. And the reverend is distributing the vegetables from the altar display at the church this morning. I'll make some brawn later and a pottage for this evening.'

Charlotte smiled without looking up. 'A young man needs his victuals.'

'I'll look after him, Charlotte.'

'I know you will, love. And I ain't never seen him so happy. He's just bone weary. You'll see.'

Reassured, she fetched two still-warm loaves from the bake-house and packed Jem chunks of fresh bread and cheese in a tin beside pickles and an apple. Then she made tea and poured it into a bottle with a tight-fitting stopper. Putting all into a basket, she made her way to Ruddle's. The noise in the yard was deafening, the air thick with dust and the smell of grease and sweating horses. Jem was bare to the waist, pitching sheaves up to the top of a huge machine as if his life depended on it. She skirted the circling horses and drew closer. Sweat beaded on Jem's brow, his dark hair slick-wet and his back glistening with rippling muscle.

He saw her and faltered mid-pitch. She pointed to her basket and then to a place by the wall of the barn. He nodded, and she blew him a kiss. He smiled briefly, blew one back, and resumed pitching.

Charlotte was right. He was just working too hard. He wasn't like Harry, who'd used her for his own lust and nothing more: she had nothing to worry about.

***

Jem's heart thudded near to bursting as he pitched sheaves for the last hour of the day. It was Friday, almost three full days since their disastrous outing to Newhay Copse. Joe's wife had been asking if anyone had seen her husband as he hadn't come home on the Tuesday, and she was sure he'd be found with his brains blown out. Her enquiry had led to a search, and, yesterday, Joe's body had been found. They were calling it murder. How long before George, who'd seen them up by Newhay, heard the news? Why the hell had they gone to Newhay Copse after the man had warned Cal the keepers could be there? What if George pointed the finger in their direction?

Sweat chilled on his skin, sticking his breeches to his buttocks. He'd promised to keep Ella safe, look after her. How could he do that swinging from the gallows?

He pitched another sheaf, but Nat failed to catch it. He looked where Nat was looking. Ruddle was talking to a group of men. One of them was his lordship's head keeper. Nat had gone as white as one of their landlord's swans. Cal, who'd pleaded a wrenched shoulder, and was passing sheaves for pitching rather than pitching-up himself, dropped the sheaf he was holding. Ruddle grabbed the bridle of one of the horses, bringing the sweep to a standstill, and the thresher clattered and whined to a halt.

Nat climbed down from the thresher and stood beside him. 'We're done for, Jem.'

'Shit.' He wiped clammy hands on his trousers and swallowed, sick to his stomach, and made a show of examining his pitchfork handle. Ruddle was walking towards him, five men following him: three of the men were police constables. The older one looked to be their superior officer.

Cal looked at his boots. 'Don't let on as you know anything.'

The officer in charge approached with a swagger. 'I'm Chief Constable Goddard.' The officer held himself straight, like a ramrod. 'Nathan Denton, Caleb Brafield, and James Weston, I have information that leads me to believe you may be involved in a suspicious death. I'm therefore arresting you on suspicion of the wilful murder of Joseph Upton. You don't have to say anything. Come with me, please.'

***

Ella answered a sharp rapping on the front door. A man in a police uniform stood in the lane. Jem hadn't poached any pheasants: not even a hare. He'd been working close to the open belts that drove the thresher. Her head swam. 'Has there been an accident?'

'I'm Chief Constable Goddard. I need to search the house.'

Jem's mother rose from her chair. 'I'm Charlotte Weston. Why

123

do you need to search my home? What are you looking for?'

'There's been a murder. I believe your son, James, may be involved.'

'Oh, Charlotte.' Her hand flew to her mouth. 'A murder? Who's been murdered?'

'Mr Joseph Upton. A gamekeeper for the Marquis of Northampton has been shot and killed. Where was James on the night of Tuesday last – October sixth?'

Charlotte glanced at her. 'He was here, I expect, same as always.'

Goddard looked from Jem's mother to her. 'And you are?'

She bristled at his tone. She wasn't ashamed of her and Jem. 'I'm James's wife, Ella Weston. His common-law wife.'

Goddard nodded and looked around the small room. 'I'll start upstairs.'

She watched Charlotte as the chief constable thudded up the stairs. Jem had hated Joe Upton. 'Jem wouldn't, would he?'

Charlotte shook her head. 'Him and Upton have tangled before. Upton got him convicted and fined. It's common knowledge they hate each other, and Harry's been stirring it with Joe, I heard, Jem being accused of poaching and all. Dear Lord, that boy will be the death of me.'

Convicted? Jem had mentioned owing the court money. 'But he wouldn't. Not Jem.'

Charlotte gripped her daughter-in-law's shoulders and whispered beneath her breath. 'He went poaching on Tuesday. It was the night he came home late, stinking of beer.'

He'd gone to bed as soon as he'd come in. He'd been gone when she woke. Her heart thudded. She'd known then there was something wrong. 'Who did he go with?'

'Nathan and Caleb, his cousins. They can be a bit wild when

they've had a few beers. Oh please, Lord. Don't say they met up with Joe in the Chase.'

'But Jem doesn't have a gun.'

'Caleb has one, Ella.'

'Do you think –' A thud on the stairs silenced her. Goddard searched the living room and then the outhouses. He came back inside. 'There's nothing here. I'll bid you good day.'

'Where's Jem, Chief Constable?' Her voice shook.

'He's been arrested. My men have taken him to Castle Ashby.' The chief constable's face was emotionless. 'If he can answer our questions to our satisfaction, he'll be released later today.'

She shut the door behind the police officer and leaned back on it, shaking. 'It can't have anything to do with Jem. He'll be home for his tea, Charlotte. You see if he isn't.'

***

'Joe's dead?' Harry couldn't take in what his father was saying.

'Shot in the head and had his brains bashed in, apparently. Three lads have been arrested.'

'Who?'

'That Jem Weston that Ella's hitched herself to. Him and his cousins.'

'Nat and Cal?'

'They're the ones.'

'They were seen killing him?'

'Not that I know of. The evidence is strong though.' His father smiled. 'If you still want her, this is your chance to get young Ella back.'

'She won't abandon Jem. The girl's obsessed with him.'

'Then see to it he isn't here to be obsessed with. The killing happened in the copse – right on our doorstep. You're the obvious person to have seen what happened.'

'But I didn't see.'

'For fuck's sake, use your brains, boy. Do I have to wet nurse you all your life? You tell the sergeant you saw those boys with Upton on Tuesday night. Herby Longfellow reckons they were in the Rose and Crown till gone five, and Jem wanted to borrow a gun off him. George Whitehouse says he saw them coming this way from the Olney Road, a bit after that. Sixish, he reckons. All the police need is for you to say you saw them with Joe, sometime after six o'clock. Maybe heard raised voices. There's ill-feeling enough between James and Joe to make any jury convict him with that evidence, Harry.'

He smiled. 'Jem hangs, and there's no-one to stop me taking Ella.' His smile spread wider. 'And Jem will know he's helpless to stop me.'

'Now he gets it. Give the boy a prize.'

Half a head taller than the older man, he gripped his father's shoulder. 'I get her back, and you don't rape her again, right? She's mine, and you'll respect that.'

John Cartwright shrugged off his son's hand. 'Whores are cheap, Harry. I don't need Jem Weston's castoffs, even if you do.'

***

Jem rode the short distance to Castle Ashby on the police cart. Three constables accompanied them, one to each prisoner, and they allowed no talking between them. Cal and Nat were taken away by two of the constables. He was held by the other constable in an office.

It was three o'clock in the morning, after he'd dozed fitfully in a chair, before anyone came to question him.

The man introduced himself. 'I'm Superintendent Young of Northamptonshire Constabulary. You are James Weston?'

'Yes. Has my wife been told I'm here? She'll worry if I'm not

126

home.'

'Both your wife and your mother have been informed, Mr Weston.' The superintendent sat opposite him. 'A statement has been made implicating you in the murder of Joseph Upton. Anything you say will be taken down and may be used in evidence against you. Do you understand?'

This couldn't be happening. He nodded.

'Where were you on Tuesday night with Brafield and Denton?'

He swallowed. What had the others said? Stick to the truth as far as he could? 'Cal and I met Nat on the road from Yardley to Olney, and we went to Newhay Copse. Cal went off, and after a while, we heard a gun fired. Me and Nat went towards the place the sound had come from and saw Cal. He said he'd been shot by Joe Upton. Nat went after Upton and collared him. Tried to throw his heels up but couldn't. They had a scuffle and Nat's gun went off.'

'Did Upton move after that?'

'He tried to get up.'

'And someone hit him. They broke the gun.'

'I can't say who struck Joe after he were shot or who broke the gun.'

'You don't know, or you can't say?' Superintendent Young paused and glanced at the constable to ensure he was taking notes. 'And what did you do afterwards, James?'

'After he were dead. Nat and me dragged him into the wood. Nat had him by the legs, and I had hold of one arm. When Nat fired, Cal and me were about three yards off. I didn't have a gun or a stick.' God would judge him, but it had been Nat who'd shot Joe, not Cal or him, and he had to be here for Ella and keep her safe. Harry mustn't get her back. 'I didn't hit Upton. That's all I know.'

The superintendent nodded and then read back the statement. 'Is that correct, James?'

127

His tongue scraped a dry mouth. 'Yes, that's what I said.'

***

The carrier's cart was packed with anxious people. Ella sat at the back with Jem's parents. Cal's parents and Nat's wife and family made up the remainder of the space. Today was the committal hearing, and they wanted to be there. Reverend Buchanan had travelled separately with Mrs Downs. Someone said Joe Upton's family were being driven to Northampton in his lordship's coach.

The cart stopped by a row of coaches and carts that stood outside the courtroom. They climbed down, and the carrier drove away promising to return for them that evening. Rows of stark windows stared across the road. Somewhere in there, Jem was held captive.

Inside they were met by a court official.

Cal's father spoke for them all. 'We're here for the committal case against our sons. Where must we go?'

She gripped Charlotte's hand. 'I'm James Weston's wife. This is his mother. Can we see him?'

'That won't be possible. You won't be allowed into the committal proceedings, I'm afraid.'

A man in a black coat hurried past, nodding to the official who obviously knew him.

'He's allowed in. Why can't we go in?'

'He's from the *Northampton Herald*, covers all the trials here. You'll be able to read about it tonight, Mrs Weston.'

She wasn't leaving. 'But we can stay? Someone can tell us what's happening?'

'You can wait here. I'll come back and let you know what charges are brought. It may be some time. There are witnesses to speak, evidence to be examined, and the inquest results to be read.'

'We'll wait.' She was near Jem even if she couldn't see him.

'Can someone tell James, Caleb, and Nathan we're here?'

The man nodded. 'This must be very hard for you all. I'll make sure they get to know you're here. They'll be bringing them up soon.'

She sank onto a bench and buried her head in her hands. She was so tired; she'd barely slept. A tap on her arm made her lower her hands.

Mrs Downs smiled down at her. 'I'm sure the reverend will speak for them, Ella. They're all regular churchgoers. It may help.'

Her heart rose. If Reverend Buchanan spoke for their characters, it must help, surely. These were boys, not murderers. There had to be some explanation for what happened to Joe Upton in Newhay Copse.

***

Jem stared into blackness. The cell was gloomy, his future gloomier. His prison was small with damp stone walls and a stone floor. He lay on a wooden platform at one end of the cell. Along the side wall was a bench fixed with iron brackets. A bucket stood on the floor in one corner, and a jug of water and a mug were the only other home comforts. The air stank of must, mould, and rot, infused with years of fear and bodily waste. A crust of bread had been shoved through the iron bars in the door, but other than that, he hadn't eaten since lunch the previous day. He hadn't seen Cal or Nat since the ride to Castle Ashby. Where were they? What had they told the police constables?

He'd stared at the oppressive weight of darkness for what seemed like a lifetime, reliving the events of the previous Tuesday in Newhay Copse and the questioning he'd undergone, yesterday and this morning. It must be Saturday now, unless he'd lost a day? Where was Ella? What would she be thinking? Would she hate him for what he'd done, or would she watch him hang and weep for him?

Dawn filtered through a barred window high up. A clank of iron on iron and the thud of boots on stone flags brought him to a sitting

129

position. He was pretty sure he was below ground: there had been steps leading into darkness, and he suspected he'd been brought to the Northampton County Gaol in George Row.

'Stand back, Weston.' The door to his cell swung open with a creak. 'Come on. You're up for your committal hearing. Make a move, man.'

He was cold, stiff, and sore. He shambled towards the door, eager for a breath of clean air and a high, clear sky. 'Has Ella asked after me?'

The gaoler fitted manacles with chains around his hands and shackled his legs. 'Who's Ella? Your sweetheart?'

'She's my wife.'

'Then I'm sorry for her. You got kids?'

'No.'

'That's a blessing.' His gaoler's eyes softened. 'She'll find someone else, lad. She'll get over you, in time.'

He shuffled forward and up the stone steps, the weight of the irons dragging at his feet. Sunlight through a window made him squint. The sky was high and blue. *'She'll find someone else.'* Yes, that's what she must do now. Their life together was over, whatever happened to him. *'She'll get over you, in time.'* He'd never get over her as long as he… His skin prickled: as long as he lived. The walls of the passage passed by in a blur as he pushed unwilling legs to his doom.

The courtroom was smaller than he'd imagined; rows of benches filled the floor, but there were raised seating areas, too, behind oak panelling. To the front of the room was a structure reminiscent of a pulpit but lower and wider.

His gaoler led him to one of the raised areas. 'Sit here. And keep quiet unless spoken to.'

Cal and Nat were led in and told to sit beside him. Their gaolers stood behind them, watching their every move. Cal and Nat looked

130

pale and drawn and stank: he must look and smell much the same. No-one spoke. People began filling the seats. Some, he recognised from the village and from the Castle Ashby estate. A small group of well-dressed men entered and took seats at the front. Reverend Buchanan was among them, and judging by the rector's demeanour, the men were important people. He caught a breath: the Marquis of Northampton had come to see justice done. If Cal, Nat, and he were found guilty, would the marquis put their families and Ella out of their homes?

His heart thudded: according to his gaoler, this was a committal hearing to determine what charges would be brought against them. A report of the inquest on Joe would be given and their statements read out. He hadn't told the entire truth but then had Cal and Nat? He didn't know exactly what had happened when Cal had been shot. He only had Cal's version of events. What had the others said? How much had they confessed?

He glanced across at his cousins; both were quiet, their eyes downcast. The trial itself could be weeks away: weeks of rotting in a cell away from God's good earth, away from Ella. It would be better if they hung him now and got it over with: better for everyone.

Chapter Twelve

Jem sat up straighter when his lordship's head keeper, Ernest Barritt, was sworn in to give evidence.

The magistrate looked up from the papers he'd been reading on the desk in front of him. 'Mr Barritt, you knew the deceased? How would you describe him?'

'Yes, sir. I did know him. Joe Upton was a watcher of game for the marquis. He was about thirty-five years old, well-built, and strong. He was vigilant in his duty.'

'Can you tell the court what happened on Wednesday afternoon of last week? That would be October the seventh.'

'Yes, sir. Joe's wife came to my house to ask if I'd seen Joe, as he hadn't been seen since four o'clock the previous day. I told her I hadn't. She said she thought we'd find him with his brains blown out.'

'Why did she think that?'

Mr Barritt looked across at the dock. 'Joe had a run-in with the prisoner, James Weston, some time back that put James in court. James vowed to blow Joe's brains out.'

'And what did you do then?'

'I went to acquaint his lordship with the fact that Joe was missing and that he'd been seen the previous evening in Howcut Lane according to someone Joe's wife had spoken to. Lord Northampton directed I take some men and search the woods next morning.'

'That would be Thursday last. And did you find Joe Upton?'

'Yes, sir.'

'Describe how you found him?'

'We went into Newhay Copse and down a riding. Some way in we found blood on the ground and, by it, part of the stock of a gun.'

'Did you recognise the gun?'

'Yes, sir. It belonged to Joe. I called to the rest of my party. As they came towards me, Mr Scriven called out, "Here he lies.". I went towards them and found a hat. It were about fourteen yards or so from the body, and it were Joe's hat.'

'And can you describe the scene? The disposition of the body?'

Ernest Barritt gripped the top of the oak panelling in front of him. 'He were lying on his back, his head all bloody. One hand was clenched over his breast, and the other arm was stretched out on the ground. Mr Scriven, Mr Dixon, and Mr Steward, the rest of the search party, will tell you the same.'

'Thank you, Mr Barritt. That will be all for now.'

Barritt stood down and glanced across at him as he went to sit at the back of the courtroom. Nothing Barritt had said connected him or the others with the crime, though the scene he'd described haunted his nightmares.

The magistrate turned over a sheet of paper. 'Mr Harry Cartwright?'

What did Harry know? Nothing. That wouldn't stop him lying to get him hung.

Harry put his hand on the Bible and muttered the oath.

'Please confirm your name and place of abode.'

'Harry Cartwright of Newhay Farm, just by Newhay Copse.'

'You were at home on the night in question?'

'I'd just finished tending calves in the barn and had walked down to a pasture close by the copse. I was about to cross the lane when I heard Joe's voice. Then gunshots and shouting. I went up

133

the riding and saw the accused running away. They had shotguns. I thought they were poaching and had been spotted by Joe. That's Joe Upton, the deceased, his lordship's keeper. I assumed Joe had fired warning shots. I didn't know he'd been shot.'

Harry had seen them? It had been dusk, surely hard to be sure who they were at a distance. Harry turned and stared at him, a slow smile spreading across his lips; the man was lying through his teeth, but he had no way of proving it. Bad feeling between him and Harry would count for nothing. Harry was dismissed and stepped down.

'Mr Scriven, please.'

Scriven swore his oath, his hand shaking on the Bible.

'Mr Scriven. You went to Newhay Copse and found Mr Barritt and a search party?'

'Yes, indeed, sir. Ernest, Mr Barritt, that is, called out. I went over. Joe were lying with his legs crossed and his head to one side. There was a large wound in the back of his head, and his jacket was pulled up as if the body had been dragged to where it lay. The gun lock was half-cocked.'

The magistrate held up a gun lock. 'This is the lock found by the deceased's head?'

'Yes, indeed, sir.'

'The lock belonged to Upton's gun?'

'Yes, sir.'

The magistrate frowned. 'And it being half-cocked suggests the intention of being ready to fire the gun?'

'I suppose so, sir. But many keepers carry a gun that way, because of magpies. They take pheasant eggs and chicks.'

'It's been confirmed that there are traces of blood on the lock. Mr Scriven, you returned to Newhay yesterday.'

'Indeed, sir. After the inquest, I met one of the gamekeepers who'd seen the prisoners near to Newhay on Tuesday night, the night Joe went missing. We found the gun barrel.'

'Which information also led to their apprehension.' The magistrate showed Mr Scriven the barrel of the gun. 'This is the gun barrel you found?'

'It is.' Scriven's voice was firm, as if his nerves had steadied. 'Can I add that James Weston was asked, in my presence, whether the statement he'd made last night was made voluntarily? It was read out to him, and having been told it would be used in evidence, he confirmed that it was correct.'

'Thank you, Mr Scriven.' The magistrate nodded his dismissal. 'Now, let's proceed to the findings of Mr John Pell, surgeon.'

Which of them had dealt the fatal blow? A dapper gentleman in a black coat came forward and took the oath.

The magistrate cleared his throat. 'Mr Pell, please describe your findings. You were present when the body of the deceased was found, were you not?'

Pell nodded. 'I was. There was a severe wound in the back of the skull and dreadful bruising to the head. On closer examination, yesterday afternoon, I found cuts to the eyelids, a wound on top of the head, and another under the right ear, which must have knocked him down and was sufficient to produce insensibility or even death. There was a gunshot wound in the neck, which must have been caused by a shot fired downwards, either when the deceased was on the ground or the assailant on an eminence, above the deceased.'

Upton hadn't been on the ground when Nat fired. But Nat was tall and the keeper off-balance because Cal had thrust the gun barrel aside. Joe had been on the ground when Cal and he had hit him.

The surgeon continued his report. 'The charge passed through the victim's collar bone and dispersed into the scapulary muscles.' The man paused and looked across at them. 'There was also a tremendous lacerated wound on the back of the head which had

135

caused an irregular fracture of the skull, penetrating to the brain.'

That had been him, hadn't it? The moments when rage had taken hold of him were confused and unreal. He desperately wanted it not to be true.

The magistrate's voice broke through his desperation. 'Can you say what might have produced such an injury, Mr Pell?'

'A violent blow with a weapon, like the gun produced, would cause such a wound. It was probably the fatal blow.'

Nat and Cal had shot at Upton, but it had been him as killed him. He lowered his eyes, wanting to hold his head in his hands and weep like a baby.

The magistrate turned to the prisoners. 'Caleb Brafield, do you have anything you'd like to ask Mr Pell?'

Caleb didn't raise his head. 'The person who shot Joe stood on the ground.'

The magistrate glanced at Pell. 'Not on an eminence?'

Cal shook his head. 'No, sir.'

The magistrate frowned. 'Are you saying the deceased was on the ground when Denton shot him?'

'No, sir. He was not.'

The magistrate turned back to the surgeon. 'Mr Pell, can you add anything else?'

'The deceased was dragged some way. There were burrs in his hair, Also, judging by the state of the blood on his clothes, I believe he *was* shot while on the ground.'

The magistrate nodded. 'Thank you, Mr Pell. Chief Constable Goddard, your testimony, please.'

The chief constable put his hand on the Bible and swore. He told how he'd gone to Ruddle's after receiving information that led him to suspect the prisoners and had arrested them. He cleared his throat and continued. 'I went to Denton's home and, in an upstairs

136

room, found a pair of cord breeches, wet in places with bloodstains recently washed out. There are marks of blood on them now. Then I visited Brafield's home and found a jacket in his bedroom with spots of blood on the left arm and shoulder. I found nothing incriminating at Weston's home.'

He hung onto those last words like a drowning man clutching at duckweed. The chief constable had found nothing incriminating. Not that it would help him much after what he'd admitted that morning.

'Can you say whose blood was on Denton's clothing?'

'The amount of blood on the breeches suggests it was Upton's, but acting on information received, after the search I went to Castle Ashby to examine Brafield. He had more than thirty gunshot wounds in his back and arms. I asked him how he got them, and he said Joe Upton had shot him, and he wished the shot had gone into his head, not his shoulder. I asked how it happened, and he said, "I saw him with his gun. I presented mine." Like this.' The chief constable posed as if firing a shotgun. 'Brafield told me they both fired together and he, Brafield, dropped. As he was getting to his feet, the other prisoners came up and collared Upton. Upton presented his gun to Denton, and Denton fired. Upton fell, and Denton and Weston dragged the body into the wood. Then they all left. Superintendent Young took down Brafield's statement, and the prisoner was cautioned.'

Cal hadn't mentioned him hitting Joe with the gun barrel.

'And your examination of Weston?'

The chief constable consulted a notebook. 'Weston had this to say. "Brafield and I met Denton on the road from Yardley to Olney, and we went together to Newhay Copse We split up but after a little time we heard a gun fired, and Nat Denton and I went towards the place, and saw Cal. Cal said Joe Upton had shot him. Nat and I went after Joe and collared him, and Nat tried to throw his heels up but couldn't. They had a scuffle and afterwards separated. Nat Denton then fired and Upton fell. He afterwards struggled and tried to get up. I can't say who struck Upton after he

137

was shot or who broke his gun. After he was dead, Nat and I dragged him into the wood. I had no gun or stick with me and did not strike Upton. This is all I know." That concludes Weston's statement'

'Mr Weston. Do you have any questions for this witness?'

Mr Weston: that was him. He flushed and lowered his eyes again: his hands shook as if with a palsy. Having lied would look bad for him. 'No. That's what I said.' He looked up as Isaac Keene, the police constable at Little Houghton, was sworn in. His testimony concerning Nat's statement was read out and confirmed much of what he and Cal had already said, adding that Cal had struck Upton on the head with the butt end of Joe's gun. He held his breath. Cal had hit Upton too. Nat had shot Joe before Joe could shoot him. Could they be sure who'd dealt the fatal blow?

The magistrates consulted briefly, and one spoke up. 'There is some doubt as to the admissibility of this evidence as the questions partake of the character of an examination. The court will adjourn while we consider this matter. Please clear the room.'

The prisoners were led from the room. They sat with their gaolers in a corridor: Cal had his head in his hands, Nat stared at the wall opposite, and he leaned back against the wall, weak and trembling.

A man approached. 'I thought you lads would like to know your families are outside the court, waiting for the results.'

'Is Ella here? Did she come?'

'She's here. They're all very distressed, obviously, but I promised I'd let you all know they'd come.'

'Thank you. Tell her…' What could he tell her? He was guilty, and he had no excuse except rage: at the Cartwrights, at Upton, at the game laws, and at himself. 'Tell her I love her.'

'I will, son.'

The court reconvened and the chief constable resumed his testimony. 'I asked Denton if Weston did anything. He said

Weston hit Upton over the head after he was down. I asked if he saw Weston strike him with any weapon. He said Weston struck him on the back of the head with the gun barrel. I asked him if the lock was then to the barrel, and he said he thought it was. I asked him how near he was when he fired. He said about three yards. I asked him whose guns they were. He said they were both Caleb Brafield's. I then asked if he knew where the guns were, and he told me one was in the wood, near the spot where the murder was committed, and the other was in a close in the tenancy of Mr Longfellow, near the Bedford turnpike road.'

The chief constable cleared his throat. 'I went this morning, in company with assistant keeper Steward, and I found the gun in the ditch, in Mr Longfellow's close. I couldn't find the one in the wood, but part of a broken ramrod was found later near the spot where the murder was committed. In the presence of the three prisoners, I asked Brafield whether this was the gun he used on the evening of the murder. He said it wasn't. I asked Denton whether that was the gun he fired at Upton, and he said it was. This morning, Weston admitted to striking Upton while he was on the ground.'

The magistrate looked over his glasses at his prisoners. 'Do any of you have any questions?'

None of them answered. He stared at his boots and shook his head.

The magistrate addressed Cal first. 'Caleb Brafield, you are charged that, on October the sixth of this year, you did wilfully murder Joesph Upton. Anything you say will be used in evidence.'

Cal straightened beside him, broader and a head taller than he was. 'I'd like to tell the story from the beginning to the end.'

***

Ella paced up and down the passage outside the courtroom. They'd been in there all day, and it was getting late. Nat's baby was grizzling quietly: hungry, no doubt. Sarah produced a twist of cloth containing a little bread soaked in milk for the child to suck on: it

139

seemed to soothe the infant.

She paced back, but the swift tread of boots made her turn in her tracks. 'What's happening?'

The man they'd spoken to earlier stopped beside her. 'They've been charged with wilful murder.'

'All of them?'

'All three. I'm sorry. They've been committed for trial at the next assizes, and the witnesses have been bound over to appear.'

'When will that be?'

'When the circuit judge is next here. I can't say when.'

'Can we see them?'

'Not now. They'll be held in gaol or in the lock-ups, in town. Maybe you'll be able to visit them.' He turned to walk away and paused mid-stride, looking back at her. 'You're Ella?'

'Yes.'

'James said to tell you he loved you.'

'How romantic.' The sarcastic voice made her stiffen and turn.

'Harry. What are you doing here?'

'I'm a witness. Newhay Copse is right by our farm, or had you forgotten that? You can forget your lover, Ella. He's going to hang for Joe Upton's murder. I'm going to make sure of it. And then I'll make you pay for humiliating me.'

Chapter Thirteen

'Ella.' Reverend Buchanan beckoned her into his study. He walked over to the window and stared out as if composing himself. 'What can I do for you?'

Ella sat on the chair he'd indicated and brushed aside tears. 'You were in the courtroom. What happened? Is what they say in the newspaper true?'

His shoulders tensed. 'The statements that were read out suggest they're guilty, but there'll have to be a trial, of course. Justice must be seen to be done.'

'Did you manage to speak up for them?'

He turned to face her. 'Speak up for them? They're trouble, Ella. They broke the threshing machine, got drunk, and then went poaching and killed a man. How many more misdemeanours do you need to convince yourself James Weston isn't worth defending? Thank the good Lord you're not legally married to the man. I would suggest you throw yourself on the mercy of your husband and see if he will take you back.''

'Better a life alone than a life being abused by my husband.'

'This was never your choice to make, Ella. Harry has rights. You took an oath before God to obey him when you married.'

'And God will judge me, not a village rector.'

'Mind your tongue, Ella.'

She examined her fingernails. 'I'm sorry. You've been good to me, Reverend. You don't deserve my anger. Does John Cartwright have a right to abuse me?'

'No. Harry failed to protect you, but I've spoken to them both. It won't happen again, Ella. You'll be quite safe there, or John

Cartwright will answer to God.'

He'd certainly never answer to the law. 'I love Jem. I should never have agreed to wed Harry. It's Harry and Joe Upton taunting Jem that began all this trouble. It's my fault.' Part of her was proud of Jem for standing up to Upton on her behalf – the man had spat at her and called her a whore. The rest of her wished to God he'd stayed home and left her insulted.

The reverend sighed. 'If it hadn't been this, it would have been something else. This isn't the first altercation James and Joe have had, and if Joe had lived, it wouldn't have been the last. You know James threatened him?'

'It said as much in the newspaper.'

'He'll have a defence lawyer, it being a murder charge. The court will appoint one.'

'Do you think they'll be found guilty? According to the paper, Joe Upton shot Cal first. Maybe they were defending themselves.'

'They'll have a chance to explain their actions before a judge and jury.'

'This lawyer... We don't have money.'

'Poor prisoners can secure legal representation by applying to defend *in forma pauperis*, if they can't find funding for legal assistance through a benefactor.'

'A benefactor?'

'Don't look at me for aid, Ella. My stipend isn't large, only eighty pounds, and much of that I give to the poor. What's more, I truly believe the sooner that man is out of your life, the better. You must face the facts, Ella. James Weston and his cousins are murderers, and they're going to hang.'

'They can't hang him. I love him.' She ran from the room, out of the rectory, and along the road. She ran along the track all the way to Cold Oak Copse. Briars and brambles tore at her coat and legs as she pushed through the narrow animal-tracks Jem had

142

showed her between the trees. She felt close to Jem here in the place he loved. She walked on, kicking at yellow and russet leaves. Reaching an ancient oak, she slumped to the ground and buried her head in her hands. 'Jem, please tell me you didn't do what they say you did.'

She'd read the report of the committal in Saturday's *Northampton Herald* over and over. Jem had admitted striking Upton while he was down. What kind of man did that? How well did she really know Jem?

Treetops laced the sky with a dense filigree of branches in an intricate random pattern only God could design. She pushed her hair from her eyes, and a white rump flashed on whirring wings above her. A feather floated to the ground. It was blue, a jay feather like the one Jem had found for her. She plucked it from the ground and stroked it softly against her cheek. Jem loved her, and whatever had happened in Newhay Copse, he was still the only man she would love, and nothing would change that.

She hurried back to the village. The carrier's cart was outside the blacksmith's shop, and the driver was helping unload a heavy box. He nodded to her. 'Mind yourself, miss. Don't want to drop this on your toes.'

'Are you going to Northampton?'

'You want to go?'

'Yes.'

'Soon as I've finished here. You can jump up, if you like.'

She hoisted herself onto the seat at the front of the cart. She had a little money left from the allowance Mr Josiah had given her before she'd married Harry, but she'd have to find work if she wanted to visit Jem often, always supposing they'd allow her to see him.

The carrier's horse was slow, and the drive to town took two hours. The driver directed her to the county gaol in George Row. 'I'll be leaving for Bedford in a couple of hours. You can find me

143

by St Sepulchre's if you want a ride back to Yardley Hastings.'

'I know it.' She walked to George Row, through the imposing door of the gaol, and accosted the first officer she saw. 'I'm here to see James Weston.'

'He a prisoner?'

'He's been accused of murder. I need to talk to him.'

'And you are?'

'Ella Weston. I'm his wife.'

The man looked doubtful. 'It's not a nice place for a young woman to visit.'

'Please. I have to talk to him.'

The man took a bunch of keys from a hook on the wall and attached them to his belt. 'This way.' He led her down stone steps. The air grew dank and foul as she descended. It was gloomy with only light from small, barred windows, high up, and it was cold.

The man's broad back blocked her view, but he led her past a number of stout oak doors with tiny grills in them. 'You keep people down here? I wouldn't keep a pig in a place like this.'

The man grunted. 'Pigs aren't criminals.' He stopped outside a cell door and banged on it with his fist. 'Weston, you got a visitor.'

'Jem?'

A pale, grimy face appeared at the grill; hands, with knuckles clenched white, gripped the bars. His eyes were wild like an animal at bay, his cheeks sunken and hollow. 'Ella? Is that you?'

The warder grunted again. 'Five minutes.'

Her hands closed over Jem's. She couldn't take her eyes from his. 'Aren't you going to let me in?'

The gaoler snorted. 'You don't want to go in there, missus. Honest to God, you don't. Five minutes. Say what you have to say.' The man stomped back up the steps.

144

'Ella…'

'Jem…' Now she was here, she didn't know what to say. 'Jem, I love you. I can't believe this is happening. Tell me it isn't true.'

'I won't lie to you, Ella. Not to you. Cal, Nat, and me – we all had a go at Upton, but I reckon it were me as done for him. I were that mad at him. He'd shot Cal, and he'd called you a whore, spat at you in church. It was like something took a hold of me, seeing him on the ground after Nat shot him. Like I was at the threshing with a flail in my hand. I picked up the barrel of his gun, and my arm just came down. If I could go back and change it, I would.' Tears made pale tracks down Jem's cheeks.

She reached through the bars and thumbed away a tear. 'Jem, I know you've done wrong, done a terrible thing, but you were provoked. Sorely provoked. Surely, the judge will see that.'

'The charge is murder, Ella. I'm going to hang. Loving you is the best thing as ever happened to me, but you have to let me go. You have to get on with your life. Promise me?'

She reached beneath her coat, beneath the neckline of her woollen dress. 'I found this in Cold Oak Copse.' She held out the jay feather. 'It's not as blue as the one you gave me, though.'

He took it and stared at it. 'It's beautiful, and I'll treasure it always, but it makes no odds. You have to forget me.'

'Never. I'll love you till the day I die, Jem Weston. I'm going to do everything I can to get you out of here.'

'There's nothing anyone can do, Ella. Face it, please, sweetheart.'

'No.' She reached for him with both hands and drew his face towards the bars. Her face pressed against cold iron as her lips found his, and his hands tangled her hair.

'Time's up, Mrs Weston.'

A hand on her shoulder. Jem's lips, soft, warm, urgent. A blue jay feather. Chilling cold and the stench of filth and corruption.

'Don't give up, Jem. Know that I'll be fighting for you. I love you.'

His hand reached through the bars to touch her face. 'I love you, too, Ella, but I'm a dead man walking. That's why you have to forget me.'

'It isn't just you I'm fighting for, Jem. I never knew my father. I want our child to know you.'

'Our child?'

'I think I'm pregnant, Jem. A midsummer baby. You're going to be a father.'

***

Ella jumped down from the carrier's cart at the crossroads, her mind made up. 'Can you wait for half an hour?'

'Make it a quarter. I have to be back in Bedford before dark.'

'Please don't leave without me.'

Reverend Buchanan had mentioned free lawyers, appointed by the court, but how well would such a man defend Jem and the others?

She ran to the cottage she still shared with Jem's parents and threw open the door. 'Charlotte. I'm going to Bath. The carrier's waiting for me.'

'You're leaving?' His mother frowned. 'I know Jem's done wrong, but it'll destroy him, Ella.'

'I'm going to get him the best lawyer in the country.'

'We can't afford no lawyer.'

'We can afford this one. My mother's employer is a lawyer. He has offices in Bath and London. He'll help Jem. He has to, if I have to get down on my knees and beg.'

Her feet flew up the oak stairs. She dragged out one of the bags Mr Josiah had given her and threw in spare clothes. If she was lucky, there'd be a stagecoach or mail coach leaving Bedford for

Aylesbury or Oxford at dawn, and from there she could catch a coach to Bath. She could be there in two days, three at most, and if she couldn't afford the fare, she'd walk all the damned way. Mr Josiah had to help them: he just had to. She'd throw herself on his mercy. She'd do anything he wanted. Anything at all.

She crossed the living room towards the front door.

Charlotte pushed a packet into her hand as 'Something for the journey. God bless you, child, and Godspeed.'

She gave Charlotte a brief hug and ran out, clutching her bag. The carrier was where she'd left him: she climbed up beside him. 'Thank you for waiting.'

He smiled. 'Anything for the course of true love, Mrs Weston. It's a bad do, but it's not my place to judge. I hear people talk, and your young man and his friends have a fair amount of sympathy among ordinary folk. Life's hard enough without his lordship's gamekeepers and these damnable game laws.'

She hadn't expected a common sympathy, but she'd seen first-hand the struggle of Jem's parents to feed themselves and put by enough money each week to pay the next quarter's rent. She doubted they were unusual in that; some of the villagers were desperately poor. Was it any wonder there was ill-feeling between those hunting the Chase for game to eat, and the keepers who protected it for those who hunted for sport? Her life as her mother's helper in Bath had been safe and comfortable in comparison to the villagers of Yardley Hastings.

She spent the night in an inn in Bedford and was up early, after a sleepless night, to catch the coach. The coach driver took pity on her and let her spend the next night in the coach at Oxford so she could afford the fare to Bath the following morning. She woke cold, stiff, tired, and hungry to the sound of hooves on cobbles. It was barely light. Bleary-eyed, she peered through the coach window. A pair of chestnuts and a pair of greys were led out ready to be harnessed. Grooms holding lamps were checking them over, running their hands down slender legs and over muscled shoulders where the collars would fit. Harnesses were brought from the harness room and hung on hooks on a wall. There was no sign of the driver yet, so she stumbled to the privy and relieved herself. A splash of cold water from the pump in the yard freshened her face and wetted her throat, and a crust of bread, saved from Charlotte's generous provisions, broke her fast.

She walked around the yard, conscious that she would be sitting all day, her legs and back still cramped from the day and night before. Yesterday, she'd been an insider, travelling in relative comfort and warmth on thinly upholstered seats. Today, she could only afford to be an outsider, perched on a wooden bench at the rear of the carriage, and open to the weather. She shrugged her coat tighter around her and searched the dawn sky for signs of rain.

Soft snorts of breath, the shake of a head, and the jangle of metal made her look round. The team was harnessed and stood patiently waiting. The door of the coaching inn opened, an oblong of light and warmth against the dawn chill: figures, huddled into cloaks, left the warmth and crossed the yard towards the coach.

'Did you sleep, Mrs Weston?'

She swung on her heel. 'A little, thank you.'

The driver smiled. 'We'll be off in ten minutes. Have you had breakfast?'

'Yes, thank you.'

He walked around the coach, tugging at each wheel in turn. Satisfied, he checked the horses' harnesses and adjusted the odd strap. He patted the neck of one of the grey lead-horses. 'Everyone aboard, please. We leave in five minutes.'

Chapter Fourteen

Bath hadn't changed: the imposing front door to Mr Josiah's home hadn't changed either, though why she'd thought it might have done, she wasn't sure. Maybe it was she who saw things differently. She'd left here not three months ago, a protected and loved member of the Barton household, surrounded by polite society with all its niceties: an innocent virgin unversed in the ways of the world. She returned a married woman who'd seen poverty and privilege: a despoiled, raped, and adulterous pregnant harlot, her heart given to a murderer and consumed by a hunger her old life couldn't satisfy. Would the reverend have acquainted Mr Josiah with her failed marriage and Jem's arrest? What kind of welcome would she receive?

She tugged the bell pull and waited.

Annie answered the door. 'Miss Ella... I mean, Mrs Cartwright. I'm sure Mrs Maundrell isn't expecting you.'

'I didn't have time to write. Is Mr Josiah at home?'

'Is that Ella?' Her mother's voice from the drawing room. 'Come on in, dear.' Her mother looked up from her mending, threw down the garment, and jumped to her feet. 'Ella... why didn't you write you were coming?' She hugged her and then held her at arm's length. 'What's wrong... why are you here?'

'You haven't had a letter from Reverend Buchanan?'

'Should I have?'

'Maybe he thought better of writing. I've left Harry, again. For good this time.'

'But...' Her mother's face went through confusion and disbelief to despair.' 'Oh, Ella. He was a good catch. I thought you'd sorted your differences.'

'I – He…' Rage gave way to grief, and her mother held her as she sobbed.

'Oh hush, now. It's nothing that can't be sorted, I'm sure.'

'Nothing can sort this. Mother, I've been so stupid. I should never have married Harry. He treated me worse than a breeding sow. His father…' She took a deep breath, determined her mother should hear it all. 'John Cartwright assumed what belonged to his son belonged to him, too.'

Her mother's brow furrowed, and then her eyes opened wide. 'He didn't? He made you? He took you against your will?'

'I left the same day. That's why I came here before Mr Josiah took me back.' She wiped away tears she'd been determined not to cry. 'I can't go back again, and anyway Harry…'

'Oh, love, any man would be honoured to have you. What John Cartwright did isn't your fault. Harry will see that.'

'I don't love Harry. I love Jem. James Weston. We married over the brush, after I left Harry. Mother, I'm pregnant.'

Her mother sat heavily on a chair. 'Oh, Ella. Whose child is it?'

'It's Jem's.'

'And this Jem will look after you? He's willing to raise your child.'

'He's in prison accused of murder.' She sank into a chair beside her mother and buried her head in her hands. 'He's going to hang.'

'Oh, dear God.' The colour had drained from her mother's face. 'Ella, whatever have you got yourself into? What are you going to do?' She shook her head as if unable to take it in. 'If you've come home – Mr Josiah sent you away for a reason. That reason hasn't changed.'

'But maybe he'll realise he was wrong to send me to Yardley. Maybe he should have let me marry Ralph. Ralph's a good man, a good friend. He loves me, and I'd never have known better.'

'It would never be allowed.'

'And it wasn't me who wanted it. I don't love Ralph in that way. I never have. He's like a brother to me. I need Mr Josiah's help. Jem needs his help. That's why I'm here, not for Ralph. I want no-one but Jem, not now, not ever.'

'What can Mr Josiah do?'

'I want him to defend Jem and his cousins, Caleb and Nathan, when their trial comes to court. I want him to come to Northampton and save the man I love from the gallows. I think that's the least he can do, since he sent me there without any good reason that I can see.'

Her mother sighed. 'I'll speak to him. Wait here. I'll get Annie to make up your bed.'

Discordant voices rose and fell from Mr Josiah's study, but whatever they were saying was too quiet for her to hear. Mr Barton valued his reputation above all else: would he see her or throw her out in the street for bringing disrepute upon him? Her mother returned, her mouth in a taut line. 'He's busy so just say your piece and don't keep him long.'

She nodded, only too conscious that her mother's livelihood and home were in Mr Barton's gift. She pushed open the door to his office and studied her former employer with fresh eyes. He was very like Ralph. Dark hair, greying now at the temples, swept back from a broad brow. His eyes were deep-set, and he was tall and, as always, immaculately dressed. He looked up from a pile of papers and set his quill pen in its holder. Her hand went to her heart where the blue jay feather Jem had given her nestled between her breasts. He stared at her for a long moment, his grey eyes penetrating and questioning.

'It's good to see you, Ella. I'm sorry the circumstances aren't better. Your mother has acquainted me of your difficulty.'

She slumped into a chair at the side of his desk. 'Mr Josiah, I need your help. I came all the way from Yardley to beg for it. Jem and the boys – they're not bad, just young and hungry.'

151

He frowned. 'I'm not aware of the full circumstances of the crime.'

She laid a copy of the *Northampton Herald* in front of him. 'That's the report of the committal hearing. Jem and his cousins made the mistake of drinking when the threshing machine broke, and they were laid off. They probably weren't thinking too straight when they decided to go poaching. Their families are so poor, Josiah, and the marquis has so much. What's a brace of pheasants to him? It's eating or not eating to these people, yet the keepers are paid to stop them, shoot them even.'

'I am well aware of the law regarding game, young lady.'

'But are you aware of what it's like to be hungry?'

'Hunger is no excuse for murder.'

'And do you know what it's like to be young and drunk and do something you regret? I know Jem did wrong, but *murder*? He didn't go out intending to kill someone. It's not fair!'

He raised his eyebrows and then shook his head. 'I'll read the report. Run along now. Your mother will have extra cooking to do with you here.'

'I can stay?'

'For tonight. It's late, and you must be tired after the journey.' He reached across his desk and covered her hand with his broad, smooth one. 'I too was young and foolish, once. I never regretted it, but that doesn't mean I've eschewed responsibility, as you and Jem will have to face the consequences of your actions.' He withdrew his hand. 'Try not to worry, Ella. I'll see what can be done. We'll talk about it in the morning.'

Smooth sheets caressed her skin as she sank into the goose-feather mattress. Without Jem by her side, it might as well have been sackcloth on stone. How was he? Could he stay sane cooped up away from the woods he loved, for God knew how long? If she could take him Mr Josiah's promise of help, it would give him hope. She'd done what she could, and tomorrow was another day.

She closed her eyes and let sleep take her, to dream of the gibbet and Jem's stiff corpse swinging by the neck in a silent breeze.

***

Mr Barton called Ella into his study before breakfast. 'Sit down, Ella.' He tapped the newspaper. 'The evidence presented so far is pretty damning. They've admitted killing Joseph Upton. All of them had a part to play in the poor man's death.' He steepled his fingers, reminding her of the reverend, and looked over them at her. 'I'm sorry to say it looks as though it may have been James who dealt the fatal blow.'

'He's not a murderer, Mr Josiah.'

'I dare say not. And it seems there was some provocation and hot-headedness, on both sides. I don't know if I can sway a judge and jury, but I will look into the case further, speak to the boys myself, and see if a lesser crime might be pled.'

'What lesser crime?'

'Manslaughter.'

'But they'd still be convicted.'

'Manslaughter doesn't carry a death sentence. It's probably the best we can hope for.'

'What sort of sentence would they get?'

'Life.'

'But he'll… He can't spend the rest of his life locked up. It would kill him.'

Mr Josiah shrugged. 'Take it or leave it, Ella.'

'We'll take it. I can't lose him, not now. I love him, and this child needs a father even if we do have to visit him in gaol.'

'I doubt…' Mr Barton seemed to think better of what he was going to say. 'Where are you living?'

'With Jem's parents.'

He nodded. 'I can see why you wouldn't want to be at Newhay, in the circumstances. I'll do my very best for you both. Now, enjoy the day with your mother. I've given her the day off.' He pushed some coins into her hand. 'Go shopping in town. We leave tomorrow at dawn for Northampton. I'm sure Charles Buchanan can be depended upon to provide lodgings.'

***

The journey back to Yardley Hastings was more comfortable than the journey to Bath had been, travelling as insiders on padded seats and with comfortable beds in the coaching inns en route. The carriage Mr Josiah had hired in Bedford stopped outside the rectory, and Ella's former employer helped her climb down.

Mr Josiah pushed open the gate and strode to the front door. He rang the bell and stood back to take in the generous frontage of the building. The door opened and Mrs Downs stared out, lost for words judging by her silence.

'Please tell the reverend that Mr Josiah Barton is here to see him, with Miss – I mean Mrs Ella Weston. No, I mean Cartwright.'

'Yes, sir. You'd better come in, I'm sure. This way, Mr Barton. Ella.' Mrs Downs showed them into the sitting room.

'Thank you, Mrs Downs.' She'd cleaned and dusted this room: she'd never expected to be sitting in it. She squirmed uncomfortably on the sofa.

'Josiah, good to see you again.' Reverend Buchanan took his friend's hand and pumped it like he was drawing water.

'Charles, my dear friend. You're looking well.'

The reverend turned to her, more sober-faced. 'Ella?'

Mr Josiah inclined his head. 'Ella came to me to ask for my help. She put her case well. I couldn't refuse her.'

The rector shook his head. 'You indulge this girl too much, Josiah. No good has come of it.'

She clenched her fingers. 'This isn't about me. This is about

154

three young men of your parish, Reverend. Don't they deserve a chance of life?'

'Didn't Joseph Upton?'

She took a deep breath. 'How will three more deaths undo what's been done?'

'It's called justice, Ella.'

Mr Josiah coughed. 'Justice is only done when all the facts of the case have been heard and carefully weighed, when a jury has deliberated and come to a conclusion, and when a judge has decided just punishment. The days of an eye for an eye and a tooth for a tooth are gone, Charles.'

'More's the pity. This whole affair could be over and forgotten by now if swift justice had been administered. As it is, this silly young girl lives in some false and tortured hope of redemption, which only God can grant.'

She held onto a shred of hope. 'I won't give up on him. Jem is all I have.'

Mr Josiah sucked his top lip. 'That isn't quite true, Ella. Charles, she's expecting James Weston's child.'

Reverend Buchanan threw up his hands. 'I wash my hands of you, Ella. Really, I do. I warned you where your seductive behaviour would get you. You've made your bed, and now you must lie in it.'

'Charles, that's a bit harsh. As this young lady reminded me, youth can be a little hot-blooded. You can't blame youth for being young.'

'If the girl had had a father to teach her right from wrong, birch her occasionally, I dare say we wouldn't be having this conversation. The wickedness of the mother bears fruit in the child. Mark my words, Josiah, the devil looks out of her eyes.'

Mr Josiah put a hand on her shoulder before she leapt to her mother's defence. 'Mrs Maundrell has behaved impeccably during her employment and has been all but a mother to Ralph. With the greatest respect, Charles, you don't know the woman. I'll not have her spoken about this way.'

The reverend bowed his head. 'I'm sorry, Josiah. I meant no offence. It's this business with the Cartwrights and Joseph Upton. Ella here stirred quite a wasps' nest, leaving Harry for James, and then the murder in Newhay. It's split the village down the middle. There's bad feeling on both sides, anger at the game laws, and I'm at my wits' end to broker any kind of peaceful solution.' He moved to a sideboard upon which stood a Tantalus and glasses. 'You'll have a drink with me, my friend? Ella, go and prepare a room for Mr Barton, and tell Mrs Downs there'll be two extra for supper.'

***

Jem squinted as daylight flooded down the steps. A visitor? What kind of visitor demanded the comfort of a room away from the stench of the cells? He'd never put much store by washing, until he'd met Ella, but even he reeled at his own body odour. His legs were used now to the weight of chains, and he walked up the steps more easily. He entered the small room with a sense of confusion, for the man seated at a small table was smartly dressed and obviously wealthy.

The man waved him to a seat. 'James Weston?'

'That's me.'

The man brought a small box from his pocket, opened the lid, and held it briefly beneath his nose. 'I'm Josiah Barton, a lawyer from Bath.'

'Ella's Mr Barton?'

'The same. She arrived on my doorstep last week and begged me to help you.'

'And you came. I'm very grateful to you, sir. You find me in a poor state.'

'Ella loves you very much. I'm here to see if you're worthy of that affection. Whether I leave you here to face the gallows, and

156

good riddance, or whether you are worth trying to save. I care greatly for Ella. Tell me why I should help you, James.'

'To tell you the truth, sir, I've pondered that a good deal.' He sighed. 'You should leave me here to rot, and good riddance, to use your own words. I ain't worth shit, and Ella would be better off without me.'

Josiah Barton smiled. 'It seems you're honest, at least.'

A small laugh escaped his lips. 'And you wonder why an honest man is locked up as a criminal?'

'What was going through your mind, James, when you attacked Joseph Upton? What were you feeling?'

'Nothing that makes much sense now. I was angry. I love Ella, I have since I first met her, but I knew she was too good for me. Harry offered his hand, and I stood aside because I thought he could give her things a woman like her ought to have. Her own household to run, comfort, but...'

'But? What changed?'

'Harry didn't treat her right. He hurt her. If I'd spoken up to Ella, she wouldn't have married him. Her getting hurt was my fault.'

Mr Barton leaned back in his chair. 'What was Joe Upton's involvement? I know he was a gamekeeper, and you'd had run-ins with him before, I read the newspaper report, but why such an apparently frenzied attack?'

'He was a friend of Harry's. Joe said awful things about Ella. Called her a whore, spat at her in church. He'd been goading me for months, one way or another, even got me arrested and convicted a couple of years back, saying I'd had a pheasant what his lordship's got any number of. I was fined ten pounds. That's half a year's wages. He took a pot shot at me, not three months since, but I got away with a brace. Then, dammit, if he ain't shot Cal in the shoulder.'

'This is Caleb Brafield?'

'Yes. And then there Upton was, on the ground at my feet. He'd pointed his gun at Nat, and Nat had shot him afore Joe could discharge a barrel. Cal had hit him with the gunstock and broke it. It all happened so quick. Something just snapped inside me. I picked up the barrel of the shotgun and brought it down like a flail on a stook of corn. I just couldn't keep all that anger in any longer.'

'So, Joseph Upton shot Caleb, first. Then Nathan Denton shot Joseph, and then Caleb and you hit him. Is that the correct order of events?'

'It is, sir.'

'And you'd all been drinking?'

He nodded. 'And Joe Upton must have got wind of us talking about having a spree up the Chase, after rabbits, and set off to catch us a-purpose.'

'Rabbits aren't game.'

'No, sir. They ain't.'

Grey eyes bored into his. 'You lied in your first statement to the police. You maintained you hadn't hit Upton.'

'And all I've done is landed myself here, in more trouble, where I'm no use to no-one.' He stared at his hands. 'And I'm ashamed, sir. I was thinking of Ella, how I need to be here to protect her from the likes of Harry and John Cartwright. Word gets around, even here. John Cartwright raped her, sir. That's why she ran away.' His knuckles clenched white. 'I'd die to protect Ella.'

'And you very well may. What John Cartwright may have done is hearsay, James, unless Ella accuses him in a court of law. And, if you didn't know of it when you killed Upton, I can't use it in your defence. Still, I may be able to make a case for your state of mind and the fact that Upton began the affray that led to his death.'

'You're prepared to defend me, sir?'

'I can see why Ella loves you. You have passion, and you're not

158

the first young man to do reckless and stupid things.' Mr Barton got to his feet. 'I'll defend you and the others. I'll speak to both of them, get their side of the story, but I suspect the best we'll achieve is a verdict of guilty of manslaughter. You won't hang, if we can convince the judge, but you know what the punishment is likely to be?'

He hung his head. 'I do, sir.'

'Does Ella?'

'I don't know, I'm sure, sir.'

'Then I shall have the unhappy duty of informing her. Goodbye, James.'

'Must she know yet?'

'She should be prepared, but maybe it can wait a while longer. The situation is bad enough without making it worse.'

'Tell Ella… tell her I keep her feather next to my heart. Tell her I'll always love her, but she must go where life takes her and not be bound to me or her memory of me. She told you she's pregnant?'

The man nodded. 'She did. It's a complication she could have done without, but… Who knows how life will play out? Some good may yet come of it. Don't give up hope, James. Ella loves you, too. And the love of a good woman is worth more than gold.' He nodded again as if taking in his own words. 'Yes, indeed it is. More than gold.' Mr Barton placed a careful hand on the shoulder of his client's filthy jacket. 'You have the courage of your convictions and that makes you a better man than I am, James.'

'Mr Josiah, can I ask something of you, sir?'

'You may, James.'

'You won't let Harry get her back, will you? You'll see she's safe.'

'Legally, she's still Harry's wife. My hands are tied.' Mr Barton stood to leave. 'I'll speak to Harry, though. I'll do what I can for

159

her, within the law, I promise.'

***

Harry opened the farmhouse door to find a well-dressed man in his fifties on the doorstep. He was familiar, but from where he couldn't immediately bring to mind.

The man held out a calling card. 'Josiah Barton. Your mother-in-law's employer.'

'Of course. I'm sorry. You gave Ella away at our wedding, and you brought her home.' He held out his hand in greeting, but Mr Barton ignored it.

'I'm a solicitor. I have offices in Bath and London, and I'm defending James Weston, Caleb Brafield, and Nathan Denton against a charge of wilful murder, at the request of your wife.'

Where in God's name had Ella got the money to hire a solicitor from Bath?

He must have looked as astonished as he felt for Josiah Barton continued, stern faced. 'I'm also Ella's benefactor. She's like a daughter to me, and with James locked away, I need to know she'll be treated fairly and with kindness.' Mr Barton frowned. 'She's put me in a difficult position, but I feel responsible. I sent her here to avoid a liaison with my only son. I feel duty-bound to see she's happy.'

'I heard Ella had gone to Bath. I didn't know why. She's back?' He stepped into the yard and closed the door behind him. 'I want her home. She's my wife, and I can treat her how I want.'

'I'm aware of that, Mr Cartwright, but I shall take it as a personal favour if I hear from her that she's being treated with respect. Forcing a woman who is not your wife to have intercourse is rape, a serious charge, and, should Ella decide to bring charges against your father, I shall see to it the full weight of the law crushes him and this entire family. Do I make myself clear, Mr Cartwright?'

The daft mare couldn't refuse to come home, now Jem had been

160

committed, unless this man stood in her way. His fists clenched of their own accord. Damn his father for raping Ella. 'I shall make sure my father knows not to touch her. Where is she? I'll fetch her home this afternoon.'

'She's staying with me, at the rectory. I believe she wishes to reside with the Westons, at least while the trial's pending. Reverend Buchanan will watch over her when I return to Bath. If he hears you are ill-treating Ella, he will inform me. If she wants to live with Jem's parents, I suggest you let her for the moment.' He sighed. 'Jem isn't likely to be found innocent. He won't always stand between you and Ella. She'll get over this infatuation, I'm sure, and realise where her duty lies.'

'I'm sure you're right, Mr Barton.' He smiled, certain of the fact. Patience wasn't his strong point, but he'd have to bide his time or deal with the reverend and Mr Barton. 'I'm a reasonable man, but I've missed her, and I can't wait to have her back.'

Chapter Fifteen

The dark days of winter had given way to the blustery winds of early March. Primroses turned their hopeful faces towards the sun in sheltered nooks and crannies in Cold Oak Copse. Half-built nests balanced precariously in bushes and skeletal treetops, as birds, large and small, flitted through the branches with beaks full of hay, wool, and twigs. Rooks, building a treetop city above her, cawed and Ella looked skywards.

What Jem wouldn't give to be free and here with her. She visited him whenever she could and kept his memory of the woods alive by describing her walks to him. His eyes lit when she talked about the people and places he loved. Last time she'd seen him, she'd smuggled in meat and cheese, and he'd managed to reach a thin arm through his bars to place a hand upon her belly and feel their child move. She'd thumbed away his tears from gaunt cheeks. They should have been tears of joy, not heartbreak.

She placed her hand where Jem's had been, and the baby moved again. 'Your father loves you, little one.' Would he live to see their child born? Could Mr Josiah sway a judge and jury? She turned for home and breakfast. Today, at midday, the trial would begin at Northampton Assizes, and carriers' carts and hay wagons had been commandeered for the day. The whole village was intent on travelling to court and seeing justice done though views on what constituted a just verdict were varied. In an earlier, less-enlightened time, Jem and his cousins would have been strung up on a gallows tree on the turnpike road months ago.

After breakfast, she and Jem's parents boarded a farm cart along with Cal's and Nat's families. It spoke volumes that outside the Upton's cottage stood a carriage sent by the marquis and that the reverend, obviously remaining neutral in the matter, was taking Mrs Downs and Doctor Hayes in his pony trap.

Rows of carts and carriages crammed the street outside the court, and purveyors of cold meats and pies hawked their wares. A throng of people milled about outside the entrance to the courtroom. Judging by the picnic baskets clutched to bosoms, it seemed some villagers were making a day out of it. Jem's mother had packed bread, cheese, and cold tea, but she didn't imagine any of them would feel much like eating.

'Lucky heather, dearie?' A small, sun-browned and wizened woman held out sprigs of dried heather. 'Cross my palm with silver.'

'Silver? I don't have silver.' She fumbled in her purse for coppers. Luck, she needed, but a gypsy curse was the last thing she wanted. 'Here, will that do?'

The old woman grinned toothlessly and selected a sprig. 'You'll marry and have children.'

'I am married, and I'm six months pregnant.' She bit her lip at the admission. She'd avoided walking abroad in recent months, and when she'd been forced to walk in the village, had hidden her pregnancy beneath a voluminous winter cloak.

The woman's smile faded. 'That's as may be, but what I say is true. The rest of your future is dark, too dark to see.' The woman pressed the coppers back into her hand, along with the heather. 'I wish you luck, dearie. You're going to need it.'

Shaken, the woman's sprig of lucky heather grasped tightly, she followed Charlotte into the courthouse. She and Jem needed luck; with Jem's wage gone, the Westons would be hard-pressed to pay the rent due on Lady's Day. They were ushered into a room made gloomy by oak panelling and small windows. She squeezed onto a bench, the room already full to bursting, with more people cramming through the door and standing in the aisles between seats. The air was taut with expectation and humming with a buzz of conversation. Already the room felt airless.

Mr Josiah caught her eye and hurried towards her. 'Ella, Mr and Mrs Weston. I'll do my best for James. I think I can bring a good

163

case, but you should be prepared. Even if the boys get off with manslaughter, they're still likely to get life.'

'At least they'll be alive.' Her hand went to her stomach again. 'At least I'll be able to visit Jem, and he'll get to know his child.'

'That may not be possible.'

'What do you mean? Why not?'

A staff rapped on the boards 'Pray silence for the Lord Abinger. Please be upstanding.' The rapping came again, louder. 'Silence!'

Mr Barton hurried away and took his place. The hum subsided and heads turned towards the front of the room. One by one, villagers got to their feet and fell silent. Jem's father whispered to her. 'That's the clerk of the court. The man in the red robes is the judge.'

The stout man in scarlet robes, who was wearing a black scarf and a full-bottomed grey wig, sat behind a raised panelled desk. The clerk rapped his staff again. 'This court is now in session. There will be silence in court. Pray be seated.'

Feet shuffled, room was made on benches. Her eyes were on Jem, who followed Cal and Nat into the court, head bowed as he mounted a raised platform. They all wore chains on their legs and had their hands manacled. Tears pricked her eyes. He looked subdued, lost, and weakened by captivity.

Mr Josiah glanced around the court, met her eyes, and smiled. He turned to Lord Abinger. 'If it pleases your lordship, the prisoners would like to challenge three of the jurors.'

'On what grounds.'

'Mr Freeman is an employee of Lord Northampton, for whom the deceased worked. Mr Cartwright is the legal father-in-law of Ella Cartwright, who is the defendant, Weston's, mistress. Mr Cartwright was also a friend of the deceased. The third juror, Mr Rutherford, is a gamekeeper by trade.'

'Accepted. Will Messrs Freeman, Cartwright, and Rutherford

stand down? Will the clerk please swear in three new jurors?'

She let out a breath, thankful she'd persuaded Mr Barton to help, even if he had called her Jem's mistress. John Cartwright, for one, would have found Jem guilty without hearing the evidence, and his opinion was respected locally among those of his class.

The new jurors accepted, the clerk stood. 'Sergeant Adams will open the case for the prosecution.'

The prosecutor bowed briefly, glanced from the judge to the jury, and addressed the court. 'I shall confine myself to a simple statement of the facts. The duties of myself and Mr Barton, the council for the prisoners, are different. He is bound to do all in his power to avert impending danger from the prisoners. I must lay out a clear and unexaggerated statement of the circumstances. The jury must ignore anything the defence says unless it is borne out by evidence.'

Her heart sank again. She'd hoped Mr Josiah could sway them with a fine speech. The facts, as she understood them, would bring the death sentence.

Sergeant Adams addressed the jurors directly. 'You and Lord Abinger must decide whether the circumstances of the case, and the hot blood in which it originated, might reduce the offence to the lesser crime of manslaughter. I would be very happy if that were the case.' Sergeant Adams sat down.

Jem's mother gripped her hand and she squeezed back, reassuringly. Her heart thudded in her ears. If the prosecution weren't pushing for a verdict of murder and the death sentence, maybe there was a chance.

'Call Mr Herbert Longfellow.'

She leaned forward in her seat as the first witness, an elderly man in a patched jacket, was sworn in and began his evidence. 'On October the sixth, at around two thirty, I was at a public house in Yardley Hastings, where the prisoners were drinking. Weston asked me several times to lend him a gun. I said I wouldn't. Then he pressed me to sell him one. He was very anxious to get one and

165

said he must have one that night as they were going on a spree.'

Jem hadn't told her this, but he'd told her he was going to get a rabbit or two, or a pheasant, so why wouldn't he want a gun?

The next to be called was only a boy. He looked scared, and her heart went out to him. 'I were playing with a friend on Tuesday the sixth of October, near Nat Denton's house. I saw Denton getting over some poles, and a gun barrel fell out of his pocket. I were about ten yards from him. He caught the barrel afore it hit the ground and put it in his pocket. I followed him a ways, and he went up to the close and met Jem Weston and Cal Brafield.'

Lord Abinger nodded. 'Thank you. You may stand down.'

The clerk looked up from his papers. 'George Whitehouse, my lord. A labourer at Yardley.'

Jem's eyes met hers. She couldn't read his expression. Fear, guilt, remorse?

George cleared his throat. 'I met the prisoners in Lett's Close, on the Tuesday evening, about a mile from Newhay Copse, in which direction they were heading. I told Cal – Caleb Brafield – if he were going that way, he should look out for himself, as the keepers were gone that way. He said "Bugger their eyes, they'd better take care of themselves." Then he called to the other prisoners. "Why the hell don't you come on? We shan't get taters dug for Sunday's dinner." This was a little after six o'clock, and about half past, I heard two gunshots close together. Somebody screamed, and while the screaming and shouting was going on, I heard another shot, and the screaming stopped. This gunshot had a very dull sound compared to the others. That's all I can say.'

Charlotte Weston's grip on her hand tightened. This put the cousins at the scene of the crime, but George hadn't seen what happened. And she was clutching at a blade of grass while drowning in the brook. George stood down and was replaced by Harry. She glanced at Jem, but he was staring at Harry taking the oath.

'Harry Cartwright, you stated that you heard shots and shouting

166

and saw the defendants running from the scene of the murder on the evening of the sixth of October. Where were you when you heard the shots?'

'I farm at Newhay, off Howcut Lane, close to Newhay Copse where Joe was killed.'

'And what time was this?'

'I'd finished feeding the calves, and I do that after milking, so it would be some time after six o'clock. I'd taken a walk down towards the copse – we farm land down there. I didn't have the time about me, but the grandfather in the hall struck seven when I got in afterwards.'

'And you heard raised voices?'

'I heard Joe Upton's voice. And then shouting and gunshots. I went up the riding and saw three people running away. I thought they were lads out poaching and Joe had fired warning shots. I didn't know he was shot.'

'You didn't think to check Mr Upton was uninjured?'

'Joe could handle himself with poachers. And I was late for my supper already.'

'I see. And you recognised these people. Can you see them in this court?'

'Yes, sir. I can. They are in the dock, the accused, sir.'

'That's all. Thank you. You may step down.'

Next up was a tall man, broad of build, dressed in a smart country coat and breeches. Jem glanced from Cal to Nat and then to her. She gave him what she hoped was a smile.

The man glared at Jem and his cousins, who met his stare. 'I'm head gamekeeper to the Marquis of Northampton. The deceased, Upton, was a watcher of game under me. Upton's wife informed me that the man was missing, and I informed his lordship of this. Upton had been seen in the direction of Howcut Lane, and his lordship sent a party of us to look for him there. I went into

167

Newhay Copse, where I found a quantity of blood and part of the deceased's gun. I called to the rest of the party and, as Mr Scriven and Mr Dixon approached, they found the body. Upton's hat lay nearby. He was lying on his back, his head all bloody. One hand was extended on the ground and the other clenched to his chest.'

Mr John Pell, a surgeon, told the court he was present when the body was found. 'I didn't make a minute examination as the man was perfectly dead. On the following day, I subjected the body to a strict investigation.' He perused a paper in his hand. 'There were cuts on the eyelids, another wound to the head, and another which had severed the right ear. A gunshot wound in the neck had passed through the collar and dispersed in the scapulary muscles. There was also a lacerated wound to the back of the head, about four inches long, connected with an irregular fracture of the skull, and penetrating the brain. A violent blow from a gun or any other blunt instrument would produce such a wound.'

She felt sick. Jem had done this, and she was partly to blame.

The surgeon paused and addressed the judge. 'The bruises might in some conditions produce immediate death, but the fracture to the skull was, in all probability, the cause of it in this instance. That concludes my findings as reported to the inquest.' The man left the witness stand.

She recognised the man who took his place as Chief Constable Goddard, the man who'd searched the cottage after Jem was arrested. The chief constable read from a notebook. 'I found the prisoners working at a threshing machine on the premises of Mr Ruddle, near the Rose and Crown at Yardley. I took them to Castle Ashby, where they were held while I searched their lodgings. At Denton's home I found this pair of cord breeches.'

A wiry young man, possibly one of the constables, held up a pair of breeches and handed them to the jurors.

'They were quite wet in places, with marks of blood having been recently washed out. Then I searched Brafield's house and found a jacket with spots of blood on the left arm and shoulder. I found nothing at Weston's cottage. I brought Brafield to a harness room in Lord Northampton's stables and left him with a constable. I returned later, with Superintendent Young and his lordship's head gamekeeper, and examined Brafield. I found some thirty gunshot wounds in the centre of his back and on his arms. He told me Joe Upton had given him them. When I asked how, he said, and I quote. "I saw him with his gun, and I presented mine. I don't know which of us fired first, Upton or me. We both fired together and I dropped."'

The chief constable waved a hand at the young constable, who produced the jacket and a gun.

She frowned. How did Cal have gunshot wounds on his back if he and Joe fired together? Cal must have fired, missed, and then turned away as Joe shot him? Or Joe had shot him in the back before Cal fired?

'The jacket still has marks of blood on it. The gun is the one used by Denton. It was sold to Brafield by Herbert Longfellow seven weeks before Upton was murdered.'

The chief constable, having completed his statement, stepped down, and Lord Abinger banged on his desk. 'I think this would be a good time to adjourn for lunch. We shall reconvene at one of the clock, sharp. Court dismissed.'

The court erupted into a babble of voices. Jem, Cal, and Nat were led away, not having had the opportunity to say a word in their defence. And when would Mr Josiah speak up? 'Ella...' Jem's mother gripped her sleeve. 'I need some air, Ella.'

She knew the feeling: the court was hot, fetid, and airless, crammed as it was with sweating bodies, the inhabitants of Yardley not being so particular with their hygiene as the residents of Bath. She led the way out into the street where the ranks of purveyors of victuals had swelled fourfold. Her head swam, and she swallowed, pushing down a desire to vomit. Jem had been right: he was a dead man.

***

Jem couldn't face food, not that he'd been offered anything more

169

than bread and water since his arrest. He drank a little water to wet his dry throat, the manacle rubbing at his wrists as he lifted the mug to his lips. The gibbet loomed large in his mind's eye. Ella's face, as she'd listened to the evidence, loomed larger. How could she love him now, hearing what he'd done? He'd broken a man's skull in anger. However he tried to look at it, whatever Upton had done to provoke him, he'd done wrong. He deserved to die.

His gaoler tugged at his chains. 'Court's reconvening.'

He struggled to his feet and followed the man back into court. Cal and Nat were already there. They both looked as drained as he felt. The wait would soon be over.

Cal's statement spiralled him back to Newhay: the smell of leaf mould and autumn, the rank scent of fox and badger, and the sounds of birds at dusk. A hare standing and a gunshot. Upton bearing down on them and them scattering like rabbits before him.

'I ran up the quarter to an old riding, called the Ring Riding.' The clerk's voice, reading, not Cal's. 'Upton was there, and we had a word with one another. Then, somehow he cocked his gun, and I cocked mine, and whether his went off first or mine, I can't rightly say, but I think mine did. It ain't worth telling a story about. His gun caught me on the shoulder, and I was on the ground. Upton walked past me and swore at me something dreadful.'

Cal had shot first, even if he'd missed. That must be the nail in their coffins. He closed his eyes, as the clerk read on: they'd come upon Joe Upton. He wished they hadn't: with all his heart, he wished it. He licked his lips, trying to clean them of the memory of the metallic taste of blood. Fingers clenched, he relived the picking up of the gun barrel and the bringing it down with an ominous crack.

'Denton.' The clerk turned to the prisoners. 'Do you approve this statement?

Nat nodded. 'I do, sir.'

'And Weston, do you approve it?'

170

His nails bit into his palms: it wasn't only his life on the line, it was Nat and Cal's, and Ella's. 'That's about right. That's what happened. Only I believe Upton was as much at fault as us. If he hadn't interrupted Cal, we wouldn't have interrupted him, I'm sure.'

Reverend Buchanan was called as a character witness. The man tried to find good things to say about the three of them, but the rector's words didn't fill him with confidence.

Mr Josiah Barton stood up: his only hope now. 'I am greatly obliged to the learned sergeant, who opened the case for the prosecution, for his cautious abstinence from making any remarks that may have tended to inflame the minds of the jury. Nothing could be more temperate or just than the observations of the learned gentleman.' He drew himself up, a striking figure in his smart robes. 'However, I deeply regret that it was thought necessary to refuse my application, on the prisoners' behalf, to have copies of their statements. This refusal has placed me in an embarrassing position. And I beg the indulgent consideration of Lord Abinger and the jury if, unprepared with these, I fail in the proper handling of the nice distinctions of law involved in the present case.' Mr Barton smiled, flashing white teeth.

Jem had seen copperplate engravings in his mother's *Family Magazines* of sharks, washed up on beaches, with gentler smiles than the one on Mr Barton's face. He hoped his lawyer had a shark's bite.

Mr Barton's smile faded. 'I contend that the crime of the prisoners at the bar cannot possibly be construed into anything other than manslaughter, an aggravated case, certainly, but still only manslaughter.'

A stifled gasp escaped from some of the listeners. Joe's widow, Elizabeth, stared at Nat, Cal, and him with ill-concealed hatred. If she'd loved Joe like he loved Ella... He looked away.

'Silence in court.'

Whispers drifted like autumn leaves to the ground and lay

171

silent.

Mr Barton eyed each juror in turn. 'If the prisoners had gone out with the intention of committing an unlawful act, and the unfortunate deceased had fallen by their hand after he had warned them off the ground they were trespassing upon, then in that case, with a result so fatal as the present, the prisoners might be convicted of murder. Here, however, there is not the slightest evidence that the deceased said anything to the prisoners in his capacity of keeper. The case is therefore reduced to a common quarrel among parties, and allowances are always made by the law for actual provocation and heated blood.' The lawyer paused, turning to face Lord Abinger. 'The law considers that a person receiving from a person a blow was not answerable to the crime of murder if, in the heat of passion, he snatched up a weapon and destroyed his opponent. Even if, still excited, he jumps furiously upon the breast of his fallen opponent and death ensues, still, the provocation considered, the crime is still manslaughter.'

His heart thudded like a galloping horse. Voices rose around him, jostling for attention. Was it possible what he'd done wasn't adjudged murder? It was manslaughter in a moment of madness? Would the judge and jury agree?

Voices murmured, some assenting and some in dissent, as Mr Barton quoted several cases where a verdict of manslaughter had been brought and then addressed the court. 'I believe this jury will be directed by his lordship to return a verdict of manslaughter only.' Mr Barton bowed slightly to Lord Abinger and sat down.

Joe Upton's family shouted their disgust. John and Harry Cartwright weren't alone in being vocal in their condemnation.

The clerk to the magistrates called for silence. Lord Abinger banged on his desk. 'The prisoners are in peril of their lives, and it causes me much pain that while men stand in these dreadful circumstances, people are making a rude and thoughtless noise.'

Voices faded, one by one, and Lord Abinger continued. 'I trust I shall hear no more of it.' He looked around the court, waiting for complete silence. 'Members of the jury, you have heard the facts of this dreadful case, and you have heard the prisoners' statements and the plea for clemency on their behalf by my learned friend, Mr Josiah Barton. These young men, having drunk a quantity of beer, set off to Newhay Copse with no proven intent of murder. There is no evidence that they were warned off the land for trespass. The fact that Joseph Upton, the deceased, presented his gun and shot Caleb Brafield is not under dispute, nor is the fact that he presented his gun to Nathan Denton. The conclusion I draw from this is that this was a crime committed in hot blood, after some provocation, and I would direct you to return a verdict for the lesser offence of manslaughter.'

Nat and Cal sat rigid beside him as Lord Abinger directed the jury. Ella looked drawn and pale, but she was hugging his mother as if she thought he was safe. Had Mr Barton spoken to her about his likely sentence? Life was better than death, no matter where he lived it: he would be grateful if he was spared, but it would be a living death without Ella and his child.

The jury huddled together. He tried to hear what they were saying, but their words were whispered, their glances around the room furtive. No-one looked directly at the prisoners. His hands were clammy with cold sweat, his stomach churned, and his head swam. Ella was staring straight ahead, her face taut with tension. He wanted to hold her one last time.

The jury returned to their seats. His heart thundered in his ears, fit to burst.

Lord Abinger cleared his throat. 'Have you reached a verdict?'

One of the jurors stood. 'Yes, my lord. We find the prisoners guilty of very aggravated manslaughter.'

He was going to live.

'Is this the verdict of you all?'

'Yes, my lord.'

'So be it. James Weston, Caleb Brafield, Nathan Denton. You have each been found guilty of very aggravated manslaughter. I

173

sentence you all to transportation for life. Take them down. Court dismissed.'

The court erupted. He caught sight of Ella as he was led away in chains. She fought her way through the milling crowd towards him, reaching for him. 'Jem, I love you.'

'Forget me, Ella. Look after our child and find yourself someone else.' Chains weighed arms weak from lack of honest toil. His fingertips brushed hers for a moment before she was swept aside by a crush of people making for the street.

She was torn away, tears streaking her cheeks. 'Jem… There'll never be anyone else. I'll find you. Whatever it takes, I'll find you.'

Chapter Sixteen

'Where will they send him, Mr Josiah?' Ella sat in the small living room of Jem's parents' cottage, absent-mindedly pulling loose threads from her cuff. 'How will I see him if they send him away?'

'They'll take him to a port down south, Plymouth or Woolwich, probably, and he'll spend some time on a prison hulk, moored in the harbour, or in a prison onshore. When there's room for him on a convict ship, he'll set sail for Van Diemen's Land.'

She'd heard the name. 'Where's that?'

Mr Barton accepted the cup of tea Charlotte held out to him. 'It's the other side of the world, Ella. Even if he survives the journey, Jem is lost to you. You must accept that. He can never come home.'

Charlotte sank into her work chair. 'The journey is dangerous, Mr Barton?'

'I'm afraid so, Mrs Weston. Conditions on board convict ship are harsh. It's a four-month voyage, and the seas are perilous. I won't lie to you... Lives can be lost before they even reach Hobart. They have to round the Cape of Good Hope, survive the roaring forties... I've heard the storms can be ferocious.' Mr Josiah put his cup down on the table at his side. 'Ella, what are you going to do?'

She tugged at a pale thread, snapping it. 'He'll make it, Charlotte. He'll survive.' She wouldn't believe she'd never see Jem again, never hold him, love him, or raise their child with him. He'd begged her to find someone else. How could she forget him and love another? 'I'm going to wherever they take Jem. I'll find out where he is. I need to be near him.'

'Ella, be sensible. You're going to have a child in three months. How are you going to live in a strange town, alone? How will you look after a child on your own? You need a husband and a home. Harry will take you back.'

'You've spoken to him, Mr Josiah?'

'I made it clear he's to treat you with respect. He's your husband, Ella. You belong to him.'

'I'm not going back to Newhay. I'll find a way to do this by myself.'

Mr Josiah sighed. 'I feel responsible, sending you here. If you need to come home for a while... Or I can give you a small allowance to help out, here. At least think about it before you go off at half-cock.' He sighed again. 'James will have to make a new life out there. You must do the same here.'

He was right, part of her knew it, but she was in no mood to admit it even to herself. 'I'll think about it, all right?' She didn't have the fare, anyway, but, if she promised to stay here, and Mr Josiah was as good as his word, she soon would have. 'Yes. You're right, of course. I'll stay here if Charlotte will have me.'

Charlotte raised a small smile. 'Of course, we'll have you.'

'Then I'll arrange for funds to be made available.' He consulted a pocket watch. 'Now, I must make ready to return home. A carriage will be calling for me at Charles's.' He stood to say his farewells. 'If you need anything, Ella. Anything at all, write to me. You know you're like a daughter to me.'

She moved towards him and gave him a hug. 'Thank you for everything, Mr Josiah.'

His arms closed around her, uncertainly, and he planted a brief kiss on the top of her head. 'Take care, Ella. I'll bring your mother to visit when the weather is more clement for the journey.'

'You're very kind, sir.'

He turned towards the door and hesitated. 'There's something you should know. I'm not sure now is the right time to tell you, but James said something that made me consider who I am and what's important. You must know I have great affection for your mother. I've asked her to marry me. I hope you don't mind.' His eyes crinkled, and his mouth curved. 'She accepted my proposal.'

She smiled despite her own heartbreak. Her mother deserved happiness and security. 'You're a good man, and I know you'll make her happy. She's very fond of you, too.'

He let out a breath. 'Maybe you could call me Josiah?'

All her life, he'd been the nearest thing to a father she'd had. 'I'd like that, Josiah.'

***

The prison wagon was a square, black, enclosed box on wheels with hard benches running the full length of each side and small, barred windows that let the wind and rain slant through. Jem left Northampton with Cal, Nat, and three other prisoners, and they'd squeezed in four more at Oxford. According to his gaoler, who'd manacled and chained him before pushing him up onto the footplate and into the wagon, they were bound for Plymouth and were bloody lucky they didn't have to walk all the way, in a chain gang, as some prisoners did.

He was glad of fresh air on his face and a glimpse of trees, sky, and green fields after six months of being cooped up in filth and gloom. Walking would have been a pleasure, but the jangle of the horses' harnesses was sweet on his ears compared to the moans and cries that had emanated from the cells of his fellow prisoners. Even so, he was bitterly aware that every turn of the wagon's wheels took him ever farther from Ella and the home and family he would never see again. He'd accepted this was his future: six months with nothing else to think about had convinced him of the futility of wishing things were different. His only hope now was that he'd been able to convince Ella: she still seemed to harbour false dreams of a future that could never be.

'A penny for them, Jem?'

'What?'

177

Cal tried to stretch his back into a more comfortable position. 'I said a penny for them. Your thoughts.'

'I was thinking of Ella. You?'

'I was wondering if they'll separate us when we get wherever we're going. Six months' solitary was hell. I don't want to go through that, again, ever.'

It had been hell: not seeing Ella would be worse. 'Me neither. It helps having you and Nat here.'

Nat continued to stare silently at his boots.

'You all right, Nat?'

'This is forever, ain't it? We ain't never coming home.' Nat palmed tears from his eyes. 'I can't get Sarah's face out of my mind. She was distraught. She'll get a divorce eventually, I expect. She can claim one after seven years, my dad reckons, and I can't blame her for that, but...' He dragged a grubby sleeve across his nose. 'Someone else will watch my son grow up. I always reckoned me and Sarah would grow old together.'

Cal plucked at Nat's sleeve. 'I heard as how as convicts' families could follow them out if they was well-behaved, the convicts, that is.'

Nat looked up sharply. 'You think so?'

Was Cal right? Could he or Nat ask so much of their loved ones? To abandon everything and everyone they knew and cross the globe for love? Nat's words had brought home the finality of their situation: saying the words no-one had wanted to voice. Silence fell on the prisoners in the wagon: each turned inward, dreaming their own dreams of their past and a future that would almost certainly never be.

***

'Did you see Jem? How's he bearing up?' Charlotte's voice was anxious.

Ella flopped into a chair and buried her head in her hands. 'He's

178

gone.'

Charlotte dropped her bobbins. 'Gone? Already? You didn't see him?'

'They said the prison wagon left at dawn. Him and Cal and Nat are on their way to Plymouth. What are we going to do, Charlotte?'

Her mother-in-law knelt at her side and took both her hands in hers. 'We have to let him go, Ella. I'm sure he'll write, if he can, when he can. We'll have to make do with that.'

'But even if he's allowed a letter, it will take forever. Josiah said it takes four months to sail to Van Diemen's Land. Even if Jem wrote straightaway he got there, and the letter caught a ship coming home, it will be at least another four months before word gets back to us. That's the best part of a year before we know if he's alive – if we ever get to know.'

Charlotte stroked her hands. 'Ella, James will be all right. He's resourceful. He'll make the best of his situation, whatever that is. Us pining over him won't change a thing. We have to get on with our lives, best as we can.'

'I know you're right but – I thought I'd be able to say goodbye.'

'Jem knows how much you love him. He's trusting you to do the right thing by your baby. That's what's important now.'

She had to get out of the house. Getting up out of her chair was not so easy now. Her back ached if she sat too long or if she worked too long: it would be better when the child was born, but that would present a whole new bucketful of problems. How would she support a child, never mind herself, away from here? Yet she couldn't stay where the memories of Jem drove her to her knees. She walked through the village: without Jem, it wasn't home anymore.

The sound of cartwheels made her step aside. The horses, a chestnut and a grey, stopped just past her. She swirled her cloak around her to hide her full shape and looked up to see Harry's smug smile. 'They got what they deserved, Ella. James Weston is

179

out of our lives forever, and good riddance to him. Now, get up here, and I'll take you home.'

'Were you telling the truth about seeing the boys in the copse the night Joe was killed?'

'I might have been.'

'You testified just to spite me. You could have had them hanged. What sort of man are you, Harry?'

He drew his lips back from his teeth in a snarl. 'A man who won't be bested by a low-life like Weston. Get up in this cart now! You're coming home, and you'll tell the reverend how happy you are to be at Newhay with me, or I'll see to it the Westons are turned out on the street.'

'Never. You wouldn't dare.'

'If you're worried about Father, he won't touch you again. I beat the living daylights out of him. I'm master at Newhay now. He does my bidding, and Mother'll do the same. You'll be mistress in your own home. Our children will have everything you want for them.'

'I'd rather die or live in the poorhouse than live with you or bear your children, Harry Cartwright. And the Westons are good people. They'd rather live on the street than…' She'd almost let slip she was pregnant. Charlotte wouldn't want her grandchild brought up by Harry, whatever the cost to her family. 'I can't even bear to look at you.' Her mind made up, she turned around and went back to the cottage. Harry had done his worst. Maybe, if she wasn't around, he'd be satisfied with that and leave her and Jem's parents alone.

Charlotte looked up from tending the fire when she walked in. She straightened. 'I can see by the look on your face as how as you've made a decision.'

'I'm going to Bath, to stay with my mother and Josiah, until the child is born.'

'I can't say as I wasn't expecting it, but I'll miss you something
180

awful, Ella. You will come back, won't you?'

'Of course, I will. It's just…'

'Your bed's empty without Jem in it?'

She smiled. 'Something like that. And I need to get far away from Harry. I'll write every week.'

'And I'll look forward to your letters. I ain't much of a reader or writer, myself. Bill, neither, but I dare say as the rector will read them for me and pen a reply to you.'

'I'll pack what I need. I'll catch the carrier, if he passes through this evening, and get lodgings in Bedford.'

'Do you have enough money? I've a little saved towards next quarter's rent.'

She waved the generous offer away; Charlotte could ill afford it. 'Josiah gave me a little to tide me over. I should have enough to get to Bath.'

'I'll make you up a parcel of victuals.' Charlotte turned away and busied herself in her larder.

She'd miss Charlotte, but she needed her mother, and the longer she postponed the journey, the less likely she'd be fit to travel. And, anyway, she'd made Jem a promise she didn't intend to break.

The journey to Bath was tiring and took three dawn-to-dusk days. She arrived sore and aching. Josiah's maid, Annie, answered the door to her. 'Miss Ella. The master's away in London, but the mistress will be so pleased to see you.'

Master and mistress? Had the wedding taken place already? Annie knocked at the door to Josiah's sitting room and then opened it. 'Miss Ella's here, Mrs Maundrell.'

That answered her question about the wedding. Her mother rose to greet her, setting aside her mending. 'Ella, you got my letter… You're here for the wedding?'

181

'No, I haven't received any letter, I must have left before it arrived, but I'm glad I haven't missed your wedding. I'm so pleased for you both.' She hugged her mother, who then stood back to inspect her.

'You're looking tired.' She moved to the bell pull and tugged it. 'Annie will bring us tea. I'm so sorry about James. Josiah did his best for him, you know.'

'I know. He probably saved James's life. I can't thank him enough for that.'

'Can you stay long? What are your plans?'

'Jem's been sent to Plymouth. There's no point me being in Northamptonshire any longer. I hoped I could stay here for a while?'

'Of course, you can, Ella.'

'You're sure Josiah won't mind?'

'He loves you, Ella. He always has. He thought he was doing the right thing, sending you to Charles Buchanan, but I'm sure he realises his mistake. He should be home tomorrow. He won't turn you away.'

The door opened and Annie wheeled in a loaded trolley. 'I had the kettle on the range already. And there's two kinds of cake. Can I get you anything else?'

'No, thank you, Annie. Why don't you make up a bed for Ella and then take the rest of the evening off, dear? Ella and I can finish up down here.'

'Thank you, Mrs Maundrell. If you're sure. Mr Ralph's just come in. Shall I bring an extra cup and saucer?'

'Please, dear.'

Annie closed the door behind her.

She leaned forward and rubbed her aching back, not sure how she felt about seeing Ralph again. 'I shall be glad of my bed,

182

tonight.' She was making excuses to avoid him already. 'How has Ralph been?'

'He buries himself in his work. The practices are doing well. Josiah's very proud of him.'

The door flung open and Ralph strode in, a cup clasped in one hand. 'Just in time for tea, Mother.' He grinned his irrepressible grin.

Her mother tutted. 'Cheeky young whelp.'

Ralph put down his cup and turned to her, his smile faltering. 'Ella, it's good to see you.'

'It's good to be home, Ralph.' She hadn't realised how good until he'd walked into the room. It was as if her troubles melted away, as if her childhood innocence had been restored. She shook the notion away: it was far too late for that. 'You're looking well.'

He took her hands and pulled her to her feet. 'And you look tired, Ella.' His eyes showed his heartbreak as he surveyed her full figure. 'It must have been a long journey.'

'The coach was delayed, a broken wheel. It took three days.'

Her mother poured tea and handed Ralph his cup. He sat down, patting the sofa beside him for her to sit down next to him. Her mother broke the awkward silence. 'Ella's staying.'

'For a little while. I don't know how long Jem will be held in Plymouth.'

'But you can't be thinking of going to Plymouth?' Her mother stared at her, an eyebrow raised. 'You'll stay until after the baby's born, surely.'

Ralph didn't look up. 'When's it due?'

'Around midsummer. Jem could sail at any time. I have to see him.'

Her mother frowned. 'It would be reckless to travel anywhere until the child is a few months old.'

183

Ralph nodded his agreement. 'Prisoners can be held in prison hulks for months, years even, before they sail for Van Diemen's Land. And even if you do drag yourself all that way, and see him before he sails, then what will you do? Go back to Reverend Buchanan?'

'The reverend has made his feelings quite clear. He wouldn't take me back and, anyway, it would put him in a difficult position. The murder, or should I say manslaughter, has split opinion in the village. He needs to be able to remain neutral. He can hardly do that with me and Jem's child in his home.'

Ralph looked thoughtful. 'I suppose not. What about Jem's family?'

'They'd welcome me with open arms, but they're very poor, and I can't be a burden to them now they've lost Jem's wages.'

'So you'll come back here, once Jem's sailed.' He looked across at her mother. 'It makes sense. It's not as if we can't afford it.'

Her heart swelled with love for her childhood friend. She wanted to be gentle with his feelings. 'That's a kind thought, Ralph. I'm not sure it's what I want.'

Her mother tutted again. 'A young woman in your predicament has little room to have wants. You have to forget this young man of yours. You need a home, warmth, and food, and so will your child. If you won't return home to Harry Cartwright, you are entirely reliant on Josiah's generosity and love, as are we all. Gift horses should not be discarded because they're not the right colour or have long teeth.'

Ralph laughed despite his obvious concern. 'Stay with us, Ellie, please. I'll find out who to write to, concerning James. Maybe, I can accompany you to Plymouth to see him. You may be able to settle better here, knowing you've said your goodbyes.'

Would it make a difference to how she felt? The voice of sense and reason joined forces with her maternal instincts and warred with the voice of desire and loss: reality reared its head, and how

184

could she resist Ralph when he called her Ellie, like he had when she was little? 'It may be that caring for a child alone will seem more daunting when it's here. I intend to see Jem, if I can, but I won't make a rash decision, Ralph. I promise.'

***

Ella was up early next morning, happy to help her mother and Annie. She found she tired easily, and it didn't take much to make her back ache. Also, even in a feather bed, sleep was hard to come by. Either she couldn't get comfortable for tiny, sharp elbows and knees moving across her belly or thoughts of Jem had her tossing and turning. She needed rest, but it wasn't in her nature to stand aside and let others work.

She stood from brushing the mat in front of the sitting room hearth and straightened, stiffly. It was one of the lighter tasks.

Annie took the brush and dustpan from her hands. 'Sit down, Miss Ella, and rest, for the love of God. I'll bring you a cup of tea.' The maid bustled out of the room and returned with a pot of tea and two cups. 'Mr Ralph's here. I thought he could amuse you while I do the beds.'

Ralph breezed in and sat beside her on the couch. 'Shall I be Mother?' He poured, pausing mid-pour to look at her when she didn't reply. 'Sorry. I don't suppose you find that amusing at the moment. Annie said your back hurts.'

'It's nothing. Just pregnancy.' She took the cup he offered. 'Thank you.'

Ralph took a sip of his own tea. 'I've been thinking, Ellie. You know how I feel about you. How I've always felt about you. I thought one day we'd marry. We used to pretend, remember, when we were little?'

She smiled. 'I remember. I made the mistake of marrying a man I didn't love. I won't make that mistake again, Ralph.'

He reached for her hand. 'Ella, I love you. I know you love me, too. Haven't we always been friends?'

185

'I love you like a brother, Ralph, not a husband. If all I wanted was a good man, a friend, someone I could trust with my life, I would choose you above all others, but I love Jem.'

'I know you do. I'm not asking you to love me in any other way, but – damn it, we're a firm of solicitors – if Dad and I can't get you a divorce from what's his name, Harry Cartwright, who can? And damn the scandal. I can give you a home if we marry. I'll raise your child with as much love as if it were my own. We could have a good life. I won't ask you to give me children, if you find the thought abhorrent. We can have separate rooms. I just need you to be safe and loved.'

Tears trickled down her cheeks, unhindered. 'Ralph, you are the kindest, sweetest man I know. It's the most wonderful offer, and sensibly, it's hard to refuse, but you deserve to be loved the way I love Jem. Someone who would go to the ends of the earth for you.'

'As you would for Jem?'

Her mind was in a whirl. This wasn't just about her: this was the future of her child. *Look after our child...* 'Even if I agreed, your father would never allow it.'

Ralph looked down his nose. 'He's marrying your mother. He can hardly complain you're not good enough for me!'

She laughed at his indignation. 'I suppose not.'

He got down on one knee.

'Ralph, please.'

'Ella Cartwright, will you marry me?'

'No!' Josiah Barton stood in the doorway. 'No, stop this now. You can't marry Ella.'

Ralph turned on his father in fury. 'Why not? I love her.'

Ella's mother pushed past Josiah to stand beside him. 'You can't marry Ralph, Ella.'

She didn't want to marry Ralph, but she resented being told

what she could and couldn't do. Reverend Buchanan had tried that with disastrous consequences. 'I'll marry who I like and you can't stop me.'

'You can't marry Ralph, because he's your ha

lf-brother.' Josiah's face crumpled. 'Ella, I'm your father.'

Chapter Seventeen

Ella stood, mouth open, her eyes moving from her mother to Josiah. 'You're my father?'

Josiah gripped her mother's hand. 'I should explain.'

'Explain?' She looked at Ralph, but he was as stunned as she was. 'How can you explain eighteen years of lies?'

Ralph's face showed his confusion. 'But Mother was still alive when Ella was born.'

'Ralph, you were a baby. Your mother was very ill for a long while. Ella's mother – Deborah helped nurse her, looked after you, kept the house running, and kept me sane. It was a terrible time. We became very close. Deborah loved your mother too. We comforted each other and one thing led to another.'

'Did Mother know?'

'No, though she made me promise I'd find someone who could be a wife and mother. She wanted you to have a mother, and she wanted me to be happy. She was very fond of Deborah. I don't think she would have denied us our love.'

Her fingers clenched. 'So why keep it a secret all these years? Why deny my mother her status and me my birth right?'

'I was starting out in the world. A new practice. The scandal would have finished me before I got started. We agreed she'd remain my housekeeper in name, and we invented a dead husband. It was a respectable arrangement, and we got to stay together. We raised our children together. No-one was hurt.'

Her heart hammered. 'No-one was hurt? You let Ralph have feelings for me. You sent me away. You lied to me and sent me away. For the love of all that's holy, I married a man who treated me like the dirt on his boot. His father pushed me up against a wall and raped me. The man I love killed a man and is being sent to the far side of the globe. Almost certainly, Harry's treatment of me, and Joe Upton's remarks, contributed to it. How on earth can you say no-one got hurt?'

'I'm sorry, Ella. It seemed the best thing to do at the time. If Ralph hadn't fallen for you, neither of you would have been any the wiser.'

Ralph crossed the room towards their father. 'And that makes it all right, does it? Have you any idea the pain you've caused.' Ralph turned away, fists clenched, then swung round, caught Josiah a glancing blow across the jaw, and stormed from the room. The front door slammed shut, and silence dropped like a wet blanket from the clothesline.

Josiah made for the door, but her mother put a restraining hand on his arm. 'Leave him, Josiah. He's angry and rightly so. He'll come around when he cools off. He knows how much we love him.'

'And I know how much you love me.' She fled up the stairs to her room, leaving the accusation hanging: it was her they'd sent away, her they'd deprived of a father.

She collapsed onto her bed and sobbed. The years when she'd longed for a father, and brothers and sisters, poured into the void inside her, overwhelming her. She needed Jem. He'd be in Plymouth by now, and she didn't have the fare to get there. She loved her family more than life, but she couldn't stay where she was an inconvenience, a scandal, a bastard child. Would Josiah give her the fare? She doubted it: he'd consider it ill-advised. If she asked Ralph, he'd want to go with her, and that wasn't fair. He should be looking for a wife and establishing his career, not trailing after his half-sister like a hastily packed, last-minute travelling bag.

Josiah kept cash in a box in his study. She repacked the bags she'd only unpacked the day before, eager to get out of the house before anyone tried to change her mind. The study door was open.

189

The box was kept in a locked drawer, and the key was kept in a pot on the windowsill.

The lock clicked, and the drawer slid open silently. The box was small and made of tin. It too was locked. She cast about for a hiding place for its key. Would Josiah carry it with him? His jacket hung over the back of his desk chair. Her fingers closed over a small hard object in a pocket: a brass key. She glanced at the door. Voices came from the sitting room and she stiffened as footsteps rang along the tiled hall.

The footsteps faded, and she opened the box. Twenty gold sovereigns gleamed. That was more than a year's wages for a housemaid, almost two years, in fact. She took two and slipped them into her pocket. She'd need money for the fare, food, rent, clothes for her baby. She took two more. Josiah could afford it. This was like coppers to him. It would keep her until she could find Jem and get work. Would she be able to work with a baby? She took two more. Surely Josiah wouldn't begrudge her six month's wages after all the unpaid labour she'd provided over the years.

The sovereigns safely stowed in her purse, she took a sheet of vellum from a pile, dipped Josiah's quill pen in black ink, and stabbed at the vellum.

Dear Mother and Father. I have taken six sovereigns and am going to Plymouth to find Jem. I'll write you when I am settled. One day, I may be able to repay you. Your affectionate daughter, Ella Weston.

She sprinkled pounce from a silver shaker onto the wet ink, blew away the powder, and placed a glass paperweight on the letter. Satisfied, she retrieved her bags and left the house. She looked back at the house that had been her home. Would she ever see it or her family again?

***

Jem stared out of the prison wagon's barred window. Plymouth, if it were Plymouth, was a town such as he'd never seen. The

190

cobbled streets were a throng of smart carriages pulled by matched teams, people afoot, and horses drawing high-piled carts carrying all manner of goods for sale. The clatter of hooves, the grinding of wheels, and the babble of voices almost drowned out his own thoughts. Buildings crowded a low shoreline that was deeply cut with inlets filled with ships of all sizes; masts stuck up like a dense forest of pine trunks that had been stripped of branches ready for felling or like quills on a startled hedgehog. Sun sparkled from the water, and the sea stretched as far as the eye could see: a broad blue, as blue as the sky above it. Guarding the mouth to the harbour sat a small island ringed with fortifications that had probably been built to repel the French. Over everything hung the smell of fish, dung, human waste, and something blowing in on a sea breeze that he'd never smelt before.

The prison wagon drew to a halt. He nudged Cal awake. 'I think we're there, wherever there is.'

A prisoner, who'd joined them at Oxford, leaned over to peer through the bars. 'It's Plymouth Sound. I've an uncle in the navy who sails out of Plymouth. This is Plymouth Dock. I never thought to come here in a prison wagon.'

The rear door of the wagon opened. The guard motioned them to hurry. 'Out.'

He squinted in the bright light that reflected from the water. Ships, taller than houses, rose above him, their masts seeming almost to pierce the sky. Some bore flags that fluttered in the breeze. Everywhere men bustled about their business, and workers carried stone to a harbour wall they were building. A couple of ruined ships lay burnt out, listing at anchor, and on the dockside, some buildings also showed signs of a fire.

A hand in his back pushed him onwards. 'Get a move on.'

He urged his shackled legs forwards to a small room. A man held out his hand. 'Caption papers.'

His guard handed over a handful of papers, and the man perused them. He looked up. 'I see we have three lifers.' He glanced back at the papers. 'Weston, Brafield, and Denton... Take them to Stirling Castle.'

They were ushered outside. Cal looked around. 'We're going to a castle, Jem?'

'That's what the man said.' He searched the shoreline and the higher land that swept either side of the sound, but they boasted no castles. The guard led them to the dockside and down steps into an open boat that rocked violently as they stepped into it. He glanced at Cal and Nat's pale faces. None of them could swim, and even if they could, their heavy chains would send them straight to the bottom of the harbour. His leg and back muscles were stiff from the tension of the journey in the prison wagon, and the unaccustomed movement of the boat found every ache.

He was handed an oar and told to pull on it. He'd never been in a boat, but he watched a guard and pulled when he did. The shore receded as they heaved, his arms and back burning with the effort. Impossibly huge ships rose on either side of him as they drew farther from shore. Where the hell were they being taken? How far would they have to row? The thought of rowing all the way to the other side of the world lodged in an insane part of his mind as reality slipped from his grasp. Beside him Cal heaved doggedly, and he matched his cousin stroke for stroke, concentrating on the task at hand and not his uncertain future.

'Ship oars.'

The command brought him back to reality, and he copied the guard, who'd pulled his oar from the water. He twisted round as the boat bumped into something solid. A wooden wall curved up and up. Above him, two long rows of windows followed along the ship's side towards a graceful upsweep of bow and, above those, a haphazard arrangement of what appeared to be sheds made the whole thing look top-heavy. Masts rose from among the wooden structures, and all about were strung ladders and ropes bearing small fluttering flags. He could just make out the words *Stirling Castle*. A rope ladder snaked down towards them. The guard moved among them, unshackling them. 'You. Up you go.'

192

'Are we sailing straightaway?' He'd hoped to be able to write to Ella before he sailed.

The guard laughed. 'In this? I doubt she'd make Land's End. She was a seventy-four gunner, a great ship, once. She's been a prison hulk since thirty-nine. Seen better days. You'll be kept here until a convict ship docks. Go on, man, and be quick about it.'

One by one, the ten prisoners climbed the ladder to be dragged aboard ship and re-shackled. He glanced shoreward: the open boat was already halfway back to dock. Captivity was suddenly very real. There was no way he could get back on land.

They were herded like cattle towards an opening in the deck. 'Down into the hold. Hurry it up.' The climb down the open treads was slow and made difficult by his chains and the descent into gloom. The stench of human waste made him gag: moans rose from the darkness. As his eyes adjusted, he made out what looked like cages along the sides of the hold. Men stared at him like trapped animals from behind bars. A door was unlocked, and he was pushed inside with Nat and Cal close behind him.

A man shuffled aside to make room, grunting his displeasure. 'Welcome to purgatory. Next port is Hell.'

He swallowed. 'Hell?'

The man spat onto the oak boards. 'Van Diemen's Land.'

***

Ella had been in Plymouth for a week before she found her way to the docks. Her lodgings were a mile walk from Plymouth Dock, where, she'd been assured, convicts were taken, and the way through the busy streets was perilous. Several times she'd almost been run down by teams of horses hauling heavily laden wagons to and from the port.

A labourer carrying a baulk of timber on his shoulder pointed her to a small building on the quayside. She hurried across the busy space and entered a low room. A man looked up from his desk. 'Can I help you, miss, or is it missus?'

'I was told prisoners were brought here.'

'That's true.'

'Was a man called James Weston brought here?'

'Weston? Brother? Husband? Father?'

'Husband.'

He thumbed through a pile of papers. 'When would that be?'

'About a week ago?'

He pushed himself out of his chair and reached for a leather-bound ledger. 'James Weston, aged twenty-one, convicted of manslaughter on March sixth of this year at Northampton?'

'He is here.'

The man moved across to the doorway and turned her to face the harbour. 'See that ship? The one with all the cabins on top? That's the prison hulk, *Stirling Castle*. That's where he is.'

'How do I get out there?'

The man laughed. 'You want to go out there?'

'I want to go where Jem goes. I'm his wife.'

'You don't want to go out there, missus, believe me. There's cholera, dysentery…'

'Dear God.' Bile rose in her throat. 'These are human beings.'

'They should have thought of that before they broke the law of the land.'

'He's not a bad man. He doesn't deserve this.'

'I dare say the man he killed didn't deserve it either.' The man shook his head but his features softened. 'They come ashore for hard labour most days. Those that are fit. If your man's not here on the quayside, I suggest you come back tomorrow morning and every morning. Sooner or later he'll be sent ashore. They're building new harbour walls along the way, and there's work turning the cranks in the rope walk or picking oakum.'

194

'Oakum?'

The man limped towards his chair. 'Picking apart old, tarred ropes for caulking. Hard, tedious, dirty work.'

'Thank you.'

'You take care, though. They're a rough lot that work the docks.' His eyes glittered. 'You mind they don't get you behind the rope walk and have their way with you.'

She put a hand to her stomach. Her warm cloak barely concealed her bulging belly. 'I have to see Jem. How long will it be before he's sent away?'

'It could be days, months, or years. It depends what ships dock and who gets picked to go. Some spend their whole sentence on the hulk.'

Her heart rose at the thought of him not leaving though how he'd survive disease and deprivation on the hulk, she had no idea.

'The man traced a finger down the open page in the ledger. 'Transported for life. He won't stay here. He'll be sent to Van Diemen's Land.'

'But what if he leaves before I give birth. I need him to see his child.'

The man sighed. 'Families don't always have to be split.'

'What do you mean?'

'Sometimes, just occasionally, wives go with their husbands.'

'I could go with him to Van Diemen's Land?'

'You could apply. You have your papers?'

She shook her head. 'I'm Jem's common-law wife.'

He frowned. 'So you're not legally married?'

'No, well, yes. I'm married to Harry Cartwright, but I left him.'

The man shrugged his shoulders and closed the ledger. 'Not much I can do, then. Sorry.' He nodded towards men in chains who were hauling rocks. 'I hope you find your man.'

She made her way along the quayside, trying to keep out of the way of wagons and horses. Men stared at her as she passed, and she clutched her cloak tightly around her, her hand over the purse she'd hidden next to the blue jay feather beneath her bodice. She searched the haggard faces of gaunt men. She couldn't see Jem or his cousins.

She spent half a day wandering the vast dock area. It wasn't just one dock. It seemed a multitude of large and small inlets made up the port of Plymouth. How would she ever find Jem in such a maze?

She returned to her lodgings, exhausted and in despair. She couldn't give up on him. Her resolve hardened. She still had most of the money she'd taken from Josiah's desk: if she couldn't travel with Jem as his wife, maybe, there was another, more comfortable way she could follow him across the globe.

Chapter Eighteen

Harry's bed was still empty. Ella had been gone more than a week, and it seemed likely that she wasn't coming back to Yardley. He hadn't got Ella back even though Jem Weston had left. The girl had vanished.

'You should have broken the filly in properly, Harry. A girl like that needed a firm hand. A man's hand, not a boy's.'

'I'll get her back.' His clenched fist hardened. 'I'll wipe that smug smile off your face, Father, and make you eat your words.'

'Words are cheap, Harry. You want my respect, you'll have to earn it. I've worked hard to build this farm, as have you, as did my father before me. Do you want the tenancy, the herd, all this sweat and blood, to go to some other buggers when you're too old to work? You need legitimate heirs, sons, if you want this place and all your hard work to stay in the family. Ella's your wife. If you want legal heirs, you need Ella and no-one else. Get her back here and tie her down with a brood of children. Hell, tie her down with a halter rope and shut her in the root cellar if you must, but get a child on her.' Familiar contempt curled his father's lip. 'Or do you want me to do that for you as well?'

The barb hurt. 'You'll not touch her, Father.' He drew himself up, taller than his father. 'I'll show you what stuff I'm made of, damn you. I'll make you proud of me.'

John Cartwright smiled and clapped him on the shoulder. 'That's what I needed to hear, Harry. I'll see to the farm. You go and find your wife.'

'I've a load of feed to take to Ruddle's. I'll call on the Westons. They're sure to know where she is.'

'Or the reverend. That Barton is a friend of his.'

197

'I'll try the Weston's first.' He harnessed the cart mare, loaded the cart, and then headed towards the turnpike road and Yardley. Across the street, Charlotte Weston was walking alone. He hauled the mare to a halt. Charlotte was without the protection of her husband, Bill, whose knuckles he hadn't wanted to risk. His broken nose was still bent from Jem's attack, despite Doc Hayes setting it.

He jumped down from the cart and hurried across to her.

She turned at the hand on her shoulder, her face betraying her fear. 'What do you want?'

'I need to know where Ella is.'

'I don't know.'

'I don't believe you. I want to know where she's staying. In Bath with her mother? I want her address.'

'I don't have it. Ella promised she'd write, but I haven't heard from her yet.'

He breathed in her face. 'If you're lying, I'll have a word in the ear of the estate manager. Us Cartwrights have influence. I'll see you out on the street.'

'Do you worst, Harry Cartwright. I wouldn't tell you where Ella was if I knew.'

He gripped her shoulder harder. 'The rector will have heard. He's a friend of Mr Barton. He'll know where she is. I'm going to fetch her home, Charlotte. No Weston gets the better of a Cartwright.'

Charlotte Weston smiled. 'I think you'll find James already has the better of you. He has Ella's love, and that's something you'll never have.'

He curled his lip. 'I don't need her love. As her husband, I demand her obedience.'

Mrs Weston laughed. 'Good luck with that, Harry.' She shrugged away his hand, and he let her go. The woman wasn't

198

worth talking to. He'd get what he wanted from Reverend Buchanan.

He lashed the mare into a trot, hauled her to a stop outside the rectory, and hammered on the front door, bruising his knuckles in his anger.

'What's the emergency?' Reverend Buchanan opened the door wider. 'What's happened, Harry?'

'I want to know Mr Barton's address in Bath.' He pushed past the rector into the hallway. 'I'm going to fetch Ella home, and no-one is going to stop me.'

Reverend Buchanan closed the front door. 'Calm down, Harry. There's no point you going to Bath. I had a letter from Josiah only this morning. Ella was in Bath, but she's left. Took six sovereigns and left without a word. Josiah doesn't know where she's gone.'

He stared at the reverend. 'But she can't just disappear.'

'I fear that's exactly what she's done, Harry. She and Josiah had some sort of argument, apparently. I don't think Ella wants to be found.'

'According to the *Herald*, Jem's been taken to Plymouth to a prison hulk. You think she's gone after him?'

'I'm afraid it's quite likely.'

'So if I find Weston, I'll find Ella.'

'I dare say.'

Plymouth and back would take more than a week, and it could take weeks more to find her. 'I can't leave the farm for the length of time it could take me to find her. I have crops to think about, not to mention the herd.'

'It will do no good running after her if you don't know where to look. If I hear anything about Ella, I'll let you know, but there's something else you should know. Ella's with child, Harry.'

'A child?' Ella was his wife, and he'd had her before Weston

199

had. He pushed aside the thought that his father had had her as well. 'I have to get her back, Reverend. That could be my son and heir she's carrying.' And anyway, he'd promised her he'd be her first fuck and her last, and he wasn't about to break his promise. It could be his child, couldn't it?

***

Jem lay on his back on a hard bunk, staring into darkness as he'd done every night for what seemed like a lifetime. Days blurred into weeks, and he had no idea how long the hulk had been his prison; there were no trees or wildflowers to show the passing of the seasons. He guessed it must be late spring or early summer judging by the haze of green on the higher ground in the distance. Ella would be close to birthing.

He turned onto his side. Every muscle hurt, and his wrists and ankles were raw from the manacles. Sleep evaded him, for the night wasn't quiet. The hulk creaked and groaned as it moved with the tide; men moaned, whimpered, snored, and farted. His own stomach rumbled ominously: hunger or the onset of dysentery? The clanks of iron and rattles of chains were a constant in his life, and even now, he was chained to his bunk to prevent his escape.

The fact that he couldn't swim wouldn't necessarily have stopped him trying. He'd probably be better drowned than existing in this hopeless, brutal half-life. Nat moaned on the bunk below him: he'd angered the guard by slopping his latrine bucket on deck and had been flogged.

He shut his eyes. It seemed less dark that way. His fingers closed over the quill of the jay feather Ella had given him. He tried to picture home and Ella, something that was becoming more and more difficult. An image formed: an eye, the line of her lips, and the tilt of her nose. What was she doing now? Was she sleeping, her dark lashes brushing her cheeks, her auburn hair spread across her pillow, or was she lying awake in the dark thinking of him, his jay feather in her fingers, as hers was in his? Thoughts of her consumed his every waking moment: one day, for a moment, he'd thought he'd seen her on the far side of the dock. He was probably losing his sanity.

Despite being tired as a work-weary dray horse, he couldn't wait until morning, so he could get off this hulk and into fresh air. The smell of fouling from latrine buckets clogged his lungs and clung to his clothes. From the bows, where a man couldn't even stand straight, came the ravings of delirium. Dysentery, cholera, or typhoid? He found himself wishing the man would die, so he didn't have to listen to what would almost certainly be his own fate.

The ravings and moans quietened at last. Ella's face filled his mind: they were walking in Cold Oak Copse. Spring sunshine lanced through the fresh green of spring, wood anemones and primrose raised their heads, and the bright spears of bluebell leaves thrust through the leaf mould. He could smell the damp earth, the musk of fox and badger, and the scent of Ella's freshly washed hair. His lips brushed hers, her body warm and soft against his.

A bell clanged far away. Yardley church?

It tolled again, louder, nearer, and was followed by the rattling of chains. 'Get up, you lazy dogs. On deck with your latrine pails. Get your rations.' Guards moved among them, releasing chains, kicking at buckets. A whip cracked, snapping the brittle air. 'Come on. Get a bloody move on.' The guard laughed. 'Only the dead are excused.'

Ella's image faded beyond his grasp, leaving him bereft. He picked up his bucket and climbed up onto the deck. Washing facilities were non-existent, and rations would be short if he wasn't quick.

Breakfast over, he swilled his cup, bowl, and spoon in a vat of murky water and handed them back to the officer in charge. A lump of bread and a bowl of thin, barley gruel weren't much to do a day's work on, but it might be all he got. At least, on the docks, he'd be away from the stench of human waste, though he doubted the waters of the harbour were clean after the hundred or so ships at mooring had emptied their latrines into it. The tide swept the waste out to sea, as it would the unwanted prisoners once a convict

201

ship arrived.

He shrugged the thought away: it was all out of his control now. He stood in line to climb the rope ladder down to the open boat that would take his gang of men to their day's work. Cal and Nat descended in front of him, and he joined them adept now at climbing rope ladders. He pulled at his oar with a will, eager to get ashore and feel solid ground beneath his feet.

On shore, they were shackled together in a chain gang so none could escape. Today's work was passing rocks down the line to workers building the new harbour wall. Turn, hold, swing, and let go; turn, hold, swing, and let go. Cal, at his side, swayed and dropped his rock.

A guard ran across, whip raised. 'Pick it up, you lazy cur.'

Cal swayed again and fell.

'Get up.' The man raised his whip.

'No… Cal's ill.' He moved in front of his cousin. 'How will whipping him help any?'

The whip lashed across his face. He fingered the raised wheal. The image of Joe Upton lying prone at his feet made his fists clench. If he had a gun barrel this man would die.

'Less of the mouth, dog. I'm watching you, and don't you forget it.' The guard unshackled Cal from the line and dragged him aside.

Beyond the line of waiting men walked a familiar figure. Ella? He shook his head: he was dreaming. The figure turned towards him. It was Ella. He bowed his head and moved behind the guard. He couldn't bear for her to see him like this. Why wasn't she getting on with her own life as he'd begged her to? Why did she have to come looking for him? Some of the men called to her lewdly. Ella was close enough now for him to see the blush on her cheeks. She was big with his child, and he could do nothing to protect her from these men, from life. He'd failed her and would continue to drag her down to his state if she found him. He

202

hunched into his jacket hoping she wouldn't notice him.

Another man shouted to her. 'How much do you charge, girl? I'll give you a farthing.'

She caught her coat around her and hurried on, away from him and the laughter and jeers. He breathed again; he'd have done anything for Ella, once, but now all he could do was let her and his child go.

***

Ella walked slowly back to her lodgings. Another day she'd failed to find Jem. She knew he was still here, but that was as much as she'd been able to discover.

'Evening news! All your weekly news!' The newspaper seller on the corner of her road yelled his wares, though it sounded more like Eenun noooooz! Allyuwklynoooz! She gave the man four and a half pence in exchange for a broadsheet: it listed ships docking and sailing and was four and half pence well spent. She scanned the shipping reports. No convict ships were reported due to dock in the next week, only passenger ships and cargo vessels.

An advertisement caught her eye.

Under Her Majesty's Commissioners. Entirely Free Emigration to Van Diemen's Land and New South Wales. She read on hungrily. **Mr Firth of Plymouth is desirous of obtaining immediately a large number of Emigrants belonging to the class of Mechanics, Handicraftsmen, Agricultural Labourers, Carpenters, Quarrymen, Masons, and Domestic Servants. The Emigrants must consist principally of married couples. Single women with their relatives are eligible and, in certain cases, single men. The age of persons accepted as Adults is to be not less than 14 nor, generally speaking, more than 35, but the latter rule will be relaxed in favour of the parents of children of a working age.** It went on to describe the colony in glowing terms. In large capitals, it read **NO CHARGE FOR CHILDREN.**

It didn't say when the ship was sailing, but it gave an address for Mr Firth. She probably didn't qualify, unless her unborn infant counted as a relative, but it wouldn't hurt to enquire. A foot kicked her belly. 'I haven't forgotten you. How could I when you keep kicking me?' She rubbed the spot gently with her hand. 'I will not let you grow up without your father. I promise.' She needed to deliver the child safely before she could travel, but if this ship sailed before she could travel, and there was a demand for domestic servants, there'd surely be other emigrant ships.

Next day, she took a carriage to Plymouth Hoe instead of her daily walk to the dockyards. The house in St Andrews Street was half-timbered, a survivor from an older time. Mr Firth seemed to have survived with it – not that he was half-timbered, at least, not as far as she could see through the open door.

He smiled broadly and invited her into his office. 'What can I do for you, Mrs…'

'Weston.' She shook the hand he extended and sat in the broad chair he indicated. 'Ella Weston. I want to emigrate to Van Diemen's Land.'

He dipped a quill pen into an ornate bronze inkwell. 'I'll need to take some details. Husband's name?'

'James Weston.'

'Age?'

'Twenty-one.'

'What's his trade?'

'Bricklayer, farm labourer.'

'Excellent. We need bricklayers. I need a character reference. His employer?'

She faltered. 'He works on the docks.'

The quill pen hovered. 'He's employed by the dockyard authority?'

'Not exactly.'

Mr Firth frowned. 'Are you trying to avoid telling me that he's

204

a convict?'

'Is that a problem?'

He laid the pen in its rest. 'I'm afraid wives of convicts aren't included in the government's free-passage scheme, unless the prisoner has earned the right by good conduct to have you join him. You can only travel on a convict ship.'

'I asked about sailing with him, but I was told I couldn't. I'm Jem's common-law wife. I don't have marriage papers.'

'Ah.' Mr Firth's face brightened. 'You're a single woman? You have relatives wishing to emigrate?'

'No, but I'm legally married to someone else.'

He frowned. 'But you're not travelling as a couple.'

'No.'

'Then you're not eligible.'

'I have to be with Jem. How else am I to get to Van Diemen's Land?'

'Do you have money?'

'Yes.'

Mr Firth smiled. 'Passage to the Australian colonies is about nineteen pounds, and most passenger ships leave from London. You wouldn't have to pay for the child.'

'I don't have that much. That's nearly two years' wages for a housemaid.'

'You could try for assisted passage. The government pay a bounty on single women of eight pounds, though whether they'd accept you, being still married.'

'I'd still have to find eleven pounds. I have less than half that.'

Mr Firth rose to his feet in one surprisingly graceful move, not as half-timbered as he looked. 'I'm afraid I can't help you, Mrs Weston.'

She walked back to the docks, aware she'd wasted precious money on a carriage and a new warm cloak. Her legs dragged and her back ached: she clasped her hands beneath her belly to support the weight. Jem might not leave Plymouth for months: if she worked once the baby was born, she could save the fare. The baby could come any day now, and maybe someone would need a wet nurse. She still had to find the cost of a midwife, and the rent on her room was due today.

The long shed that housed the ropewalk was ahead of her. A group of workers were taking a break outside. One of them spat tobacco at her feet. 'What have we got here, then? What's a pretty young thing like you doing out unchaperoned?'

She stood her ground. 'I'm looking for my husband. He's a prisoner here.'

'You want to forget him, lover.' The man eyed her as if summing up her wealth. 'Though if you've got money, I might be able to ask around for you.'

'I can pay.'

The man's eyed glittered and she realised her mistake too late. He took her by the arm and hustled her behind the ropewalk shed.

'Please, I'm with child… Don't hurt my baby.'

'It's your money I want, lover, not your body.' His hands tugged at her clothing.

She brought up her knee, aiming for his groin, but the man avoided her attack effortlessly. He pressed his body hard against her, squeezing her belly uncomfortably. She stifled a sob. 'Please, you're hurting me.'

'Then give me your money, or I'll do for you and your brat.'

Gasping for breath, she reached inside her bodice. The man grabbed at her purse and threw her to the ground. A blue jay feather floated to the ground beside her. Her fingers closed around it as the world went dark.

Ella came to groggily: she was lying on a heap of discarded ends of rope in an alley behind the rope walk. Sitting up carefully, she breathed in the stink of tar and rotting fish guts. Her new cloak was stained and torn. She placed a hand on her belly. Was her child unharmed? Her fingers unclenched to reveal a crushed jay feather. She stared at it, wondering why it was in her hand. Her heart thudded. Her money! The place beneath her bodice where she'd kept her sovereigns was empty.

It served her right for stealing them. They hadn't been hers to take, however angry she'd felt towards Josiah, and it had taken a thief to catch a thief. How stupid she'd been, coming here to look for Jem when she had no hope of finding him and no hope of following him. She'd put their baby at risk when the only thing Jem had asked of her was to look after it. She hadn't even the fare to go home to Bath and face her parents.

She eased herself to her feet and made her way back to her lodgings. Not having the fare to go home was the least of her worries. How would she pay her rent? How would she eat? She didn't even have the cost of a letter to Ralph, who would surely help her. Would she have to give birth alone in the gutter?

'Oh Jem, I'm sorry.' Despair streaked her cheeks. She would have to throw herself on the mercy of her landlord.

Back at her lodgings, she gathered together what wealth she had: the silver-backed mirror her mother had given her, a second-hand silver card case she'd bought having once naively thought to use it for her calling cards, and the cameo Harry had given her that had belonged to his grandmother. She stared at them hopelessly. Her landlord would be wanting his rent today, and this was all she had to offer him.

She descended the stairs and knocked at his door. It opened, and a tall gentleman stared down at her. She took a deep breath. 'Mr Jessop, I wonder if I might have a word with you?'

He smiled. 'Mrs Weston, come in. How can I help you?'

She refused the seat he offered and held out her mirror, cameo and card case. 'I was robbed today. My money was stolen. I can't pay for my room. This is all I have.'

He frowned. 'You want me to sell them for you?'

'If you could take them as rent...'

'They're not worth much. Maybe a week's rent.' He stared pointedly at her bulge. 'How will you pay after that with a baby at your breast? And how will you eat?'

She shook her head. 'I don't know. Maybe you could find it in your heart...'

'I can't afford to keep you and a baby, even if I wanted to. Don't you have family? What about your husband?'

'My family are in Bath. My husband – I came here looking for him.'

Mr Jessop's eyebrows rose in question. 'He left you, alone and pregnant?'

'He...' There was nothing to gain by lying. 'He's on *Stirling Castle*.'

'He's a sailor?' Her landlord's eyes opened wider. '*Stirling Castle*? Isn't that the prison hulk? He's a convict?'

She clutched at the back of a chair. Her head hurt where she'd hit it when she'd fallen, and a twinge in her stomach made her gasp. 'He was sentenced to be transported. I tried to find out about an assisted passage, so I can follow him, but convicts' wives don't qualify for help. And because I'm only his common-law wife, still married to someone else, I can't go with him on the convict ship like legal wives can.'

'From what I've heard, you wouldn't want to, and certainly not with a young baby. If you want my advice, go home to your family.'

'I don't have the fare.' Another twinge cramped her stomach. 'Anyway, I don't think I'm fit to travel.'

Mr Jessop handed her back her mirror and card case. 'You can stay tonight, but you'll need care while you birth. I can't afford to pay a midwife either.' He pursed his lips. 'Your best course of action is to throw yourself onto the mercy of the parish.'

'What do you mean?'

'There's a poorhouse in Stoke Damerel, not far from here. Duke Street. I suggest you approach them first thing in the morning. They'll look after you and your baby.'

'But the poorhouse...' Her mother had told her of her grandmother's last years. A shudder ran down her spine. 'My grandmother died in the poorhouse.'

'It's your best option, Mrs Weston, if you don't have a husband who will provide for you.'

She nodded. Much as she hated the idea of charity, she had a baby to consider, and she had a feeling she would birth early. 'It will only be for a while. I'll find work, eventually, and be independent again.' She flopped into the chair she'd refused and held her head in her hands. 'Am I ever going to be able to follow Jem? Am I stupid to even try?'

Mr Jessop patted her shoulder. 'Love is a powerful support, but your child will need you more than your man does.'

She palmed aside a tear. What chance was there of following her heart now?

Chapter Nineteen

By the time Ella reached the poorhouse next morning, the pains in her stomach were frequent. She bent double as another pain seared through her. The spasm receded, and she looked up at the grim, grey building with its single forbidding door and its rows of mean windows. What if they turned her away? She put down her bag of belongings, pulled the iron bell pull, and waited.

The door opened, and a severe-looking woman in a black dress and white apron looked her up and down. She sighed and shook her head. 'You young girls... You get yourself knocked up and then crawl to us for help.'

'I...' A contraction took away her breath. 'I'm...'

'In labour. So I see.' The woman's voice was as grey as the sky. 'Never trust a young man who promises you the world to get you to lie with him. They always let you down.' The woman grabbed the bag from her hand. 'The porter's just stepped out. Come on in, girl. Have you eaten today?'

'I'm not sure I could.'

'This way.' The woman led her down an echoing corridor, past doors that opened onto long rooms with straw and rags on the floor, and then pushed open a door and sat behind a desk. 'What's your name?'

'Ella Weston.'

'Sit. I'm Mrs Clement. I'm matron here.' Matron opened a leather-bound ledger, dipped a pen into her inkwell and made an entry in copperplate. 'Ella Weston. Age?'

'Nearly eighteen.'

'Parents alive?'

'They live in Bath. I had money, but it was stolen. I can't afford to travel home, and anyway…'

'You'd give birth on the coach by the look of you. How strong are the pains?'

Words were strangled by agony.

'Strong, then. How far apart?'

'Every few minutes. Not far.'

'We'll find you a bed, Ella, in the infirmary. I can assess you properly and take your parents' details later. I take it the father has left you?'

A bed, not straw. She nodded. It was easier than trying to explain. Wetness soaked her undergarments and pooled on the floor. 'Oh… I'm sorry.'

'Your waters have broken.' Mrs Clement sighed. 'Don't worry, dear, we'll look after you. You're not the first young girl to come to us pregnant, and you certainly won't be the last. Come on. This way.' Matron grabbed the bag and put it on a shelf. 'You can have this back when you leave. You'll be bathed and issued with regulation clothing once you've given birth. No point ruining another dress.'

A large dormitory held rows of iron bedsteads. Most were empty, but some held women who were obviously unwell. Their shaved heads suggested they'd had lice. She opened her mouth to enquire if this was a sanitary place to give birth and closed it again. Gift horses and teeth came to mind. She was lucky to have a bed, someone with her who knew what they were doing, and a place to birth in.

'This bed's free.' Mrs Clement pointed to a pallet with a flock mattress and a rag for a coverlet. 'Now, I have work to do. I'll send Biddy to tend you.'

A baby cried at the far end of the room, and a young, shaven-headed woman in drab grey clothing plucked it from its crib and suckled it. This was home for the foreseeable future, and she must

211

make the best of it. It was doubtless better than Jem was enduring.

***

Ella's pains continued through the long night. Around her, women slept or complained her moaning and cursing kept them awake. In the early hours, she felt a sudden need to push. 'Biddy!'

Her scream of terror brought Biddy, the night nurse, hurrying along the rows of beds. Biddy examined her briefly. 'I can see the head. Right mop of black hair.'

Black hair, like Jem. 'It's coming.'

'Don't push yet.'

'I have to.'

'Pant. Like this.' Biddy panted like a rabid dog. 'Next contraction, push like you're shoving a chimney sweep up the flue, Ella.'

She pushed.

'Again.'

Her strength deserted her. 'I can't.'

'Do it, girl. Think of someone you hate… Push them up the bloody flue.'

John fucking Cartwright and Harry. Reverend bloody Buchanan. Josiah pompous Barton. Joe wretched Upton. She garnered her rage and pushed. A huge slithering sense of relief was followed by a plaintive mewling. 'Is it…' She was too tired to finish the question.

'You have a son, Ella.'

She struggled to raise her head. 'A boy. Is he – is he all right?'

'Perfect.' Biddy laid a tightly wrapped bundle onto her chest.

'Hello, William.' She closed her arms around her son.

'William Weston.' Biddy smiled. 'It has a ring to it.' Her nurse cleaned her best she could and helped her sit up. 'See if he'll take a nipple.'

A woman in the next bed turned over, pulling her rag cover around her ears. 'For the love of God, can we get some bloody sleep now?'

A tiny nose pressed against her bare breast, the mouth searching. She offered her nipple and William began to suck, feebly at first and then stronger. She leaned forward to kiss his head and whispered softly. 'Your father will know you, William. I promise.'

***

Jem wiped black sweat from his brow with a black sleeve and stabbed the rounded point of his shovel into a mountain of black lumps in the bowels of a coal hulk, newly docked at Plymouth. Coal dust gritted his eyes and throat and rubbed sores where sweat stuck his shirt to his back. Somewhere above him, Cal and Nat off-loaded the filled sacks from the hulk onto carts waiting on the quay. He coughed and spat black phlegm onto the boards beneath his boots.

Stab, push, heave, twist, and dump. The motion had already become automatic, his muscles remembering the order of their flexing and stiffening, and, though he revelled in his returning strength of arm after six months languishing in a Northampton jail, the mindlessness of the repetitive task gave him too much time to think.

Where was Ella now? He hadn't seen her around the dock area for more than a month. Had she had the good sense to give up looking for him and go home to her mother? Part of him hoped so. He liked to imagine her in a nice house in Bath, under the protection of Josiah Barton, her mother's employer. Or she could have gone back to Yardley to be with his parents, but that he doubted with John and Harry Cartwright close by: that was surely a part of her life she'd want to forget. Would she forget him, too, given time? His heart wept at the thought, yet that was what he'd asked her to do.

Stab, push, heave, twist, and dump. A black-faced convict heaved the full sack onto his back and made for the ladder up onto deck as another prisoner took the man's place and held open the mouth of a new empty sack. Stab, push, heave, twist, and dump. Had Ella had their baby? Supposed she hadn't survived the birth? Childbirth was fraught with danger for both mother and baby. Or suppose the child had died, and she was grieving alone, or…

Stab, push, heave, twist, and dump. That way lay madness. He blinked away sweat, or was it a tear? No, he had no time for tears, no room in his heart for grief or regret. He was here because he was a murderer, an outcast to be punished. A spasm of coughing left him doubled. He straightened at a touch on his shoulder.

Nat's grimy forehead creased. 'Here, give us that shovel. You take the sack up on deck. Get a breath of air. It ain't raining, Jem.'

He nodded, grateful for the chance of air without getting drenched to the skin and having clothes that refused to dry. He couldn't remember a wetter summer. 'Thanks, Nat.' He held the mouth of the sack, as Nat filled it, and then hefted it over his shoulder and bent into his load like one of Ruddle's black Shire geldings. The taste of salt on his lips was a welcome relief from the taste of coal dust. He took a deep breath and coughed again. Spitting black from his lungs, he crossed the deck and walked the gang plank to the quay. The carrier's cart stood half-loaded, and the grey mare harnessed to it stood with her head hanging low, resting a hind leg and dozing. He thumped the sack onto the flatbed of the cart making her twitch one ear back towards him. As he turned, he saw Ella.

His heart skipped a beat, and he gripped the cart's flatbed to steady himself. She was talking to a dockworker, close to the dockyard offices. The man waved an all-encompassing arm, as if trying to impress on her the vastness of the docks, the impossibility of her search.

She turned towards him. She was wearing a striped dress and white apron and was carrying something in her arms. He leaned away from the cart to see better, and her eyes met his. He wanted to run and hide, not let her see him like this, but he couldn't make his feet move. She took a step towards him, and the man grabbed her arm, gesticulating. She shook it off and pointed. The man looked where she pointed and, shrugging his shoulders, turned back towards the office. Ella walked towards the coal hulk, back into his life.

'Ella…' He began to hobble towards her, his leg irons dragging at his feet. 'Ella…' He coughed.

She stopped a few paces from him. 'Jem. Dear Lord, Jem, what have they done to you?'

He must look as filthy as a coalman. 'I'm all right, Ella. It's the coal dust.' He couldn't take his eyes from the bundle she carried. 'Are you well? The baby… Is that…'

'This is William. This is our son.' She stepped closer and held out the bundle.

He was afraid to take him. 'I'm filthy.'

'This may be the only chance you get to hold your son, Jem. I promised him he'd know his father.' She pushed William into his coal-blackened arms, and he accepted her gift of trust and love. Tears coursed down his cheeks. 'He's beautiful.'

'He has your hair.'

'And your nose.' He smiled through his tears. 'Thank you.'

'What for?'

'For finding me. For giving me this memory.' He wiped a black sleeve across his mouth and planted a gentle kiss on his son's head. So soft. So heartbreakingly soft.

Ella moved closer, and he put one arm around her, cradling his son in the other. Her lips found his, and the world lurched beneath his feet.

'Miss, you shouldn't be here, and this is no place for a baby.' The voice was not unkind, though the face was stern. It was the guard in charge of the gang, the one who called him by his name

215

not his number. 'Back to work, Weston, before the gaffer sees you slacking.'

Ella pulled away. 'Just five minutes, please. He's not seen his baby before.'

'Sorry, missus. See that lot?' He pointed to the gang of convicts. 'They have families, too.'

Ella faced the guard. 'But Jem may never hold him again. Please...'

The guard's hand gripped his shoulder.

'He's right, Ella.' He was thankful Nat was down in the hold: he had a young wife and baby back in Yardley he'd never see again. He dug deep for every shred of courage he'd ever had and pushed William into Ella's arms. 'Go. Look after our son. Make a new life and forget me. I can't be the man you want me to be. I can't be a husband and father. This is my lot now. Go and find your own life.' He thumbed a tear from Ella's cheek, leaving a black smear. 'I'll never love anyone like I love you. Please, do this for me. I want to think of you safe and happy.'

The sun sparkled on unshed tears in Ella's eyes. 'But I love you, Jem.'

'Promise me, Ella.'

The guard gripped his shoulder harder. 'Back to work, Weston.'

**

Young William thrived despite the poor rations and insanitary conditions in the workhouse. At night, he slept on straw on the floor beside Ella: no beds but a patch of straw now she'd been discharged from the infirmary. During the day, she carried him in a sling fashioned from her old dress and held close to her chest. The monotonous movements of her work, crushing bones to make fertilizer or picking oakum from old ropes with a spike for hours on end each day, seemed to content him. Her hands were rough and sore and discoloured with dark pine tar, the flesh had dropped from her slight frame and, like Jem, she'd developed a cough from

216

dust, though she was breathing in powdered bones not coal.

She had little time to herself, and the only way she could leave the workhouse was to discharge herself and William in the morning and then apply for re-admittance at night: a risky strategy given the huge numbers of needy in Plymouth due to a general depression in employment and the relentlessly wet weather driving the homeless off the streets. The town seemed full of wounded soldiers, back from the wars, and agricultural workers laid off by the growing mechanisation of tasks that had once needed many hands. In the end, she'd been forced to give up all hope of seeing Jem again at the docks in favour of the security of having food and shelter for herself and William.

Pattie, the woman next to her, coughed and wiped her mouth with her sleeve. 'Damned dust gets right in your lungs, don't it, Ella?'

'It's no wonder there are so many ill with coughs and consumption.' She pummelled a cracked bone with a stone and a small cloud of dust rose.

Pattie spat as William snuffled and coughed in sympathy. 'It can't be good for the little un.'

'I'd leave if I could. I don't have the money. I can't find employment with a baby.'

'You could always leave him on the orphanage doorstep.'

She stared at the woman in shock. 'I couldn't!'

Pattie shrugged. 'Your choice. You want to stay here and be slave labour, you keep the little bastard.' She crunched another bone to shards and coughed again.

'I don't have a bloody choice. At least, here, I have food and somewhere to lay my head. At least, here, I'm safe from the men who'd take advantage of me. I'm prepared to work for that.'

'It still costs the parish to keep us. I heard they like to get rid of paupers to the colonies.'

She looked up sharply. 'How do you mean? What colonies?'

'New South Wales.'

'Van Diemen's Land?'

Pattie shrugged again. 'So they say.'

'Free passage?'

'We're paupers, aren't we?'

Her heart rose. She hadn't made Jem any promises, the guard had forced him back to work before she'd answered, but maybe she could keep her promise to William.

That evening, after supper, she knocked on the door to matron's office and waited.

'Come in.'

She entered and stood quietly while matron finished her writing.

Mrs Clement raised her head at last. 'What do you want?'

She cradled William, patting his back as if it were he who needed comfort. 'I understand the parish transports paupers to Van Diemen's Land. I want to volunteer to go.'

Matron frowned. 'Why would you want to do that?'

'My common-law husband is being transported there. I can't go with him because I'm not his legal wife. I'm still married to someone else, and I can't afford the fare.'

Mrs Clement rocked back in her chair and clasped her hands over her ample stomach. 'You left your husband? Were you born in Plymouth?'

'No, ma'am. I was born in Bath, but I've been living in Northamptonshire.'

'And where is your husband's parish?'

'Yardley Hastings, ma'am.'

'It would depend if the parish is prepared to stand the cost of transporting you.'

'This parish?'

'Why should we pay to keep you, or transport you, if your husband's parish will foot the bill?'

And why would the worthies of Yardley pay when she was no longer a burden to them?

'Is there someone we can contact in Yardley Hastings? Your husband, perhaps? Maybe he'll come and fetch you home? Or your parents. You said you have parents. Bath, wasn't it?'

'My father wouldn't want me, and I can't go back to Harry.'

Matron sighed and shook her head. 'You young girls don't have the sense you were born with. A name I can write to?'

Reverend Buchanan was respected in the parish. Would he approve her request, to get rid of her, once and for all? It was worth a try. 'Please write to Reverend Charles Buchanan at The Rectory, Yardley Hastings.'

Mrs Clement wrote down the address and nodded. 'I'll see what I can do. The colonies need housemaids, and you and your baby cost this parish dearly.'

And worked her like a slave. 'I can't pay for the postage.'

'No matter.' Matron waved her away. 'I'll let you know if I get a reply.'

'Thank you, ma'am.' She walked back to her patch of straw and rags with a lighter step. The reverend would persuade the men of the parish to send her to the colonies after Jem: the man had a heart, somewhere beneath his stiff exterior. 'You will know your father, William. I promise, if I have to beg, borrow, or steal to follow him.'

A sudden thought chilled her. Reverend Buchanan would inform Josiah Barton. If her mother discovered she was living in the poorhouse, she'd want Josiah to bring her home to Bath. They surely wouldn't force her to go back to Harry Cartwright, but could she persuade them to help her travel to the other side of the world? More to the point, as she was underage and had proved herself reckless, could she persuade them to help her to take William with her?

Chapter Twenty

Harry looked up at the sound of hooves in the yard. He grabbed the horse's bridle, forcing it to a halt. 'Reverend, have you heard something?'

'The parish has received a request for funding from the poorhouse in Stoke Damerel.'

'Where's that?'

'Plymouth. Ella's claiming pauper assistance to get passage to Van Diemen's Land under the Poor Laws.'

He had to admire his wife's perseverance. 'But you won't allow the parish to give it to her?'

'She isn't entitled, being your wife and your responsibility. But we know where she is, now, Harry.'

He wiped spittle from his lips. 'Looks like I have a long journey. She's in the poorhouse, you say? She'll be glad to come home.'

'You will respect her, Harry? It's no good you fetching her home if she's going to run off again. John, your father…'

'He knows to leave her be. She and I will be fine now Jem's gone. And she'll see sense now she's had a taste of poverty.'

The reverend let out a breath. 'I'm relieved. She's a handful, that one. I shall be glad to see her settled, to have fulfilled my duty towards her.'

He smiled. It would be good to have a woman in his bed again. 'And I mine, Reverend.'

'One more thing, Harry.'

'She's had the baby?'

'The poorhouse didn't mention a child, but I wrote to Josiah Barton to acquaint him with Ella's whereabouts. I doubt her mother will allow Ella to remain in the poorhouse. I suspect you would be advised to travel via Bath. Ella may be there by the time you arrive.'

'Thank you, Reverend. I shall make haste to Bath. I shan't come home without her.'

***

Ella knocked on matron's door, her heart thumping wildly. It had been barely a week since the letter had been sent. Surely, she wouldn't have an answer already?

'Come in.'

Was matron's voice surlier than usual, or softer? She turned the doorknob and pushed open the door. A broad-shouldered man sitting in front of matron's desk turned to face her. She stifled a gasp. 'Ralph?'

'Ella. God, what's happened to you?' He paused to take in her appearance and his eyes came to rest on the bundle in her arms.

She turned the child to face him. 'This is William, your nephew.'

Matron cleared her throat. 'Mr Barton has come to take you home, Ella. I've signed you out, so you're free to go.'

'But...'

Matron pointed to the battered bag Josiah had given her what seemed like a lifetime ago. 'Your belongings are all in there. Take your uniform to the washhouse before you leave.' Matron moved to the door and held it open, interview over. She shook Ralph's hand. 'Pleased to make your acquaintance, Mr Barton. Good luck, Ella.'

She had no choice but to do as matron instructed, and it would be ungrateful, irresponsible, to spurn Ralph's generous offer of help. She'd lost her place in the poorhouse: it would already have

222

been allocated to another unfortunate, for spaces were few, but what welcome awaited her in Bath? Ralph waited outside the dormitory while she changed out of her uniform and into a clean dress, and then he picked up her baggage and escorted her to a waiting carriage. He helped her onto the seat, holding William for her until she was comfortably settled. She took the child from him as he climbed in beside her.

'You're skin and bone, Ella.' Ralph's accusing tone hurt. 'Is this any way to bring a child into the world? Why didn't you come home? Are you trying to punish Father?'

'Punish Josiah? You think I'd put my son at risk for spite?' She cradled William protectively. The springs bounced as the carriage wheels bumped over cobbles. 'I just want him to know his father, Ralph. I don't want him growing up without one, like I did.'

'Father regrets denying you and your mother.' Ralph sighed. 'He had his reasons. He was protecting you both as much as himself. The scandal...'

She put a rough, tar-stained hand over Ralph's soft, beautifully manicured one. 'Thank you for caring, Ralph.'

He smiled. 'I came as soon as Father received the letter from Reverend Buchanan saying where you were. Why didn't you come home to have the baby, Ella? Father wasn't angry at you for taking the sovereigns. He felt he owed you that much and more.'

'I had no money for the fare home, not even enough for a letter. It was stolen on the docks, and anyway, this is where Jem is. I found him, Ralph. He's on the prison hulk out in the harbour. He works in a chain gang on the quay. I've seen him.'

'And you're prepared to live like a pauper to stay close to him?' Ralph frowned. 'The letter said you'd asked to be transported and wanted the parish to pay your fare under the poor-relief laws.'

'I'm going to follow him to Van Diemen's Land. You can't stop me.'

'Father showed me the reverend's letter. The parish won't pay,

223

Ella.'

'Why not? I thought they wanted rid of paupers.'

'You're Harry's wife. Even if he threw you out penniless for cuckolding him, the parish would consider you the common-law wife of a convict. There's been no such thing legally for decades, but the concept lives on, and it's a loophole they'd exploit. You're not entitled to poor-relief assistance for transportation. You can't go after him, Ella, and the sooner you accept that, the sooner you can make a life in Bath for yourself and your son.'

Her shoulders sagged as defeat welled up and engulfed her. 'I can't get assisted passage because I'm treated as the wife of a convict. I can't go on a convict ship because I'm still legally married to Harry. This was my last hope. The full fare for the passage is nineteen pounds, Ralph. Even if I can find employment, how am I ever going to save nineteen pounds?'

'I hope you never save it.' Ralph's tone was harsh. 'And don't look to me or Father for a loan. Neither of us will allow you to go to the other end of the world. Have you any idea how dangerous the journey would be? How many souls are lost to shipwrecks? What hardships and deprivations you'd face in the colonies? The whole idea is madness. How you can even consider taking a baby, I don't know.' Ralph threw up his hands in frustration. 'What kind of mother would risk her child's life for an ill-educated murderer?'

Her fingers clenched in the dirty rag that was William's blanket. 'But you don't know Jem like I do. He's loving and gentle. He may not be educated by your standards, but he knows all the trees of the Chase, all the birds, and the ways of the countryside. I love him, Ralph, and he loves me.'

'If he really loves you, he'd have told you to let him go.'

She brushed away tears. 'He did. He asked me to promise I'd make a life for myself here and forget him.'

Ralph put an arm around her, his expression softening. 'Then keep that promise, Ella. Make a life in Bath with a family that loves you. Be happy.'

224

She rested her head on his shoulder, safe and loved. She hadn't promised anything, except to William. She'd find a way, somehow.

***

Life on the prison hulk had settled into a hellish routine. Jem kept his head down, aware conduct reports were being kept on every prisoner. He worked hard from dawn to dusk and ate whatever was slopped into his bowl. He attended religious services twice a week in the hulk's chapel and had eventually learned to sleep through the asphyxiating nights of stench, pain, moaning, and rattling of chains, shackled to his bunk with the blue jay feather Ella had given him close to his heart. Still, Ella walked through his dreams beneath the green shade of Cold Oak Copse, and each night, the dream turned to nightmare – blood on his hands, blood he couldn't wash away.

He roused to the familiar sound of two bells and a pause followed by two more bells, the metallic smell of Joe Upton's blood mingling with the stench of the latrine buckets. It was six o'clock, and a shaft of light caught the dust motes dancing in the stagnant air as the doors to the hold were thrown open. Heavy boots thudded down the ladder and along the walkway.

'Time to get up, my pretties.' The man's voice was familiar, hated. 'Which of you pretty boys wants a stiff 'un up the arse this morning? Last one on deck is mine.'

Hundreds of feet hit the boards in unison. The guard's threat was not an idle one, as he'd almost discovered to his own cost. He waited at the side of his bunk for the man to unlock his shackles, his eyes downcast, trying to avoid notice.

The man paused at his side. 'How about you, pretty boy? Maybe, I'll keep you chained to your bunk. Maybe no bugger'll disturb us this time.'

'Please, let me go.'

'What was that? I didn't hear. Speak up, boy.'

225

'I need the latrines.' He raised his head and looked the guard in the eye. 'I've got the shits. I think I might be coming down with dysentery.'

The guard unlocked the shackle. 'Better get moving, then.'

'Thank you.' He relieved himself in a latrine bucket and followed the other dregs of stinking humanity up the ladder to the deck, bucket in hand. He waited in line to empty his bucket over the side. Out in the harbour, a three-masted ship came slowly into port. It reduced sail as it came closer, and a pilot tug approached it from the dock to tow it to its mooring. A small knot of men stood in the prow of the three-master, watching the quayside.

It was an old ship and looked as if it had seen better days. He struggled to read the name and smiled despite his predicament. HMS *Tortoise*, a fitting name judging by the speed it was coming in. Not a ship to outrun a clipper or a storm.

The slop that masqueraded as breakfast eaten, his gang for the day climbed down the rope ladder and into the rowing boat to go ashore. He gripped an oar. Two bodies in shrouds lay in the bottom of the boat: two more unfortunate souls who'd succumbed to the slow death aboard the hulk. They were far from the first to be rowed ashore to be buried on land.

'Pull.' His shoulder muscles tensed at the gang-master's voice. The boat moved away from the hulk. 'Pull!'

Pull, push down, lean forward, relax. Pull, push down, lean forward, relax. Pull.

They drew closer to shore. Would Ella be there with William? There was no sign of them, as there had been no sign since the day he'd held his son in his arms and told Ella to make a new life without her convict husband. How long ago was that? It had been high summer, a wet summer, the leaves a deep green on the trees on the hill beyond the port. Now the hillside held the bronzed tones of autumn, and the shadows hung lower in the trees and fingered darkly across the fields. The air was damp and the mists spoke of September.

'Pull!'

His muscles tightened across his back and shoulders. Six months of living in the hold of a convict hulk, and slaving in the docks, had taken its toll on him. He was leaner and prone to debilitating shits and coughing fits. He found it harder and harder to remember the oak trees of Cold Oak and the fields and streams of home. Harder and harder to see Ella's face in his mind. What did William look like now? What would Ella tell their son about the father he'd never know?

Murderer, outcast. The shroud of despair cloaked him in grief. He'd be better dead in the bottom of this boat than living in this hell.

'Ship oars!'

He lifted his oar from the water in time with the others, like marionettes whose floppy limbs were controlled with sticks, and held it away from the stonework as the rowing boat glided towards the quay alongside the ship *Tortoise*. He peered up at the bulk of the ship towering above him, the prow and masts rising gracefully to pierce the sky amid a spider's web of rigging. A row of gun ports ran along the ship's sides, and two cannons poked out their muzzles, one to port and one to starboard.

Once on the quayside, his gang was detailed to carry stores from the warehouses to re-provision *Tortoise*. He caught snatches of conversation between sailors and dock officials as he carried wooden boxes and hessian sacks back and forth.

'Captain Hood.' An official looked *Tortoise* up and down. 'She looks a bit beaten up. Where was your last port of call?'

'We left Chatham on the twelfth of last month after repairs and refitting.'

'What cargo are you carrying, Captain?'

'Orders are to proceed with convicts to Van Diemen's Land.'

The official nodded. 'A long trip. Where are you bound after that?'

'From Hobart we sail to Te Karo Bay, New Zealand, for kauri spars and timber for the admiralty.

'You're picking up off *Stirling Castle* before you leave?'

'Aye. Room for twenty. Convicts...' Captain Hood spat. 'All the old ship's fit for now. She was a proud ship once. The *Sir Edward Hughes* she was, a thousand tonnes with her guns. Belonged to the East India Company before she was given to the admiralty. Saw action in service, but she was built nigh on forty years since, and she's past her best. Bad luck to change a ship's name, I reckon.'

Convicts? They carried passengers on this old tub?

The official rubbed his beard. 'She's teak, then, if she was an East India?'

'Aye, teak. She's sound enough, despite her age, and well-found. She was a coal hulk at Milford for a while, and then a store hulk. Now this. Bloody convicts. Stores and coal are less trouble.'

'And more profitable.'

Captain Hood smiled. 'Now there's a bounty paid for each one disembarked alive, it can be quite a profitable venture, as long as not too many die on the way. Make that twenty-four. I'm sure we can find room.'

'You're welcome to them. Hobart can have them, all of them, may God forgive them.' The official glared at Jem, obviously annoyed at a convict loitering and listening.

The man's mocking voice echoing in his head, he stumbled on, carrying a box stamped *salted herring* on one shoulder,

Hobart? Was that in Van Diemen's Land? He supposed it must be if convicts were being shipped there. Somehow, while he was still in England, seeing his family again hadn't seemed impossible. But once they were on different shores... Would he be one of the twenty-four? Was Tortoise, a storm-battered old coal hulk, demoted to a convict ship, to be the vessel that took him away from his beloved Ella and William, forever?

228

Chapter Twenty-One

The pale stone façades of Bath hadn't changed, but Ella's circumstances had. She'd left an independent woman with hope in her heart and sovereigns in her purse. She returned penniless with an illegitimate babe in her arms: a charity case, a failure.

The carriage drew to a halt outside Josiah's home. Josiah's, not hers, despite her having been born and brought up here. Ralph helped her down and fetched her baggage from the rear of the carriage. She stood, cradling William in her arms, staring at the imposing front door and feeling like she had when she'd waited to be admitted to the poorhouse in Stoke Damerel. Whatever the welcome, the lodgings couldn't be as bad as the poorhouse.

The door flew open and her mother ran down the steps. 'Ella!' She flung her arms around her and then stepped back to look at her. 'For pity's sake, Ella. Just look at the state of you. Come inside. I'll get Annie to fill you a bath.' Her mother turned on her heel. 'Annie? Annie!'

She followed her mother up the steps and into the front hall with its polished tiles and mahogany chairs. Her mother hadn't asked about the baby. 'Mother, this is William, your grandson.'

Her mother sniffed. 'I'm sure he's beautiful, Ella, but he stinks to high heaven. I'll find something to make a napkin. Perhaps, we'd better bathe him first. Annie! Where is the girl?'

Annie arrived in a bustle of starched white apron. 'Yes, ma'am?'

'Take the big tin bath up to Ella's bedroom and heat water, lots of water. And fetch the little bath to the scullery for the baby and a fresh bar of Pears. We'll bathe him in there first. Ella will help you fetch soft water. Fill everything…' Annie hurried away and her mother turned back to her. 'Bring water to the kitchen and I'll heat it. If your father sees you both in this state, he'll have a fit. What Ralph must have thought when he found you, I dread to think. A poorhouse, of all places.'

Ralph found her drawing buckets of soft water from the tank that collected rainwater from the roof. He closed his hand over hers. 'I'll do this. You can carry the pails to the range.' He smiled down at her. 'You'll feel better after a bath and in clean clothes.' He squeezed her hand. 'I can't imagine what you've been through, Ella. Talk to Father. I'm sure he'll do what he can to help you. He does love you. And he'll love William, too.'

An hour later, she lay in the bath, a clean and fed William asleep in a wooden drawer on the rug at her side. The hot water was luxurious against her skin, the bar of fine, translucent soap smelt slightly of summer as she rubbed up a lather, a world away from the pine tar smell of oakum that impregnated her hands. She scrubbed at her fingers and nails, scrubbing the memory away. That part of her life was over, done with. She had a hard choice to make and luxuriating in hot water, with a contented child safe beside her, wasn't making it any easier.

***

'Close the door, Ella.'

Ella pushed the door closed and stood straight, staring ahead. She felt naked without William slung at her breast, but the child was in the kitchen being cooed over by Mother and Annie. She pushed her carefully brushed hair away from her eyes and took a deep breath as she stood before her father. 'Sir.'

'Sit down, child.'

'I'm not a child.'

Josiah straightened his pens, lining them up beside his ornate inkwell, and then steepled his fingers. 'No, I suppose you're not. You're a mother and, as such, have responsibilities. It's certainly time you grew up.'

230

'Yes, sir.'

'Could you bring yourself to call me Father, Ella?'

'No.'

'Josiah?'

'I could call you Josiah, sir.'

He smiled. 'Josiah will be fine. Ella, I know I should have recognised your birth right. I was a coward, but I've always tried to do right by you.'

'I shouldn't have taken the sovereigns. I'm sorry.'

He brushed the indiscretion away with a careless hand. 'It's not important. Petty cash…'

'I wanted to follow Jem.'

Josiah sighed. 'I know, Ella. I understand you love him, but going to Van Diemen's Land after him isn't a viable solution, even if you had the fare. And, while the poorhouse in Stoke Damerel tried to shift responsibility for the cost of keeping you to Yardley Hastings, Harry's parish, you deserted your husband. You're entitled to nothing under the poor law.'

'But I love Jem. Doesn't that count for anything?'

Josiah's expression hardened. 'Think about William if you won't think of yourself or your mother. Here, he can have a wonderful life. He can be part of the partnership, if he wants, when he's old enough. His whole future could be mapped out for him.' Her father's hands made an expansive gesture. 'He could be a man of influence, education, wealth. The world is at his feet. Will you deny him that by taking him to the ends of the earth to suffer all manner of danger, ignorance, and deprivation? And for what? A man who will probably have forgotten you already or at least knows you and William are lost to him? He'll probably marry the first girl he meets in Hobart, once he's free to do so. He is only your lover, after all. You are still married to Harry Cartwright.'

She sat on the upholstered chair before her father's desk and leant forward, her elbows on the polished mahogany, shaking her head in denial. 'About that, Josiah. Ralph said you may be able to get me a divorce.'

'A divorce?' Josiah's face reddened. 'Have you any idea what you're asking? The church regards divorce as an offence against God. You have no right to ask such a thing. In fact, you have no rights at all, in law. You belong to Harry. The man would be within his rights to drag you home, give you a beating, and lock you up for the rest of your life. You would have no legal redress.'

A tremble started deep inside her. 'He could do that?'

'There are only three possible reasons for divorce, and all are at the mercy of the church court, not a civil one. I have no influence in a church court.'

'So divorce is possible?'

Josiah nodded, donning his solicitor persona like a well-worn cloak. 'One way is if the marriage is nullified, through impotence, insanity, or potential incest. The church permits those divorcees to remarry, but any children would be illegitimate.'

Her and Ralph would have been incest. The thought horrified her. 'And the second?'

'In the case of adultery, sodomy, or physical violence… The petitioners wouldn't be allowed to remarry but would be permitted a separation.'

'So, even separated from Harry, I can't marry again? That isn't fair.'

'You are not even legally separated. Are you saying Harry was physically violent towards you or committed adultery?'

'No, but he forced himself on me.'

'You're his wife! You took vows to obey your husband. Procreation is his right and your duty.'

'Even if his father rapes me?'

'That was unfortunate.'

The memory of John's breath on her face rose bile in her throat. 'Unfortunate?'

'It wasn't Harry's fault. It's not grounds for divorce, even if Harry consented to the rape. You are his property to do with as he pleases.'

'Do I have no say?'

'It is possible to get a separation and then sue for adultery. If successful, Parliament sometimes eventually allows a divorce without making the children of the marriage illegitimate, but only the very wealthy and influential can afford such a strategy – members of the peerage. And if there was no adultery on Harry's part...' Josiah held out his hands palms upwards. 'There are no grounds for a divorce, Ella, and the church certainly wouldn't consider your plea. You deserted your husband. You are the one in the wrong.'

'And I have no rights?'

Her father shook his head. 'Why would you need rights? You're a woman. Your pretty little brain isn't equipped to deal with important decisions. You need the protection and support of a man, a husband. This is why, in the eyes of the law, everything you have, not that you have much, belongs to Harry. Even the allowance I've given you in the past. It's for your own good. If you and he had children, even they would belong to him and not you.'

'Then thank God we didn't.'

'Indeed, but it remains that you have and deserve the same legal rights as a lunatic, an idiot, an outlaw, or a child... In fact, you are an idiot and a child, and your recent behaviour only proves that. It further proves, in my mind, that you're not fit to make life-changing decisions, especially on behalf of your child.'

And there it was, the thing she'd been afraid of as a mere woman, a lower form of life, a second-class citizen. Whatever decisions she was allowed to make for herself, she wouldn't be allowed to make for William. She couldn't go back to Harry, or stay in Bath, while Jem spent the rest of his life in a far country, and she wouldn't leave without her son.

***

Jem stood in line, on the deck of *Stirling Castle*, with a large group of prisoners all dressed in clean clothes and told to look their best. He stood as straight as his sore back would allow, fit to drop now they'd finished loading *Tortoise* with stores and barter goods. A portly man, wearing a waistcoat and sporting a gold watch chain, strode along the line examining each man in a perfunctory fashion and pulling a few out of the line. The hulk's surgeon pointed out some, saying they were fit to travel, even though those men had been in the hospital quarters for a week. Were they trying to get rid of problem convicts?

The portly man waved a sick man aside. 'He looks scrofulous. He wouldn't live to see the Cape.'

The prisoner, seeing his chance of getting off the hulk disappearing, grabbed the man's arm. 'No, sir. I got a cough, that's all, and that's the truth of it.'

The portly man shook off the offending hand and moved on, stopping in front of Cal. 'This man is free from cholera, dysentery, and typhus? You have his medical certificate?'

'I'm waiting for the shore authorities to release them.'

'He looks healthy to me. Step forward, young man.'

Cal took a stride forward. The portly man pulled Nat from the line, and then stopped in front of him, Jem Weston. 'Is this man clean and of good behaviour?'

The hulk surgeon nodded. 'His records show he's had no serious illness and his conduct is good.'

'Step forward.' The portly man did a quick head count and turned to the hulk surgeon. 'I can embark twenty-four. I'm disembarking three who are too ill to travel farther. They'll need berths in a hospital. I need four more. Which do you suggest?'

Together the two men continued along the line, examining the prisoners as if they were prime beef and pulling out four more. Twenty-four. That was the number to be embarked. Were they taking the lifers or the fittest?

A guard faced the twenty-four men. 'Quick march. Come on. Move your lazy arses.'

Cal managed a smile. 'At least we're all going together, Jem.'

He smiled back. 'That's worth a lot, Cal.' He followed Cal and Nat across the deck and down the rope ladder to the waiting rowboats. On the quay, a gangplank sloped up to the deck of *Tortoise*. This was it, then: he was finally setting sail for the colonies. He looked back at the bronzed hill, golden in the evening light, and the bustling quay beneath it, pain constricting his heart. He'd never see Ella again, never press his lips to William's soft mass of black hair, or hold Ella in his arms.

He swallowed tears. In front of him, Nat wiped a hand across his face. Behind him, Cal sniffed. They wouldn't be here, none of them, but for Joe Upton: Joe had started this back in thirty-seven, with his false accusations against Nat, and made matters worse getting him that huge fine the year before last. At least he'd never have to pay that now. He swore beneath his breath. 'Damn your poisonous soul to hell, Joe Upton.'

On deck, they formed an orderly queue, and their leg irons were removed by a guard and replaced with those to be worn on *Tortoise*. A bundle of clothes was pushed into his arms. 'Change into these. Surgeon Brownrigg will see you later. Below decks.' The man pointed to where Nat was already headed.

He followed, his legs accustoming to the different weight of the shackles. Cal's breathing was loud in his ears. Open treads led down into darkness. Another ship, another prison, this one low-roofed, between decks: another country, another prison, another guard. This was his life and nothing was going to change.

Bare inches above his head, the door to the prison hold slammed shut. He paused for his eyes to accustom themselves to

235

the gloom. Nat, who was taller, bent so his head didn't crack on the beams. Open vents spilled light that illuminated dour faces and let in a breath of salt air. Berths lined the ship's sides in two tiers and made messes, separated by planks, where eight men could sit around a table. Towards the bows of the ship, the ceiling lowered even more, and iron bars made a cage behind which a man crouched, wild eyed. The beams above the central space had iron hooks to string hammocks: some were already hung up and bulging with prone bodies. There were the usual moans and groans of men in despair and pain, and the hold stank of unwashed bodies and the privies, but it was nothing like as stuffy or oppressive as the hulk had been. Maybe, this wouldn't be so bad.

A burly man stood lazily to confront them, his face hard, aggressive, and his eyes glinting in the light from the vents. 'The bunks are nearly all taken. You young 'uns get the hammocks.'

He wasn't about to argue the point. He smiled slowly. 'That's fine by us.'

The man smirked. 'You ever used a hammock?'

'No.'

The man laughed, a deep guttural belly laugh. 'Should be fun, boys. These wet behind the ears youngsters ain't never used a hammock before.'

A smaller man sided with the bully. 'Yep, should be fun, Knocker.'

Knocker smiled, showing a black gap where his two front teeth should be. Had he earned his name fighting?

Nat straightened. 'We ain't looking for trouble, mister. And you don't want to get the wrong side of Jem, here. I like the idea of a hammock. Jem, you can have the bunk, if you want.'

'Like I said, fine by me.' This would be a long and difficult journey as the butt end of jokes or, worse, the butt end for a pervert. 'I'm Jem Weston. I ain't no pushover, Knocker. I bashed a man's brains out.' He nodded to his friends. 'That there's Cal and

236

that's Nat. Nat shot a man. Cal, too, and broke a gunstock over his head.' He lowered his voice, and spoke slowly, in the hope he sounded dangerous to cross. 'We're here because we murdered a man. We ain't none of us averse to making it two.'

***

Ella walked back to the house she shared with her parents, her new dress wrapped in a brown paper package. Her father's generosity hadn't gone unappreciated and neither had her mother's offer to mind William while she went for her final fitting. She was still thin, but her waist had thickened slightly since the seamstress had made her wedding dress, and the new dress she'd made for her had needed a little alteration. Now, it was perfect.

The walk into town had made a welcome distraction. Her determination to follow Jem hadn't diminished, but she needed rest, good food, and clothes before she made the attempt. She still had no idea how she was going to arrange it: the nineteen-pounds fare was as far from materialising as it had always been, bar stealing it, for Ralph had made his feelings on her emigration clear, and her father made sure he kept the key to his cash box on his person at all times.

She rang the front doorbell and waited. Annie opened the door a fraction and then threw it back, her face animated. 'Miss Ella, great news. Your husband's here.'

'Jem's here? He's been released? Where is he?'

'He's with Mr Josiah, in his study. I'm so happy for you.'

She thrust her package into Annie's arms and pushed past her, not daring to hope. Suppose Jem had escaped... Could they hide him? Would her father aid a criminal for her sake? She pushed open the door without knocking.

'Jem!'

'Ella...'

Her heart thudded in her throat. Her skin went cold. The man turning towards her wasn't Jem. 'Harry?'

'I had a visit from Reverend Buchanan. He said you'd be here with your mother. Mr Barton, here, was kind enough to let me wait for you to return. We need to talk, Ella.'

Harry wouldn't know Josiah was her father. 'Anything you wish to say to me you can say in front of Mr Barton.'

'As you wish. I understand from Mr Barton that you have a child.'

She nodded. 'I have a son, William. He's none of your concern.'

'I'm your husband, Ella. Of course, he's my concern. How old is he?'

'He was born at midsummer.'

'Is he mine?'

'No, Harry. He's Jem's child.'

'I don't believe you. Where was his birth registered?'

'I don't think it was. Stoke Damerel spike-house didn't bother with that sort of thing.'

'Spike-house?'

'It's what we were known as, spikes, because of picking oakum with a spike.'

Harry waved her explanation aside. 'I've no idea what you're talking about. So, you can't prove the child's date of birth?'

'No, but he's not yours, Harry, or your father's. Believe me.'

Harry frowned, his face dark. 'The reverend always said you were a wanton. Couldn't get enough of it, could you?'

Her hand connected with Harry's cheek leaving a livid red mark. 'How dare you? Your father raped me, Harry, and I'm not the first. Ask your mother. He couldn't bear for you to have a woman when he didn't.'

Harry fingered his cheek, his eyes wide. He seemed to be

238

holding his temper with some difficulty. 'What my father did wasn't my fault. I've treated you as any man would treat his wife, and now you're trying to keep my son from me, to spite me because of what Father did.'

She looked at her father in desperation. 'Josiah, tell him William isn't his.'

Josiah frowned and paced the room. 'Ella, I'm sorry, but young William might be lawfully considered to be Harry's. You hadn't been separated from him for very long when you consummated your relationship with young James. The child's paternity has to be disputable.'

She froze. 'He's Jem's child, not Harry's. There is no dispute.'

'Harry disputes it and without a birth certificate to prove his age...'

'But...'

'Harry is your husband. The child is legally his.'

She turned on Josiah in fury. 'You mean he could take William? Is that what you're saying?'

'He's within his rights.'

Harry's gloating smile told her everything. He didn't care about William. He was out for revenge. She sank onto a chair. 'But you wouldn't take him from his mother, Harry. You wouldn't do that.'

'William comes home to Yardley with me. I'm sure you'll want to come with him, after everything you've been through. Mother and Father will be pleased to welcome you home.'

Her vision swam. This couldn't be happening. She turned to her father, her legs giving away, her voice weak. 'Please, Josiah, if you love me, help me. I can't go back there.'

Josiah looked lost. 'It's only your word against Mr Cartwright's, Ella, and Harry has promised me you'll be safe. You brought no charge at the time, and even if you had, you wouldn't be the first young woman to regret her position after her wedding

239

night. Who would a court believe? You, when it's clear you didn't marry Harry for love and were maybe looking for a way out of your marriage-bed duties, or an upright and respected member of the community like John?'

'Don't let him take my baby.'

Her father turned away and stared out of the window, his back ramrod straight. 'I can't go against the law, Ella. I'm sorry. My –'

'Reputation?' She clenched her fists. 'I don't care about your reputation! This is my son you're giving away.'

'Harry's your husband, Ella, as I keep reminding you. You promised to obey him. I suggest you keep that promise. Jem wanted you to forget him and get on with your life. This is your chance. Take it and be grateful for a second chance and someone to look after you both. I'm satisfied that you'll be treated with respect. Harry's made a magnanimous gesture, which I applaud, considering William may not be his blood. I cannot, will not, come between husband and wife.'

Harry smiled. 'Annie has taken my bag up to your room. We'll leave in the morning. Now, I'd like to see my son.'

She fled to the kitchen and scooped William from his crib. 'Mother, Harry's to take me and William to Yardley. I can't go back there. I need to follow Jem. What am I to do?' She cradled William against her breast, her tears wetting his black hair, so like Jem's. 'Please, God, don't let me lose my baby. For pity's sake, Mother, what am I to do?'

Chapter Twenty-Two

The door opened. Ella held her son protectively. Mother had gone to speak to Josiah on her behalf, and she was alone in the kitchen. She cringed as Harry crossed the room towards her.

He looked down at William. 'So, this is young Harry.'

'His name is William.'

'Not James?'

'No.' James was his second name, but Harry didn't need to know that.

'If Jem Weston was the father, you'd have called him James. That proves you can't be sure whose he is.'

'He has Jem's colouring.'

'That proves nothing. My mother had dark hair before she went grey.' He smiled at the baby. 'William's a strong name. 'William Harold. I like it. We'll have him baptised as soon as the reverend has time. You can't do these things too soon.'

It was true: too many babies died in their first year. She held William tighter. He was all she had left of Jem. 'He's not yours, Harry. Please, you don't need to take my son.'

He smiled at her: a long, slow, vindictive smile. 'No, but I can. You made me look a fool, running off after our wedding night. If I have William, I have you, and then I can get a son on you I'm sure is mine. I can tell people you came crawling back when you realised you were carrying my son, and I forgave you. As Mr Barton says, very magnanimous of me under the circumstances, you running off with a murderer, but a father will do anything for his son.'

She bridled. 'Like yours does for you? Your father raped me.

Doesn't that mean anything to you?'

'We've always shared our women. I confess I was a bit put out he didn't ask me before he had you, you being my bride. As long as you're a dutiful wife, I shan't let him have you again. Fail to give me sons' – Harry's tiny lapse didn't fool her; he knew William was Jem's – 'More sons, and...'

She shook her head in disbelief. 'You're an evil man, Harry Cartwright. I wish I'd killed your father with that colander. Maybe I'd be in a kinder prison now than the one you have in mind for me.'

'Women should know their place. You'll soon learn yours. Now give me my son.'

He stepped forward and wrenched William from her. 'I need hot water for a wash and shave. Bring it upstairs now. I'll take William to our room.' He turned and left, leaving her arms bereft.

Defeat weighed her heart. She had no option but to obey Harry. She had no means to support herself and her son independently. Josiah had already made his position clear, and she doubted there was anything her mother could say that would change his stance. The law was the law, and Josiah's reputation rested upon being seen to be upholding it. She heated water in a pan and carried it up two flights of stairs to her – their – room. She wiped tears from her eyes with the back of her hand and pushed open the door to her bedroom. Harry lay naked on her bed.

Her heart lurched. 'Where's William?'

'In the old nursery, in the attic.' He smiled and fingered a small key on a thong around his neck.

'That's the key to the attic.'

'It will never leave me while we're in Bath. Now come here.'

'I hate you.'

'Be nice, Ella, and William will be safe and cared for. Disobey me and... There are plenty of childless couples wanting children.

242

A strong young lad like William would fetch good money.'

Her fingers clenched round the handle of the pan. 'You wouldn't. Not even you...'

'Try me. Now put that pan down and do your duty. Pleasure me the way a wife should.'

Throwing it at him would achieve nothing. She put the pan down on the marble-topped table by the window. Her feet occupied her attention as she removed her clothing, anything to avoid looking at Harry's erection. She sat on the edge of the bed, trembling, waiting for him to force her down beside him.

He seemed to read her mind. 'No. I want you willing.' He lay back against her pillows, his arms crossed above his head. 'Ride me like you'd ride a stallion, Ella.'

Tears blurred her vision. Jem was lost to her: damn him for bringing her to this. She knelt astride Harry and lowered herself onto his member. Her body betrayed her, her muscles clenching as she rode him, the pace quickening as he bucked and writhed beneath her, driving her onwards, no whip needed, to a frenzy of need. They climaxed as one, and she collapsed panting against him, sobs choking her.

Harry's fingers stroked her hair. 'See, that wasn't so bad, was it?'

She couldn't speak. Harry's chest was wet with her tears. She'd betrayed the man she loved with a man she detested, for her own profit, and had derived comfort from the act. During those moments of passion, her need for physical contact had been sated, the pain of losing Jem briefly forgotten. The fact that she'd had no choice if she was to keep her son didn't figure; part of her had needed it, enjoyed it almost. Reverend Buchanan had been right. She was wanton and prey to her own base lusts: a whore, plain and simple. She no longer deserved Jem's love. And if she couldn't have Jem, then any man could have her.

***

243

Ella followed Harry into the farmhouse. He'd made a point of ensuring everything she'd done was being done willingly, as if she had a choice in the matter. Harry's mother, Jane Cartwright, took William from Ella's arms. Having travelled from dawn to dusk for two days, and walked the length of Howcut Lane from the turnpike carrying William, she no longer had the energy to fight her future.

Harry dumped their bags on the passage floor. 'What do you think of your grandson, Mother?'

Jane Cartwright shot her a doubtful look. 'He has my colouring, don't you think, Ella?'

She held out her arms for her son. 'He needs feeding. I'll take him upstairs.'

Jane released him with obvious unwillingness. 'You must both be tired. I'll bring you up a cup of tea, Ella. Harry, take up the bags.'

She tried not to show her surprise. Jane was waiting on her? She must look as exhausted as she felt. She climbed the stairs and sank onto a low chair in her and Harry's room. Loosening her clothing, she exposed a breast and let William find a nipple. She stroked his head, absently, as she contemplated their future.

Mother had promised that Josiah would write to John Cartwright and Reverend Buchanan in the strongest possible terms. Would it make a difference to how she was treated? Maybe Jane's softer demeanour meant she would prove to be an ally in this awful house. Maybe John would leave her alone. Maybe... She rubbed her forehead. Maybe Christmas would come at Easter: it would be as likely.

Harry arrived with the bags. He left them on the floor and sat down on the bed. 'This is all I want from you, Ella. To be an obedient wife and raise our children. It could be a good life.'

'You know it isn't what I want. I don't love you.'

'I don't need your love, just your obedience. Do I have it?'

'Yes.'

244

'Good. These are my rules. You never leave this house with William unless accompanied by me, Mother, or Father. You work for your keep. I have my name on William's birth certificate and no-one knows he may be Jem's. You satisfy my needs and carry out my instructions. In return, you and the child are fed and housed, and William will have an equal share of any inheritance with his future siblings. Agreed?'

She nodded tiredly. 'Agreed.'

'Disobey me, and you'll never see William again.'

She would die for her son. What Harry asked was no more than she'd promised when she married him. Her heart would always belong to Jem, but she no longer cared who used her body if it profited her and William. Maybe, if she bided her time, he'd grow complacent, and she'd find some way out of this hell.

There was a knock on the door. 'Can I come in?'

'Mother.' Harry opened the door. He took the cup from his mother's hand. 'Ella's tired. I think she should rest.' With that he closed the door and put the cup on a small table by the bed. 'I'll be back later. I want you rested and ready for a ride.'

She was too tired to think straight. 'We're going somewhere? What about William?'

He put a hand on her thigh. 'Not that sort of ride.'

Her cheeks flushed with heat, and something wicked stirred deep inside her.

***

Sunday, sunshine: the church bells rang, summoning the faithful to prayer. St Andrew's would be full. Green, gold, and blue light painted the white christening gown William wore and fell on the tiles on which Ella had knelt when she'd married Harry. One hand went to the blue jay feather she still kept close to her heart, and the other arm cradled her son. Did Jem keep his feather close to his heart?

The Cartwrights hurried to their accustomed pew, latecomers due to William soiling himself just as they were about to leave the farm. Prayers were said and hymns sung: she joined in half-heartedly. Reverend Buchanan beckoned, and Harry put a hand beneath her elbow, helping her to her feet. Together, they walked towards the south aisle of the church, all eyes on them. She supposed they made a handsome couple, happy on the day of their son's baptism. No-one knew the truth of why she was here, except Harry. A gasp at her side made her look round.

'Ella?' Jem's mother looked up, her expression questioning. Beyond her sat a young man.

'Jem?' She gripped the pew end with a shaking hand.

The man smiled Jem's smile. 'I'm Jem's brother, Tom.'

Charlotte's eyes fixed on the baby in her arms. 'Is that…'

She shook her head, hoping Charlotte would pick up on the warning, and quickened her step beside Harry. Her head spun: seeing Tom, so like Jem, had unnerved her.

At the side of the plain, octagonal font, Reverend Buchanan waited, his face composed and his hands clasped before him. He smiled benignly as she drew closer. He took William from her arms and addressed the packed church. 'It is with great pleasure that I welcome this child to God's house. Let us pray.'

She bowed her head. Her prayers hadn't yet been answered.

'Heavenly Father, by the power of your Holy Spirit you give your faithful people new life in the water of baptism. Guide and strengthen us by the same Spirit that we who are born again may serve you in faith, and love, and grow into the full stature of your Son, Jesus Christ, who is alive and reigns with you in the unity of the Holy Spirit now and forever.'

Where was Jem now? Did he pray to God and have his prayers unanswered? Or was this what he prayed for? A father for William. He'd have wanted her to be happy. She joined in the refrain without really listening to the words. 'Amen.'

'People of God, will you welcome this child and uphold him in his new life in Christ?'

Murmurs spilt from the lips of the faithful. 'With the help of God, we will.'

William snuffled restlessly. Reverend Buchanan made the sign of the cross on the baby's forehead. 'William Harold Cartwright, God claims you for his own. Receive the sign of his cross.'

She bit her tongue. William James Weston. His name was William James Weston. No matter what Harry did or claimed, her child would always be Jem's son.

The reverend droned on. 'May almighty God deliver you from the powers of darkness, restore in you the image of his glory, and lead you in the light and obedience of Christ.'

Please, almighty God, deliver Jem from darkness. She knew what it was to spend hours picking oakum, but what must it be like, cooped up in the hold of *Stirling Castle*, if he was still on the hulk.

Reverend Buchanan dipped a small bowl in the sanctified water in the font. He held the bowl over William's head. 'William Harold...'

William James... His name's William James.

'Cartwright.' Harry's voice, claiming Jem's son publicly.

Reverend Buchanan glanced at Harry and continued. 'I baptise you in the name of the Father, and of the Son, and of the Holy Spirit. May God, who has received you by baptism into his Church, pour upon you the riches of his grace, that within the company of Christ's pilgrim people you may daily be renewed by his anointing Spirit and come to the inheritance of the saints in glory.'

She gulped back tears. God knew who William was. At least his immortal soul was safe in his saviour. 'Amen.'

It was done. Her son was a Cartwright in the eyes of the world,

247

and now she must protect him against their indifference to honest decency and kindness the best she could. When William was old enough, she'd tell him how she'd failed in her promise to him, and about his father, and how much he'd loved them both. Maybe, one day, if she couldn't make the journey, William would find his own way to Jem and keep her promise.

Outside in the fresh air and sunlight, she blinked through blurred eyes. A touch on her shoulder made her turn.

'We need to talk.' Charlotte Weston pushed something into her hand. A letter?

She concealed it beneath William's shawl. 'I'll try to get away.' She moved on quickly before Harry and the Cartwrights, who were talking to the reverend, noticed. She joined their group. 'That was a lovely service, Reverend.'

'It's my pleasure, Ella. I'm glad to see you back where you belong. Confessing your sins is good for the soul. Pray to God for forgiveness.'

'I do, sir. Every day. Thank you for your kindness.'

He beamed at her, obviously pleased to welcome an errant ewe back to the fold. He didn't know she'd sold herself, body and soul, to the devil.

Chapter Twenty-Three

Ella sat on the privy and opened the letter Charlotte had passed her.

Dear Ma and Dad,

I hope you don't think too badly of me. I ain't bin much of a son to you, and that ain't no bugger's fault but mine. Anyhow, I'm in Plymouth, and will be for a week or more. I'm on a ship called HMS Tortoise, docked in Plymouth Dock, and due to sail around the twenty-third of this month according to them as knows.

Thing is, relatives are allowed aboard to say goodbye. I ain't never going to see you again, Ma, or my darling Ella. It would mean a lot to me to see you all one more time afore I sail, but I know it ain't likely you'll be able to make the journey. I have a baby son, Ella brought him to see me, but I don't know where they are now. Whether they're still in Plymouth, or if she's gone to her parents in Bath. I don't know their address, but the reverend does. If he could get a message to her, I'd be grateful.

Your grandson is called William and he looks like you, Ma. I wish you could know him.

I shan't never forget you. I'll write when I can but letters will take months to arrive so don't worry if you don't hear for a while.

Your loving son.

James. Convict no. 42,363

She reread the letter, tracing the words with her fingers, trying to connect to Jem. She counted on her fingers. In four days' time, Thursday, Jem would be gone. The Westons had no chance of getting there any more than she had.

She pushed the letter inside her bodice, next to the jay feather, biting her lower lip as a plan came to mind. Tonight, she'd pleasure Harry like never before, get him in a good mood, make him dough in her hands, but, first, she had to work on his parents.

William was in her and Harry's room: he should sleep for an hour or more. Jane was visiting friends at Roundhay Farm. She had time to find John before Harry finished the afternoon milking.

He was sweeping the barn. She took a deep breath. 'John. I've had a letter. Reverend Buchanan passed it to me after church. It's from Mr Barton. My mother's ill.' She wiped a non-existent tear from her eye. 'She's not expected to live. I have to go and see her, and I have no money for the fare.'

John looked her up and down. 'What do you expect me to do about it?'

'I thought you might speak to Harry. Make him see I have to go to her. Just for a few days. I'll come back, I promise.'

He leaned on his broom. 'What's it worth?' His eyes followed the curve of her hip and the swell of her breasts. 'You're a fine woman, Ella. I thought that the first time I saw you. You know me hearing you and Harry fucking in the next room drives me wild.'

She'd promised herself she'd do whatever it took to see Jem one more time. That any man could have her. Could she really do this? It would only be the once. Just once to see her beloved for the last time. She looked up to the hayloft and then lowered her eyes provocatively. 'Harry's busy. Jane's out.'

'You're offering?' He raised an eyebrow. 'I promised Jane and Harry I wouldn't force you again but if you're offering.'

She smiled and shot his own question back at him. 'What's it worth?'

'I'll see you get to your mother's.' John's hand went to his belt. 'Get on up there, girl, and be quick about it.'

She climbed the ladder to the loft ahead of him and lay back on a pile of hay. It tickled her neck and ears. She kicked off her shoes, removed her bloomers, and pulled him down on top of her before her courage failed her.

He wrenched at his trousers and pushed up her skirt. 'You're eager all of a sudden.'

The devil inside urged her on. She was doing this for her fare, but also she needed to lose herself again, hurt herself, anything to dull the pain in her heart. She ran her tongue across his ear. 'I need a real man, John.'

His erection pressed against her thigh. Her hand caressed its hard, silken length and guided it, as she'd seen Harry guiding the bull's erection. He plunged into her, and she bucked beneath him, the way Harry had bucked, thrusting her hips in time to his and moaning with pent-up desire. 'More, John. More. Harder.'

John responded with a ferocity that took her breath away. Experienced, brutal, he gave her what she wanted, needed, what she deserved, and she responded with abandon. 'Ella... Oh God, Ella!' He exploded inside her, a shared orgasm that left him limp and her breathless. He sank onto her breasts. 'Oh, Ella... sweetheart.'

She had him. He was hers, and now she knew what a man wanted, she knew how to capture Harry and make him as weak and pliable. 'You'll speak to Harry?'

He nodded and caught at a breath. 'Tonight, come here when Harry's asleep?'

'You'll have the money? I'll need enough for the fare to Bath and back.'

'You shall have it. You know he won't let you take William.'

'But he's not weaned. I have to take him.'

'William stays here. Harry will insist upon it. We'll find a wet nurse.'

Let someone else suckle her child? She'd promised herself she'd do anything. 'Jane will love having him to herself for a few days.'

251

'I'll persuade her if she objects.'

She needed Jane on her side too. 'She's a good woman, and she asks for so little for herself. She deserves more.'

'I'll buy her something nice. That always puts her in a good mood.'

Guilt gifts, no doubt, given what Jane had told her about his illegitimate children.

He swallowed. 'You *will* come tonight, Ella?'

'I'll need money for overnight lodgings, as well, and food on the journey. It will take two days there and two days back, if not more.'

'You shall have as much as you need. Just say how much. Tell me you'll come.'

She smiled at his helpless, little-boy plea, relishing her newfound power: the devil's bride. Once she had the fare, John would die before she gave him her body again. 'I can't wait.'

***

Ella laughed. It had been so easy. Harry even believed she was growing to love him, she'd pleasured him so enthusiastically that afternoon, after milking. She'd gone straight from the hayloft to Harry's bed, undressing him from his work clothes in her haste to practice what she'd learned from John. At last, in the throes of orgasm, she'd found moments of blessed relief from the pain of losing Jem.

Harry hadn't changed his mind about letting her take William out on her own, but he'd allowed her to walk to the village with a letter for Josiah to say she was leaving on the next stagecoach, though whether the letter would arrive before she did was uncertain. Harry had thought the stiffness in her walk was down to him, and had teased her. She'd smiled, dutifully, praised his lovemaking, and wondered how sore she'd feel if she was forced to perform all over again with John before she left.

She deposited the letter, neatly affixed with a new penny-black stamp, at the post cottage to be passed on to the Royal Mail coach. It wasn't addressed to Mr Barton, as Harry thought, but to Mr J. Weston, Convict no. 42,363, HMS *Tortoise*, Plymouth Dock. Hopefully, he would get it before he left England forever.

John hadn't yet produced the money he'd promised her, but she didn't doubt he'd provide it for fear she'd withhold her favours or cry rape again to Jane and Harry. With luck, she and Charlotte would get to say their farewells to Jem.

She glanced around before knocking on Charlotte's door. It opened wide. 'I don't have long, Charlotte. Can I come in?'

'You read the letter?'

'I hope to have the fare for both of us to go to Plymouth.'

'But… Both of us? Where did you get that sort of money?'

'Best you don't know. Will you come with me?'

'Like a shot. God bless you, Ella.'

'Meet me up on the turnpike. We need to find a cart or carrier going to Bedford this evening, if we're to catch the morning stage.'

'Will we get there in time? To Plymouth, I mean.'

'I shall never forgive myself if we don't try, Charlotte.'

'I'll pack a bag and be there within the hour, Ella.'

She nodded and turned to leave. 'I'll meet you there as soon as I can.' She hurried back to Newhay and John. She needed to leave before her assignation with John that night to stand a chance of reaching Plymouth by Thursday, but she'd do whatever she must to get the money she needed.

***

'You promised, Ella.' John dangled a small leather purse of sovereigns in the air above Ella's reach. 'This has to be worth something.'

John didn't need to know how desperate she was. 'You think

253

I'd leave without keeping my promise?'

'Jane's in town, buying a new dress with the money I gave her. I sent Harry with the cart to the blacksmith for a new wheel rim.'

They were in the scullery, the place where he'd raped her. The colander hung on the hook on the wall, one side dented where she'd hit him. It was a pity she hadn't killed him: she'd probably be on her way to Van Diemen's Land by now. She couldn't kill a man in cold blood, could she? He dropped the purse on the flagstones and unbuckled his belt. She backed him to the wall, the way he'd backed her to it, and knelt before him. The purse lay by her hand: she tucked it into her bodice and then unbuttoned his fly.

He put his hands on her shoulders, breathing heavily, as she lowered his trousers and undergarments and let them fall to his ankles. Cupping his balls in her hand she took his erect member in her mouth. He groaned as she worked at him, sucking as if his penis were a carrot, sweet from the garden, and squeezing his balls like a ripe plum. His hips began to thrust, making her gag, as he lost all control.

'John, you there?' The front door slammed shut behind Jane. 'Ella?'

His sudden orgasm choked her, and she swallowed involuntarily. He pulled up his trousers and buttoned his fly, his fingers fumbling. 'Not a word, Ella.'

Her heart thundered in her ears, but she smiled, patting her breast, and helped him buckle his belt. 'Not a word, John.' She blew him a kiss as he left the scullery, closing the door behind him. Alone, she retched in the sink and wiped her mouth on her sleeve.

Voices came from the passageway. 'There you are, John. Have you seen Ella? There are dishes to be done.'

'I think she's upstairs with the baby or out in the privy. She's going to see her mother for a few days. She has to leave this evening. Poor woman's at death's door, apparently. I need you to look after William while she's away.'

254

'Who's going to nurse him?'

'Ruddle's herdsman's missus has had a baby. I reckon she'll wet nurse him for half a crown.'

The voices faded towards the kitchen. She let herself out of the scullery and hurried upstairs to pack. Leaving William would break her heart, but there was no way she could take him with her, and she'd return as soon as she and Charlotte had seen Jem.

***

My darling Jem,

I can find no way of following you to Van Diemen's Land, and have spoken with your mother, who received your letter. I have arranged for her and myself to travel to Plymouth. She needs to say her farewells, as do I. I'm sorry I can't bring William, as the journey at this time of year would be too dangerous for the tiny mite. I know this will grieve you, but I also know you will understand. He will be well cared for while I'm away, and returning to him will give me much-needed solace.

Pray for God's speed that we may arrive before you sail, but if we should not then hold my love close to your heart.

You must travel where life takes you:
Bend, 'ere love breaks you
And tears the ties that bind you.
Though we dwell on different shores,
My heart's forever yours,
And, one day, I shall find you.

Your loving wife, Ella Weston.

Jem sniffed back tears and reread the letter for the tenth time, holding it to the light that came through one of the air vents. If Ella and Ma didn't arrive today, they'd be too late. Loading of stores had stopped, presumably completed; during his hour on deck, earlier that afternoon, he'd taken note of the last-minute preparations. The ship's master, Captain Hood, kept scanning the sky and testing the wind as if worried about suitable conditions. The appearance of another ship, moored in the sound and presumably waiting to dock, gave further credence to *Tortoise* leaving sooner rather than later. Nat and Cal sat despondently on a bench by their small mess table. He didn't see how their parents, or Nat's wife, would afford the fare and still pay the Michaelmas quarter's rent. They didn't have a rich benefactor as Ella did in Mr Barton. Ella's mother must be looking after William, in Bath, while she was away travelling.

He'd grown accustomed to the slight rise and fall of the ship at mooring and the creaking of the wooden hull, but what it would be like on the open sea, he had no idea. Caught snatches of conversation between deckhands spoke of fever, typhus and scurvy, and high seas and shipwreck. He swallowed a need to vomit at the thought. He'd never even seen the ocean before he came to Plymouth, never had to endure such dark, damp, cramped quarters until he boarded *Stirling Castle* and *Tortoise*. The gaol in Northampton seemed like a long-distant luxury.

The barricade to the upper deck hatch creaked open. 'Forty-two, three-six-three!' There was a pause and the voice yelled louder, sharper. 'Forty-two, three-six-three. Let's have ya.'

That was him. He tucked the letter away and stumbled to the ladder and up onto deck. He blinked as his eyes accustomed themselves to the light.

Guards stood by the hatchway, and one re-shackled his legs. 'Visitors. Make the most of it. We put out in an hour.'

The huddle of relatives assembled on deck to say their farewells was pitifully small. He searched the deck. There was no-one he recognised. No, wait... 'Ma?' The Michaelmas quarter's rent surely wouldn't get paid unless Mr Barton had paid her fare as well as Ella's. 'Ma!'

His mother turned to face him, joy in her face: he smiled back, but he only had eyes for the slim figure standing beside Ma. 'Ella...' His heart thudded as he pushed towards them. He caught

256

Ella up in his arms and hugged her and then hugged his mother. 'Ma, thank you. How did you find Ella?' Ella moved back into his arms, and he kissed her and his mother, hugging them both tight as if his sanity depended on it. This moment had to last a lifetime, and he soaked in the feel of them, the smell of them, and the sound of them, and drank in their smiles. 'You came. I can't believe you both came.'

'The devil himself couldn't have kept us away.' Ella's eyes penetrated his soul and then dropped away as if unable to bear what she saw there. If she'd noticed his shackles, she made no comment. 'You look pale. Are you well?'

'I'm not so bad. But what about you and William. How's William? Is he growing?'

'He's a sturdy lad. He looks like you, Jem.'

He nodded. 'I wish I could have held him one last time.' He smiled through a blur. 'Ma, how's Dad and the others.'

'They're well, Jem.' His mother put an arm around him. 'Son, I've missed you so much. I love you so much.'

'And me, Ma.' He swallowed noisily. 'I miss you all. I can't tell you what it means to see you.'

Ella held herself with great restraint, giving his mother this time with him, and he loved her the more for it. 'So how did you arrange this? Did Ella visit you, Ma?'

Ella answered for her. 'I took William to see his family. It was fortunate I was there when your letter came. I shall be travelling back to Bath soon. I'm sorry I thought the extra travelling would be too much for our son.'

'I thought maybe your mother was looking after him. I'm glad you're going back to Bath, Ella. I'd hate to think of you anywhere near Harry or John Cartwright.'

Ella's shoulders tensed. 'I loathe the sight of them.'

'So, where's William, now?'

His mother looked at Ella questioningly but said nothing. Ella bit her top lip. 'I left him with Mrs Downs. I hate being away from him, but you understand, don't you? The journey is just too far.'

'You did the right thing.'

She nodded. 'I didn't feel I had a choice. What about you? What are your quarters like? Are they feeding you properly? Do you know how long the voyage will take?'

They bombarded him with questions, when all he wanted was to hold them in his arms and never let them go. He longed to make love to Ella one last time. So much to want and so little hope of ever getting it.

'Time to go ashore. Say your goodbyes.' The captain's voice was not unsympathetic. 'Hurry along now. We leave on the tide.'

Ella glued herself to him. He tangled his fingers in her long hair and looked over her shoulder to his mother, who had tears streaming down her face. 'I'm so sorry... I'm so sorry.'

Ella's face turned up to his, and he put a finger beneath her chin. Their lips met in a kiss so full of promise and passion his knees almost buckled. His embrace tightened, making them both breathless. 'I love you, Ella.'

'I'll never love anyone else, Jem.'

'I know. Be happy, Ella. Promise me.' He turned to his mother. 'I'll write when I get there.'

Ma nodded wordlessly.

Ella kissed him again. 'Wait for me, Jem.'

He shook his head, setting her free. 'You have a life to lead, Ella. Live it, for me.'

She nodded, her mouth trembling. 'I will. Stay strong, Jem. William will need his father one day.'

His heart overflowed. He had a son, and that meant he had a future. Dare he hope that one day William would find him?

A hand gripped his shoulder. 'Time to go.'

He crushed Ella to him, tasting her lips one last time. The hand on his shoulder tightened, wrenching him from Ella's arms.

She stood as bereft as he. Her hand reached for him, soft in his. 'I love you, Jem.'

He couldn't see for tears. Her fingers slid across his open palm, along the length of his fingers, lingering briefly on his fingertips, her touch tingling. The connection broke, and he stumbled away with the guard's hand still on his shoulder, the feel of Ella's fingers burning his, and the chains on his heart dragging heavier than mere shackles. He turned at the open hatch to see Ella standing by his mother. This was to be his last sight of them. Unable to speak, he raised a hand in final farewell and descended into darkness.

Chapter Twenty-Four

Ella put her hand in Charlotte's. HMS *Tortoise* left the dockside behind a tug and raised sail as it headed for the sound taking her hopes and dreams with her. Once out in the sound, the ship lowered its sails and appeared not to move farther. What were they waiting for? Another ship took *Tortoise*'s place at the quay, and they were shoved aside as men hurried to unload the new vessel.

Charlotte squeezed her daughter-in-law's hand. 'We ain't doing no good standing here maudling, Ella. Best we get on home. Jem has his own life to live now, and us standing here like a pair of broken mangles ain't going to change that.'

She sighed. 'And I should get back to William.'

Charlotte walked beside her, away from the quayside. 'You are all right over at Newhay with Harry? You are planning on staying?'

'I have no choice, Charlotte. Harry has laid claim to William, and I must stay with my son no matter what.'

Jem's mother nodded. 'If there's anything I can do…'

She didn't want Charlotte worrying, and she could look after herself: she had to. 'I'm fine, really. I'm fortunate Harry took me back and let me stay with William. It's not so bad there now.'

'If you say so. Now, we'd best find a room for the night. We have to be up early to catch the coach.' Charlotte glanced back towards the ship moored out in the sound. 'I really appreciate being able to say goodbye, Ella. I can't ever thank you enough.'

'Thank you for not telling Jem where I'm living. He'd only worry.' She palmed away tears. 'I'm glad you could come with me. I don't think I could have done it alone. Just remember that Harry mustn't know about this. If anyone asks, my mother was ill,

260

feared dying, but has recovered. You came with me for support.'
She walked on purposefully. 'Mr Jessop was kind to me when I
was here before. Maybe he'll have a room we can have for the
night.'

Mr Jessop greeted them cordially, and she and Charlotte
squeezed into a single bed until dawn, when they took the stage for
Oxford and then home. She bade Charlotte farewell at the cross on
the turnpike road and walked on alone to Newhay Farm, and
William, and Harry, and John.

***

The glow of an oil lamp shadowed the beams of the old ship and
picked out the spider's web the night had woven with fat-bodied,
dextrous legs. Jem didn't much like spiders. He lay on his back on
his narrow bunk, his hands folded across his chest beneath his
blankets, and stared at the narrow strips of paler night between the
heavy bars of the hatch cover. The creaks and groans of the
timbers kept time with the rise and fall of the low ceiling and the
nausea in his stomach, which was made worse by the stench of
bilge-water, rotting timbers, and sweating bodies. The heat of the
bodies around him had kept the worst of the night chills from his
bones, but the damp air ate at them. Cal and Nat, their faces in
shadow, slept on hammocks slung from hooks in the beams and
swung gently to the rhythm of waves: too gentle to be at sea, so
they must still be moored in Plymouth Sound.

His fingers traced the grooves he'd scored in the teak plank
beside his bunk and counted ten. The ship hadn't moved for ten
days which, he figured, made it October the third. Sunday, by his
reckoning, so a day interspersed with sermons and praying. Ten
days cramped and cooped up like hens in a basket for market, ten
days of darkness with only an hour or so of daylight on deck, two
if they were lucky: ten days of grief, and fear, and praying. Two
bells rang. The ship came alive, before the next two sounded, with
souls that already had the shipboard routine engraved on their
hearts. Six o'clock. Would today be the day they sailed?

He dressed in his regulation clothing, a luxury after the hulk to

261

have clean clothes and a washed body. A jacket and waistcoat of blue kersey went on over a linen shirt, and duck trousers of a coarse linen were yanked over yarn stockings. He donned his woollen cap and stood ready, hunching into his jacket. It still felt damp after yesterday's exercise on deck in the rain. He shivered: after the heavier clothing of the hulk, the cold ate at him, and winter was coming on. According to the surgeon superintendent, who'd issued the new clothes, he was better cold than dead: the flannel and woollen garment of the hulks harboured disease, and disease was something to be avoided at all cost on a long voyage.

The hatch cover creaked open and sprinkled pale stars across the pre-dawn sky; a half-moon was framed in the hatchway. The moon disappeared behind the black shape of the hatch guard. 'Let's have you.' The guard peered down into the gloom. 'Get a fucking move on.'

He rolled up his bedding, a thin mattress, two thinner blankets, and a pillow, and tied it with sennit, two lengths of plaited grass, and then helped Cal and Nat turn their small area of tween-decks into a mess for eight men. Cal grabbed their bowls from the storage locker and laid them out on the table that hung from the beam, above which a hammock was strung at night. The guard opened the barred barrier, which admitted little light. 'Come on. We ain't got all day. Bedding on deck.'

The bedding roll slung over his shoulder like a dead sheep, he mounted the ladder to the deck. A cold gust slapped his face with the promise of more rain, and fine, wind-blown spray glittered in the yellow light of the oil lamps hung along the deck. Clouds darkened the sky seawards with ominous foreboding, and shoreward, the soft glow of lamps could be seen lighting the deck of *Stirling Castle*. On the dockside, pinpricks of lamplight showed the slow progress of dockhands on their way to work.

'Stop gawping, man. Get in line for the tub.' The guard's rough voice brought him back to now and the area set aside for bedding. Already men swabbed the decks, and hundreds of bedding rolls were being covered with worn hammocks which gave little protection against the promised weather.

His bedding stowed, he undressed, piled his clothes neatly where he could see them, and stood naked and shivering. On deck was a bath tub. A dripping man climbed out of it, and it was his turn. He got in and waited for two prisoners to throw buckets of water over him. The cold shocked his body, sending it into spasms of shaking. He rubbed himself down with a piece of coarse towelling and threw on his clothes with trembling fingers.

'Hurry along, man. Get your rations and get below.' The guard moved on to harass the next man.

'I'm coming as quick as I can.' The words were muttered beneath his breath as he joined the queue for their rations. As mess captain, volunteered by Cal and Nat, it was his job to see the mess was kept clean and tidy, and to stand in line for his mess's ration of breakfast gruel. He shivered in the pre-dawn chill as he put his wooden hub, the container for their rations, on the serving board. He didn't begrudge Cal and Nat their warmth below: it would be their turn in the tub all too soon, and the sky above his head and the glimpse of the familiar, dark shoreline were worth the cold.

'You want your grub or not?' The surgeon superintendent, Mr Brownrigg, pushed the half-full wooden hub of gruel towards him, and a surly kitchen-hand, who'd already been at work for an hour and a half, slopped gruel into the next one.

Hugging the rough wooden container, he moved along, sure the ration was bigger than at breakfast the day before, when Mr Brownrigg had been called away. He'd watch the kitchen-hand in future: he was probably saving extra for himself or trading it for tobacco. It was light by the time he shambled back down to the tween-decks gloom where the others, shivering and barely dry themselves, were waiting. Cal, ravenous as ever, doled out the contents into the tin pint-mugs. He gulped down his own, relishing the sweet, buttery taste. While they were at anchor, boats had brought fresh meat, butter, and vegetables daily, but once they were at sea, that would stop: what provisions they had preserved aboard would be all they had for many months.

263

The ship shuddered suddenly and lurched, making the lanterns swing and the dancing shadows leap like stalking monsters. He grabbed his mug to stop it falling to the floor. The sound of flapping came from above, and the ship moved beneath his feet. Waves slapped at the hull, and *Tortoise* heeled over, trembling along its length, and turned seawards. His breath built in his lungs, and he grabbed a timber to steady himself. This was it, then. They'd set sail. A journey into the unknown and a lonely future without his family or the woman he loved.

***

Tortoise rolled and pitched as she ploughed through the waves under full sail. Jem vomited over the side, wiped his mouth on his sleeve, and staggered to maintain his balance as he went about his duties, an easier task now they were clear of the sound and his leg irons and manacles had been removed. Land, his last breath of English air, diminished to a long, low, blue haze to his right, to starboard.

Bed boards, already stowed on deck, had to be scrubbed and scraped. The prison deck, the tween-decks squeezed between the upper deck and the hold, had to be holystoned with chunks of smooth sandstone and swept clean of scrapings. Now they were in open water, the movement of the hull caused some of the old ship's seams to leak, darkening the stains already running from the caulking and making the foul air stink of dank rot and mould.

Prayers were said, hymns sung, and he half-listened to the sermon, taken back to Yardley Hastings, Reverend Buchanan's Sunday oratories, and watching Ella from the corner of his eye. He sighed; too late now for regrets.

School began midmorning for those who couldn't read or write, but he was set to picking oakum, a job he hated as his hands were never clean and everything he touched tasted and smelt of pine tar; others mended clothes or washed dishes or were busy cooking the midday meal. Cal had been sent to the bows to help in the hospital quarters. Nat was perched on a bench opposite him knitting socks and concentrating hard on turning a heel. Above him, boys scaled

264

the rigging and tended the sails.

All around them, guards watched, pistols at their sides and knives in scabbards. Others, not on duty, threw dice and gambled their rations. Looking up made him dizzy, and he staggered to the side to puke again, the deck slippery from those who hadn't made it. A wave shuddered the hull and sprayed across the deck: icy water trickled down his neck. He hated ships.

'You!' He looked round, and the ship's barber beckoned him. 'Over here. Sit down.'

He staggered to the bench and sank down. The deck was dark with littered clumps of hair. It was time for his twice-weekly shave and a haircut.

The man wiped a cut-throat razor on his thigh, gripped his victim's chin, and dipped the blade in water. The steel was cold against his cheek. He held his breath. The deck tilted and the blade nicked his flesh. 'Keep still, damn you.'

Having his throat cut seemed preferable to four months on the open sea. 'Just get on with it. Do your worst.'

The barber must have honed his skill on many voyages, for the blade slid across his cheek and above his lips in time with the peaks and troughs of the waves. The man tilted his victim's head to expose his throat. The blade rasped through the stubble as *Tortoise* pitched and yawed. The barber produced scissors and he closed his eyes. The point of the scissors could take one out. The blades sliced next to his ear. 'There, done. Next.'

Eight bells: noon and a change of watch. The guards pocketed their dice and their winnings and took up their positions. Nat said the ship held about a hundred pensioner guards, bound for Van Diemen's Land to guard the prison camps. Some had brought their wives and families to make a new life in the colony. His heart bled at the sight of women and children. Ella and William were safe in Bath. He must be content with that.

Noon meant food and a much-needed ration of water. Maybe even a ration of wine.

'Get in line.' A hand cuffed his ear. 'Keep in line.'

He ducked and side-stepped, keeping his eyes down; this guard could be one of his warders for years to come, and it wouldn't pay to antagonise him.

'I were here before you.' Knocker's surly face pressed close to his.

He smiled an easy smile: he wouldn't allow this bully to intimidate him. 'After you, mate. I ain't pig enough to be in no hurry to eat this swill.'

Knocker's face contorted; his breath came slow and deep. 'You calling me a pig?'

'Your words not mine, mate.'

Knocker took a swing at him. He ducked, letting the swing go over his head, and caught the bigger man a punch in the gut.

A hand grabbed his collar. 'Enough of that. What's your number?'

Knocker smirked, showing the gap in his teeth.

He tried to struggle free. 'Forty-two, three-six-three. And he tried to hit me first. I didn't ask for no trouble.'

The guard propelled him along the deck and shoved him into a tall, narrow box, just big enough to stand in. He closed the door on him, leaving him a small grill for air. 'You can stay in there till you cool down.'

'I were only protecting myself.' The thud of boots faded. 'Hey, let me out. It were Knocker as started it.'

Through the grill, one of the masts almost filled his field of view. A guard dragged Knocker to the mast and lashed him to it, exposing his back, his smirk gone. The crack of a whip, followed by the thwack of leather on flesh tensed his muscles. Knocker's back had a red wheal across it. The lash came down again and again. Thirty-six lashes, and the man's back was striped with bloody wheals.

266

He felt sick and trapped, dizzy and claustrophobic. His legs sagged but he had no room to sit. He braced his body the best he could against the walls of his prison within a prison and rode out the nausea and the rolling deck. His body shook with exhaustion, hunger, and thirst, and he prayed to God for salvation or a merciful death. Stars pricked a pale night sky before the door to his cage opened, and he fell half senseless to the deck.

***

Ella had only been home a day when John cornered her in the scullery. 'I'm in need of a little loving, Ella.'

She pushed him away. 'I'm busy.'

He barred her exit. 'Women like nice things. Don't you want presents, Ella?'

'You really think presents will make me happy?'

A trace of the hurt little boy shone from his eyes. 'What is it you want, Ella? I'll do it, if I can.'

'You know what I want.'

He grabbed her arm and kissed her, grasping her breast. She pulled away. Was he so egotistical? 'Not that.'

'What then?'

'I want my freedom.'

'You still mooning over that Weston boy?'

'I want to be with the man I love.'

'James? That isn't possible.'

'Then I'll do the impossible.'

John laughed. 'How do you propose to get to the colonies? Murder someone?'

She glanced at the colander. 'The thought had crossed my mind. I'm going to earn the fare. One day, I shall have enough to take me and William, if it takes me until I'm old and grey.'

John stroked his stubble with a broad hand. 'I know you don't love Harry, and he doesn't love you, but he needs you. He needs his legal wife to give him a legitimate son.'

'He has one, now he's claimed William.'

John waved her assertion aside. 'He knows as well as I do William isn't his. He needs a legal heir, or all this' – he embraced the whole farm with a gesture – 'is for nothing. He won't let a son of Jem's inherit the herd and the tenancy, and nor will I.'

'He promised William would share any inheritance, but I know he wants a son of his own'

'Suppose he can't give you one. He had mumps as a young man. Some say it can make a man sterile. Ella, I have a proposal for you. I'll make sure you get with child. I'll pay half your fare to Van Diemen's Land when you become pregnant and the rest when you deliver a healthy son. You leave the boy with us and take William with you. I'll help you get away, and Jane and Harry will never know the boy isn't Harry's. We all get what we want.'

She could have the fare in as little as nine months? 'Suppose I have a daughter?' She couldn't leave a daughter anywhere near John Cartwright. She bit at a thumbnail. Could she bear John a son, for money, and leave England without him?

John gave her a lewd smile. 'I hope you have a string of daughters. I keep fucking you till you have a healthy son. That's the deal.'

It was a deal but not one she intended to honour. Ten pounds would be a huge step towards Van Diemen's Land and Jem. She'd get the rest, somehow, before she gave birth to another baby. She'd already prostituted herself to Harry and John. If she could get one man to pay for her body, there would surely be others willing. She moved closer and breathed on his neck. 'I want half, now. I want ten pounds before you touch me again.'

***

October, and a chill wind whipped Ella's hair across her cheeks and heaped golden leaves against gravestones. Inside the church, it was cold, and she huddled into her winter coat, cradling William close in his shawl. Harry strode beside her, a hand possessively on her elbow. The family pew, towards the front of the church and not far behind Lord Northampton's, was conspicuously empty. As a young father, Harry had taken a more prominent role in the Cartwright family, relegating John and Jane to the older generation. Roles had been reversed somewhat since William had joined the family.

Reverend Buchanan smiled and nodded as they seated themselves and waited for Harry's parents to sit in the remaining space. She glanced around, sensing that others had noticed the change. It was as if Harry had gained in confidence and stature and was proud. Of her and William?

Guilt flushed her cheeks. She was damned and double-damned for what she'd done. Harry was kinder to her now she excited him in bed and was looking forward to her being with child. Did he deserve her and John's betrayal? William snuffled, and her resolve hardened. She was doing this for William's future. She'd promised him he'd know his father.

The reverend waited for the congregation to fall silent and then clasped his hands together. 'Today we remember a fallen friend. It is almost a year to the day that Joseph Upton was brutally killed in Newhay Copse. Almost a year since three more of our own sons were taken from the village forever. Guilty though they were, our thoughts are with their families, as well as with the family of Joseph, and I know I speak for all when I say the whole village grieves at this time.

He scanned the faces of his flock. 'Caleb, Nathan, and James are bound for Van Diemen's Land. Joe's body lies in the churchyard, but his soul is with our Lord, and on the day of judgement, the dead in Christ will rise first.'

She glanced across at Charlotte, who returned her glance before looking down hastily. Had she told anyone they'd seen Jem?

The reverend continued. 'The thoughts of their families go with
269

those young men. But let this be a warning to all who dare to break God's commandments, for surely your sins will find you out. God, in his infinite wisdom, will punish all ye who repent not of your sins. Yet Luke tells us that Jesus answered the Pharisees and the teachers of law thus: "It is not the healthy who need doctors but the sick. I have not come to call the righteous, but the sinners to repentance." Let us all repent of our sins.'

And God would judge her, not Harry or John, or the reverend. Harry nudged her, and she stood. She'd sung hymns learned by rote and missed most of the sermon. Outside, Reverend Buchanan made small talk.

Harry shook his hand. 'Thank you, Reverend. That was an enlightening sermon.'

'Thank you, Harry. Ella, you must bring young William to visit. Mrs Downs would love to see you both. She's grown quite fond of you, young lady, as have we all. Come and have tea. Say four o'clock?'

She could see tea at the rectory written all over Harry's face. His mother had never been granted such hospitality.

Harry smiled 'I shall be busy as you know, afternoon milking, but Ella will be delighted, although I'm afraid William is too young for two long outings in one day. Maybe we can both bring him another time.'

'Of course. Ella, four o'clock?'

She nodded, and Reverend Buchanan moved on to another group of parishioners. He hadn't actually invited Harry, and he gave scant regard to Mrs Downs wishes, so what did he want with her?

Ten minutes to four saw her walking through the front gate and up the long, straight path to the imposing front door. She'd been invited, and her husband was a man of means; she wouldn't go in by the servants' entrance.

Mrs Downs opened the door to her. 'Ella. Come in, dear. I've

270

baked gingerbread. The reverend's in his study. I'll bring tea in shortly.'

She followed Mrs Downs to the study door, as if she didn't know the way well enough. Mrs Downs knocked and opened it. 'Miss Ella. I mean, Mrs Cartwright, Your Reverence.'

'Thank you, Mrs Downs. Give us half an hour, there's something I need to discuss with Ella.'

Mrs Downs hurried back to her domain, and the reverend beckoned her into the room. 'Sit down, child. How are things at Newhay Farm? Young Harry seems happy.'

Heat flushed her cheeks. 'Harry and I are getting on better.'

'And John?'

Her cheeks burnt hotter. 'What about John?'

'I had a letter from Mr Barton, and I'm informed John Cartwright had one as well. You can tell me if John asks more of you than is right for a woman in your position.'

The reverend might be surprised at some of the positions. The ten sovereigns burnt the mark of Satan in her breast. 'John is a perfect gentleman. He's been very kind to me since I returned.'

'Ella...' Reverend Buchanan's gaze fastened somewhere above her bosom. 'You're very fortunate Harry took you back, after James... I'm glad that unfortunate incident is behind you.'

Her eyes smarted and pain clamped her heart and throat. 'I miss him, Reverend. I miss Jem. The pain is too much to bear. He'll never be in my past.'

'He will, child. You have a family here to keep your mind from James.'

She dabbed at her eyes with a handkerchief. 'I miss him holding me. I long to be held. Just to be held.' She leaned forward, her full breasts rounding, and the reverend's eyes fixed upon them.

'You're a beautiful young woman, Ella. I'm sure physical

271

contact won't be an issue.'

'But to be truly loved, the way Jem loved me, and to love. I need…'

He swallowed. 'You need?'

'It's only when… Only then can I forget him.' The reverend put his hand over hers, and she placed her own over his. 'I need to forget him. Help me forget. Please, help me forget.'

'Ella…' His voice sounded hoarse. He closed his eyes. 'Do not lust after her beauty or let her captivate you with her eyes.'

The stirring inside her wouldn't be denied. She needed to escape, if only for a few brief moments, and the reverend wouldn't be able to deny his need either. She walked around the desk and sat on it in front of him. 'It would be a mercy. God is not merciful?'

He breathed in her face. 'The mind governed by the flesh is death, but the mind governed by the Spirit is life and peace.'

'But you will ease my spirit. Is it a sin to give life and peace?'

'God has sent you to me in your need. God is indeed merciful.' He pushed back his chair and loosened his belt. He released his erect penis from his clothing and turned her away from him, as if unable to look into her eyes. He pressed her face down over his desk, scattering inkwells, quills, and fine sand onto the carpet, pushed up her skirts, and then parted her thighs with a knee. 'But each person is tempted' – his breath was hot on her neck – 'when he is lured and enticed by his own desire.'

Her hair fell across a leather-bound and embossed family Bible. A heavy crucifix lay beside it. She turned her head away, and her hand caught a globe of the world. It spun on its stand; vast expanses of Atlantic Ocean and Antarctic Ocean lay blue between her and Australia. Somewhere, Jem sailed ever farther away from her. Reverend Buchanan pulled down her bloomers, and his fingers found her aching for release. Her breath came in shallow gasps. 'Yes, Reverend, yes.'

His breathing grew heavy with long-denied lust. 'Desire when it has conceived gives birth to sin.' He slid his hands beneath her hips and lifted her with the force of his penetration, holding her around her stomach so he could thrust. 'And sin when it is fully grown...'

She was an object to him, as she'd been to Harry and John. She would change that. She would change the way men thought of her. She would make them pay: show them she had worth. She began to writhe, to lose herself in the act, to feel him deep inside her. She urged him on, again and again, and he gave his all.

He released her and sank back onto his chair. 'When it is fully grown brings forth death. May God forgive me for my wicked lust.'

She stood up and straightened her clothing. 'But to die without ever having lived or loved is a sin against God, who gave you life.'

He panted and opened the Bible, his fist thumping down on a page. 'Galatians five: "Now the works of the flesh are evident: sexual immorality, impurity, sensuality, idolatry, sorcery, enmity, strife, jealousy."' His finger stabbed at the texts. '"Fits of anger, rivalries, dissensions, divisions, envy, drunkenness, orgies, and things like these. I warn you, as I warned you before, that those who do such things will not inherit the kingdom of God."' His shoulders slumped, and he looked at her with pleading eyes. 'Am I damned, Ella?'

She sat on his lap and stroked his hair. 'Was that drunkenness, wickedness, or an orgy? It was an act of compassion. An act of love.' She searched her own knowledge of the scriptures. 'If we confess our sins, He is faithful and just to forgive us our sins and to cleanse us from all unrighteousness.'

He held his head in his hands. 'Oh, God, forgive me. Ella, my life has been a fallow field until now. I have denied myself love in God's service. Why would he deny me love?'

'He wouldn't. This is between us and God, Reverend. We can help ease one another's pain. No-one else...'

A sharp knock at the door made him thrust Ella from his lap. 'A

273

moment, Mrs Downs.' He buttoned his fly and waited until Ella was seated again in her chair. 'Come.'

She pushed an errant lock of hair behind her ear and smoothed her dress. She'd made a useful ally, and next time she visited the reverend, she would ask some sort of payment in exchange for her body. She needed at least nine more sovereigns for her fare to Van Diemen's Land, and she had little time to earn it; her flow was late, and it seemed there might be a second midsummer baby.

She didn't know if it were Harry's or John's, but at least, if she were pregnant, she had no worries about the reverend getting her with child. God might forgive Reverend Buchanan for his carnal lust, but would He forgive her for prostituting herself for her son and the man she loved? She put a hand to her breast where the blue jay feather accused her. Would Jem forgive her?

Chapter Twenty-Five

Ominous clouds built in the west as *Tortoise* ploughed through ever taller waves and deeper troughs, her sails taut and straining and her ropes singing. Jem clung to a rail and made his way from the spray-soaked deck to the tween-decks hatch with lunch for his mess. They were two days out of Plymouth and approaching the Bay of Biscay, according to one of the crew, and already the sea had turned against them. He waited for the ship to hang for a second before he moved to the next handhold. His stomach came up as the ship plummeted, and he retched. He hadn't kept down anything more than water since they'd left Plymouth Sound. Half a globe of open sea loomed before him, fraught with peril.

His plea to his maker was lost beneath a crashing wave. 'Dear God in his mercy, protect us sinners.'

'Shorten sail.' Captain Hood's voice was half-drowned by the howl of the wind in the rigging. There was a loud crack, and sailcloth flapped and billowed before dipping into the dragging waves. Voices relayed a command, and boys scampered up the rigging to cut loose the sail. The captain yelled at one of the guards. 'Get the prisoners below. Batten down the hatches and close the vents.' Captain Hood cupped his hands around his mouth. 'Get that sail down before it de-masts us and we turn turtle!'

Jem staggered to the hatchway, weak from lack of food, and half fell down the ladder to tween-decks. Two prisoners followed him, and the hatch cover thudded closed behind them. His eyes adjusted to the gloom. Lamps swung arcs of yellow light into corners that light never normally penetrated and showed old timbers glistening black with wet and green with slime. Seawater slapped across deck boards slick with vomit, and the old ship creaked and groaned in protest. Somewhere, from a gloomy corner, a voice moaned in sympathy. Knocker, still groaning from his lashing? The man had spent a day in the hospital quarters lying on his stomach, according to Nat who seemed to know everything that went on aboard ship.

He slopped what food he hadn't spilt already into waiting bowls and handed out knives. Potatoes and some sort of meat. He gripped the side of his bowl and forced his share down with no hope it would stay there. The bowls licked clean, he collected the knives ready to be returned: each one to be accounted for.

Cal slung his hammock above the table and made a fair stab at climbing into it. The thing swung about violently, adding to his feeling of dizziness and nausea. He lay down on his bunk, not sure if it were better than the hammock he'd managed to avoid, and closed his eyes, letting the rise and fall of the ship wash over him. The ship suddenly heeled over and pitched him onto the deck. 'What the fuck?'

Nat's eyes were wide. 'We're sinking. We're trapped. Jem, we're going to drown.' His cousin crossed himself and murmured promises to the almighty.

'It's the sail as broke loose and went in the drink. It's dragging us down!' He put a hand to his breast pocket where the blue jay feather nestled. 'Ella...' But he'd set Ella free. Would she mourn him?

Cal lurched to the hatchway and hammered on the underside. 'Let us out. For pity's sake, don't leave us here to drown.' His only answer was the howl of the wind.

Tortoise levelled out, throwing them one against another, picked up speed, and ran before the storm. Bells rang the watch changes. Night fell, day came with no light, and night fell again. For two days the old ship limped on, leaving the prisoners locked below in the dark with only their prayers to light their way when the lamps ran out of oil. With the vents to the outside closed against the waves breaking over the deck, the air in the quarters was damp and fetid. No-one manned the pumps that brought fresh air down below, and no-one brought them food or water while the ship's crew fought to keep her alive. In a floating coffin, about ten

276

paces across by twenty paces long, and a mere six feet in height, four hundred humbly repentant men waited to meet their god.

***

Jem woke to a calm rocking motion; sunlight poured through open air vents. Two bells, a pause, and two more. The hatch opened, making him blink. His head and belly ached, and his throat was raw.

A voice cursed. 'Come on, you stinking scum. Get them bed boards up on deck. Tub time and breakfast.'

'Breakfast? I could eat a horse.' He rolled his damp bedding, tied it in a neat bundle, and followed Cal up the ladder.

Cal swore. 'What the fuck?'

Tall masts speared the sky like bristles on a yard brush. Drake's Island guarded the way, its cannons pointing out to sea. He squinted against the bright light. 'This is bloody Plymouth.' He'd thought England lost forever.

'We're waiting on a berth.' The guard grunted and glanced up at shattered timbers. 'Captain Hood turned us back for repairs. Looks like we'll be here a while.'

The convict souls assembled on deck were a sorry sight. Some lay on the boards too weak to move, able only to give thanks to God for their deliverance; Surgeon Brownrigg and his assistant, Surgeon Domville, walked among them. The sick were helped to the hospital quarters, a tiny room with tiered bunks. The rest had their shackles replaced and were given a double ration of water. The guards thought they had the strength left to try to escape?

'Best Thames water.' A guard doled out his ration. 'Make the most of it. Only a barrel a man to last the voyage.'

'A barrel for four months?' He gulped it down anyway, wondering how river water would keep for four months even if strict rationing made it last that long, and then stood in line for the morning gruel. Later they'd be watched over as they drank their daily ration of wine but, for now, water, even Thames water, and

277

gruel had never tasted so sweet or been more welcome.

The ship slipped back into its daily routine while carpenters repaired and replaced the damaged timbers, new ropes were stowed aboard, and sailmakers stitched a new sail to replace the one lost to the storm.

With calmer water, food and drink stayed down, and gradually his strength returned. The physical health of the prisoners improved, but the storm had unsettled them, and all now dreaded facing the open sea again. Even Knocker had withdrawn into himself and could be heard muttering in his sleep. Each day was a day closer to sailing, and tempers on board were brittle with fear. They'd been in the sound just over a week, and the wind was rising again, when tensions came to a head.

Knocker's eyes were wild. 'I'd rather take my chances here than out there. There's no way I'm going.'

'You planning on getting a pardon, then, Knocker?' One of his cronies laughed. 'How are you going to swing that?'

Knocker clenched his fists and pulled at his shackles. 'I'll die here rather than sail. What do you reckon?'

He backed away, not wanting to be caught up in whatever was about to happen. The guards bore pistols and wouldn't be averse to shooting a mutineer. There was no way men in shackles could overrun a hundred armed guards.

Knocker looked from face to face. 'Well? Are you with me?'

Knocker's crony stood forward. 'I'm with you, Knocker.'

Knocker looked from one to another. 'You're all lily-livered cowards. You deserve a watery grave.' He shuffled to the side of the ship and hauled himself up and over the gunnel before the guards realised what was happening. His friend followed him. One splash followed another.

A guard ran to peer over the side. 'Man overboard! Lower a lifeboat! And get those convicts below deck!' Guards ran to their stations.

He shambled to the place where Knocker had jumped, dodging through a crowd of men and guards. Men were shouting, egging Knocker on. Could he make it to the docks or to Drake's Island?

Guards pushed the men back, but he struggled against them and strained to see the water far below. 'Can you see them? I can't see them.'

A dark head broke the surface briefly before disappearing beneath it. A guard laughed. 'Damn fools. How the hell do they think they'll swim ashore with ten pounds of iron around their legs? They're dead men, for sure.'

One by one, the prisoners on deck fell silent and watched the waves, but Knocker and his friend weren't seen again.

***

Ella prodded bubbles of cloth back into the grey water of the boiler, heaved the sheet out on the end of the copper stick, and watched the soapy water pour back into the boiler. She slopped the sheet onto the washboard and scrubbed at a stubborn stain with a bar of soap.

Jane dropped a wicker clothes basket onto the floor. 'You need to get a move on, girl. Weather won't hold all day, and there's a line full of washing still to be hung out.'

She straightened, rubbing her back with red hands. 'I'm working as fast as I can.'

Jane frowned. 'Is there something you want to tell me?'

She bent back to her task, not daring to look Jane in the eye. 'Like what?'

'You haven't washed any cloths this month.'

Her cheeks heated, and she scrubbed harder. 'My flow's eight days late.'

Jane beamed. 'Eight days… Harry's to be a father? I never thought I'd see the day.'

279

'Why not?'

Jane's smile faded. 'I wasn't sure he was capable.'

She laughed. 'Oh, Harry's well capable, I assure you.'

Jane smiled again briefly. 'You're a lucky woman, Ella.'

She put a damp hand on Jane's bare arm. 'I know you and John… It must be hard.'

'I'm past childbearing, Ella, but he still won't touch me. I expect he's found a younger woman, somewhere.'

She pushed her sleeves farther up her arms, gathered the sheet, and plunged it into a sink of cold well water. 'He's an old fool, Jane. He should be grateful for the love of a good wife, not go out looking for what isn't his.'

'Men's lusts need satisfying, Ella.'

'And women's?'

'Ella!'

'Aren't we allowed to have feelings, needs?'

'It's not proper, you saying such things.'

She pummelled the sheet to force out the soap and began wringing it from one corner, working her way along it, as if it were John's neck she was twisting into a long rope. 'I'll say what I like and do what I like. I answer to God not man.'

Jane crossed herself. 'As God's my witness, no good will come of you, Ella Cartwright. You mark my words. I rue the day Harry fell for the likes of you, with all your fine airs and new-fangled ways.'

She emptied out the soapy water and followed Jane outside to draw clean to repeat the process. 'You wanted a brood mare and a skivvy. If I'm pregnant, I'm having Harry's baby. What more do you want from me?'

Jane eyed her shrewdly. 'This *is* Harry's baby, isn't it?'

She yanked the pump handle up and down, and water gushed into the bucket. The baby would probably look like Harry. She sighed as her life closed around her like a snare around a rabbit's neck; if she couldn't find another nine sovereigns before midsummer, this would be her lot. A baby a year, if Harry was capable, and a life of manual servitude. Everything she'd promised herself she'd avoid. 'Cross my heart and hope to die. I mean, I rarely ever go anywhere. Who else's would it be?'

'Does Harry know?'

'Not yet. I was waiting till I was sure.'

Jane smiled again. 'He'll be happy as a pig in mud. It'll make a man of him. John always says as much.'

'Don't tell John, yet. Please, Jane. Harry should be the first to know.'

Harry's sexual appetite proved he was all man, but if he were infertile, then any child must be John's. She slopped water into the sink and pummelled the sheet again, angry with herself for agreeing to John's plan. She wouldn't let his baby trap her, any more than she'd let Harry's. She straightened and a shaft of sunlight caught the ring on her right hand: the ring Jem had given her. Maybe she could use this possible pregnancy to her advantage. The reverend wouldn't know it wasn't his. Nineteen sovereigns, plus another four or five for coaches, and food until she was settled, and she and William would be gone for good, midsummer baby or no midsummer baby.

***

A spider swung from a beam in the hay barn, trying to reach a strand of web, spinning a thread of silk and descending lower and lower. Ella admired its determination and the beauty of the intricate web it wove.

John caught her arm and hurried her towards the ladder that led to the hayloft. His lips were moist, the bristles of his stubble coarse and rough, but she let the kiss linger. 'John…' Her voice was a whisper.

281

His mouth cut her words and took her breath. He grabbed her wrists and held them before he released her lips. 'Quiet. I want to fuck you, not talk to you.'

'But I need to talk to you.'

'Later.' His voice was a strangled moan. 'Get up there.'

She climbed the ladder, and he pushed her to the floor, standing over her as he unbuckled his belt. 'I want what I've paid for.' He heaved above her, his face close to hers, the smell of milk cows and manure on his clothing, and the coarse cloth of his breeches rubbing against the inside of her thighs. Next to her heart, nestled between her breasts beside the blue jay feather Jem had given her, what seemed like a lifetime ago, lay her purse of coins. She'd added barely a sovereign to the ten John had given her, scrimped from bartering in the village. At this rate, she'd be an old woman before she made it to the colonies.

She wrenched her attention back to John and reached for his neck, pulling him closer, bucking beneath him as he grunted with effort. 'John…'

Orgasm when it came was a blessed relief. He sank against her panting. 'I'm listening.'

'I'm pregnant.'

John stared at her. 'Already?'

'Jane's guessed.'

He looked at her sharply. 'She knows you're with child?'

She nodded.

'Have you told Harry?'

'Not yet. I've been waiting until I was sure. And I wanted to warn you.'

'Harry and Jane mustn't know about us. That's part of the deal. If she finds out, you don't get the other ten pounds, boy or not.'

'Our secret's safe with me, but…'

282

John's face darkened. 'But what, Ella?'

She waved a disparaging hand at the hay barn. 'I was brought up in Bath. I'm used to finer things than this.'

'You want nice clothes. Is that it? Ten pounds not enough?'

John stiffened again inside her and began to move slowly. The spider descended on its silken thread towards them. 'That's for my fare, as you well know. I'm used to having an allowance. Money to spend as I wish. Stuck out here in this back of beyond... Well, there's not much to spend it on, is there?'

He glowered down at her. 'So why do you need money?'

'I'd like to feel I could visit my mother from time to time, even if I'm not allowed to take my son to see his grandmother. You know she isn't well, still. The fare is expensive, and I can't go to Bath wearing clothes like this. And I miss the finer things.' Her dress was perfectly adequate, but John seemed willing to throw cash at Jane to keep her happy. She pursed her lips and lowered her eyelashes in a manner she hoped was alluring but probably only looked petulant. 'Mr Josiah Barton gave me a handsome allowance until I married Harry. It reflected very well on him that Mother and I were always dressed impeccably in polite company. A man of your standing...'

John paused, puffing out his chest like a cock turkey. 'An allowance... Yes, why not? After all, just because you're pregnant doesn't mean I won't expect you to pleasure me. The deal was until you deliver a healthy son. It's not as if you won't earn it.' He smiled and put his hands beneath her buttocks, pushing deeper. 'You will earn it, Ella.'

She put a hand against his chest. 'How much?'

'Half a sovereign a month.'

At that rate, it would take her the best part of two years to earn her fare and enough money to live on until she was settled somewhere near Jem. 'That's not even a housemaid's wages. A prostitute in town earns far more, according to Harry.'

'You get free bed and board already, girl. Half a sovereign, and for that I have you any way I fancy.'

It was more than she'd hoped for, but less than she needed if she were to get passage before her child was born at midsummer. She swallowed and smiled. She might sell her body, but her heart was Jem's. 'We have a bargain.'

'We do.' He removed his hands and spat on one, holding it out for her to seal the transaction. She spat, and he grasped her hand. 'Now, turn over. I want you on your knees.'

Hay tickled her nose and embedded itself into her cheek. He knelt behind her, held her hips firmly, and pushed into her with as much finesse as a bull mounting a cow. But then Jane was the wife he loved, whereas prostitutes were two a penny…or rather, half a sovereign a month.

Chapter Twenty-Six

The oak panelling in the reverend's study shone like horse chestnuts fresh from their shells in the afternoon sun that slanted through tall small-paned casements. Ella moved across the room to the window. Cattle lowed in the pasture behind the church, and the trees were burnished copper. It was October, a little over a year since Joe Upton's untimely death in Newhay Copse. Where was Jem now? She turned back to the reverend's desk and idly turned the globe with one finger. Off the coast of Africa? Farther? Maybe the Cape of Good Hope?

She stared at the shapes on the globe: countries she couldn't begin to imagine. The Antarctic Ocean looked vast and empty. She wouldn't have been surprised to see here be dragons written there. Could the old ship, *Tortoise*, even make the crossing? She sighed. So much had happened to her since she'd first arrived in Yardley Hastings. She'd found love. She'd married into a family of good standing. She was pregnant again. It should have been a life she was content with. If the love she'd found had been Harry's, life would have been perfect: the heaven on earth about which Reverend Buchanan preached. As it was, her life was a nightmare, a living hell.

Reverend Buchanan put down his quill pen and pushed himself up from his chair. He stood behind her, put his arms around her waist, and traced the curve of her right breast with his fingers. 'You seem distracted, Ella. What's wrong?'

She put her hand over his, cupping it around her breast. 'There's no easy way to say this.'

His fingers stiffened. 'Please, Ella... Don't tell me you won't come anymore. I couldn't bear it. I live for our stolen moments.'

She nestled her head against his shoulder: Jem's shoulder had been more muscular, safer, stronger. An ache started in her stomach and clenched her heart. How had she allowed this to happen to her? Why hadn't she kept Jem at home that night? 'I'm with child, Charles.'

He turned her to face him. 'You're with child?'

She took a deep breath. God would strike her dead. 'It's yours, Charles.'

His lips moved silently, blush-rose against a blanched face: a prayer to the almighty? 'What are we to do, Ella?'

'What are you to do, Reverend?'

He stared at her as if the full consequences of their lust added the last piece of the jigsaw to the puzzle. 'You're a married woman. You claim it's Harry's, of course. I'd have thought that was obvious. I'll be defrocked if this gets out. It would ruin me.'

'And what about me? You think I want this child?'

His hands fell to his sides. 'What choice do you have?' His face paled further, if that were possible. 'You mean get rid of it? Abortion is an abomination. I couldn't countenance such a thing. It's a sin against God!'

She shrugged. 'What's one more sin? I'm damned anyway.'

'No! No. I won't hear of it.' He paced across the room. 'You must confess your sins and find forgiveness. You must go away – leave Yardley. You don't love Harry, so what's to keep you here?'

'How am I supposed to do that? Harry won't let me out of the house with William. Even if I had the money, I won't go without my son.'

'Maybe I can help.' Reverend Buchanan paced across the study. 'I have a little money put by. Not much but enough to get you back to Bath and your mother.'

'Josiah won't let me stay. He says I belong to Harry, William too. I have no rights, Charles. None. Not even over my own son, Jem's son.'

286

His hands clenched behind his back, he stared out of the window. He didn't turn to address her. 'Then I'll set you up somewhere else. Far enough away to be no trouble.'

Trouble? Is that all she was to him? She stood beside him and gripped his arm, making him face her. 'Give me the fare to Van Diemen's Land, and you'll never hear from me again.'

'That's out of the question. My stipend isn't that generous. And Josiah would never forgive me.'

She bit her upper lip. She needed money, and Josiah had made his feelings clear: she was now Harry's responsibility. 'I heard there's a woman in Denton who gets rid of unwanted brats. She's not cheap, but it would be a permanent solution.'

Emotions warred across his face, and his lips moved in silent prayer. 'No-one need know?'

'Not if I pay her enough.'

'And we could still see one another?'

If he paid enough for her silence, she wouldn't need to give her body to this hypocrite for the small gifts she sold; she'd be on the first ship out with William and her unborn child. 'Of course.'

He moved across to his desk and unlocked a drawer. 'May God forgive us, Ella.'

***

The guards aboard *Tortoise* had been doubled since Knocker and his mate drowned. Jem stared into a stygian darkness waiting for the bells to sound the end of his night's captivity. The rattle of a chain suggested he wasn't the only one awake. He fingered the new set of grooves above his bunk; by his reckoning, it was around the twenty-sixth of October, give or take a day, and for the tenth night in a row, all prisoners had been shackled to their bunks. He needed a piss, and from the stench mingling with the smell of rot, slime, whale lamp oil, foul breath, and unwashed bodies, some of the men hadn't been able to wait until they were allowed to the latrines.

287

The thud of boots overhead suggested the watch was about to change. Light filtered through the grill that led to the upper deck, faint but discernible. Voices shouted, the ship shuddered, and the long, slow rattle of the anchor chain being raised suggested they were about to move again. Were they sailing at last?

A slow rocking motion began, and he closed his eyes, trying to ignore the heaving in his stomach. The crew said men got used to it, that the seasickness would only last a few days, but last time he'd wanted to die, he'd felt so ill. Maybe the sea would be calmer. Maybe…

He tried to picture Ella's face, to recreate the feel of William's soft hair on his lips, to breathe in their warm comforting smell. His fingers twined themselves through Ella's hair, her body silken against his; his lips found hers. 'I love you, Ella.'

The ship heeled over, and the timbers creaked, echoing the straining of the rigging and the tautness of the sailcloth. Two bells rang, followed by a pause and two more rings. The hatch opened and guards strode down the centre of the tween-decks unlocking the chains that bound them to their bunks. The sound of chains being drawn through rings would haunt his dreams forever. He joined the dash for the latrines, running with the short legs apart stride that moving in shackles dictated.

Guards stood by the latrine entrance, hurrying them in and out as if afraid, even at dawn, that the unnatural practices they abhorred would take place if they didn't watch the men constantly. A shiver ran down his spine: men without an outlet for their natural urges took their pleasure where they could, and he avoided going to the latrines without Cal or Nat, even when the guards were watching.

By the time he was on deck with his bedding roll, Plymouth Dock was lost in a low layer of autumn mist, and above it, like ears of corn held high above the earth at harvest, the masts of the ships stood tall, their flags fluttering in the slight breeze. The roofs of the houses of Plymouth Hoe, hanging above the trailing wreaths of mist, shone orange in the low sun. If this was to be his last vision

288

of England, it was a beautiful sight.

He swallowed and steadied his balance to the gentle movement of the ship. Waves slapped blue-green against the ship's sides, and a trail of white spume stretched behind them where the bows had parted the waves like a plough cutting a furrow and turning the damp clods to shine smooth in the sun. They were almost out of the sound now.

'Look lively, there.' A guard pushed him along the deck to where the bedding was stored. He sighed, beyond tears. Bed boards to scrub, decks to holystone, oakum to pick, and rations to wait for anxiously, if he could keep them down this time. Such was his life now. He glanced back at Plymouth as the sea mist engulfed it and it was lost to him forever. 'Goodbye, Ella. I'll never forget you.'

***

Ella counted the coins in her purse. Thirteen pounds. It was enough to get her to Plymouth or London but not enough for her fare or to keep herself and William away from Newhay, where she was fed, housed, and clothed. Her pregnancy was certain now, her breasts tender, and her mood swung from determination to despair. She tucked the purse back into the cleft between her breasts and knocked on Charlotte Weston's door.

'Door's open!'

She pressed on the latch and pushed open the door. The interior of the cottage was gloomy.

Charlotte sat at the table by the small window, her head bent over her work. She turned in her chair. 'Oh, come in, Ella. Kettle's on the hob. Don't mind me if I carry on. I've a piece of lace to finish for her ladyship. '

The lace pinned out on the cushion was intricate, fine and beautiful, and Charlotte would be paid a pittance for it. Her ladyship could afford to pay more, living as she did in a fine house on a large estate; her ladyship didn't have to sell her body to afford nice things. Had she tempted a rich husband with her favours, or

289

had he married her for her dowry? She doubted love came into the equation with estates and money involved and heirs needed. Did her ladyship consider herself a whore or a chattel?

'Kettle's boiling, Ella?'

'I was admiring your work.' She moved across to the range. 'I'd never have the patience.' She warmed the teapot and spooned a careful measure of leaves into it. 'My fingers are more used to scrubbing than lacemaking or needlework.'

Charlotte glanced over her spectacles. 'You didn't bring William to see me, Ella. Is he well?'

She splashed boiling water into the pot. 'I'm still not allowed to bring him out alone. Harry doesn't trust me.'

'You have to make him trust you, or you'll be a prisoner in your own home.' Charlotte went back to her work, her fingers flying across the delicate patterns, moving pins from place to place. 'You have to forget James, Ella. It's what he asked you to do, and for good reason. Make a life with Harry. You could do much worse.'

'Am I being unreasonable, wanting to follow Jem?' Cups and saucers clattered as she set them out on the table. 'Wanting William to know his father? Am I chasing shadows?'

'Ella, my dearest girl.' Charlotte's voice was soft and sad. 'You don't need my permission to fall in love with Harry.'

'Is that what I'm doing?' She let a spoon fall to the tiled floor. Harry wasn't entirely the monster she'd first thought. She shook her head. 'No... no... I don't love Harry. I love Jem.'

Charlotte picked up the spoon and wiped it on her apron, then poured the tea. 'It's possible to love two men in your life. Think about it, Ella. Give Harry a chance, for yours and William's sakes. The boy needs a father. I've seen the way young Harry looks at you and William in church.'

It was true that Harry was kinder to her now. Was he growing to love her? Deep inside, despite her love for Jem, there was a part of her that had grown fond of Harry. If he did love her, then she'd

290

abused his love, and the truth would destroy him. Her hand went to her breast; beneath it lay her purse of immoral earnings and the blue jay feather that drove her lust for money at any cost. 'You think I should settle for Harry, for second-best?'

'Few of us are fortunate enough to live all our lives with the one we love. You've had your time with Jem. Be thankful for what you had, not live in regret for what you don't have. Death or disaster parts most of us before our lives are run.' Charlotte stirred a chip of sugar into her cup. 'There's many a widow or widower will tell you as much.'

'I know you're right, it's just...'

Charlotte went back to her work. 'You're still in love with Jem? You always will be, Ella. You always will be.'

How much should she confess to Charlotte? 'I'm pregnant.'

Charlotte dropped a pin, sending it tinkling to the flag floor. A blackbird sang outside the window. Charlotte rubbed her hands over her eyes. 'That settles it then, Ella. It can't be James's child. Your life is with Harry. Does he know?'

'I haven't told him yet. I was hoping he'd never need to know, but saving the fare to follow Jem will take months – years even.'

'Taking a child from him will break his heart, Ella. You have to put your own desires aside, and put your children and Harry first.'

'Yes, I know. You're right.' She broke off a small piece of sugar from the loaf and dropped it into her tea. She sighed heavily and stirred.

'I am right. I love James as much as you do. Do you think I don't lie awake nights, worrying? All that sea and that small ship. Is he being fed? Is he unhappy? You'll drive yourself mad if you let yourself dwell on it. He asked you to get on with your life, and that's what I'm doing best I can. It's what he'll be doing. He did a bad thing, and he's paying for it. I have to put the rest of my family first now.' Tears rolled down Charlotte's cheeks. 'We have to live our lives without him.'

291

It was what she'd wanted to discuss with Charlotte. Had she expected the poor woman to support her desire to take two young children, one of them her grandson, to the colonies? Was she being selfish even contemplating it? She stared into the brown liquid still swirling gently in her tea cup, wondering if the tealeaves would tell her something she wanted to hear. Her mind went back to the gypsy woman whose palm she'd crossed outside the court in Northampton and who'd told her she'd be married and have children. The Romany had given her back her coppers, saying she'd need her luck. What would the old woman have read in the tealeaves?

Chapter Twenty-Seven

Thirteen pounds· Ella couldn't make the coins amount to more, however many times she counted them. She needed more. She'd told the reverend – Charles – that she hadn't been able to abort her child. She'd had no intention of doing such a thing, but how could she get him to part with more coin? He'd already succumbed to gentle blackmail, giving her small presents which she sold or exchanged for something more saleable, but her purse seemed to get no heavier.

She stared into the small mirror in her bedroom. Her bosom was rounded and filled her underbodice. She was still in the full bloom of youth. Still desirable to men like Harry, Charles, and John. There must be other men, well-to-do men who would enjoy what her body had to offer. No-one in Yardley Hastings came to mind, but farther afield, where she wasn't known... She dressed in her second-best dress and ran down the stairs.

Jane looked up at her footsteps, her hands covered in flour, and frowned. 'There's work to be done, girl. Pies to be made. No time for you to go tripping off into town.'

'Harry is allowing me to visit my mother.' She hadn't asked him yet, but her husband seemed to be gradually falling under her spell. Before long, if she kept him dangling on her sexual tether and pretended she was happy, he'd agree to her taking William out alone. She flounced out of the house, knowing how it would annoy Jane, and picked her way to the cowshed.

A hand grabbed her arm and pulled her behind the building. John's rough hands snagged the fine material of her bodice and fondled her breasts. She pushed him away. 'I need to visit my mother. You'll help me persuade Harry and Jane I should go?'

He fiddled with his fly. 'You know what I want in return. For what I pay you...'

She leant her back against the cowshed wall and raised her skirt out of the dirt. It was the price she must pay for half a sovereign a month. 'Be quick about it, then. I need to catch the carrier to Northampton.'

He hitched up her skirt and pulled down her undergarments. She stepped out of them and he lifted her bodily, holding her beneath her thighs. His breath on her neck was hot and rapid, his thrusting hard and driven. He came inside her and withdrew, letting her fall to the ground, then buttoned his flies, and held out a hand to help her up. One shoe had come off and her underclothes trailed in the dirt. 'Quick, get them pantaloons on before someone comes. It would be easier if you didn't wear the bloody things. We could have a quick fuck, anywhere, no messing.'

She adjusted her clothing. John seemed to take pleasure in taking what belonged to his son. 'I'll keep that in mind, John, for next time. Now, back me up when I talk to Harry.'

***

It was evening by the time Ella arrived in Northampton. The lamplighters were out with their long poles lighting the gas lamps in the streets. She walked around the town, wondering where to find suitable lodging. As far as the Cartwrights were concerned, she was in Bath and wouldn't be back for several days. How much could she earn before she had to go home?

But for William, she'd never go home: she'd stay in town and earn what she needed. How many men must she pleasure before she could steal William away and set sail for the far side of the globe?

An inn seemed like the place men might frequent, but women weren't allowed inside such places. She stood under a sycamore tree and watched the patrons coming and going. One or two looked her way. Across the road, carriages stood in rows outside an imposing building. These would have well-to-do owners. She moved closer, watching the door of the establishment. It seemed it was a gentlemen's club. What morals would such men have, where money could buy anything they desired?

She raked her fingers through her hair, letting her long auburn curls fall loose. Ella Weston would never contemplate what she was about to do, but Ella Cartwright had no scruples where men were concerned. Men's laws had forced her to become a legalised prostitute for Harry. John's lust had paid scant respect to her person or her wishes. She had no right to protect herself against such ravishing. Now, though they thought they used her, it was she who used them. They were her ticket to Van Diemen's Land: nothing more and nothing less.

A man walked towards his carriage, a fancy affair drawn by a pair of matched bays. She lifted her skirt clear of the ground with one hand. He glanced towards her, and she lifted it higher, exposing an ankle and calf. Her stomach tightened as he changed course and came closer. He was portly with a ruddy complexion and side whiskers and was dressed in a silk waistcoat and fine breeches, with a topcoat cut similar to the latest Bath fashion. This was a man of some import, a man of wealth.

He looked her up and down. 'Will you come with me?'

She smiled and nodded. A housemaid's wage was about twelve pounds a year, which was a pound a month. Two hundred and forty pennies for thirty days, say twenty-six days, given that Sundays were reserved for two visits to church and tea at the rectory. That was less than ten pence a day. What was the going rate for a whore? How many men could she tempt in a day? Two, three, more? 'I'll come with you for a shilling.'

He waved a gloved hand and escorted her to his carriage, where his coachman waited patiently for instructions. 'To the Golden Lion, Adams.'

The coachman flicked his whip, and the matched bays leant into their harness and high-stepped away from the square, their heads held unnaturally high by bearing reins, as was the fashion among the well-heeled.

'What's your name, girl?'

'Ella, sir.'

'How old are you?' He smiled, not unkindly.

'Eighteen.'

'You don't look like the other whores. Have you done this before?'

'You're my first, sir. I'm only doing it because I need the money. I have a child to support, and my husband's been sent to the colonies. I hope to please.'

He shook his head and put a finger beneath her chin to lift her face to look at her better. 'Oh, you'll please, Ella. You'll please very much.'

The carriage rumbled to a halt outside the Golden Lion. The man helped her down and escorted her inside the inn. He approached the innkeeper. 'Room four, my good man.'

The innkeeper made a slight bow. 'Certainly, Mr Summers. It's ready for you.'

'The key?'

The innkeeper nodded towards the ceiling and Mr Summers smiled. 'Excellent. We don't wish to be disturbed.'

'I understand, sir.'

Mr Summers slipped the man a florin. She'd only asked a shilling to have this man grunt and sweat between her thighs: no wonder he'd taken her up on her offer. She'd ask more, next time. Much more. A hand beneath her elbow propelled her up wooden stairs and along a corridor. He pushed open a door at the far end of the passage and held it for her to enter the low room. Four men lounged on leather chairs. They looked up when she entered.

'Who are these men?' The reverend's sermon about the *social evil* came to her mind unbidden. Prostitution was frowned on, forbidden by the church. Was this a trap set by the clergy?

Mr Summers closed the door behind her. 'These are my friends, Ella.' He pushed her farther into the room. 'I've brought you a real treat, as I promised, gentlemen. This here is Ella. She's only eighteen, and this is her first time, so be gentle with her.'

Be gentle with her? One of the men patted the bed and loosened his breeches belt. Another ran his tongue across his lips. The awful truth dawned on her as they gathered round. She'd come looking to sell her body and sell it she would. She couldn't afford to be choosy: money was the only important thing. She forced her mouth into a smile, her heart thumping wildly, and sat on the edge of the bed. 'It's a shilling each this time. If you want me again, it'll be extra.'

***

Tortoise had followed the coast of England until the land had faded from sight. Locked in the heaving dark for twenty-two hours out of the twenty-four, Jem had little idea of where they were or how far they'd travelled. A globe of the world had sat on the schoolmaster's desk when he was a boy; he wished he'd taken more notice of his teacher.

Every day, the routine was the same: up at four bells, cleaning and scrubbing the decks and bed boards and then back into the dark with his pot of gruel for breakfast and a holystone to scrape the tween-deck. A second hour was allowed on deck later in the day, when they had sermons on the moral wickedness of their ways, or oakum to pick, or socks to knit. Every day saw the same level horizon, though the outline of land to port suggested they were off the coast of northern France, or Spain, or West Africa. He stared at the blue hills beyond the coastline. Could they have sailed as far as Africa yet? The little he knew about the continent from his schooling suggested the land was full of slaves: black men, savages, the like of which he'd never seen.

He closed his eyes and tried to picture Ella's face, concentrating on moving with the ship so his stomach didn't heave. She'd be safe in Bath with her mother, caring for William. It eased his mind to think of her loved and secure and warm. It was bitterly cold on deck with the wind off the Atlantic chilling the November air, but at least up here it was fresh. As they sailed south, one of the guards had warned, it would get warmer and decidedly less pleasant below deck. It was already suffocating due to the proximity of bodies and the poor ventilation.

According to the grooves he'd scratched above his bunk, they were eleven days out of Plymouth which would make it November the fifth. Bare, craggy mountains rose straight out of the sea to the east, the cliffs reddish-brown in the dull light of morning. The wind blew from the southwest bringing with it light rain and a hope of sunshine. Had it not been for the fear of suffocating, or being thrown overboard in a storm, and the uncertainty of life in a penal colony without Ella and William, he'd have been quite excited by the adventure of sailing halfway around the world with Cal and Nat.

'Cape Verde Islands.'

'Pardon?'

A guard pointed to the craggy islands to their east. The man was one he'd spoken to before; he had a pregnant wife on board, and he'd asked after her welfare. 'Cape Verde Islands. Another week, Captain Hood tells me, if we don't get caught in the Doldrums, and we should make St Peter and Paul Rocks.'

'How far will we have sailed? How far is left to go?'

'I reckon we've come the best part of two thousand miles. That's about twelve thousand still to sail. We've barely begun, lad.' The guard shook his head. 'Barely begun.'

'And how's your wife? When's the baby due?'

'It's kind of you to ask, considering your own plight. Hopefully, it'll be born on board.'

He raised an eyebrow. Surely no woman would want to give birth on a convict ship. 'How so?'

'Surgeon Brownrigg is a competent surgeon. I doubt the hospital on Van Diemen's Land is as well attended.'

298

'Is it your first child?'

'Yes. It's a worry – a difficult time.'

He nodded, his eyes smarting. 'My son, William. He's just a baby. I only ever held him the once. Keep your family close, mister. Don't do what I done.'

The guard put a hand on his shoulder and squeezed it. 'What's done is done, boy. No good dwelling on it.' The man released his grip. 'Time for you to get below and let some other poor devils up in the fresh air.'

He nodded, dreading his incarceration, shambled towards the hatch, and descended into fetid darkness.

***

Five more scratches adorned the bulkhead above Jem's bunk. Five days and a thousand miles farther from Ella. The ship shuddered as it changed direction yet again. The Doldrums, according to the guard, was an area of ocean with changeable currents and winds. Thunder rumbled, and a crack of lightning lit the inside of the tween-decks for a moment, picking out pale, anxious faces. Muttered prayers rose in a whispered chant. The air was thick with sweat and fear, and the thunder rolled on, echoing and rumbling. Water, rainwater or sea swell, dripped from the ventilation holes in large drops.

'Suppose a mast gets hit?' Cal voiced his own fear. 'Suppose we're de-masted and capsized. Suppose…'

'I can't swim.' Nat's voice. 'Never learned how.'

'We won't need to swim, Nat.' Jem laughed, the sound high-pitched and nervous against the murmured prayers. 'Trapped down here, we'll bloody drown afore any bugger lets us out.' The ship lurched again and righted as the fey winds caught at the sails. Were they still sailing south?

The hatch opened and feet descended the ladder, blocking the brief square of daylight. 'Time for the next batch above. Get your lazy arses up here.'

299

He followed Cal and Nat in their rush for fresh air, jamming the bottom of the ladder as the previous group of convicts climbed down.

'Get a move on.' Cal pushed a man out of the way in his haste to get topside. 'Let me out.'

'Keep your shirt on, mate.' The man, taller and broader than Cal, shoved back at him. 'You think I want to be down here? Keep a civil tongue.'

Cal braced his shoulders and shoved the man's chest. It had little impact. 'Or what?'

'Or I'll break your sorry arse.' Light from the ventilation hole caught the man's brow, furrowed like a ploughed field. 'You watch yourself in the latrines, mate. Just watch yourself, all right?'

'You there. Less of that. Get up here, now.'

Cal shinned up the ladder towards the guard and comparative safety; Cal had made an enemy, not wise in a ship full of men with frayed tempers. Like rats in a trap they were beginning to turn on one another.

He followed Cal topside; he'd have to watch his cousin's back until things calmed down.

Up on deck, Surgeon Brownrigg surveyed the gathered men. 'It's been brought to my attention that some of you men are indulging in practices abhorrent to God. Men have urges which must be controlled. You have three months before we make land, and then you'll be in a penal colony separated from women. Masturbation may be an evil before God, but it is the lesser evil. If you have urges, then...' He waved a hand vaguely. 'Better see to yourself than risk syphilis and other such diseases. The guard at the latrines will stand twenty-four hours in four-hour watches. Be warned. Anyone caught indulging in buggery will have a day in the sweatbox on deck.'

He'd already had a spell in the hotbox, thanks to Knocker. He didn't envy anyone the experience, especially as the weather had grown much warmer.

He let Brownrigg's sermonising drift over his head as he picked oakum and, instead, kept one eye on the distant islands. Were they St Peter and Paul Islands, of which the guard had spoken? If so, they were on course. Rain fell in large splashes on the deck, and he shivered despite the humidity. Lightning seared the sky, and thunder rumbled in the distance. The storm was moving away.

The islands grew steadily larger, but the ship changed direction with the wind and current so often they seemed to make little headway. Above his head, the sails flapped abjectly as the wind fell and the waves calmed. The crew ran to trim sail, to make the most of what little breeze there was, but it made no difference. They were caught in the Doldrums, and it seemed possible, in that singular moment, that *Tortoise* and her passengers would be trapped there, in purgatory, forever.

Chapter Twenty-Eight

Ella twirled the globe on the reverend's desk with one finger and stopped it in the middle of Australia. Where was Jem now? She sighed. She'd profited by twenty shillings from her stay in Northampton, and was still sore from the experience. Lodgings had cost her dear, though she'd found a madam in Market Street happy to give her bed and board for a cut of her earnings.

'You still miss him, don't you?' Charles's voice behind her was soft, sympathetic.

'I will find him, one day.'

'This obsession, Ella. It can lead you to nowhere but more grief, for you and William, not to mention Harry.'

'I can't forget Jem.'

'I'm sure Harry's smitten with you.'

The thought kept her awake at night. 'I should be happy if he's grown to love me. Part of me has grown to love him too, but…'

'James was your first love. I understand.' Reverend Buchanan put a chaste hand upon her shoulder and twirled the globe with his other hand. It came to rest showing the South Atlantic and the Antarctic Ocean. His forefinger pointed to an expanse of empty blue, somewhere around the second T in Atlantic. 'He should be around here, I would think. He's far beyond your reach, Ella. This feeling will pass, with time. Trust in God and do his will. Don't let James Weston ruin your life. Let yourself love Harry.'

Tears trickled down her cheeks. Charles turned her towards him and thumbed them away. 'You know how much I love you, Ella. What I feel for you isn't just lust. It began that way, God forgive me.'

She squeezed his arm. 'I know. You're a good man, Charles. God will forgive us our fall from grace. Our need for physical comfort overcame us when we should have sought spiritual comfort in our Lord.'

'What made you so wise, child?'

'Life. Loss. Love.'

The reverend let out a deep breath. 'Are you determined to follow Jem?'

'Yes.'

'And nothing I say will stop you?'

'No.'

'What about the child?'

'It isn't yours. I'm sorry. I said it was to get money out of you for an abortion.'

He frowned. 'You'd abort Harry's child?'

'No. It's my child too. I'd never abort a child. I was just after your money. Everything I do is for the money. I've fourteen pounds and the fare is nineteen pounds.'

'Fourteen pounds. How have you saved so much?'

She lowered her eyes and hesitated a moment too long.

'Ella?'

She pursed her lips.

'You've not stolen it?'

'No. I'm not a thief. I've earned it.'

'How?'

Heat flushed her cheeks.

'You sold the gifts I gave you?'

She nodded. 'I need money, not presents.'

'They were but trinkets...' He frowned. 'I'm not the only man you've given favours to, am I?'

'How else can I earn the fare before I'm old and wrinkled? Tell me how, and I'll do it gladly.'

'The child *is* Harrys?'

She shrugged. 'I don't know. It might be.'

'But he thinks it is. I bet he's crowing like a cockerel.'

'He doesn't know I'm pregnant. It's early days and anything could happen. And...'

'And?'

'If I get enough money quickly, he'll never need to know I am. He won't grieve the loss of what he doesn't know he has.'

'You can't hide this from him.' The reverend walked across to the window, stared out of it for a moment, and then turned back to face her. 'Who else's could it be, if it isn't mine or Harry's?'

'I can't say.'

'Ella, prostitution is the social evil of our time. It's a crime against God. It's dangerous. Men are dangerous. There are cutthroats and pickpockets out there, and you could catch all manner of awful diseases. What's more, you could pass them on, to me, to Harry. For all you know, you may even harm your child.'

She'd really hoped she could leave before her pregnancy became obvious but, in all likelihood, the child would be born before she raised the fare to Van Diemen's Land. She wouldn't be able to hide it from Harry. Anger pushed down guilt. 'According to the church, any woman living with a man who isn't her legal husband is a prostitute. I've been called a whore before, so I may as well earn the title, and it isn't against the law. Hell, even Harry and John have used whores. Even you use me, a whore.'

'Mind your tongue or suffer God's righteous wrath, Ella.' His anger at her blasphemy faded. His eyes showed his hurt, his remorse. 'But hell is where we'll all go. Ella, please, if you love your son, give up this ridiculous notion about following James. Go home to your husband and baby. Be a proper wife. Tell Harry he's to be a father. Tell him now, or I shall.'

***

The low fogs of November mingled with wood smoke from the farmhouse chimneys. The air was dank and cold, bringing with it the reminder that winter was hard on its heels. After a wet summer, winter wasn't something Harry looked forward to, except the long nights gave him more time with Ella. He'd left her lighting the range ready to cook breakfast for the family and staff. She was throwing herself into her life, now that James Weston was gone and forgotten. He smiled inwardly: he had Ella, and Jem's son, while the murdering bastard rotted on a convict ship, never to return. William might not be his own flesh and blood, but he was fond of the child, and it was good to have a baby in the house. Maybe soon, he'd have his own son: a son who favoured his looks.

His good humour extended to Josephine, the latest milkmaid, as the last cow ambled out of the milking parlour. She was a slight girl, dark-haired, and dark complexioned, and, he guessed, barely fifteen, but stronger than she looked and a good worker. 'Get the calves fed, then take yourself off for breakfast, Jo.'

She smiled back shyly, looking up at him beneath long, black lashes. 'If you're sure that's all?'

'All till after breakfast. Go and eat. Look at you. There's nothing of you.'

'Mr Cartwright reckoned you might have need of me. He said if I was to keep my job…'

He raised an eyebrow. Before Ella came back into his life, he'd have had the girl on her first day, after he'd held her down for his father. He'd had plans to turn the tables and have her first, make his father see him for the man he was. 'Come here.'

The girl stepped towards him and looked down at her feet. 'What do you want of me, sir?'

305

His cock quickened involuntarily. He put a finger beneath her chin and lifted her face. Her eyes were a dark, liquid brown, like Damson's. She was pliant and willing, the stuff of which good, childbearing women, wives, were made. How could any man refuse what she offered? 'You're a maid?'

She blushed. 'No, sir.'

'My father?'

She said nothing, a sure sign his father had sworn her to secrecy on pain of dismissal.

'I wouldn't have wanted to rob one so young of her maidenhood. How old are you?'

'Thirteen, sir.'

He'd thought her older. He'd never had such young flesh, and he was only taking what was his due as an employer, what his father had already taken. His lips found hers, soft and yielding, yet nervous, tentative, but her body felt thin and bony beneath her clothing. Ella's lips had passion. Ella's body was sensuous and tantalising. Ella did things to his body, heart, and soul he'd not thought possible. He pushed the girl gently away: she was just another whore. 'Go and feed the calves, Jo. Then get some breakfast up at the house.' Ella was his life. She'd made him care for her, and no other girl, however young and innocent, would ever inflame his passion so again.

He turned, aware of a presence at his side. 'I told you, I'm done with you here.'

'Harry?'

'Ella...' He fumbled for the right words. 'I thought you were Jo. I've sent her to feed the calves. Is breakfast ready?'

Ella bit her top lip, a habit she had when uncertain. 'You and Jo? You weren't just...'

Ella cared that he might be unfaithful? 'I never touched her, Ella. I swear. She offered...' He waited for the explosion any wife might be expected to have, faced with such a blatant attempt to seduce her man, but Ella shrugged.

'She's too young to be so willing. I'll speak to her. You speak to your father. She's to be left alone.'

'I think it's too late for that.' He threw up his hands. 'That man will fuck anything with a skirt. Anyway, you came to tell me breakfast was ready?''

'I have something to tell you first.'

'Oh?' His heart skipped a beat. He'd been watching Ella carefully these last months, and something about her had changed. William was five months old, time enough for her to be with child again. 'You're pregnant?'

'You guessed?'

Now let his father crow over his bastards and call him a failure. He grabbed her by the waist and swung her round. 'Ella, that's wonderful news. I'm going to be a father.' He kissed her on the lips and then drew her closer, kissing her harder and deeper. 'God, you're beautiful.' Already aroused by Jo, he wasn't to be denied. His hands felt for her skirt, pushing it up as he backed her towards the cowshed wall. Her skin was soft, and he traced the curve of her hip and the gentle swell of her belly. Beneath her dress, she was naked. He released his erection, parted her legs with his knee, and pushed into her, moaning beneath caught-at breaths. 'I love you, Ella. God, how I love you.'

***

Ella balanced William on one hip and jiggled him. He was getting heavy for her to carry and, at five months, could sit on the floor unaided if she surrounded him with feather cushions, but today he was grizzly. He was teething and had kept her up most of the night.

He was a good child and normally happy to be with any member of the family, probably because she always had to leave him if she went abroad in the village or town.

She sang as she ironed a shirt, one-handed, on a blanket on the kitchen table. Harry had declared his love for her in a moment of elated passion. Did he mean it, or had his lust overcome his head? He treated her and William with kindness. Part of her, the parent and wife, the sensible part, wanted to settle for a simple life: the part of her that was a woman in love schemed her escape from drudgery.

Reverend Buchanan had forced her hand. Harry was so excited about the prospect of fatherhood that she hoped the child was his, but could she take his child? She knew what it felt like to think she might lose William. Could she do that to him?

She sighed. It was a decision she would have to make, before or after the child was born, but her mind ran in circles like a tethered goat, and she could find no release. She'd been obedient towards Harry, loving even, since she'd abandoned herself to her deeper physical needs: the need to be held, touched, and wanted, and the need to forget her grief if only for a few precious moments. Whatever her decision, she wanted more freedom from the constraints of the farm and to be able to take William with her. Could she persuade Harry to trust her to come home if she took the child to see Mrs Downs or Charlotte?

At breakfast, she broached the subject. She poured tea into Harry's cup. 'Harry, would you mind if I took William for a walk in the copse, now it's stopped raining at last? There may be some late sweet chestnuts blown down in the wind. I'll wrap him up warm.'

Jane frowned. 'There's floors to scrub, Ella, and the riding will be muddy. Gallivanting can wait.'

Harry swallowed a slice of belly pork and wiped the grease from his mouth with his sleeve. 'I say where she can go, Mother.' He beamed and sat taller in his chair. 'A woman with child needs her fresh air, as does William.'

Jane clapped her hands, feigning surprise. 'I'm so pleased for you, Harry. Ella…'

John glanced at her, at Jane, and then at Harry. 'Yes, well done, son. I knew you had it in you.' John's tone was a notch above dour. 'Don't let the girl down, Harry. You have responsibilities, now.'

Harry reached for the last slice of bread, beating John by a hair's breadth. The look of quiet triumph on his face when John withdrew his hand was unmistakable. She'd given Harry his ace card, and he knew it. 'Just to the copse, Ella. You're not to go towards the village.'

She smiled and kissed him on the top of his head. 'Just to the copse. I'll only be half an hour or so.' She picked her son from his highchair and wrapped him in a blanket. Outside, the fog still shrouded the ghostlike trees. Moisture dripped from skeletal branches, the air damp on her face. She shivered and turned up her collar, holding William closer. She'd won a small victory but a victory nonetheless. Once she'd shown she could be trusted to take her son out alone, and return with him, she'd be able to take him where she liked, when she liked. Van Diemen's Land, where her heart and hope resided, was one step closer.

She had maybe three months to earn the fare if she was to arrive in the colonies before her midsummer baby was born. She had to do this sooner, rather than later, or risk being trapped here forever.

'I promised you your father would know you, William. God willing, we'll be in Van Diemen's Land by midsummer.'

Chapter Twenty-Nine

Jem lay on his bunk, his clothes sticking to his back, his throat parched, and his lungs struggling for air. It was hot as hell itself. Tar from the caulking between the planks of the hull oozed down the sides of the ship, fouling clothes and bedding. Some even dripped from above, burning the skin where it touched. The mingled smells of tar and the latrines defined every waking hour, and the oppressive heat made sleep impossible. Nat's arm hung limply over the side of one of the hammocks strung from the ceiling, and from the bunk above his own, where the heat was even worse, quiet, laboured breaths echoed his own.

Men no longer had the energy to moan or pray, and an uneasy silence had settled over the tween-decks making the creaking and groaning of the hull ominously loud in the dark. The faltering sound of the air pumps, manned day and night to bring air down to the prisoners, laboured with the exhausted efforts of the men turning the handles. It was as if *Tortoise* was a hulk of dead men or men slumbering into death.

The weather had grown hotter and muggier, and the thunderstorms more frequent, the closer they got to the St Peter and St Paul Islands. The wind had settled into a prevailing south-easterly pattern, but *Tortoise* still shuddered whenever a violent gust veered suddenly to the south or east, setting the lamps and hammocks swinging and the prisoners gripping anything that was nailed down so as not to be hurled across the deck.

The ever-present bank of cloud hanging over the equator had, for days, turned the sea near the horizon grey and forbidding, and when sunrise came, it arrived suddenly. Sunset blanketed them in darkness in the same manner, with little twilight. Everything around them seemed strange and unnatural, and the prisoners lived in constant fear of the future. The guards and crew were as exhausted and debilitated as the prisoners: tempers were short and arguments many.

Two bells and then two more. On a hammock over the gangway, Cal stirred, cursing incoherently.

'You all right, Cal?'

'I can…can't…'

He levered himself into a sitting position. 'Can or can't what?'

'Can't…' Cal rolled over and landed on the floor. He lay there, waving an arm feebly. 'So thirsty… Head's banging. Give my right arm for a point – a pint. Can't get up.'

'You've sweat buckets. We all have. We need water. You have to get on deck for your ration. They won't give the bugger to me, or I'd bring it to you.'

Nat swung down from his hammock with practised ease and put a hand beneath Cal's arm. 'He's a deadweight.'

He tried to help lift Cal. He'd become so weak. 'If we can't get him topside, maybe we should tell the surgeon.'

Cal struggled onto his hands and knees. 'Gotta get out.' He began crawling towards the hatch. 'There ain't enough water. That's why they ration it. It won't last us out. We're all gonna die.'

'There isn't enough water?' A man's voice from somewhere farther to the bows. A northern accent.

'We're going to die.' Another voice, Arthur by the sound of it, took up the fear. 'It's hot as hell. We're as good as damned.'

The man in the bunk above him hadn't moved or uttered a word. 'Frank! Four bells. Wake up, man.'

There was no answer. He grabbed the man's arm and shook him. The arm fell limp, the skin odd to the touch, clammy, cold even. No sound of a breath. 'Dear God. Frank's dead.'

Nat echoed Cal's words. 'See, we're dead men. All of us.'

Men struggled from their beds and yanked down hammocks.

311

Bodies pressed in the gangway and pushed towards the hatch.

'Four bells have sounded.' The northerner's voice rose in panic. 'Why haven't they opened the hatch?'

'We're trapped.'

'They're leaving us here to die.'

'They'll take our water.'

A crash, and a square of paler dark sprinkled with stars, showed the hatch had been thrown open. Lamps illuminated upturned faces and wild eyes. Bed boards and bedding forgotten, men surged for the ladder that led to the deck, fresh air, and water, pushing others out of the way in their desperate efforts to survive.

A harsh voice shouted from above. 'One at a time, damn you, or there'll be a flogging. One at a time, I said. Guards!'

'There's a dead man down here.' He could hardly make himself heard above the raised voices.

A man shoved him aside. 'He can wait. We can't. We need water, or this hellhole will be full of dead men.'

He made it on deck at last and inhaled deeply, the dawn breeze a welcome relief. Guards, pistols drawn, ringed the hatch, while others pushed men into line to receive their ration of water, the doling out overseen by Surgeon Brownrigg. His turn came, and he reached for the mug and gulped the tepid Thames water, a taste of home.

A guard stood over them. 'One mug and get below for your bed boards and bedding. Any more trouble, and there'll be a lockdown.'

'A man died last night.' He stood his ground. 'Cal here can barely stand. He needs the surgeon to look at him. It's hot as hell down there. We can't breathe.'

Surgeon Brownrigg waved him out of the line and handed Cal a mug of water, holding the mug while he drank it. 'Take him to the hospital quarters, and I'll look at him when I've finished here.' He

312

glowered at the guard. 'I don't want another man dead on this voyage.'

Cal was a deadweight, but he helped his cousin back down the ladder and along to the hospital quarters, a small room about twelve feet by six feet with four bunks in two tiers. Three of the bunks were occupied. Cal collapsed onto the fourth, his clothing dark with sweat.

'Wait here for Surgeon Brownrigg. Nat and me'll see to your stuff.' He left his cousin and helped Nat carry the boards and bedding rolls up on deck. Some of the men had already stowed their bedding and taken their breakfast hubs back down to tween-decks.

On deck, a fight was in progress.

'You had more water than me.'

No, I didn't. I only had my share.'

'You'd already been in the queue once.'

'I hadn't, I swear.'

A guard fired his pistol, and the shot embedded itself in the main mast inches above the heads of the two men: the tableau froze. The captain of the guard strode forward. 'Manacle the prisoners. That man to the sweatbox. This man for a flogging.'

The convict was dragged away and the sweatbox door banged shut, leaving only his face visible through a small window. He'd spent time in the sweatbox. In this temperature, the man wouldn't survive. 'For God's sake, sir, the man will die in there.'

A guard snarled in his face. 'Quiet, or you'll get another taste of it yourself, scum.'

Surgeon Brownrigg put a hand on the guard's arm. 'The health of these men is my responsibility. I refuse to allow this.'

Major Cumberland snorted. 'And discipline is mine. These guards are under my command.'

Captain Hood joined the argument. 'My duty is to make the crossing in as short a time as possible without endangering the ship with mutiny. I have Kauri spars to load for the admiralty, at Te Karo Bay, after I've disembarked this cargo. Delay costs me dear.'

Cargo: that's all they were to Hood. He looked away, not wanting to be seen listening, and faced the stern of the ship, looking north to where his heart lay. To the east, the sun struggled from the clutches of the ocean, and to the north, the North Star hung barely above the horizon, waiting to be swallowed by the same empty Atlantic that spewed forth the sun. If the sea gave little indication of them moving south, the heavens were a dire warning of them leaving behind all that was familiar and dear.

Captain Hood's voice rang with irritation. Arguments between Hood, the guard's captain, Major Cumberland, and Surgeon Brownrigg were frequent and heated and were getting worse the farther south they sailed. *Tortoise* was not a happy ship.

Surgeon Brownrigg faced the captain. 'And I repeat, sir. It's my duty to see that the cargo…the prisoners, guards, and crew aboard this ship arrive in good health. The colonies need men, not corpses.'

'I'm aware of that, Brownrigg, and of the bounty paid for each man embarked alive. If we stop off at the Cape, the delay will cost the admiralty.'

The Cape? The two men seemed to be continuing a conversation they'd begun earlier.

'I need only that we moor long enough to bring aboard fresh supplies. The men are already showing signs of scurvy. In a weakened state, they may succumb to all manner of fatalities. I'll take a boat in myself, if need be.'

'One day, and that's all, Brownrigg. Or, by God, I'll sail without you.'

'Sir.' Brownrigg drew himself up to Hood's height and clicked his heels. 'My report will show you an able and compassionate captain. Keeping up the prisoners' morale will accomplish much that discipline won't.'

Hood nodded. 'As you will, Brownrigg.'

'Thank you, sir.'

Captain Hood hadn't finished. 'Major Cumberland, ten lashes only for this man, and the sweatbox punishment is to wait until sundown. Let that man out.'

The surgeon strode towards the group of prisoners. 'You! You, there, who spoke up for this man.'

Would Jem Weston never learn to keep his mouth shut? He looked up and wiped sweat from his eyes with the back of a manacled hand. 'Me, sir?' He was one of the lucky group still to be on deck, feeling the sea breeze on his skin. And lucky not to be the man being tied to the mast. Those below, awaiting their turn on deck, were stewing in their own juices.

'Yes, you, sir. What's your name?'

'Weston, sir.'

'Weston, tell the prisoners if they wish to write home, to have a letter written by the end of the second dog-watch, and I'll deliver them ashore when we moor off Cape Town. Someone will bring paper, quills, and ink and collect the missives.' Brownrigg turned on his heel and addressed the captain in a loud voice. 'These men are human beings, Captain. The temperature tween-decks is over a hundred degrees. Please ensure the air scoops are kept open, and the pumps working, so the poor bastards still down there can breathe. Better still, allow them all to sleep on deck at night.'

'I'll see the scoops are kept open whenever the seas allow it and make sure their time on deck is increased. The admiralty won't be happy if I let water into the holds and scuttle the ship, Brownrigg, and Major Cumberland won't be happy at extra guard duties for the men of the ninety-sixth.'

'The security of the ship is your concern, Captain. The health of the ship is mine. Cumberland has three officers and ninety-nine Regulars of Foot. He can surely guard four hundred prisoners who have nowhere to run and are too exhausted from the heat to do so anyway.'

Hood pulled back his lips in a grimace. 'They aren't the only ones suffering from the heat. The children are restless, the women fractious, and the crew mutinous: one of the guards' wives has gone into labour, and the whole ship is at breaking point.'

'Will we have enough water, Captain? I'm rationing it, but the men are desperately thirsty and this heat makes it worse. Maybe we can bring aboard a few extra barrels at Cape Town?'

'See it's done, Brownrigg. One day moored only, though.'

'Thank you, Captain Hood. Now I'll see the prisoners, crew, and guards get paper and ink, and I'll see to my sick. And get that hatch open. You, Weston!'

'Me, sir?' He'd been waiting for the altercation to end, but Brownrigg's tone still made him jump.

'Yes, dammit. Go with the guard to fetch paper and ink, and take it below. And get two men to bring up that body. Letters will be collected at the end of the second dog-watch, remember. That's eight bells to you landlubbers.'

The hatch was thrown open, and heat and stench rose from the opening, shimmering the air like heat from a fetid bread oven. Men clamoured to be let out for their turn on deck as his group was forced back down into a hole as hot as hell.

***

The men took turns at a makeshift desk to write their letters home to their loved ones by the light of the open hatch and an oil lamp that swung the paper from light to shadow and back again. Jem held the pot of ink still as quill tip scratched on paper and each man sought to comfort those he'd left behind with a lesser truth. Those that could write penned letters for those that couldn't, to be marked with a cross. He tried to think what he should say and where to send it. He'd known Ella's parents' address in Bath, but he couldn't bring it to mind, now. Would Mr Josiah Barton,

316

Solicitor, Bath be enough to find her? And, if he wrote there, would Josiah pass the letter on? He wouldn't blame the man if he burnt it.

Or was he being selfish, writing to Ella when she should be forgetting him? His mother would be worrying, and Joe Upton's family deserved an apology he hadn't yet made. He'd taken a man's life in a moment of rage. No excuse. Perhaps writing to the Uptons would ease his nightmares: nightmares of blood, splintered bone, and Joe's lifeless face.

Eight bells sounded the end of the second dog-watch. Feet on the rungs of the ladder heralded guards. He folded his letter in half, wrote the Upton's address on an envelope, and slipped the letter inside it. It would be a month, maybe two, before it arrived in Yardley, and by then, he should be nearing Van Diemen's Land. He'd begged Mrs Upton to let his mother know that he was well. His hand found the blue jay feather, bedraggled and stuck to his chest with sweat. He smoothed the feather between his fingers and drew it across his lips. Did Ella think of him? Would she tell young William about his father?

It would be sunset soon, the day gone almost before it had begun. Another night of breathless sweating.

'Roll up your bedding and take it on deck.' The guard strode down the centre of the tween-deck. 'You're sleeping on deck tonight, and I've got to stand a watch. I'll put a shot through the first man who causes me trouble.'

Their bedding rolls laid out in haphazard rows, Arthur leaned across Nat. 'Frank's dead. How many more of us are going to end up in the deep?'

Cal, released from the infirmary, rolled towards him. 'I thought I was a gonna, Jem.'

He couldn't bear the thought of losing Cal or Nat. 'All we can do is pray.' He didn't think it would help much.

'Pray?' Arthur touched the side of his nose. 'The only thing written in stone is your epitaph. That's what my old dad used to

317

say. I doubt leaving our fate to God will alter much, Jem.'

He frowned. 'What are you suggesting?'

Arthur lifted his hands to show his manacles. 'If we all behave for a few days, they'll take these off us again. There are four hundred of us to one hundred of them.'

'You're suggesting mutiny?'

'Not all the guards are happy going to Van Diemen's Land. If I can get a couple of them on our side and get the key to the arms store...'

Whispers spread through the prisoners stretched out, unsleeping, on deck.

'How many of us can use a pistol?' Cal had a point.

Nat leaned in close. 'How many pistols are there on board, Arthur?'

'I'll find out. Jem, ask about, see who are our best shots and who has the nerve to pull the trigger.'

'Count us in.' He nodded to Cal and Nat. 'We three killed a man who shot at us. It's why we're here.'

'But can you kill in cold blood, if you have to?'

Joe Upton lay dead at his feet, killed in a moment of madness. He'd do his part. He must. 'If I have to.'

Arthur nodded. 'Then I'll talk to the guards and find out what we need to know.'

Nat rubbed his forehead. 'Do you really think we can do this, Jem?'

He looked around at the prone forms lying beneath the stars. 'There are enough desperate men aboard to pull this off.' He took a deep breath. 'We all have families we want to see again. I'm not doing this for me, I'm doing it for Ella and William. I'll see them again or die in the attempt.'

Nat reached out and gripped his arm. 'Then, so will I.'

Cal's face showed his concern. 'But we're exiled for life, Jem. Even if this mutiny succeeds, we can't go home.'

Arthur wasn't deterred. 'Plenty of people have aliases. The island of Trinidade is only days away. It's the last land we'll pass close to before the Cape of Good Hope. If we can take the ship, we can land on Trinidade or make our way to South America and up the coast. Go anywhere we damn well please. If we wait until the hue and cry has died down, we can go home.'

Fear made him cautious. 'We need a fool-proof plan in place, tomorrow at the latest. We need to know all the prisoners are up for it. Nothing must go wrong.'

Arthur smiled. 'We'll have pistols, powder, and shot. We know when the watches change. If we plan to take the ship at midnight, when the crew and guards change, and the sympathetic guards make sure they're on duty, what can go wrong?' His friend's confidence was contagious.

Ella called to him. He'd make his way back to her after a safe period of time. Use an alias, send word to her, and they'd start a new life together under new identities. It must be possible. Like Arthur said, plenty of people used aliases.

St Peter and Paul Islands rose out of a vast, empty sea. Barren, craggy islands and rocks tore holes in the star-studded heavens, a tiny connection to the rest of the world to which he clung. The night soon left them behind and as they travelled south and crossed the equator, the wind changed, veering east and northeast. Finally, the breeze picked up and blew a gale that filled the sails and drove the ship before it.

He lay on deck, between Cal and Nat, the wind caressing his skin as the North Star sank below the horizon. Arthur, who'd been in the navy, said once the equator was crossed, Polaris couldn't be seen. Would he ever see it again? He would. He must. A day, maybe two, and *Tortoise* would be theirs.

Hope filled him with determination to make his way back to England, work his passage: walk, if he had to. In eight or nine

319

months, maybe as early as midsummer, he could be home. Ella would wait for him, if he wrote to her and told her he was coming. 'I will see you again, Ella. I promise.'

The heavens looked down on him as he listened to Cal's and Nat's gentle snoring, the quiet voices of the men on watch, and the living sounds of the great ship as she ploughed southwards through the night beneath strange stars.

The End

I'd love it if you left a review at
http://mybook.to/OnDifferentShores

For those who may like to read on, Chapter One of Book Two of
the three part series follows. Get Book Two at
http://mybook.to/BeneathStrangeStars

***

Beneath Strange Stars – Book Two of 'For Their Country's Good.'

The Barrington Prologue

From different climes, o'er wide spread seas we come,
(Though not with much éclat, or beat of drum)
True patriots all; for, be it understood,
We left our country for our country's good.

~

Henry Carter c1800

Chapter One

Upon a wild, tempestuous sea, I sail my troubled dreams of you.
Wave after towering wave crash down upon me as I sleep,
The stars are few and small,
And I shall drown.
Slowly, the storm abates, its anger tempered by the wind.
The sea looks kinder now although the stars are strange
And, clinging to my driftwood, I perceive
A distant shore.
Ever gently wash the waves over my tired mind and aching heart
And drifting out of sleep onto the beach, I wake,
And waking, find me
In a strange land.

Rebecca Bryn c1983

***

HMS Tortoise: November 1841.

Two bells: Jem turned towards Ella and let his hand follow the curve of her hip. She moaned softly and snuggled closer, putting an arm across his shoulder. Her auburn hair spread across the pillow, taking on a silver sheen in the light of the full moon through the thin curtains. He kissed her cheek, her lips, and she responded sleepily: warm and drowsy. There was time before he had to be at Ruddle's for the threshing. He rolled her gently onto her back and covered her with his body. She moved to accept him.

Two bells. But the threshing machine had broken. Ella was in Newhay Copse.

'I'll get you, you young bugger.' Joe Upton, one of Lord Northampton's gamekeepers, chased her with a double-barrelled shotgun cocked and ready.

He pounded after them, the barrel of Cal's gun in his hands. It wasn't Ella who'd done any poaching. If Upton laid a hand on her...

She lay in the mud and fallen leaves, her skirts up around her waist, John Cartwright between her thighs, and Upton holding her down. She screamed his name, and he brought the barrel of the gun down with a resounding crack on John's head. There was blood running down John's face and pooling in the cavernous wound in his shattered skull. It had splattered over Ella – his beautiful Ella.

Behind him, Harry Cartwright laughed at his father's demise. 'She's mine, now. Mine, not Father's or yours, James Weston, and you'll never see your son again.'

Ella raised an arm and held out her hand, her eyes desolate. 'Jem...'

The bells of St Andrew's had chimed four. Four bells should mean something. He had to go: leave Yardley Hastings. 'I love you, Ella.' Their fingertips touched briefly: a last lingering memory.

'Rise and shine, you lazy scum!'

He opened his eyes and groaned as the nightmare and everything he held dear slipped from his grasp. The floor beneath him bucked and rolled, and above him, taut sails partly obscured the dawn sky. His wrists were manacled, and leg irons weighed

323

him down. He was on HMS Tortoise bound for Van Diemen's Land. It hadn't been John Cartwright he'd killed, though the man deserved it for raping Ella; it was Joe Upton whose skull he'd caved in with the barrel of Cal's shotgun.

Life: that was his sentence. Him and his cousins, Cal and Nat, had all been found guilty; all had played their part in Joe's death. At least they were alive. He'd taken Joe's life in a moment of rage, while out poaching his lordship's pheasant, and they'd all been transported to the colonies for his sin. The pale stars fading in the dawn light weren't the familiar stars of home, they were strange southern stars: stars of exile.

A sharp kick in his ribs brought him to his feet. The guard pointed to his blanket. 'Get a fucking move on, you lazy bastard. Get that stowed. There's decks to holystone.'

The bleak truth brought him back to his knees: he was in the middle of the South Atlantic on the deck of a convict ship. Ella, and William, the baby son he'd held only once, were gone, forever, unless – There had been talk of mutiny in the night.

He rolled his blanket, reliving his dream as he stowed it away and shambled into line for his ration of water and gruel. Had John Cartwright raped Ella as he suspected? She'd left Harry the morning after their wedding night and sought refuge with the Westons. Though she'd made no accusation against John, something had happened to make her refuse to go back. Louisa, the Cartwright's scullery maid, had hinted John couldn't keep his hands off young girls. Certainly, several of the Cartwright's maids had left the village to stay with relatives after a few months in their employ, and village tongues gossiped. It was said the county was littered with John's bastards. Cal's Aunt Ev, housekeeper for Reverend Buchanan with whom Ella had been staying before her marriage to Harry, had been untypically tight-lipped about the

Cartwrights, a sure sign she knew something she felt she wasn't at liberty to divulge.

He accepted his group's ration, cursing the fight on deck that had led to all the prisoners being manacled and put in irons, yet again, and took the gruel to a part of the deck shaded by the sails from the rapidly rising sun. All too soon, they would be locked below decks again in the stifling heat. In the harsh light of morning, with cold iron round his wrists and ankles, the night's plans of mutiny seemed desperate and ill-founded. How could he ever hope to escape and return home to Ella and his son? Cal doled out the rations into individual bowls, and they sat in silence each with their thoughts of home.

The image of village life, so unappreciated, so carelessly and thoroughly tossed aside, sent a wave of homesickness through him. His own stupid fault. Joe Upton had been doing his job: he couldn't blame the man, not really, though he had done in the months he was incarcerated in Northampton jail and on the prison hulk, Stirling Castle, in Plymouth Sound. He'd had a lot of time to think since then, lying awake nights staring into darkness. All Joe had really done was stand by his friend, Harry, when Ella had left her new husband and found shelter with the Westons. Joe had called Ella a whore, in church, and that had been the final straw after his previous run-ins with the marquis's late gamekeeper. The man's promise to *'get you, you young bugger'* had finally borne fruit.

Life. The mood on deck was subdued. Frank had died the previous night, and if the surgeon had examined the body and concluded that no foul play was involved, Frank would be buried at sea this morning.

He huffed a short laugh. Foul play? The stifling heat and lack of air, stuck down tween-decks with inadequate ventilation holes, the interminable stench of melting tar and latrines, and sweating bodies jammed head to foot in a floating coffin, weren't foul enough? At least they were fortunate to be on deck overnight and not in that stinking hellhole. The ship was rife with cholera and dysentery, not to mention breathing problems. He coughed, not for the first time. It would be a miracle if Frank's was the last life lost aboard.

He returned his bowl and spoon to be cleaned by the galley-hands and fetched a holystone, a piece of smooth sandstone used to scrape the decks clean, a daily task that was monotonous and soothing and gave too much time to ponder his physical and emotional plight and his immortal soul.

He knelt on the deck beside Cal, as if in prayer, and let the rocking motion of the ship and the backward and forward motion of his arms relax his mind. He'd written his allowed letter to Joe's parents, not Ella, in an effort to assuage his guilt and give them some small comfort with his abject apology. It hadn't helped his nightmares.

He sighed. At least, Ella was safe now with her mother in Bath. Harry and John Cartwright would never touch her again. She was young and pretty. She'd find someone else: the man she deserved, a father for William, and be happy again. The ill-conceived hope of a mutiny gone, it was all he could ask for her and his son now: a life.

Cal nudged him. Two men carried a bundle of sailcloth tied with rope and laid it on the deck.

He got to his feet and stood silent, head bowed. 'Frank weren't a bad 'un, Cal. He didn't deserve this.'

Cal shook his head. 'Too late now. Whatever crime he did, he paid for it with his life.'

326

'He told me why he was transported.' His fingers clenched around his holystone. 'Do you know what the charge was? Obtaining a shovel by deception. Frank stole a shovel and died for it. It ain't fair, Cal. We killed a man, we deserve it, but this ain't bloody fair.'

Surgeon Brownrigg detailed two men to put Frank's body on a bed board and lift it onto the gunnel. Major Cumberland, the Captain of the Guard, and Captain Hood, ship's master, moved to stand at Frank's head. Captain Hood stood stiffly. 'This man, Francis Garland, was sent here as a punishment, but three years' exile, not death, was the punishment intended. Van Diemen's Land has lost a colonist, and England has lost a son.' Hood paused, head bowed. In prayer or thinking of his lost bounty? 'We commit his body to the deep. May God have mercy upon his soul.'

Hood nodded, and the two men holding the bed board tipped it and let the sail-wrapped body slide into the sea. The water swallowed Frank, leaving barely a ripple, barely a trace of the life so cruelly cut short.

'Amen.' He crossed himself. For Frank the nightmare was over, but there but for fortune went any one of them.

***

Ella cursed the wet days and long nights that kept Harry indoors so much. She lay back on the feather mattress and let his hands wander; it was her body he owned, not her heart. She closed her eyes and let her mind go where her body couldn't. She and Jem's mother, Charlotte, had contrived to travel to Plymouth and had waved Jem farewell on the deck of HMS Tortoise the day the ship had left Plymouth dockyard.

She'd let him believe she was staying with her mother in Bath, it being all the comfort she could give him, when that was far from the truth. He'd asked for her promise to forget him, to get on with her life, but it was a promise she hadn't been able to make. Her vow had been to her young son that he would know his father, and she'd keep that promise whatever the cost: a cost that was proving to be high.

Harry's stubble tickled her stomach. She opened her eyes and put her hands behind his neck, making furrows in his fair hair, ever the loving wife. She'd never forgive her father for taking Harry's side, for putting his own reputation above her happiness, again. Didn't he owe her for the years he'd disowned her?

Josiah, she still couldn't think of him as Father, could have given her the fare to follow Jem without making a noticeable difference to the weight of his sovereign hoard, but no. The selfish bastard had quoted the law at her, said even her and Jem's son, William, belonged to Harry, and she had no rights. '*Why would you need rights? You're a woman. Your pretty little brain isn't equipped to deal with important decisions. You need the protection of a man, a husband. This is why, in the eyes of the law, everything you have, not that you have much, belongs to Harry.*'

Harry kissed her belly, where his midsummer child grew within her. 'I think Matthew would be a good name.'

Men thought women's brains would explode if they thought too much: Josiah had said as much. '*It's for your own good.*' Well, she'd had a lot of time to think, and it wasn't her brain that was exploding; it was her temper. She held it in, keeping it in reserve; she was about to need it. 'Matt Cartwright. Sounds a strong name. What if it's a girl?'

'I need a son.'

Her fingers clenched in his hair. 'Henry the Eighth needed a son. Five of his six wives failed to give him one.'

He looked up at her. 'Then I'll get a child a year on you, every year, until we have a boy. I need a son and heir to take over the tenancy and grow the herd when I'm too old. Children to look after us in our dotage.'

He wasn't joking in his intent, and his cows were his pride and joy, but she doubted he'd father a child a year, even if his present appetite for her was insatiable. Since learning she was pregnant, he'd thrust his manhood in his father's face with almost as much pleasure as he'd thrust it into her, but this child was probably John's, given his scattering of bastards about the county and Harry having had mumps as a young man.

John laughed behind his son's back, certain he'd gotten the child on her, the thing Harry most wanted to do, but Harry's new-found, if ill-found, self-confidence had pushed his father's nose out of joint. Harry had taken hold of the reins of the farm and wasn't about to let go.

He didn't need to know the child might not be his or that hearing them in bed in the next room drove John wild with lust for her. He wouldn't know as long as John kept his promise, half a sovereign a month for sex, to augment the ten pounds he'd given her to bear his child, the heir to the Cartwright domain he feared Harry couldn't give her. He'd promised another ten pounds when she bore a healthy son, but it wasn't a deal she intended to honour. She intended to be on board ship before midsummer. There were other men all too willing to pay for her young body. Already, she had fourteen pounds towards her nineteen-pound passage to Van Diemen's Land though she needed more than that to allow her to subsist there with two young children.

A hand stroked her inner thigh, and she parted her legs every bit the prostitute Joe Upton had called her. Why did Jem have to kill the wretched man? She'd be with Jem now, at the Westons, giving

329

herself heart, body, and soul to the man she loved, not here with the husband she should never have been forced to marry. Too briefly, she'd known the passion of true love, of a body given freely and with joy.

Grasping Harry's hair, she pulled him down on top of her and bit at his lips as he entered her, bucking beneath him as he thrust. Forget Jem, forget Jem... forget Jem. *Jem*. The word almost escaped her lips. Harry's hands tangled in her hair, holding her down, capturing her, conquering her, possessing her. She responded with a passion born of anger, driving him on, wanting him to hurt her, beat her, and bruise her, like the men did in the whorehouse in Northampton. Anything to dull the pain in her heart.

He climaxed at last and rolled off her, breathing heavily

A smile painted her face while, inside, guilt tore her apart. Being unfaithful to Jem with Harry was not her choice to make; Harry was her legal husband, and she had no rights where her body or her son were concerned, but she'd sold herself to others, not just John Cartwright and Reverend Buchanan, who'd prayed for forgiveness for his wickedness and then fucked her again.

She'd sold her soul to the devil within, but how else was a girl of her age to find the fare? She'd had nothing, had been paid nothing for her duties on the farm, and was totally dependent on the Cartwrights for the very clothes on her back and the food in her belly, whereas she'd made twenty whole shillings in Northampton, whoring.

Harry's shoulder was strong against her cheek. To gain her freedom she must also gain his trust, how else would he allow her to take William away from the farm for even one second, alone? She'd persuaded him to let her take her son into the copse, on the last fine day, but he'd waited in the lane to make sure she didn't wander towards the turnpike road. She sought Harry's lips and kissed him softly. To keep her promise to William and to make her escape, she would do whatever it took.

'You do love me a bit, don't you?' Harry's searching eyes, blue not hazel like Jem's, caught her off-guard. 'You are happy here?'

She found his manhood and brought him back to arousal. 'Of course I love you, Harry.' It wasn't entirely a lie. She was going to hurt him far more than he'd ever hurt her, and he had hurt her, but then rape, imprisonment, and violence were a husband's legal rights. But there was another side to Harry; she'd seen the small boy beneath the rough demanding man, who needed to be loved.

She put her arms around his shoulders as he positioned himself above her again, needing to assuage her guilt and give him pleasure and comfort, despite everything, her anger spent. 'I do love you.' He'd been kinder to her since she'd given herself willingly: kinder still since he'd known she was pregnant. He wanted this child so much. Tears pricked her eyes; whatever the outcome of her deception, either Harry would destroy her, or she would destroy Harry.

***

Dolly, the Cartwright's white pony shook her head as Harry threaded the reins through the collar turrets and fastened the traces to the hames. He checked the rest of harness and then slipped off her halter, slid the bridle over her head and attached the reins to the bit. 'Stand girl.' The old mare stood quietly, whisking her tail at the midges that had come out with the sun despite the cold. 'Good girl.' He pushed the trap up behind her and slipped the shafts through the tugs, whistling.

Mother had one of her bad heads and had taken to her bed. Ella

331

had volunteered to go to Northampton in her stead to sell a couple of cheeses in the market if someone could look after William. One of the scullery maids had volunteered, so Ella had gone in early on the carrier's cart, and he'd taken her to the turnpike road in the trap. He would surprise her by collecting her in town and bringing her home in time to feed William, who wasn't fully weaned yet. Father could do the afternoon milking; Jo, the new milkmaid, would help the old man if he didn't spend the afternoon fucking the girl.

He shrugged. His father was welcome to the thirteen-year-old. He had a passionate woman, Ella, and no child could satisfy him like she did: Ella liked it rough. He frowned. Babies could be slipped, like calves, before their time. Suppose the passionate sex they enjoyed was harmful to the child: he wasn't about to take chances with his son. It would be a boy or, if not, Ella would deliver one alive and healthy, if it took until she'd reached the end of her child-bearing years. She was young; there was plenty of time, and daughters would be useful for labour or marrying off, but strong sons were what the farm needed.

He understood his wife's need to get away from the confines of the farm occasionally, having been used to life in Bath, so her eagerness to go to the market hadn't surprised him. He didn't mind her going as long as William stayed behind. He still didn't trust her not to run back to Bath and her mother: William was what kept her coming home.

The height and sit of the shafts checked and the belly band tightened, he climbed into the driving seat and flicked the tip of his whip. 'Get up, Dolly.' If he had to stop fucking Ella for the sake of the child, maybe he would need little Josephine after all; a man had his needs, and he was her master now, or he could renew his acquaintance with Rose and Blossom in the whorehouse in Market

332

Street. Much as he loved Ella, there was something about a whorehouse.

Some of the stalls were already packing up when he arrived in the market square. There was no sign of Ella. He accosted a stallholder who was rank with the smell of fish. 'Have you seen a young woman selling cheeses?' He raised a hand and held it at a height level with his chin. 'About so high, auburn hair, slim.'

'Young Ella?'

'You know her?'

The fishmonger winked. 'Pretty girl that one. Sold out by noon. Went off to make a bit more money, I reckon.'

She'd more likely gone to spend some while he and his mother weren't there to keep check on her. 'Thanks. Did you see which way she went?'

The man inclined his head towards Market Street and smirked. 'That way, I reckon. Hours since.'

Dolly side-stepped the two-wheeled cart in a tight circle, and he headed her out of the square and into Market Street. Ella wasn't in sight. The whorehouse was three doors down; a familiar throb started at the sight of it. Ella, almost certainly, would be waiting by St Sepulchre for the carrier to take her home. She wasn't expecting him. He had time.

He looped Dolly's reins through a metal ring in the wall and patted her neck. It wouldn't hurt to visit his old friends for an hour. 'Rose or Blossom, Dolly? Who's it to be?' He took a florin from his pocket. 'Heads, Rosie. Tails, Blossom.' And Blossom had an ample tail, and a particular way of... He hardened and flipped the coin. 'Tails.'

Rebecca Bryn lives in West Wales with her husband and dog, where she paints the coastal scenes that inspire her. She is happy to answer questions about her writing and her novels at

www.facebook.com/rebecca.bryn.novels

http://twitter.com/rebeccabryn1 and at

https://rebeccabrynblog.wordpress.com

Her first novel, *The Silence of the Stones,* was inspired by the release from prison of Angela Canning on the grounds of unsafe conviction following new medical research on 'cot death' syndrome and the disappearance of Madeleine McCann. It's availalble at

http://mybook.to/SilenceoftheStones

The poem, *The Vigil*, which prefaces this story was inspired by Madeleine's tragic disappearance on May 3rd 2007.

Her second novel, *Touching the Wire*, was written to commemorate the seventieth anniversary of Holocaust Memorial Day on January 27th 2015. And was inspired by a television report that made her examine her own feelings about forgiveness. Set partly in Auschwitz, it's a story of the courage of the women of the Holocaust.

Touching the Wire. http://mybook.to/TouchingtheWire was chosen as one of the *100 Books to Read Before You Die.* https://calebandlindapirtle.com/five-100-indie-books-read-die-6/

Her third novel, *The Child of Prophecy,* is set in the future in a world of social and religious upheaval. It was inspired by the thinking about global warming current at the time and is a tale of courage, faith, and hope.

http://mybook.to/ChildofProphecy

The historical series, *For Their Country's Good,* was inspired by a family story about a poacher who killed a gamekeeper and was transported to Van Diemen's Land. Book One, *On Different Shores,* is available at

http://mybook.at/OnDifferentShores

Book Two, *Beneath Strange Stars*, can be purchased at

http://mybook.to/BeneathStrangeStars

And Book Three, *One Common Ground*, at

http://mybook.to/OnCommonGround

The Dandelion Clock, a WW1 story of young lovers torn apart by war, was inspired by her grandparents' lives.

http://mybook.to/DandelionClock

The Chainmakers' Daughter and The Chainmaker's Wife tell of the women chainmakers' fight for a living wage and the fight for women's suffrage in the early 1900s in the Black Country of England.

http://mybook.to/ChainmakersDaughter

http://mybook.to/ChainmakersWife

Non-fiction

http://mybook.to/WatercolourSeascapes

http://mybook.to/AnimalPortraits step-by step painting
books with demos and loads of illustrations, tips, and tricks.
by my alter ego.

NB: Reviews are incredibly important to all authors. If
you've enjoyed my tale, I'd really appreciate your feedback
at the links above. Thank you – Rebecca.

Printed in Great Britain
by Amazon

72364645R00193